# Paláran

John Cheek

Armour&Armour Publications

*Paláran*
©2010 Kathryn Cheek

ISBN-13: 978-1-936541-06-5
Published by Armour&Armour Publications

Text and cover design by Armour&Armour
armour-armour.com

## ACKNOWLEDGMENT

For factual details concerning the disposition and maneuvers of Japanese naval forces on December 7, 1941, and the participation of military personnel, the author is gratefully indebted to *At Dawn We Slept: The Untold Story of Pearl Harbor* by Gordon W. Prange, McGraw-Hill, 1981

# CHAPTER ONE

**BLACK AS PITCH** was the pre-dawn. Not even faint light from a waning moon filtered through the overcast to illuminate the foamy crests of the swells of the heavy seas as the armada bore due south. In point position steamed the light cruiser *Abukuma* with its escort of four destroyers, followed three miles astern by the battleships *Hiei* and *Kirishima*, which were flanked by the heavy cruisers *Chikuma* and *Tone*. Three miles farther behind this shielding phalanx in two parallel columns protected by a swarm of destroyers came the heart and sinew of this powerful naval task force—the six aircraft carriers.

On the bridge of the flagship carrier *Akagi* silently stood four men—Vice Admiral Chuichi Nagumo, commander of the First Air Fleet, and behind him his four staff officers: Chief of Staff Rear Admiral Ryunosuke Kusaka, Senior Staff Officer Commander Tamotsu Oishi, and Air Officer Commander Minoru Genda. The time for conversation had passed. With their hands clasped behind them they stared into the darkness ahead and waited.

Below deck on the carrier *Soryu* Sublieutenant Iyozo Fujita had risen very early. A young fighter pilot with a handsome, boyish face, he had bathed the night before and now put on clean underclothes and flight uniform in order to go into battle and face death in immaculate attire, in accord with the ancient Samurai tradition. This was to be his first combat mission, and he was prepared for it to be his last. As would all the other pilots, he tied around his head a white scarf, a *hachimachi*, embellished with the Kanji characters for "*Hissyo*"—Certain Victory. Then, having placed a picture of his deceased parents in his pocket, he stepped into the corridor, closed the door to his cabin behind him and set out for the flight deck. He had been preceded by Petty Officer Noboru Kanai, the Navy's most expert bombardier, who had already spent hours at his post in a bomber going over and over the battle plan.

Overall leader of the First Attack Force was Commander Mitsuo Fuchida. As he was leaving the ready room of the *Akagi*, he paused and shook hands warmly with his friend, Lieutenant Commander Shigemaru Murata, leader of the Special Group Torpedo Force, and then headed for his aircraft across the spray-washed flight deck. He paused briefly by the Zero of the leader of the Third Flight fighter force, Lieutenant Commander Shigeru Itaya, who was sitting in his cockpit. His would be the first of the one hundred eighty-five planes to be launched. In the dim light from the bridge the eyes of the two men met for a few seconds, and then Fuchida nodded and passed on. As he approached his own plane, the senior maintenance officer handed him a specially made *hachimachi*. "Sir," he said, "this is from the crew of the *Akagi*."

At 0550 hours the six carriers and their escort vessels increased speed to twenty-four knots and swung to port to head almost due east into the teeth of the strong wind. Long swells sent spray cascading across the flight decks and delayed the scheduled launch, but at 0604 hours the wheels of Lieutenant Commander Itaya's Zero lifted off the carrier. When all of the fighters had cleared the decks, they were followed by Fuchida with his high-level bombers, the dive bombers under the command of Lieutenant Commander Kakuichi Takahashi, and finally the torpedo bombers, each group circling at different altitudes to avoid collision.

At 0620 hours Commander Fuchida led his flight across the bow of the *Akagi*—the signal for all the other aircraft to fall into formation behind him and climb to their pre-assigned altitudes. Then he set course almost due south toward slumbering Oahu.

* * *

**FOUR THOUSAND MILES** to the east the sun was shining brightly in Athens, Georgia. Mrs. Wayne Tolliver was walking her cocker spaniel along Main Street, occasionally waving at passing friends on their way home from an after-church lunch at the Palmetta Cafe. On a playing field out at the edge of town the football team of the Delta Chapter of Sigma Chi Fraternity at the University of Georgia was locked in its annual rivalry with the visiting team of fraternity brothers of the Beta Psi Chapter from Georgia Tech. It was unusually warm for early December. There was neither a breeze nor a cloud in the sky, and by two-thirty the temperature had inched above eighty degrees on the sidelines, several degrees cooler than out on the playing field.

Before calling the next play in the huddle, Bob Hanson, the Beta Psi quarterback, squinted at the opposing defensive line, trying to find a hint of some weakness to probe, an effort that had been largely unsuccessful during virtually the entire first half of the game. His key player, the fullback, a powerful six-foot-two Texan by the name of Knute McCutcheon, had succeeded in moving the ball down within striking range twice in the first quarter. But he was slow and lethargic today, and the defensive team soon learned to key on him. Both times the Beta Psi's had to settle for a field goal by "Sleepy" Sicillo, a lean and lanky Louisiana boy, who had grown up playing soccer. With the score 13–6 and less than a minute remaining, Bob knew he had time for only two or three more plays before the end of the first half. He would feel better about second-half prospects if they could get at least three more points on the board.

"All right, let's run the deep wide-out pattern. Charlie, you go right; Ken, you go left. Try to get free. And Knute, damn it, give me some protection. That left guard has been knocking me on my ass all day. Okay, let's go!"

When the ball was snapped, Bob dropped back behind the fullback and looked for his two receivers. Charlie was blanketed by two defenders, but Ken had only one on him and was leading him by several yards. As Bob cocked his arm to pass, out of the corner of his eye he saw the shifty left guard, following a consistent pattern, break around Knute's left side and charge straight for him. Bob managed to tuck the ball under his arm just before the bone-rattling impact of the tackle took him to the ground.

While still on the ground he signaled for a time-out and then began slowly getting to his feet. As the water bucket and towels were being brought in from the bench, he wiped the perspiration from his face and glowered at McCutcheon, who had sunk onto one knee and was grinning sheepishly.

"Damn it, Knute, you're going to blow the whole game. How in hell did you think that you could come stumbling in at four o'clock this morning and still be able to play? I thought we had all agreed to be in bed by twelve o'clock. And you embarrassed the tar out of me. The house-mother told me she had to let you in just a little before dawn. I would think that since the brothers were kind enough to put us up last night, you shouldn't have broken their rules like that."

Bob's relationship with his burly roommate was usually pleasant and lacking friction, for their temperaments and personalities were so dissimilar, being almost polar, that in a strange way, rather than being incompatible, they complemented each other. But Bob's body ached from the pounding he had been receiving due to his friend's omissions that day, and he was not disposed to be amiable.

"Aw, hell," Knute said half-apologetically, "I meant to be in on time, but every time I'd start to leave, that li'l honey I'd been fixed up with would do or say somethin' that'd give me hope I might be able to score if I just hung aroun' a li'l longer. When I bombed out, I was so horny I couldn't get to sleep when I got to bed."

Jack Palmer, the center, looked at Knute with only a trace of a smile and said sardonically, "Then I don't know how you ever get any sleep, Tex, because to hear you talk you're always horny."

"You said it, li'l buddy; I didn't," Knute responded with a low whistle of appreciation. "Man! These women are somethin' else down here. If I can get a date with that li'l doll again, next time I'm goin' to bring a spoon."

"A spoon?" another team member asked. "I don't get it."

"Why, sonny boy, that li'l trick is so plush, down in Texas we'd call it 'table stuff.' Ya know what I mean?" Knute winked and tossed a half-cup of water at his teammate. Bob had to grin. He was accustomed to his friend's crudities, but occasionally Knute out-did even himself. He had been watching the referee and saw him glance at his watch, so with a grunt he rose to his feet and put on his helmet.

"Okay, you heroes, we've got time for one more play. Let's try the same one we just did. Ken, I'm hoping they'll double up on both you and Charlie. Let the defenders stick with you, and break for the sidelines early. Knute, that steamroller gets by you on the left each time. Just stand your ground and block him when I cut past you on the right. That'll give me a chance to break free. Now let's go without a huddle."

As soon as time was called in, the Beta Psi's came up immediately to the line of scrimmage. The Deltas had barely got set when the ball was snapped and Bob faded back. He was pleased to see that both receivers were being double-manned, but he was concentrating more on the defensive rush. Apparently no one was expecting a draw play. As the guard cut to get by Knute, the big Texan lurched to the left and caught him with a full block, granting Bob a fraction of a second to step right and head upfield. A timely block by Palmer freed him into the secondary, and he saw running room ahead. The linebackers had been pulled wide by the two receivers and saw the developing run too late. Bob slanted toward the corner and out-ran the safety into the end zone. With three seconds remaining on the clock, Sicillo booted the extra point for a 13–13 half-time tie.

As they filed off the field, the Beta Psi's felt exhilarated and jubilant. They had done well to draw even, for their opponents were supposed to be by far the better team.

"How 'bout that li'l ol' block I threw, huh?" Knute exulted. "His gran' chil'en are goin' to feel that one. Did ya get bored, li'l Robbie? Hell, all ya had to do was stroll across the goal line."

"Yeah, sure, you're right," Bob laughed, dropping his helmet on the bench and picking up a towel. "You did the whole thing all by yourself. Come on, I've got some cold fruit juice in the car."

\* \* \*

**IN THE PARKING AREA** off to the side of the field sat the sleek beige '41 Buick convertible given to Bob by his grandmother on his twentieth birthday. It represented the last word in automotive elegance and was always enviously and reverentially referred to by Knute as "the Cock Wagon." On this balmy day the convertible top had been retracted, and two non-playing Beta Psi's were seated on the front seat listening to the radio.

"Hey, Bob," one of them called out as the two players were approaching, "come here and listen to this. Orson Welles is pulling another of his fake broadcasts about invasion and stuff."

"On Sunday?" Bob laughed. "You've got to be kidding!"

As the two drew near, they could hear the voice of an announcer.

". . . columns of smoke are rising on all sides of the harbor as waves of Japanese bombers come in from the sea. Explosions have rocked three of the battleships at anchor, and one is listing badly to the side. American anti-aircraft fire can be heard, and . . ."

"Aw, turn that crap off," Knute said, hopping up and sitting on the side of the car. "Let's get some music. I'm in the mood for Artie Shaw."

"No, wait," Bob said, leaning his elbows on the door of the car and frowning. "That sounds like it might be real. Listen, you can hear explosions and gunfire."

"Hell, the Martians were zappin' people with ray-guns on that last one of his," Knute objected but then also fell silent as the litany of disaster droned on and on and became more and more believable.

". . . this is a terrible scene. The Japanese torpedo planes and bombers are streaming in from the sea in wave after wave past Diamond Head. Five of our battleships are burning. There was a huge explosion on the *Arizona*, and it has sunk at its moorings. Only the upper structure is still visible. Many American seamen have been blown into the water and are trying to swim ashore through the oil and flames. The *Oklahoma* is listing heavily to one side, and the *California*, the *Nevada* and the *West Virginia* are aflame. There are tall columns of smoke rising from Hickam Field, which was hit by attacking planes at eight oh three. There are reports that . . ."

Sensing something momentous was afoot, other players and

spectators began drifting toward the car. A hush of incredulity fell over the scene as reports came streaming in from Washington, New York and Honolulu. The stunned silence was broken only occasionally by a soft but forceful "God damn!" or "Those bastards!"

All concern for or thought of the second half of the football game and related festivities vanished. After the initial shock had passed, people began walking and running to their cars and to buses. Bob rounded up the other two fraternity brothers who had ridden down from Atlanta with him and Knute.

"Let's get back to the frat house and pick up our clothes and gear," he said. "I think we'd better get back to school."

There was little talk until they were halfway back to Atlanta on Georgia State Route 10. The news streaming uninterruptedly from the radio painted an ever direr picture.

". . . I repeat: the last attack was beaten back at 9:45, and at present there are no attacking planes in the area. The U.S. command is not certain of the point of origin of the Japanese attack, but it is assumed a task force of carriers is lying to the north of the Islands. A state of emergency has been declared, and a general mobilization has been called. U.S. losses have been heavy. Over two hundred of our planes were caught on the ground and destroyed or damaged, for not only was Hickam Field attacked but also Wheeler Field and Kaneohe. There have been hundreds if not thousands of military and civilian casualties. All hospitals have been flooded with the wounded, and the scene is chaos. It is difficult to assemble accurate figures from all the reports streaming in, but from estimates . . ."

"They don't say anything about Japanese losses," Tim Fuller finally spoke up from the back seat.

Tim was a quiet, wiry boy from Springfield, Missouri, majoring in mechanical engineering. From a modest family background, he had managed to secure a scholarship by dint of natural ability and hard work but barely suppressed an inclination toward resentment of those he assumed had had an easier path than he.

"Where are our planes, and where's the U.S. Navy?"

"Don't worry, they'll get 'em," Knute responded. "They'll sink the whole dam' Jap fleet in two weeks. I've got a cousin who's an officer in the Navy, and he's been allowed to watch the Japs during gunnery practice. He says they can't hit the side of a barn from the inside. It'll all be over in a couple of months."

Bob was pensive as he watched the white center-line of the highway passing to the left of the car.

"I'm not so sure," he said quietly. "At any rate there'll be a big mobilization. What draft classification do you fellows have?"

Mark Wesson, the other rear-seat occupant, leaned forward and rested his arms on the back of the front seat.

"I'm sure we all have college deferments right now, but that can be changed. I bet we all get switched over to one-A."

"That might apply to you and me," Tim spoke up with a hint of bitterness in his voice, "but Bob and Knute have rich daddies. I'll bet you they don't get called up."

Knute whirled around and fixed his eyes on Tim.

"Listen, you li'l snot-nose. I'd loosen your teeth in your head right now if I wasn't afraid you'd bleed all over my buddy's car. I'll bet you fifty dollars that I'll be in front of you in that line to sign up tomorrow."

Bob broke in, wanting to ease the tension.

"Calm down, Knute. Tomorrow? We've got classes all day tomorrow."

"To hell with the classes. I'll be at the recruiting office at eight-thirty in the morning."

"Come on, take it easy," Bob said. "Don't go jumping the gun and going off half-cocked. Christmas break is coming up. Meet all your classes and take your exams. Then talk things over with the draft board and your parents while you're at home."

"Nope," Knute responded emphatically. "You guys can sit aroun' playin' with your dingus if ya like, but I'm joining up tomorrow. And I can't believe you're not."

"Hell, Knute." Bob said a little defensively, "we've only got one more semester until we graduate and get our degree. What's the rush? We'll have plenty of time."

"Li'l buddy, are you sure they're gonna let ya finish out th' year? You're a damn geology major, for God's sake. Who th' hell needs a geologist?"

"Well, they need a geologist more than a 'business administrator,'" Bob retorted even more defensively.

"I'll buy that," Knute admitted, "but that won't necessarily save your butt. I'll bet a dime to a doughnut that before the school year's out they ship your ass into the infantry. At least I'll get a chance to choose."

"Which branch are you going for?"

"Ol' Army Air Corps, man. That's my number one choice. We have a field not far from home. I like the guys an' th' way they operate."

"Do you know how to fly an airplane?" Mark asked.

"Not yet, sonny boy, but when I do learn, I'll be the best in the world," Knute answered confidently.

Bob looked at his friend and smiled.

"The Air Corps appeals to me too. So that means you'll only be the second-best in the world."

Then he leaned forward and turned up the radio volume. The four of them fell silent, and no one spoke the rest of the ride to Atlanta.

**SINCE HE HAD** an eight o'clock class, Bob got up at seven the next morning and went into the bathroom to shower and shave. Twenty minutes later when he walked back into the double bedroom he shared with Knute in the fraternity house, his friend had already gone, and the keys to the car, which he had told him he could use, were missing from his dresser. Nor did his roommate show up for their usual lunch at the student commissary or in the hours after classes.

At their return the preceding evening there was a note waiting for Bob that his parents had called. He knew the conversation with them would be long and tedious, so he delayed returning the call until after his last class. Just before dinnertime as he was sitting in the booth on the ground floor of the house reassuring his mother he was not going to do anything drastic, he heard a tap on the door. Through the glass he saw Knute's pock-marked face wreathed in a smile serving as a backdrop for a "thumbs up" sign. Pretending that someone was waiting to use the telephone, Bob finally managed to terminate his call and opened the booth door.

"Well, what went on?" he asked.

"Signed, sealed an' delivered," his friend said, waving a thick vanilla envelope. "You are now looking at a future general in th' U.S. Army Air Corps."

"When are you going to take your physical?"

"Hell, it's all done. I had th' physical early this afternoon with about six hundred other guys. I was a soldier boy by four o'clock."

Knute's face radiated like that of a twelve-year-old boy.

"I think my daddy'll be proud. He was an artillery spotter in France in World War I."

"Well, if you were through by four o'clock, why'd it take you so long to get back?" Bob said, moving toward the dining room. "I thought the recruiting office is down near the main post office."

Knute's eyes sparkled as he nudged his friend in the ribs with his elbow and said in a low voice, "Li'l buddy, I stumbled onto th' prettiest li'l heifer you'll ever see. She's a receptionist in an insurance company office in th' same building as th' recruiters. We had a chummy li'l chat while I was waiting around this afternoon, and she agreed to let me drive 'er home. You should'a seen her face when she saw that Cock Wagon in th' parking lot. I think she'd a dropped her panties right there if I'd a asked 'er."

Bob shook his head in half-mock, half-real exasperation.

"Here you are signing up to defend your country against its enemies, and you can't stop thinking about girls for two hours! You're going to burn out before you're twenty-five."

Knute pulled his chair up to the table, put his napkin in his lap and reached for one of the heaping serving dishes. As he passed the butterbeans, he leaned close and said in a hushed tone of voice, "This ain't no gal, li'l buddy; this is Woman with a capital 'W.' Wait'll ya see 'er. By th' way, she has an apartment with a blonde friend over in the Georgia Terrace. I told 'er we'd pick 'em up at eight o'clock an' tootle aroun' town a li'l bit. You gotta admit I take care of my li'l friend here, right?"

Bob put his fork down and looked at him in disbelief.

"Damn it, Knute, you know this is the last full week of classes. I've got a tough math paper to do, and I have to write up a lab experiment before Friday. I can't go out tonight or any night this week. You can borrow the car for awhile if you like, but count me out."

"Aw, come on, Robbie," his friend said entreatingly, "just for an hour. I want to sit in the back seat with my li'l sugah, and she said her roommate's a real good-looker. You'll like 'er. You'll have an hour to do your dam' studying before we leave."

Then with another elbow jab in Bob's ribs he said with the engaging grin that was one of his trademarks, "Ya gotta treat me right now, li'l buddy. Remember, I'm gonna be over there getting my ass shot at and protecting you while you're sitting over here fiddling with your friggin' rocks."

Bob laughed. "Exactly what 'rocks' are you talking about?"

"Whichever," Knute mumbled, stuffing some pork and mashed potatoes in his mouth, "but, knowin' you, they'll probably be those dam' ones you're readin' about in your books."

"Well, okay, but just for an hour, and I mean it. I've got to be back here at nine. Agreed?"

"Agreed. I knew ya wouldn't let me down. You're a good buddy. Now pass me th' turnip greens an' cornbread."


**SINCE EXAM WEEK** was coming up, after dinner almost everyone retired to their rooms to study. Only a few of the members sat around for awhile in the living room, talking and playing cards. Bob was sitting at his desk trying to organize his lab report. Knute disappeared into the shower room down the hall and was gone for almost twenty minutes. When he returned, Bob had to turn around to determine where the cloud of sweet, pungent aroma was coming from. He noticed that his friend had washed and plastered down his unruly hair and apparently after his shower had doused himself either with after-shave lotion or cologne.

"Whew!" Bob gasped. "If that stuff doesn't tone down, you'll asphyxiate that gal. What in the world is it?"

"Do ya think she'll like it?" Knute asked seriously. "She dam' well oughta. This li'l bottle cost me four an' a half dollars."

Bob grinned. He turned ninety degrees in his chair and with his arm on the back watched as his roommate sat down on his bed and busied himself with trying to polish his brown shoes.

The two of them had been rooming together ever since their sophomore year, when they had moved from the freshman dorm into the fraternity house. They could hardly have been a more disparate pair. Bob was five feet, eleven and a half inches tall, slender but muscular. He had brown eyes and brown hair and features that accorded well with his reserved, usually serious nature. He was from a well-to-do family but personally attached little importance to this fact. In the depth of the Depression his convertible was glaring proof of his family's apparent wealth, but externally there were no other obvious signs. However, there was a gentility about his bearing and manners that was far more indicative of his background and heritage. His grandfather had made a fortune in steel in Ohio and then moved to Lexington, Kentucky. Having inherited the fortune, his father never had to pursue a profession. He dabbled in various business ventures on a small scale but devoted most of his time to raising thoroughbred horses on his breeding farm, Falcrest Acres.

Bob had grown up on the farm and had always enjoyed physical labor. Instead of hanging around the country clubs with his peers, the children of his parents' friends, he much preferred to spend the time after school helping the farmhands with their chores—working the horses, pitching hay, cleaning and repairing tack, and even mucking the stalls. Although he had surprised and somewhat disappointed his parents by choosing to go to Culver Military Academy rather than to one of the "preferred" Eastern schools, he nonetheless embodied in his behavior and attitudes the picture of the "little Southern gentleman" prevalent in that era.

Knute represented a stark contrast. Fourteen months older and standing six feet, two and a half inches in his bare feet, he imposed himself on his surroundings—both spatially and psychologically. Raw-boned, coarse and frequently vulgar, he was the product of the West Texas oil fields, where his father had been a moderately successful wildcatter who had branched out into construction. As his ventures grew, the father thought that Knute, in spite of his son's considerable disinclination, should have some formal business training and insisted he try for a college degree in business administration. With the exception of brief service in France during World War I the father had been outside of Texas only twice in his lifetime. He wanted his son to be exposed to a broader range of cultural experiences than he and therefore advised him to go to a university somewhere in the "east" rather than to the University of Texas. Knute had halfheartedly struggled into his senior year at Tech, but there was no perceptible evidence that his coarseness in attitudes or behavior had to any degree been honed or polished by his three-year residence in Atlanta.

Bob's and Knute's friends and colleagues were amazed at their apparent compatibility, for they certainly represented an odd pair. It could be that subconsciously they saw a complementary function. Each to some extent envied certain traits of the other. Knute admired Bob's disciplined perseverance, his low-key but sharp intellect, and most of all his projection of culture and "breeding." Bob was by nature quiet and reserved and therefore on his part stood in awe of Knute's aggressiveness and brash confidence.

But there was another basis for Bob's genuine affection for his friend, for in spite of his dominating physical presence and overbearing crudeness there was a little-boy quality about him that partially atoned for his abrasive qualities. He represented the unlikely combination of a bull and a fuzzy puppy and frequently exhibited a wistfulness and winsomeness that won over his male friends and proved to be irresistibly appealing to women—an attraction which Knute exploited and reciprocated by a factor of at least ten. He could not be considered handsome, but his face, scarred from childhood chicken-pox and topped by a shock of light brown hair, reflected the "outdoorsy" good looks of a cigarette ad. Even those girls who were frightened and repelled by his aggressive vulgarity would have been hard put to deny his animal appeal.

Bob reached over and switched on his radio. News reports were still dominating the programs, and the news was growing more ominous with the passing of each hour.

"In his address before the joint houses of Congress today President Roosevelt has declared that yesterday will go down in history as a 'day of infamy,' and both houses of Congress, with only one dissenting vote, have declared war on the Japanese Empire. Japanese forces have launched attacks throughout the Pacific against U.S., British and French bases. Singapore was bombed yesterday. Guam and Wake Island are under heavy attack, and enemy forces are moving against the Philippines. Japanese ground troops have overrun British territories opposite the island of Hong Kong today and reportedly have landed on the northern shore of the Malay Peninsula. Siam officially surrendered this afternoon."

"When are you supposed to report for duty?" Bob asked, turning the volume down.

"I don' know yet," Knute responded, briskly applying the polishing brush to the side of his right shoe, "but the sergeant told me he can probably let me know by Friday. . . There! That shine would even satisfy the military. Jus' like a dam' mirror. If I hold my foot jus' right, I oughta be able to look up that li'l gal's dress tonight."

Bob shook his head and turned the radio off.

"I'd be tempted to say that you're incorrigible if I thought that you'd know what the word means."

"Don't go gettin' sassy with me, li'l buddy," Knute said, rising and reaching for his jacket. "Come on, let's go pick up those sweet li'l things. You're not gonna get anything more done right now anyway."

As they were walking out the door, Knute stopped Bob momentarily and looked down at him.

"Hey, do me a favor, li'l Robbie. I told this gal the car belongs to me. Don' cross me up on this, Okay? I'll tell 'er I'm jus' lettin' you drive."

Bob waited out front in the car while Knute went into the apartment to announce their arrival. The girls must have been ready, for in just a few minutes the front door opened and the three emerged. Knute had not exaggerated. His date was a stunning brunette with a narrow waist and pretty legs. Her blonde companion was shorter and more stocky and although reasonably pretty was not nearly as good-looking as her roommate.

"Robbie, I want ya to meet Peggy Wilson an' Fran Buntin. Climb in, gals. Peggy, you an' I'll sit in back. I tol' my buddy to do th' drivin' tonight."

Bob pulled out onto Peachtree and then turned left toward Spring Street. He anticipated that this concession to his roommate was going to be tedious at best and was determined to compress it into the agreed-on hour limit. A visit to the Varsity drive-in restaurant, situated close by the university, should effectively consume the time and be less boring than simply driving around. When his intent became obvious, Knute spoke up from the back seat.

"Hey, Robbie, where ya goin'? I thought we'd take a li'l spin out in the country, huh?"

"Not tonight," Bob answered firmly. "You know I've only got an hour to spare. Anyway, maybe the girls would like something to eat or drink."

As he pulled into the large parking area that circled the central preparation and distribution building, he rolled his window down.

"Oooooooooow!" came the familiar high-pitched call.

"Doodlebug!" Bob shouted, as the jacketed waiter came running up and slapped the car fender with a resounding blow, by the rules of the establishment the indisputable claim of the slapper to wait on that vehicle, placing it off-limits to all the other attendants. When he had pulled into a parking slot and shut off the engine, Bob reached out the window and joined in the stylized and traditional handshake with this most notorious carhop in all of Atlanta.

**DOODLEBUG WAS NOT** just a waiter, nor was he just a brash, gregarious and engaging personality. Doodlebug was a full-blown institution. Waiting on cars at the Varsity—at which he was the very best—was only one of the many facets of his activities. His abilities were legion, and one would find it difficult to conceive of some commission which he would not have been able to dispatch with efficiency, alacrity and infectious good humor. So catholic were his successes that it came to be assumed by everyone that he could do anything.

He was known to be an excellent cook and could even cater large parties with such skill that the host or hostess never needed to be concerned about the proper attention to the most minute detail—from linens, silverware and place-settings to table decorations and even place-cards. On short notice he could assemble dependable crews for housecleaning or maintenance and frequently "house-sat" for some of Atlanta's wealthiest citizens during their vacations. He was an excellent chauffeur and on at least two occasions was called on to substitute for the Governor's official driver. At any hour he could deliver to your door a comely companion for the evening or any type or quantity of beverage—alcoholic or non-alcoholic, foreign or domestic—that you might request. He was a perpetual-motion machine, a high revolution turbine, an indefatigable operator, and no one ever reported knowing when he dozed or slept.

Undoubtedly he could have made much more money redirecting to other activities the time he spent at the Varsity. But above all else Doodlebug was a social animal. He loved people—all kinds, all sizes, all shapes, all colors—and they usually reciprocated his esteem and affection. So engagingly appealing was his personality that within five minutes of having come to know him, the fact that he was black became inconsequential and tended to be forgotten even by those normally predisposed to the color-consciousness of the South of that era. Numberless were his acquaintances—from poor struggling students and local winos to writers and businessmen, movie stars and producers, politicians and famous athletes—and many among them were proud to count him as their friend.

There was a story that once a Hollywood producer pulled into the Varsity in a classic Bugatti he had come all the way from California to purchase. Doodlebug, an avowed automobile buff, almost bowled over four other waiters to get to it first and slap the rear fender with a resounding blow. When he approached the car window, he found the driver (unfamiliar with this Varsity phenomenon and attendant tradition) in a towering rage, fearful that the blow had damaged his costly acquisition. Yet within thirty minutes Doodlebug's charm had taken its toll, and the producer had given him the keys to the car, five one-hundred-dollar bills and instructions to drive the car to Los Angeles for him. No one knows how he did it, but six days later Doodlebug was back at the Varsity.

Bob had come to know him within his first week at Georgia Tech. It might ordinarily have taken longer, but the first time the '41 Buick convertible pulled into the drive-in, Doodlebug spotted it and made his famous charge. In the ensuing three years a mutual respect and genuine affection had developed between the two, initiated and probably solidified by an incident that occurred during the early part of Bob's freshman year. He was living at the time in one of the freshman dormitories and had come down with a serious intestinal malaise one weekend when almost all the other students, including his roommate, were away for an important football game. By midnight he had become worried by the extent of his nausea and, unable to raise any other student in the dorm, as a desperate recourse staggered to the hall telephone and dialed the Varsity, asking to speak to Doodlebug. Having detailed his plight, Bob requested the delivery of any kind of medicine that could help control his diarrhea and vomiting. Although their contact had up to that point been infrequent and superficial, in less than ten minutes Doodlebug was sitting on the opposite bed asking questions, his round face mirroring solicitude and concern. Then abruptly he jumped to his feet and grabbed the car keys off the dresser.

"Mister Bob, you just hold on; I'll be right back," he said, his white teeth flashing in a smile.

In less than thirty minutes he was back in the dormitory with a doctor in tow. The poor physician was in his pajamas and robe and had obviously been literally dragged out of bed by Bob's irrepressible agent. Diagnosis was made, medication and sedatives were applied, and Doodlebug returned the practitioner to his home, wherever that might have been. From weakness, exhaustion and the effects of a sedative Bob soon fell into a deep sleep. He was unaware of when his benefactor brought his car back, but in the morning the car keys were back on the dresser. And Bob never received a bill from the physician.


"**WHOOOEEE! THESE CLASSY** gents are sure in luck tonight!" Doodlebug intoned, bending forward and glancing into the car. "Howdy, Mister Knute. What'll it be for you folks?"

Knute passed, Peggy and Bob ordered Cokes, but Fran opted for a grilled cheese sandwich with French fries and a root beer. During the wait for the filling of the order, attempts were made at a coherent conversation, but the going was not easy. Knute ordinarily could have been counted on to carry this load, but he was preoccupied, evidence to which fact came with the sound of a forceful slapping of a hand.

"Take it easy, big fellow," Peggy said with a giggle. "Not so fast, or this could be the shortest date on record."

Bob tried without success to find a subject of mutual interest to broach with Fran. Some leavening of the tedium was afforded by his amazement at how she could intelligibly complete an entire sentence or statement without missing a single stroke on her chewing gum. This amazement turned to fascination after the delivery of the food. In spite of keen observation he never saw her remove her gum before beginning to eat, and yet after the rapid and total consumption of the edibles, it was obviously still available for mastication.

"Hey, Robbie," Knute said, obviously frustrated by the failure of his rear-seat campaign and anxious to seek an alternative, "let's drive out to the Cotton Patch and get in a li'l dancin', huh? You gals like to dance, don't ya?"

Both of the girls nodded affirmatively and giggled.

"No dice," Bob said firmly. "Some other time maybe. I've got to get back to my books. I'm sure these ladies will forgive us."

"Then I've got a great idea," Knute persisted. "Why don't you gals come to th' big dance Saturday night as our dates? Harry James an' his band are gonna be playin'. Robbie, I heard you tell somebody you don't have a date, right?"

"Well, yeah," Bob conceded reluctantly, "the date I had invited down from Lexington can't make it, but I had decided not to go at all."

"Hot dam'! Then that settles it," Knute exulted, ignoring his friend's disclaimer. "How 'bout it, gals? Are you on for Saturday night?"

"Why, sure," Peggy said, glancing at Fran for confirmation, "that would be swell."

Bob glanced back pointedly at Knute, who avoided his gaze, and then signaled Doodlebug for the bill. After they had dropped the girls off at their apartment and were driving back to the fraternity house, Bob gave vent to his annoyance.

"Damn it, Knute, you piss me off. You never listen to what I say and always go on and do things your way. I don't want to go to that dance. I've got a lot I have to do before I head home for the holidays."

"Aw, li'l buddy, now don' go feelin' that way," his friend replied. "You'll be sorry you said that soon, 'cause you're gonna miss ol' Knute when he's gone. Now, you'll do this for your ol' buddy, won't ya? An' lemme tell ya somethin'," he added, tapping Bob on the shoulder, "I'm gonna hit pay dirt with this li'l gal. Ol' Knute knows what he's talkin' 'bout. I've got a gol' mine there."

As he pulled into the parking lot behind the fraternity house and shut off the engine, Bob turned and looked at his roommate. In the dim light from the back porch he could see the steady gaze and wide grin of the big Texan.

"Okay, fellow," he said with a laugh. "This one last time I'll do it for you."

# CHAPTER TWO

**THE REST OF** the week passed rapidly. Bob was engrossed in completing the requirements for the semester and tried to work steadily, having to fend off distractions from his roommate, who had taken his imminent induction into the armed forces as a welcome excuse to abandon the academic schedule, to which he had never become addicted. By Wednesday, however, boredom had taken its toll and even he sat in on one of his last classes that afternoon. Both of them had avidly been following the somber news of that grim first week of the war and that evening sat glumly and silently listening to the details of the sinking of the British warships, *Prince of Wales* and *Repulse*, and the surrender of Guam.

On Friday exams began. Knute showed no interest in taking any of his and, having borrowed the car, left early, intending to sit and wait at the recruiting office in hopes of receiving news of the details of his induction. It was almost five o'clock before he showed up at the house again. Bob had just returned to the room, dropped his books on the desk and, bushed from two exams that day, stretched out on his bed.

"Well, any news?" he asked, glancing up as his friend entered.

"Yep," Knute answered, sitting down on his own bed with an expression on his face quieter and more sober than Bob had ever seen. "I'm supposed to report to Fort Sam Houston three days afta

Christmas for basic training. That's not too far from home, so that's good. Afta basic I'll have ta take some tests ta qualify for pilot trainin', and then I'll be on my way. I'm gettin' antsy," he added, pounding his right fist into his left hand.

"Robbie," he continued, getting to his feet, "let's skip dinner at the house tonight and grab a bite over at the Varsity. I need a li'l of ol' Doodle's horseshit to pump me up."

"That suits me," Bob replied. "I could stand a little unwinding myself."

**"OOOOOOOOOOOW!" CAME THE** wail an hour later as Doodlebug virtually vaulted over the rear of a '34 Plymouth to slap his claim on Bob's car. The ritualistic handshakes and off-beat greetings had as usual infused an air of levity by the time the orders were being taken.

"Give me a couple of cheeseburgers with fries and a Coke," Bob said, "and hold the onions."

"Gimme th' same," Knute concurred, "with th' whole works. An' put his onions on my plate."

"Gotcha," Doodlebug responded. "I'll tell Jake to do 'em up special for you gents."

Having headed for the order counter, he stopped and came back to the car window.

"If you fellows can hang around awhile, I think I'll have a little surprise for y'all later."

"Great, Doodle, we have no plans," Bob answered and rolled his window up. Doodlebug waved his hand and trotted off.

The two friends sat quietly for a few minutes without talking. A song by Vic Damone came wafting across the parking lot from a jukebox, and occasional laughter could be heard from one of the parked cars.

"You know," Bob said, breaking the silence, "our world is really going to change, isn't it?"

"Yep," Knute answered softly.

Bob turned and looked at him and was surprised at the

uncharacteristically sober expression on his face. He had never before seen his roommate in a reflective mood, and oddly it didn't seem to fit him at all.

"Are you kind of scared?" Bob asked.

Knute started, as though jolted from a reverie, and turned and looked at him.

"Huh? Me? Scared? Hell, no. Those bastards had better not mess with ol' Knute." Then after a pause, in a quieter tone he continued, "It's just that nothin's gonna be the same, ya know? I'm gonna miss all this. . . An' I'm gonna miss you too, ol' buddy. Hell, nobody else'll ever put up with me like you have."

"I can't argue with you about that," Bob laughed. "You're probably dead right."

"That's why we're gonna have a helluva final fling tomorrow night," Knute said, the typically impish grin returning to his face. "I tell ya, li'l buddy, we're gonna have us some real fun."

"Now wait a minute," Bob objected. "I've agreed to go to the dance, but it's over at twelve. And that's as far as the agreement goes."

Knute stared at him in disbelief.

"Ya gotta be kiddin'! Man, we can get us some sack time. These gals are hot to trot, believe me. You're talkin' to th' ol' master here, and I know what I'm talkin' about."

"No way!" Bob insisted. "I'm not interested in that girl. I'll let you use the car. You can drop me off after the dance and then do anything you want."

"Aw, come on, Robbie. It won't work out if ya cut out on me," Knute pleaded. Then he narrowed his eyes and stared at his friend for a moment.

"Ya know, there's somethin' I've never been able to figure out about you. Tell me, li'l buddy, are you still a virgin?"

The suddenness of the question caught Bob off balance. In spite of their closeness and the frequent allusions to Knute's astounding and checkered erotic career, the question of his own sex life had never come up. He turned and looked out the window and instead of answering merely shook his head. Knute continued to look at him.

"Well, I'll be dam'," he said. "Ya coulda fooled me. Ya sure act like one. . . When did ya luck out th' first time—las' week?"

Bob shook his head again.

"No, it was a long time ago."

"Ya gotta be kiddin'. How ol' were ya?"

"Thirteen."

"Thirteen!" Knute exclaimed with unveiled admiration mixed with a little envy. "Ya never mentioned that before. Tell me 'bout it."

"There wouldn't be anything to tell," Bob laughed. "There wasn't much to it, and you probably wouldn't even put it down on your scorecard."

Knute poked him in the ribs.

"Aw, hell, a piece is a piece, an' th' first one's pretty important. Come on now and 'fess up. This is one story I gotta hear."

At this moment Doodlebug approached the car carrying two trays, and they had to roll their windows down, leaving two inches of glass above the jamb. Doodlebug was the best "two-tray" man at the Varsity. He could hook the first tray over the window glass and adjust the outside support arm with one hand without the slightest wavering of the second tray.

"Well," Bob began, as he occupied himself with arranging the condiments on his first cheeseburger, "as you know, I grew up on a farm and spent most of my time on horseback. My dad had bought me a little filly that was the fastest pony in the county. She could fly like the wind, and I used to love to challenge all the local kids to races. I always won. The only close competition I ever had was from two brothers, sons of an alcoholic blacksmith who lived up in the hollow. They had a black gelding that was really fast. They were both older than I. Frank was an old man of sixteen, and his brother Bud was fourteen. They were really rough characters, and I don't know why I started hanging around with them. I guess in a way I kind of looked up to them. You know—their being older, and everything. Also, they taught me how to do a lot of things—some good and some bad, I guess—like cuss and chew tobacco and hunt. At forty yards Frank could hit a squirrel in the eye every time with a .22 rifle. They were terrific riders and showed me how to get better. They'd make me get up on my pony bareback and jump logs and creeks. At first I fell off so many times I don't know why I wasn't killed, but finally I learned to stay on and was a lot better rider because of it, especially after I started riding to the hounds on fox hunts."

"Hell," Knute mumbled with a mouthful of French fries, "out where I grew up, only Indians and Mexes ride bareback. A fancy saddle is more important to a man than a big cock."

A grin forced Bob to pause in taking a bite out of his burger.

"Well, go on," Knute urged, impatient at the delay occasioned by his friend's chewing.

Bob took a swallow of Coke and continued.

"There was a huge dairy barn a couple of miles from our farm, and on rainy days we used to love to explore and climb around up in the lofts and rafters. A couple of times they made me take part in a 'circle jerk'—you know, where the guys sit around in a circle masturbating. Usually the winner is the one who can shoot off first, but in our case the last one to get it off was the loser and had to 'walk the beam.' This old barn was very wide, and the support beams stretched all the way across. There were two hay lofts, one on each side, but the center section was open all the way to the floor of the barn. All the farm machinery—harrows, bailers, mowers, plows—were parked down below. You could hold onto the forty-five degree braces most of the way on the sides, but there was about a twelve-foot stretch in the middle where there was nothing to grab. The beam was only about three and a half inches wide, and if you lost your balance there, there would be about a sixty-foot drop onto the machines. You'd be a goner. Well, I was kind of a timid, shy kid, so naturally I lost every time and had to walk the beam across and back."

"Now wait a minute, li'l buddy," Knute broke in. "Beatin' your meat ain't th' same as nooky an' doesn't count."

"I didn't think it would," Bob laughed. "Well, one cold rainy day the three of us were playing in the loft with the fifteen-year-old daughter of the dairyman. Her name was Trixie, and she was a real tomboy. We'd climb up almost to the top of the roof and jump down into the hay. It was great fun. When we had almost worn ourselves out, we were sprawled on the hay talking. Frank suddenly laughed and suggested we let Trixie watch one of our circle jerks. I was so embarrassed that my face burned like fire. I said that it was late and I had to head home, but they said I couldn't leave. Bud even moved over and blocked the cutout for the ladder from down below. Frank and Trixie were whispering and giggling, and he got up and said they thought it would be a scream to make me have sex with her. I fought as hard as I could, but Frank and Bud were a lot bigger and stronger than I. She was almost as strong as they and was on their side. I don't know how anything could have happened, because I was so frightened and mortified. But with her pulling from the front and their pushing from behind, I couldn't help myself. My impressions are pretty hazy, but something must have happened, I remember having an orgasm, and then they let me go."

"Hot dam'!" Knute muttered appreciatively, taking a gulp of Coke. "An' I guess ya made out a lot with that li'l trick after that, huh?"

"No, that was the only time. After all, she cheated on me with Frank about twenty seconds later, so I considered my commitment terminated," Bob joked.

Knute pondered that for a minute, the humor passing over his head.

"Well, what about th' next gal? Was she any better?"

"There hasn't been another one."

"There hasn't been another?!" Knute repeated incredulously. "Ya mean ya don't want to do it again?"

"Sure, I want to," Bob said somewhat defensively, "but I don't look at sex or at women the way you do. My dad never talked to me about sex, but my mother did frequently: 'Son, you can't ever respect yourself if you don't respect all women'; 'Always be a gentleman'; 'Don't bring shame on the family name'; 'If a woman will let you be forward with her, then she's trying to snare you, and you will bring grief and expense to your parents'; and on and on. Did your folks ever talk to you about sex?"

"My mother never did," Knute answered, "and my old man did only once. His advice consisted of a single sentence: 'Son, get all you can whenever you can.'"

Bob had to laugh. He wanted to buy a little time to spend on his meal, so he asked his friend, "Well, what about your first time? How old were you?"

"Sixteen," Knute answered, "so ya had a three-year jump on me. But I've made up a lot a time since then."

"Tell me about it," Bob requested, starting to work on his second burger.

"It wasn't as hairy as yours. On my sixteenth birthday my dad drove me a hundred miles to a li'l whorehouse over in Barstow, Texas. All th' gals knew him there, so he must've been a regular customer. He fixed me up with his favorite."

Knute paused and was munching on his sandwich.

"How was it?" Bob inquired, genuinely curious.

"We-e-ell, I didn't know it at th' time, but it turned out to 'ave been th' worst piece I ever had," Knute responded, pausing briefly to retrieve a piece of onion that had fallen into his lap. Placing it back in the burger, he added with a soft reverence, "An' it was jus' marvelous."

Exploding in laughter, Bob almost choked on the food in his mouth.

"Robbie," Knute said after he had finished his last sandwich and French fry and licked his finger tips, "I don' mean ta be disrespectful or try ta cut ya down or anything, but it sounds ta me like you ain't really had your cherry busted yet. We're jus' gonna have ta take care a that tomorrow night."

"Oh, no!" Bob protested, "none of that now. I've already told you I'm not interested in that girl. She doesn't appeal to me at all. If you're dead set on making out with your date, then that's your business. But count me out."

"Aw, hell, buddy, I can't get 'er in bed with Fran standin' around. Ya gotta keep 'er busy at least an hour. Give 'er a bunch a your sweet-talk or play with her titties, or somethin,' but gimme a break, okay?"

Bob whistled for Doodlebug.

"Well, okay. If I can stay awake for another hour, I'll do the best I can. But if you haven't scored by then, I'm walking back to the house."

Doodlebug came walking up with a handsome man in tow. For some reason Doodlebug liked to produce and introduce to Bob people whom he thought to be different, interesting or impressive. It was a way of showing off a bit the breadth of his own contacts and acquaintances. The people he brought over could run anywhere from a Tasmanian sheep herder to a jazz drummer. The stranger this night, sun-tanned and of medium height, had a haircut and clothing style that clearly suggested, if not California, then at least someplace other than Atlanta, Georgia.

"Gents," Doodlebug said as he removed one of the trays from the door, "I want you to meet a friend of mine, Mr. Steve Brent. He's a famous movie actor from Hollywood, and I told him you fellows would like to hear some of his tales about that quiet little country town. Mister Steve, this here is Mister Robert and Mister Knute. Why don't you climb in the back seat there, and I'll bring some big cups with ice."

Knute pulled his seat back forward to facilitate Brent's entry.

Leaning into the car, Doodlebug whispered, "Mister Steve's got a little bit of liquid sunshine under his coat there. Want anything to go with it?"

When Brent produced a quart bottle of bourbon, Knute's eyes lit up, and he asked for a double cup of ice. Bob, however, just ordered another Coke; he was not too happy with this development. Drinking in cars was strictly against the law, although a common practice in drive-ins. But the Varsity was a popular place even for policemen in patrol cars, and on occasion students had been arrested for breaking this law.

After Doodlebug had mentioned the actor's name, Bob recognized him. He remembered having seen him in a series of grade-B movies several years earlier. He turned out to be not stuffy at all but very friendly, and conversation flowed freely. Actually it developed into more of a monologue under the prompting of Doodlebug, who, even eschewing a chance to claim and wait on a Bentley, stood outside the car listening attentively. (Next to people and distinctive automobiles, Doodlebug loved gossip.) Brent reeled off detailed stories of the rich and famous in the City of the Angels—the sins, the peccadillos, the rivalries, the intrigues, the scandals. Knute's unaccustomed silence gave testimony to his awe and impressibility, but as the evening wore on, Bob became more and more disenchanted. In the past he had always enjoyed Doodlebug's proffered personalities, but this time for some reason—perhaps from fatigue or subconscious preoccupation with the news of the war—he felt alienated.

Brent launched into a lengthy story concerning a challenge tennis match played in Las Vegas. The challenger, a good friend of his, was to play a best-of-five-set match against the mighty Bill Tilden and enlisted Brent to drive him to Las Vegas. Departure from Los Angeles was on the afternoon before the match, and the actor ended up in the front seat alone, acting as chauffeur, while his friend rode in the back seat with Simone Brouvet, the notoriously sexy French starlet, whom he had met at a party just the night before. Although the acquaintance had been short, Brent related that before they had reached the city limits of L.A., all he could see in the rear view mirror were the calves and high heels of the starlet, that as they passed through Baker, California, all he could see was the upper part of her body bouncing up and down more vigorously than the admittedly lack of smoothness of the highway would by itself dictate, and that as they entered Las Vegas, no portion of her anatomy at all was visible—only the face of the exhausted friend, who was moaning with pleasure.

Knute had been listening to this discourse with rapt attention, wide-eyed and occasionally wetting his lips. When Brent paused briefly to add a bit more beverage to his cup of ice, the big Texan said in a low voice, as though talking to himself, "Hot dam'! I'm gonna have ta get me a tennis racquet."

As the lengthy narrative drew to a close, the audience, already impressed by the prodigious stamina of Brent's friend, was almost more impressed by the fact that, although the great Tilden won the next day, the valiant challenger had extended him to the full five sets.

When Brent began to wax loquacious concerning some incidents that occurred during the filming of *Gone With the Wind*, Bob's mood turned increasingly sour, and he felt somewhat trapped. He motioned to Doodlebug that he wanted the check, and his grinning friend got the message.

"Mister Steve, why don't you come on with me? I've got some other folks I want you to meet. Old Doodle needs to spread you around a bit to keep up his reputation."

Having climbed out of the car, the actor amiably shook hands all around and handed Knute the bottle, still over half full of bourbon. As Bob pulled out of the Varsity parking lot into the street, Knute, sensing his friend's mood, looked at him questioningly.

"He's a helluva friendly an' interestin' fella. What got into you?"

"Yeah, he's a nice guy," Bob agreed. "I don't know. I just suddenly got turned off. The whole world's catching on fire, and we'd been sitting there for three hours talking about little else but sex. Hell, Knute, there are other things in life, you know?"

Knute rolled up his window to block out the cold breeze.

"Yeah, I guess you're right. But whatever is in second place is so far back on th' track that I can't even remember what it is."

# CHAPTER THREE

**THEY ARRIVED FOR** the dance the next evening thirty minutes late. Bob had regretted his decision to go along with Knute as soon as they stopped to pick up the girls or, more accurately, the women. He had not noticed on Monday night, but in the full light of the apartment building entrance it was obvious that both were at least in their late twenties and thus would be ten years older than the vast majority of the other students' dates. In addition they would be even more conspicuous because each had on a short cocktail dress and spike heels instead of an evening gown and dancing slippers.

Bob's premonition proved to be correct. As they filed into the gymnasium, he saw that all the other girls were in pastel ball gowns of taffeta and lace—pink, green, white, and blue—in stark contrast with Peggy's tight-fitting black satin and Fran's red mock velvet. Along the wall of the dance floor just inside the entrance sat the fraternity housemothers and the wives of university administrators, serving as unofficial chaperones to ensure that the "ramblin' wrecks from Georgia Tech" did their rambling within the limits of a certain decorum. The more proper students accepted the tradition of taking their dates down this "receiving line" and introducing themselves and their dates to each of the ladies.

Bob insisted on guiding his foursome through this routine, but when they reached the Sigma Chi housemother, Mrs. Arcy Brown, of whom Bob was quite fond, he flinched inwardly when Fran responded with a brassy "Glad ta meetcha!"

The cavernous gymnasium, packed with dancing couples, was reverberating with the superb music of the big band of Harry James. Balloons and crepe decorations festooned the ceiling and balconies, and along each of the sides, with the exception of the one hosting the bandstand, there were tables with plates of cookies and bowls of fruit punch.

Bob had always loved to dance and was swept up by the persuasive beat of the music, but unfortunately Fran's terpsichorean abilities were limited by disinterest and ineptitude. On the dance floor she was leaden and unresponsive. From observation Peggy seemed to be a good dancer, but Knute's over-enthusiastic and awkward lurching resulted in a few foot-crunching mishaps that retired them to the sidelines. After two strenuous and disastrous pieces Bob also gave up and guided his date over to join them near the punch bowl.

"Hey," Knute said guardedly and jerked his head at the three of them to follow him. He led them around behind a screen flanking the tables and pulled from his back pocket a handsome silver flask.

"This here has been in th' family for over a hundred years. My gran'daddy gave it to my pappy, an' he gave it to me when I came here to Tech. I filled it up with some a' that bourbon we got last night. Gals, y'all go an' fetch us some cups at that punch an' we'll jazz it up a li'l."

The girls giggled and went around the screen to get the four cups.

"Knute, are you out of your mind?" Bob whispered. "You know we could be suspended if they caught us drinking in here!"

"Aw hell, li'l buddy, they won' catch us. Besides, I'll take th' blame if we're caught. I'm leavin' in a coupla days anyway."

"Well, you are, but I'm not. I'm not going to run that risk," Bob said with a note of disgust. "If they kick you out, have one of the girls come and find me. I'm going to wander around a while. Ill check back with you."

The girls returned at this moment with the four Dixie cups full of pink liquid. Bob took his and drained it before Knute could embellish the contents. Knute persisted in adding bourbon from his flask to the other three, so Bob excused himself and withdrew from this potentially dangerous situation. As he walked away, his mood improved. It was as though a load had been lifted from his shoulders by his having found an acceptable excuse to break free. The music, the pretty dresses, the laughter, the whirl of the dancers—all contributed to a festiveness that was irresistible.

As he was making his way along the wall, Bob suddenly stopped, having caught sight of a girl he felt he knew. At first he couldn't place her, for, although the face was familiar and related somewhere to his past, it was far more lovely than his memory afforded. She was a fabulous dancer, and there was a long "stag line" of boys patiently waiting to break in and dance with her. By Southern tradition there was an unwritten rule that with very popular girls approximately forty seconds of time was allotted each male to break in and dance a few steps before he in turn would be "broken on" by the next stag in line. If a boor or a Northern boy unfamiliar with the tradition were to violate the code and break too soon, then he would be ostracized and made sharply aware of his transgression.

Bob stood with his back to the wall and watched as her radiant smile made each new arrival feel that he was the one for whom she had been waiting all evening. Then he recalled who she was—Nancy Garner from Lexington. The last time he had seen her had been four years earlier, and she had been a dumpy freckled-faced little girl. What a transformation! In her blue and white lace ball gown and dancing slippers she appeared to be about five feet two with a trim, firm athletic figure. Her auburn tresses, flashing with hues of burnt orange in the light from the overhead spots, reached below her shoulders on those infrequent occasions when they weren't swirling about her head as she executed the Lindy or a jitterbug "fan-out." But it was the change in her face that was the most remarkable. The wide-eyed, round-faced self-consciousness had metamorphosed into a manifestly sophisticated confidence. The freckles had faded to mere hints against the almost-translucent opaqueness of her skin and were matched by faint imitative patterns on her shoulders.

As Bob stood staring at her, their eyes met briefly as she whirled past. She did a double-take and smiled. He joined the end of the stag line and waited through almost two numbers before his turn came up to break. By that time the sweet wails of James's trumpet lamenting "You Made Me Love You" assured a disinclination to conversation, so they just danced. She immediately melted into his arms and followed him so superbly that it was almost as though she were an appendage of his own body. Bob had caught sight of the next stag starting to move toward them, when luckily the piece came to an end and he was granted the luxury of the interval between numbers.

"Hi, Nancy, I'm Bob. . ." he began.

"I know! You're Bob Hanson," she interrupted, holding onto both of his hands and smiling up at him. "It's not very likely that I'd forget, for I used to have a terrible crush on you."

"I can't believe that," he answered. "I remember you on those long horseback rides our families used to take on Sunday afternoons, but I think it's been at least four years since I've seen you."

"That's right, and I can tell you exactly where it was," she said. "It was at Sue Bennett's birthday party. You were there in your military school uniform, and all us girls were simply swooning."

"By George," Bob laughed, "I believe I do remember that party now. But I hardly recognized you. Talk about the butterfly coming out of the cocoon! What a change!"

"Not really," Nancy said. "I think I still weigh the same, but I guess I've rearranged it a little."

"A little?" Bob laughed again. "But what are you up to now? How did you end up here?"

"I'm a freshman up at the University of Virginia," she answered, "and Bill Neal—you remember him, he's a junior here at Tech—asked me down for the dance. The Neals have always been good friends of the family, and he and I used to fight all the time, but I thought it'd be fun to come."

At this moment the band launched into the opening bars of "Pennsylvania Six Five Thousand" and the two of them spontaneously fell into a jitterbug routine. The formerly frustrated and impatient stag, however, granted them only a few steps before he came up to break on them. As they parted, Nancy squeezed Bob's hand tightly and, looking him in the eye, said, "When you get to Lexington, call me, will you?"

Bob nodded his head and moved off. He circumnavigated the gymnasium several times, enjoying watching the pretty girls in their efforts to impress their dates or partners with their feigned sophistication. So pleasant was this role of detached observer that he had become unaware of the passage of time. A rude reminder was supplied by the band leader's announcement of intermission. Only then did Bob suddenly remember the trio with whom he had arrived. He pushed his way back to the refreshment table, but they were no longer there. After a hurried circuit of the gymnasium floor he passed through one of the doors into the spectator entrance hall and saw Knute braced against the wall with both arms draped over the shoulders of the girls, who were apparently partially supporting him. Obviously he had dispatched the majority of the contents of the empty flask precariously protruding from the pocket of his jacket.

"Hey there, li'l buddy. Where th' hell ya been? We been lookin' all over for ya. We thought that maybe we oughtta go back to th' gals' place. They've offered us a drink and maybe some eggs or somethin.' What d'ya think?"

Bob was very uneasy over the obviousness of Knute's inebriation. If the student government monitors assigned to the dance were to spot him, they'd be in real trouble. So he quickly agreed to the early departure and volunteered to go and get the car to cut down on the distance in which Knute could be observed to be staggering.

"The apartment number is 6C," Peggy said as they struggled to get Knute out of the car in front of the building. "Why don't you park the car and come on up? We'll try to get him on the elevator."

Bob found a space on a side street and locked the car. The elevator "in use" light was illuminated for a long time, so he had to wait while he imagined the girls' efforts to get the big Texan up to the sixth floor and into the apartment. Several minutes had passed by the time the elevator had returned to the ground floor and carried him back up. The door to apartment 6C was ajar, so he entered and closed it behind him. The small entrance hall led off to a bathroom and bedroom on the right. There was a living room straight ahead, and to the left a closed door presumably led to another bedroom.

There were muffled voices coming from behind the closed door, but no one was in sight. Feeling somewhat uneasy, Bob walked into the living room and sat down on the sofa, picking up and skimming through a *Life* magazine. He heard a door close, and in a moment Fran appeared, stopped in the doorway and looked at him expectantly.

"Well, aren't you coming?" she asked.

"Huh? Oh, yeah, sure," he answered, unsure as to her meaning but fearful that he had a good idea of what it was.

Caught off guard by the suddenness of this development, he rose and followed her hesitantly into the bedroom on the right. She took a light blue rayon nightgown from a hook on the closet door and headed for the bathroom. Noticing that he was standing awkwardly in the middle of the floor, she looked at him quizzically.

"Well, make yaself comfortable, lover," she said. "I'll only take a minute."

Bob began to undress. Since there was no chair in the room, he laid his clothes on top of a cedar chest standing to the right of a dressing table. Having stripped, he pulled back the bedspread and nervously crawled under the covers. He had only a few moments to contemplate the dire nature of his predicament when Fran entered. She hung her red dress in the closet and then slid under the covers on her side of the bed. Bob realized the seriousness of her intent when, just before she turned out the light, he saw her remove her chewing gum and place it on the bedside table.

When she moved over and wrapped her arm around him, Bob was suddenly immersed in the stiflingly sweet aroma of Sweetpea Bath Powder. He could identify it, because the family cook during his childhood in Lexington had been addicted to it and refused to use anything else, requesting him and his mother to buy it for her during their occasional visits to Kress on a Saturday morning. After a few wet and prolonged kisses Fran pulled up her nightgown, clasped him tightly and rolled over, positioning him on top of her. When she had inserted the diaphragm in the bathroom, she had apparently been quite generous in the application of a lubricant, for in spite of the fact that a pertinent part of Bob's anatomy exhibited less than ideal enthusiasm, entry was absurdly easy and subsequent friction virtually non-existent.

However, with a relentless hold on his hips and frenzied pelvic movements Fran did manage to bring him to a sufficient level of excitation to achieve a semi-orgasm. In fact the climax, if that is what it loosely could be called, came much more quickly than Bob would have anticipated and certainly more quickly than he would have wished. Totally disinterested in any further activity, with a feeling of enervation he rolled off to the side onto his back with his eyes closed. Fran turned on the lamp and moved up to sit leaning back against the headboard. Bob couldn't tell if she had re-engaged her wad of chewing gum, but he did hear her light a cigarette. With an explosive exhalation of smoke she said bitterly, "That's great! That's just great! What th' hell am I s'posed to do—make it with the handle of my hairbrush?"

Bob inwardly cringed. He sensed he had failed and suddenly realized that subconsciously he had always feared that failure, realized that very probably a sizable component of his "gentle manliness" and shyness had been based on that very anxiety. He was disappointed in himself and acutely unhappy to be lying there. He felt a compulsion to leave immediately and was about to rise and retrieve his clothes when the bedroom door opened. Peggy paused and leaned against the door jamb. A cigarette was dangling from her lips, and she had on a full-length black silk dressing gown.

"That big stud passed out on me before he could get his clothes off, and I can't rouse him," she complained, taking the cigarette out of her mouth. "How did you all make out in here?"

"Fantastic! Absolutely fantastic!" Fran snorted. "If ya like a twenty-yard dash, that is."

Bob cringed again and felt hot all over. He opened his eyes a bit and wondered if he shouldn't just get up and get dressed.

"Aw, I can't believe that," Peggy said, taking a drag on her cigarette and observing Bob through the exhaled smoke. Walking over to the bed, she sat down next to him and pulled the sheet down to his waist.

"That doesn't make sense," she continued, beginning to lightly rub his arms, chest and stomach. "Bobby here is built like a greyhound. He should be able to go the distance."

The touch of her hands mesmerized him, and he postponed his intended departure. He regarded her through half-closed eyes and for the first time fully realized how pretty she was. After a moment she patted him on the solar plexus and said, rising, "Now you just take it easy, sugah, and I'll be right back."

Bob closed his eyes again and aurally tried to follow her movements. He heard her go into the bathroom and heard the running of water. A few minutes later when he sensed she had returned to the bedroom, he cracked his eyelids and saw her approaching the bed totally nude and carrying a towel and a balled-up washcloth. Jerking the sheet all the way off of him, she sat down on the bed again and placed the hot unraveled washcloth over his inert member, cleaning it meticulously. The effect of her hands earlier had been minuscule compared to the pleasure he now felt. Continuing to stimulate his slowly expanding phallus with her left hand, she cupped the hot cloth completely around his testicles and massaged them gently with a slow rhythm. The larger his penis grew, the more smug became her half-grin.

"Aha!" she purred softly, giving him a wink. "I've always had faith in the resurrection of an erection."

Bob closed his eyes and stretched out to relish this indescribable sensation. Abruptly, however, she got up from the bed, and he felt the press of flesh against each ear followed by the insertion of the head of his member into her mouth. Startled, he opened his eyes and saw that she had straddled his head with her knees and bent forward to perform her ministrations. As varied as had been his fantasies concerning women, never had he dared dream of having such an intimate and gratuitous view of that portion of a woman's body. Shock and exhilaration flooded through him as he gazed at the panorama above. Having been raised on a farm, he had frequently observed the mating of a multitude of animals and had always considered female mammalian genitalia to be functional but otherwise unimaginative. So he was unprepared for the profound and almost existential beauty of this girl's genitals.

He would have been content to lie thus indefinitely, but this was obviously not sufficient for Peggy. Momentarily abandoning her oral exercise, with her inverted face peering at him from behind her long black hair and from between her shapely suspended breasts, she said tersely, "Don't go to sleep on me, sonny boy. You can play with it, you know. It won't bite you." Then she returned to her charitable activities.

Slowly and methodically Bob began to explore and caress her body. He admired the smoothness of the skin on her legs, the subtle beauty of the curve of the line between buttock and thigh and the pliant softness of her labia. After some hesitation and trepidation he began gently to rub her clitoris and in the next five minutes received a broad education in the erotic stimulation of women. Peggy's bodily responses could not have been more graphic or obvious in letting him know what he did that pleased her the most and what he did that pleased her less.

Suddenly she raised up, moved forward on her knees and, holding his penis erect under her, sat all the way down, drawing him up within her. Bob had never experienced anything like the sheer ecstasy of that instant. He was carried along by an almost inexorable rush to ejaculation, and only by sheer will power bolstered by fear of another failure resulting from premature orgasm was he able to pull back from the precipice. He had avoided the catastrophe by clenching his teeth, holding his breath and squinting his eyes firmly shut. Very quickly, however, he learned to rely on less-strenuous methods and soon was amazed to realize that he could orchestrate his response quite subtly through mental exercise and discipline. Luckily Peggy had sat motionless for a minute, giving him time to regroup. By the time she started moving up and down he had stumbled on a method of shifting into different levels of control. He could switch instantly from the extreme stimulation of acute awareness of his intimate involvement in sexual intercourse with a beautiful woman, through a "subjective observer" role (wherein he was outside of himself but still inside the room), then through an "objective observer" role (a third person looking in from outside) all the way to complete mental disengagement—an awareness of the patter on the window sill of the rain that had begun to fall or the sound of the auto-mobile tires on the wet pavement of Peachtree Street. He became so fascinated by this exercise and the development of this control that he purposely manipulated it. He would allow himself the delicious appre-ciation of Peggy's long dark hair cascading down her lovely back, the tiny waist pointing to the dimple at the top of each buttock and even the soft sole of her feet curled back under her. When the resultant ten-sion within him became critical, he could retreat to a safer level, if need be even to the point of risking the loss of his erection.

So engrossed was he in his newfound game that he was happily immune to whatever Peggy did or didn't do; he could control the sit-uation. It was almost immaterial to him when she dismounted and her place was taken by Fran, who sat facing him rather than away from him. For the next hour he calmly and stoically followed their requests for an incredible variety of positions and arrangements, each of the girls taking turns while chatting with each other and sharing ciga-rettes. At the time he was unaware of it, but upon later reflection he was amazed at the total mutual depersonalization of the encounter. It wasn't just he who was emotionally detached. There was no personal involvement on his part with them or on their part with him—only genital involvement—and he played no role with them except that of erotic implement. His pleasure was no longer dependent on the stim-ulation of their attractiveness, identity or beauty. He was firmly mired in pure carnality.

Finally at one point he was vaguely aware that Fran had appar-ently achieved orgasm, for she withdrew and sat leaning against the headboard. Peggy asked him to lie on his back again and remounted, facing him this time. Her movements became so violent and frenzied that Bob was in grave danger of losing his vaunted control. Franti-cally he shut his eyes and mentally withdrew to a winter day in Lex-ington and a walk in the cold rain across a barren cornfield. Rudely he was drawn back to the apartment by a sharp pain on his chest, and he grabbed Peggy's hands. She had dug her long nails into his flesh and thrown her head back, her body quivering and a low growl coming from her throat. When the spasm had passed, she slumped forward and rested her head on his shoulder, breathing heavily. Bob pulled her thick hair away from his nose and eyes and glanced at Fran, who winked at him and grinned. She lit two cigarettes and, when Peggy had straightened up and dismounted, handed one to her.

Only then did Bob realize that he was in pain. Pressure in his bladder, the increase of which he had been unaware of during intercourse, now made itself known and was intense. Excusing himself, he made his way into the bathroom. He stood for a long time over the toilet bowl, but the unrelenting turgidity of his penis rendered urination impossible. Beginning to fear that this might be a permanent condition, he moved to the sink and began to run cool water over the offending member. During this exercise he glanced at himself in the mirror and noticed two fine trickles of blood coursing down his chest from the nail wounds just received. Gradually the water treatment began to work. Having succeeded in emptying his bladder and temporarily stopping the trickles of blood, he walked back into the bedroom. The girls had moved down onto the bed and were both fast asleep, Fran's head resting on Peggy's out-stretched arm. One cigarette had been extinguished in the ashtray, but Fran's was dangling from her fingers dangerously close to the sheet. Bob removed it slowly and extinguished it also. He stood for a moment looking down at them. Incongruously there was a fresh innocence about them as they slept. Their cheeks glowed, and each had an obviously reddish spot on the right point of her chin caused by the stubble of his beard during the intensive kissing.

Suddenly Bob shivered. The temperature in the apartment had dropped considerably due to the cold rain outside. Gently he pulled up the sheet and the spread and covered the sleeping girls and then proceeded to get dressed. As he stepped into the entrance hall, from behind the opposite closed door he heard a loud snore. Sticking his head into the room, he saw Knute in just his shorts sprawled on his back on the bed with his right foot on the floor, snoring loudly. With a weary smile Bob closed the door and walked out of the apartment and to the car.

\* \* \*

**BOB AWOKE LATE** in the morning with a feeling of euphoria, with a sense that the change in his life due to the war would be equaled, if not exceeded, by the change due to his experience of the preceding evening. He knew that henceforth his view of sex, of life and, most important, of himself would never be the same. Although he had two important examinations coming up the next day, he found it very difficult to concentrate on his books and his notes. He sat at his desk with his shirt unbuttoned and occasionally would gingerly and proudly run his fingers over his superficial wounds. By mid-afternoon he had finally succeeded in getting his concentration centered on his studies when Knute came wandering in.

"Man, li'l buddy, what about that evenin,' huh? Didn't I tell ya we'd have us a good time?"

"Yep, you were right," Bob admitted with a grin. "That was really something. How did you get back? You should have called me to pick you up."

"Aw, it's not far. The rain stopped, and I figured the walk would do me good. My head was a li'l cob-webby."

"I can well imagine," Bob laughed. "You had a lot to drink, you know."

"You're tellin' me, li'l buddy! But I'm gonna hafta cut down some. I tried to talk that li'l gal into another roll in th' hay, but she said she was too sore from las' night. Hell, I can't remember a dam' thing about it and don't feel I'd been at it at all. This li'l thing is mighty pretty," he added, pulling the flask from out of his pocket, "but I'm gonna give it back to my daddy. Hell, it ain't worth it if I can't remember nooky. How'd you make out with Fran, Robbie?"

"Oh, fine," Bob answered, suddenly remembering to button his shirt. "We talked a lot and listened to records."

"Aw, hell, li'l buddy, that's kinda sad. If I wasn't leavin' on Tuesday, we'd hafta do somethin' about you."

**AT TEN FIFTY-FIVE** on Tuesday morning the two friends stood on the platform of the Atlanta train station. They had finished getting on board the bags and boxes packed with all of Knute's belongings, since he was leaving for good. A self-consciousness had descended on them and precluded conversation. The hiss of steam and the shouted "'board!" by the conductor jarred them from their silence. They shook hands warmly, and Knute beamed down at his former roommate.

"I'm gonna miss ya, li'l buddy. You take care, ya hear?"

"Yeah," Bob answered, "I'm going to miss you too. It won't be the same around here without you. Don't take any wooden nickels, and I'll see you in Berlin."

With a wave of his hand the big Texan bounded up the steps of the railroad car and disappeared. As the train began to move out of the station, Bob took one last look and then turned and walked toward the street. Suddenly he felt much, much older than he had just ten days earlier.

# CHAPTER FOUR

**LEXINGTON WAS NOT** the same.

During his last days in Atlanta and on the drive home, as an antidote to a growing restlessness and unease, Bob had yearned and hungered for a return to the comfort and security of familiar faces, familiar routines and familiar places—especially the farm where he had spent his childhood. As soon as he could break away from his solicitous parents after his arrival, he donned some comfortable old clothes and riding boots and took the pickup truck back to the barns. As usual, the reunion with the farm hands, grooms and trainers was boisterous and warm with jokes and banter and physical jostling. He had known most of them since he was a boy, and a mutual respect and affection assured a comfortable and easy rapport in spite of his frequently prolonged absences away at military school or college and his status as scion of the family.

Although it was late, he had a five-gaited pony saddled and set out on a ride along his favorite paths through the hilly, wooded portion of the estate. Somehow there was a comforting reassurance of stability in the stark wintry silhouettes of the trees, the measured trot of his well-trained horse and even the rhythmic contact of his thighs with the saddle as he posted. He reined in the pony and dismounted at one of his favorite spots, a bluff that was situated at the edge of a draw and that afforded in the fading light a wide view of the tailored fields, pastures and paddocks of the farms down below. As he had done hundreds of times as a boy, he pressed his ears against the warm fuzzy neck of the pony and inhaled its familiar aroma. Observing the small clouds of condensation emanating from its nostrils, the alternate flicking to and fro of the ears and the brown gentleness of the eyes brought back a nostalgic flood of thousands of childhood memories. This was the medicine he had been seeking, and it was partially successful. But by the time he had returned to the barn a trace of the disquietude had returned. It was already dark and everyone had left, so he unsaddled the pony, rubbed it down with a brush and a towel and rewarded it with two coffee cups-full of oats and sweet feed.

In the conversation at dinner time that evening, even though the course of the war was discussed at length, both Bob and his parents meticulously avoided bringing up the subject of his draft status or of his possible volunteering. The parents avoided it because they knew their son well and were afraid of what his response would be. Bob avoided it to spare his mother the truth of his ultimate intentions. She was the type of woman who, with all things being equal and given a choice between peace of mind and anxiety, would invariably choose the latter. Even as a child he had learned to gauge the level of her anxiousness by the frequency of the nervous involuntary raising of her eyebrows, even when she wasn't speaking. And the frequency this evening gave a clear indication of the dread of what she might hear.

The onset of the weekend afforded some insulation from the tension. Bob had wanted to go immediately to talk to Army recruiters after his return to Lexington but was forced to wait until Monday the twenty-second. This allowed the family two days in which to settle into a familiar routine and at least an air of pretended normalcy. It also granted Bob a period of reflection in which to firm up his intent—if he were successful in gaining a delay in induction until after graduation—of shielding his mother completely from the news of his signing up. He was reluctant to lie to her but wanted to avoid burdening her with six months of needless worrying.

Bob had a legitimate excuse for driving into town early on

Monday morning. He wanted to take his car in for a general checkup, an oil and filter change and a lubrication. The long wait for the completion of service would grant him a suitable length of time for the ten-block walk to the recruiting office and the anticipated hours-long process of screening. He had been surprised at the speed with which Knute had completed his enlistment, but it turned out to have been lengthy compared to his own. The long line of mostly young recruits was efficiently handled by a leather-faced but surprisingly soft-spoken and paternalistic sergeant. When he saw the indication on Bob's application of his desire to apply for pilot training in the Air Corps, he directed him to an office down the hall. A second lieutenant was seated behind a plain wooden table examining the papers of four other prospective candidates ranged on chairs along the wall. Bob recognized one from his grade school days and nodded but could not remember his name.

He took a seat and waited for thirty minutes until the four had been processed. The lieutenant finally took his file and glanced through it.

"So you're in college now?"

"Yes, sir."

"Where?"

"Georgia Tech. I'm a senior."

"Then you have a deferment—at least until you graduate. Why are you applying now?"

"By signing up now I'm hoping to get a priority for Aviation Cadet training as a pilot, sir."

"I see. But are you aware that, even if you pass the physical and your application is accepted for the Cadet program, you might not be assigned for pilot training but for that of navigator or bombardier?"

"Yes, sir, I'm aware of that. I would like to graduate, though. If I sign up now, is there a chance I could put off induction until after graduation?"

"I can almost guarantee that," the lieutenant responded, making a notation on the form. "The Army would prefer that you finish your college training. In that way, if you don't qualify for the Air Corps, then you could probably apply for Officer Candidate School in the infantry or wherever. Also, in the last two weeks we have been flooded with pilot applicants. The classification centers will be jammed for several months, so your timing would be about right. Do you know the date of your graduation?"

"June second, I believe."

"Suppose I put down the middle of June as a rough induction date. Could you make it back here by then?"

"Yes, sir. That would be no problem."

"Good. Report to the Veterans Hospital at nine hundred hours Friday for your physical. Ask for Captain Snyder. He will let you know if you pass. If you do, bring the report back to me here, and we'll grant you a deferred enlistment and notify your draft board. If the processing goes smoothly, you shouldn't hear from us again until near the end of May. Any questions?"

"No, sir. I believe that's clear. Thank you, sir," Bob answered and without thinking saluted. Then with an embarrassed laugh he apologized to the startled officer.

"I'm sorry, sir. I spent four years at a military academy, and that was just a reflex."

"That's all right, mister," answered the lieutenant, pointedly and half-sarcastically returning the salute and then continuing to scribble a note on Bob's forms. "But may I offer a bit of advice?"

"Sir?"

"Try not to be too much of an eager beaver. It's not good form—as the British would say."

"Yes, sir. I mean, no, sir. I won't, sir," Bob stammered.

The officer finished filling out a form for the physical and handed it to Bob.

"When you bring this back Friday, you can sign the papers and be sworn in. That's all there is to it. And Mr. Hanson . . ." he added as Bob backed toward the door.

"Sir?"

"Good luck."

* * *

**BOB HAD THOUGHT** that the visit to the recruiting office would calm the restlessness he had been feeling and that he would be able to submerge himself in the comfortable routines of his life at home. He did have a sense of satisfaction that at least he had made that initial step, but nonetheless peace eluded him. The pleasures of his activities on the farm left him with a tinge of guilt, especially upon hearing the news the next day of the surrender to the Japanese of the gallant garrison on Wake Island.

He resisted firmly all suggestions by his mother that he attend any of the parties or other social functions connected with the holidays. He knew he was disappointing her but considered any such activity to be trite and inappropriate. Even the mood of the family dinner on Christmas day was compromised for him by the announcement of the fall of Hong Kong and the advance of Japanese military forces in the Philippines and Malaya. As his mother was conferring with the kitchen staff after the meal, Bob and his father found themselves temporarily alone together in the library.

"Son," the elder man said, having lit a cigar and settled back in a deep maroon leather chair, "I want you to know that last week I had a long talk with my good friend George Sommers. He's chairman of the local selective service board. We discussed your status, and he was most encouraging. He said that you will definitely not be called up while you're still at Tech and that after you graduate you can be granted a deferment as an essential worker in agriculture. I've been in touch with the local War Resources Board committee, and I've submitted a plan whereby you and I are going to convert the farm to maximum food production. They like my plan, and you're going to be my overseer and manager."

Bob took his time settling onto a sofa opposite his father, leaning forward and stretching his hands out before the open fire in the fireplace. He was searching for the right way to respond, caught somewhat off-guard by the sudden need to divulge the details of his enlistment.

"Dad, I appreciate your efforts and the very good intentions of Mr. Sommers, but I'm not interested in a deferment. As much as I love this farm and want to spare you and Mom any worry and concern, I would be miserable doing anything less than taking an active role in the war. I do plan to graduate, but I want to try for pilot training in the Air Corps immediately afterwards. Knowing me, you can understand that, I believe."

Mr. Hanson removed the cigar from his mouth and stared at his son.

"Robert, I know you think you're being patriotic, and I respect that. But don't make any quick decisions. That would be a mistake. There are a lot of young men who can become pilots, But your contribution to the war effort will be just as great here in Lexington, if not greater. Raising food is going to be extremely important. I've had tests run by the state agriculture department on all of our fields and pastures, and there are four basic crops that we can raise well. Son, I'm going to need you here. We're going to need you here. Your country needs you here."

Bob stared into the fireplace, not wanting to meet his father's eye.

"I'm sorry, Dad. I've already signed up. I'm having my physical tomorrow."

After a long period of silence, his father cleared his throat.

"I've been watching you ever since you got home. I felt I knew what was on your mind and was afraid that's what you would do. Why did you rush into such an important decision? Why didn't you talk it over with me first? You haven't been sworn it yet. You can still change your mind."

Bob glanced at his father and smiled.

"No, sir, I won't change my mind, and I didn't rush into the decision. But I haven't passed the physical yet. Maybe I've never realized I have flat feet and will be classified 4F."

His father smiled weakly and shook his head.

"No, I have no hopes of that. But I want you to know that whatever you do, I'll be proud of you and will always love you."

Bob felt a slight constriction in his throat.

"Thanks, Dad. I appreciate that. And Dad . . ."

"Yes, son?"

"I won't be called in until June. I don't want to worry Mom before I have to. I won't lie to her if she should ask me, but if she doesn't bring the subject up, I see no reason to mention it. If you like, you can pretend you don't know anything about it. I won't cross you up."

Mr. Hanson nodded his head and took a long draw on his Corona Corona.

"I think that's a good idea," he agreed, rising to his feet as he saw his wife approaching from the kitchen area.

Much to the elder Hanson's credit, the subject never again came up between him and his son—neither the following evening, when Bob had returned home after having passed the physical and been sworn in, nor in the following months prior to his induction.

**AS PARTIAL ATONEMENT** for the guilt occasioned by the deception of his mother, Bob reluctantly agreed to accompany his parents to a New Year's Eve party given by a group of their friends at the Idle Hour Country Club. Cocktails began at eight, there was a five-course dinner at nine, and a dance band was to begin playing in the ball room at ten o'clock. Although the crowd included different age groups, most of the guests were from the older generations. Bob would have been bored under any circumstances, but this evening the burden of boredom was made heavier by the persistent restiveness that had been afflicting him. As soon as the dessert plates had been cleared, passing up the champagne being served, he excused himself from his table and wandered down the hallway leading back toward the golf shop. Having paused briefly, he was taking a sip from a water cooler when he heard the footsteps of someone following him. Before he could glance up, he heard the chiding of a female voice.

"Is this the way you always keep your promises, Mr. Hanson?"

"I beg your pardon?" Bob responded, glancing up and immediately recognizing Nancy Garner.

"If my memory is correct," she said with a mock frown, "you promised me in Atlanta that you'd call me while you were here at home. Did I make such a bad impression on you, or are you having to spend all your time with your girl friends?"

Bob laughed.

"Obviously the first possibility you mentioned can't be true, so it must be the second. Actually, eight of my girl friends are luke-warm toward me, but the other two are very demanding of my time. What in the world are you doing at this stodgy affair? I should have imagined that you would be ringing in the new year with a lot livelier group."

"I'm here with my folks," she said. "I have to admit I had racier plans, but my date came down with the flu. At least that's what he's told me. If I find out that he's two-timing me, he's going to end up in the morgue."

"If he's two-timing you, he shouldn't end up in the morgue but in the insane asylum." Bob grinned.

"Ver.r.r.ry nicely put, Mr. Hanson. Now give me a sip of water," she responded, holding her long auburn hair back with her hands and bending over the fountain.

Bob pushed the pedal with his foot and watched as she positioned her pursed lips just at the limit of the arc of cool water. He had no idea why, but there was something sensually suggestive about the scene, and he felt his pulse quicken. Although more sedately attired than in Atlanta, she seemed to him to be even prettier than he had remembered. Cutting her eyes at him, she noted the intensity of his gaze, crinkled her nose and smiled, the trickle of water splashing against her chin.

"Now look what you've made me do," she scolded playfully, retrieving a handkerchief from a small pocket in her skirt and dabbing at the moisture on her face. "You know, I really shouldn't even be willing to talk to you. I waited the whole second half of the dance for you to come back and dance with me once more, but I never saw you again. That's pretty rough on a girl's ego, you know."

"I'm not going to waste a lot of time worrying about your ego," Bob grinned, "with a mile-long line of panting swains waiting to cut in on you."

"But none of them could dance as well as you, and I hate to say it but I think you're smugly aware of that."

"Oh, I don't know about that," Bob rejoined. "That real tall drink of water I saw you dancing with was a helluva dancer."

"Well, he was good," she conceded, "but he and I didn't fit as well as you and I do. And now that I've got you cornered, you're going to have to do your duty and dance with me tonight."

"I can't imagine a more horrible fate," Bob laughed.

"Listen," Nancy said, seizing him by the hand, "they're playing our song. Come on!"

As Bob followed her at a trot down the hallway, he could hear the strains of "You Made Me Love You" coming from the ballroom. He spent the next two hours in a heady, intoxicating haze of pleasure. They danced every piece together. The band leader tailored the music to the more advanced average age of the guests, offering a predominance of slow pieces. This suited Bob perfectly, for, although he loved the fast dances, particularly with a partner as good as Nancy, he could not get enough of holding her close. Although there was no discernible separation of their bodies from shoulder to knee, never was there an indelicate or suggestive pressure between them. They moved in unison with the mood and tempo of whatever music was playing.

She exuded femininity in her movements and gestures, and Bob was acutely aware of her physical presence at every moment, even during the pauses between pieces when she would simply hold his hand or glance up at him briefly while speaking with some other couple. There was an impish semi-smile in her eyes when she would tease him or joke with him, and he found the occasional wrinkling of her nose—a mannerism more "little girlish" than coquettish—for some reason terribly appealing.

Both Bob and Nancy were aware that during those two hours they were under the intense and approving scrutiny of their respective parents, who had congregated at a common table to converse with each other and observe "the children." It was testimony to Nancy's attractiveness that this in no way soured the experience for Bob. In fact, he was disappointed when the evening came to a rather abrupt ending. At midnight the orchestra leader rang a bell and launched the band into a rendition of "Auld Lang Syne" there were kisses and shouts of "Happy New Year" on all sides, and everyone started wandering toward the front door. As the Hansons were waiting for Leslie, the chauffeur, to work his way down the long line of limousines to the entrance, Nancy tugged at Bob's sleeve and whispered, "When are you heading back to Atlanta?"

"On the fourth. I have to get started on my senior project."

"Will I get a chance to see you again?" she asked, touching his hand lightly.

Bob leaned over and whispered in her ear,

"Don't tell me you aren't dated up solid."

"Well, as a matter of fact I am. But I have a strange feeling that I'm about to come down with the flu for three days," she responded, giving him a half-crinkle of her nose.

"Tomorrow night?"

"What about those ten girl friends of yours?"

"They'll just have to be understanding. I'll have a talk with them."

"Seven o'clock at my house?"

"That sounds great. I'll be there at six fifty-nine."


**IT WAS ACTUALLY** six fifty-eight when Bob rang the front doorbell. The wind had shifted around to blow from the north by mid-afternoon, and Bob had headed his horse back to the stables by four o'clock because of the intense chill in the air. Snow had begun to fall as he was walking back to the house from the barn, so, after having showered and dressed, he had left early for the Garners' residence to preclude the chance of being late.

A maid opened the door and ushered him into a parlor off the entrance hall, advising him that "Miss Garner will be down directly." He had barely seated himself on the sofa when Nancy's mother walked in. She was a rather plump but pretty woman in her late thirties. Bob remembered from years past that she was a terrific horsewoman, able to ride beautifully either side-saddle or astride, a talent that stood in contrast with her typically Southern genteel mannerisms.

"Good evening, Robert," she said with a smile, offering her hand as he rose to his feet. "It's so nice of you to join us this evening, especially with the weather so bad."

"I very much appreciate the invitation, Mrs. Garner, and it's a real pleasure to see you again."

"Nancy will join us in a minute. She's almost dressed. I'm afraid it was my fault that she's a little late. She was helping me take down the Christmas tree this afternoon, and the time slipped up on us. Please have a seat. It's been quite a while since those Sunday afternoon rides we all used to take. What have you been doing the last few years? Nancy tells me that you're at Georgia Tech now. What are you studying there? Somehow I had thought that you were up East, at Princeton or somewhere. What do you plan to do after you graduate?"

Every time Bob would open his mouth to try to answer one of her questions, she would flow right into another sentence. He now recalled that non-stop loquaciousness was another of her salient characteristics. He had not succeeded in responding to a single query of hers when Nancy's entrance solved that problem for him. She was very informally dressed—a wool skirt and sweater, high socks and saddle shoes—but projected an image of casual high style; and Bob was acutely aware of the excitement he felt at seeing her and being with her again. She had on very little makeup, and her face was framed by bangs along her forehead and long straight tresses on each side turned under pageboy style.

"We hope we're not disrupting any of your plans," Mrs. Garner continued without let-up, "but Nancy's father and I would prefer that you children have dinner here tonight. She was in an accident two years ago during a snowstorm, and we've been nervous about that ever since."

Bob continued to stare at Nancy but managed to break in verbally, "There's no problem. I had planned to ask Nancy what she would like to do. But I had not heard about the accident. Were you injured badly?"

"No," Nancy laughed, "I wasn't hurt at all. It was just a fender-bender, but to hear my folks talk about it, it was at least a twenty-car pile-up."

"She's always complained that we worry about her too much," the mother smiled, "but we won't carry our concern to the point of subjecting you to the torture of having dinner with us old folks. We have a card table set up in the library near the fireplace, and I've told Katy to serve you there."

"That's very nice of you," Bob responded, "but won't that be a lot of extra trouble? I would enjoy your and Mr. Garner's company."

"Come, come, Bob," Nancy interjected, "don't over-do the politeness bit. Don't you realize our parents like to live vicariously through us? Besides, this was my idea, and I set it up myself."

**THE SCENE WAS** most inviting. The walls of the small library were paneled in walnut and lined with bookshelves. The card table, placed in the middle of the room, was adorned with a white cloth and two candlesticks complementing the place-settings. A fire was burning cheerily in the fireplace, and the blustery north wind would occasionally back up the pressure in the flue and cause small wisps of smoke to carry the aroma of the burning hickory logs throughout the room. Bob was ravenous from the day spent outdoors and was a bit embarrassed at the amount of food he ate during the dinner.

While Nancy was busy overseeing the clearing of the dessert plates and the removal of the card table and chairs, Bob sat on one end of a love-seat and stared fixedly at the burning logs and glowing embers.

"Why so glum?" Nancy asked, having re-entered the room and taken a seat next to him. "You seem pensive. Anything I've said or done?"

"No, of course not," Bob said with a smile, continuing to stare at the fire. Then after a short pause he added, "Manila fell today."

"Who?"

Bob turned and looked at her with a mixture of surprise and amusement, unsure as to whether she was serious or joking.

"Manila, the capital of the Philippines."

"Oh," Nancy remarked simply, inspecting the polish on her nails.

"I take it you don't follow the war news very avidly," Bob grinned.

"It's all so depressing," she responded almost impatiently. "Besides, we're going to win."

"I hope you're right," Bob said, his gaze returning to the burning logs, "but things don't look good. The Germans control Europe and maybe soon the Middle East and Africa. The Japanese are advancing on Singapore and moving toward Australia. If the Japs succeed in taking all of Burma and meet up with the Germans in a pincer move on India, then we would be in a hell of a mess."

"All that may be true," Nancy conceded, "but what good would it do for me to worry about it? Don't let it spoil our evening. There's nothing you and I can do."

Bob turned and looked at her for a moment.

"Each of us has to contribute what he can. I know it may not be much, but I'm going to try to do my share."

"What do you mean?"

Bob hesitated briefly and then proceeded to tell her of his enlistment and his conversation with his father, requesting that she keep the information confidential.

Nancy had a pouty look on her face.

"Well, I must say that I agree with your dad. You should stay here and protect the home front." Then with a wrinkle of her nose she laughed. "Don't tell me we're going to resemble a corny movie. Just as we've found each other, I'm going to lose you to some smelly old battlefield."

The mood became brighter. For over two hours they sat and talked, interrupted only by the occasional need for Bob to get up and poke the fire or add another log. The conversation covered a wide range—from philosophy to campus gossip, from reminiscences to plans for after the war. Bob left for home even more captivated than before, and the cumulative effect during the evening of an occasional nudge of her foot against his to make a point rendered it difficult for him to fall asleep that night.

**THE BOND BETWEEN** them continued to grow stronger. In spite of the icy roads, they had secured her parents' grudging permission to go to Lexington's only year-round drive-in movie the following night. It was a miserable time of year to make that choice, but Nancy had refused to consider any of the theaters downtown for fear she might accidentally encounter the boy with whom she had broken the date for that evening. Bob rolled the window on his side of the car up as tightly as he could against the cord of the speaker that was carrying the scratchy soundtrack and spread out over their legs a thick lap-rug he had borrowed from his grand-mother's chauffeur. But he still had to start the engine and run the heater every now and then to dispel the chill that would rapidly creep in from outside. The third time he resorted to this measure Nancy spoke up somewhat impatiently.

"That's a nuisance having to do that all the time, and you keep interrupting the movie. They have a more efficient way of staying warm up north. They call it bundling. Look, this rug is big enough to cover us both if you put your arm around me. Here, let's try it."

With a bit of shuffling and rearrangement they managed to get comfortably situated. With both his arms around her she snuggled warmly against him, and the lap rug covered them both from chin to ankle. Nancy became engrossed in the movie, but Bob was unable to follow her example. The warmth of her body against his, the periodic grip of her hand on his arm during tense scenes, and above all the increased intensity of her perfume due to her closeness obliterated any chance of his concentrating on anything other than her proximity. The soft touch of her hair against his chin was intoxicatingly pleasant, and occasionally he would brush his lips against it.

He was startled when the film ended and the lights came on in the parking area. The time had passed all too quickly. In fact it had seemed to him to have lasted only twenty to thirty minutes at most. Nancy turned back the edge of the lap rug and moved over to the passenger side of the car.

"Boy! That was great! Don't you think?" she remarked, running her fingers under her hair to fluff it up. "I think he's the best actor in Hollywood, don't you?"

"Yeah, he's good all right," Bob answered, turning on the engine and lights and easing into the long line of vehicles inching toward the exit. "How about a hamburger or a milkshake or something?"

"No, thanks," she answered, glancing at her watch. "You'd better drop me at home. The folks will be on pins and needles until I get in."

They fell silent. Nancy was apparently going over in her mind the most memorable scenes of the movie, whereas Bob was in an uncharacteristic state of agitation. How could he tell her how pleasant it had been holding her? How could he confess that he didn't want to take her home at all? How could he admit that he must see her again before he left town? As he turned into the long drive leading to the Garner home, he was on the verge of blurting out something stupid when she suddenly turned to him.

"Bob, this flu has really got a grip on me. Would your girls let you off the hook your last night in town?"

He stopped the car and looked directly at her without a smile.

"Nancy, maybe it's time for us to be serious. You don't have the flu, and I don't have girlfriends. And I would like very much to see you again tomorrow night."

She leaned over and spontaneously kissed him on the cheek.

"Tomorrow night my parents are going to a meeting of the Brook Hill Hounds. If you come by after supper about eight o'clock, I should be able to sneak out for a little while. Okay? Now, home, James. If they see us parking here, our names will be mud."


**THE NOOSE CONTINUED** to tighten. Bob even decided to forego his last ride the next day. Much of the time was spent in packing and preparing to leave for Atlanta, but he was inclined to spend what little time remained in reflections on their two evenings together. While packing his car, he once even sheepishly explored the edge of the lap rug until he found the spot that had been under her chin, evident by the faint but unmistakable fragrance of her perfume.

When he drove up to the entrance a little past eight, he didn't even have to get out of the car. She came running out the front door in wool slacks, boots and white fur parka and climbed into the car beside him.

"Your timing was perfect," she said, patting him on the arm.

"They left about five minutes ago. If I'm back in about an hour, that should get me home in plenty of time."

"An hour?" Bob said in a subdued tone. "That's pretty short. What can we do in an hour?"

"Well, it's better than nothing," she responded. "Why don't we drive around and find a place to stop and talk? I know! Do you remember that old quarry up on Cooper Road? It's got a place to park on the north side, and maybe we can see the moon on the water in the quarry."

Bob's pulse quickened.

"Why, sure. That's where all the high-school kids used to neck. Is it still there? But it used to be pretty crowded."

"It's too cold tonight. There shouldn't be many cars there," she answered, settling back on her seat. "Let's give it a try."

Bob couldn't believe his good luck—first, at her suggestion and second, at the fact that, when they arrived, there was not another car in the area north of the quarry. He shut off the engine, and they both sat in silence for a few minutes, observing the stark but pretty scene below them—the mirror-like surface of the small lake at the bottom of the quarry reflecting the sprinkle of stars and the crescent of the quarter moon. He reached over and took her by the hand. She turned her head and looked at him.

"I'm going to miss you, Bobby," she said openly and directly. Then, moving over close to him, she added, "Kiss me. Please?"

Not another word was spoken for the next thirty minutes. The kisses became protracted and successive as his hunger for them increased rather than diminished. He wanted to absorb her, to consume her. Even her breath was intoxicating to him. The level of passion within him became painful, and almost desperately he sought some position on the front seat of the car to bring more of their bodies closer together. But as his hands dropped below her hips and he sought to pull her firmly against him, he encountered resistance. Quickly she sat up and tried to restore order to her disheveled hair.

"Bobby, let's get out and stretch our legs," she suggested, throwing aside the lap rug and reaching for the door handle.

Frustrated and slightly embarrassed, Bob followed suit and joined her at the edge of the bluff. The air was bitingly cold and helped restore his mental balance. As they stood looking down into the quarry, she thrust her hand under his overcoat and encircled his waist with her arm, drawing herself close to his side.

"How beautiful that is," she said softly. "I want us to remember this always, for it may be a long time before we are together again. Can I write to you, and will you write back if I do?"

"Of course," he answered.

"Will you write down your address for me when you take me home?"

"Just address it to me care of the Sigma Chi House at Tech. That's all you need."

There was a long silence, and then she took him by the hand and started for the car.

"You'd better get me home. We shouldn't stretch our luck."

"Yeah, I know," he answered. "Also, since this is my last night, I suppose I should spend some time with my parents before they go to bed."

## CHAPTER FIVE

**IF BOB HAD** been pre-occupied and slightly troubled on his drive up from Atlanta to Lexington, he was even more so on his return trip on January fourth. Not only was he mentally agitated by the impending changes to the course and direction of his life brought on by the onset of war, but in addition images and memories of Nancy intruded insistently into his mind. Many of the pieces he heard on the radio had been played by the band on New Year's Eve, and the associations with the feel of her in his arms, the fragrance of her hair and the sound of her voice were powerful.

He was unduly susceptible to this romantic infatuation, for he had not been what could be called "in love" before. It's true that he had had a crush on a little girl in the fourth grade but no involvement since. His four years in military school had effectively reduced the frequency and duration of his contacts with girls, and then too his almost-total summertime absorption in horses ensured a certain detachment from the social activities of his peer group. As exhilarating in a way as this new experience was for him, he was not unmindful of its threatened disruption to the normally ordered pattern of his life.

And in the succeeding weeks this disruption proved to be considerable, especially when coupled with his almost constant compulsion to follow on a daily basis the grim course of the war. The quality of his academic work suffered, for many hours that normally would have been devoted to his studies were spent daydreaming of Nancy or listening to news reports and poring over maps on which he plotted the fortunes, or mostly misfortunes, of Allied forces. Then, too, the stark continuous emptiness of Knute's bed (not needed to be filled by the fraternity due to the exodus of several members) taunted him each morning and evening with the suspicion that what he himself was doing was trivial and inconsequential. He missed and in some ways envied his friend and frequently tried to picture in his mind what he was doing.

In a way the weeks and months dragged by, and yet in a way they passed quickly. Initially Nancy's letters arrived at least once or twice a week and were answered by Bob immediately; but as time wore on recourse to their limited store of shared experiences became exhausted, and the number of letters fell to a trickle of perhaps one a month. She was immersed in her life at the University of Virginia, and he had to begin a struggle to salvage what he could of the academic semester. This required a concerted effort on his part, for it was difficult for him to relate such courses as *Explorational Geophysics* and *Advanced Igneous and Metamorphic Petrology* to the reality of the world as he now saw it. When representatives from Kennecott Copper and three major oil companies made appointments in May to interview him, he had to force himself to attend the meetings and pretend to be interested. When one of the interviewers remarked on the recent downturn in his interim marks for his courses, Bob frankly and unhesitatingly admitted to his imminent induction even though aware it would disqualify him for consideration.

With the onset of gas rationing he had decided against making the trip home for the spring break. He would need his coupons for getting to Lexington after graduation, and he didn't want to spend two and a half days out of the available week on a train. Instead he went out to a small airport in Marietta, north of Atlanta, and talked to a tall dour Arkansas man by the name of Hank Pusey about taking some flying lessons. Hank was instructor, mechanic, line-boy, dispatcher and book-keeper all rolled in one and ran a one-horse, or rather two-horse, flying school with two well-used but well-maintained Piper J-3's. By dint of his acerbic personality and demands for serious and maximum effort on the part of his students, Hank had apparently succeeded in driving off most of his customers, few of whom were in evidence. But for some reason he and Bob hit it off immediately. He appreciated Bob's seriousness and dedication, and Bob for his part admired the pilot's thoroughness and conscientious professionalism. Bob spent almost the entire day every day at the field and by week's end had not only soloed but had received intense instruction in the theory and principles of flight that he later realized was on a level of quality as high as, if not higher than, that he received subsequently in the Air Corps. Due to the press of late-semester studies Bob didn't get back out to the field until near the end of May, but Hank was no longer there. A farmer next door to the field said that he had heard that Hank had signed up as a civilian instructor for training female pilots for the WASPs over in Sweetwater, Texas.

Bob's parents were insistent on coming to Atlanta for his graduation. By conserving and pooling gas coupons they had Leslie drive them down on May thirty-first. Bob had made them reservations at the Atlanta Biltmore and met them there for dinner that night. After dinner they retired to the parents' quarters to visit and talk. As Bob and his father were settling in chairs in the sitting room of the suite, the mother retired to the bedroom and came back carrying a long envelope, which she handed to Bob.

"Here, son, this came for you several days ago. I have a feeling you've probably been expecting it."

Bob glanced at the letter, then at his father and finally back at his mother, who was gazing down at him with a sad smile on her face.

"Your father and I have never discussed it, but, after having brought you into this world and watched you grow up for twenty-one years, did you really think that I wouldn't guess, that I wouldn't know? But I realize that through the ages you men have never wanted to hear of the heartache and pain of us millions of mothers who send our sons off to war. So I have kept silent and won't spoil these important days for you now."

Then she sank onto a chair opposite him. Bob stared in amazement at his mother, at the subtle change that had taken place in her. The very real cold fear that attended this potential tragedy in her life had supplanted the previous constant but vague anxiety. In place of the prior nervous habit of raising her eyebrows there was now a resigned melancholy.

"Well, go on and open it," she said, as though he were a little boy opening a present.

Bob looked at the envelope and saw that it was indeed from the War Department. Tearing it open, he removed the letter and read:

RESTRICTED

SO 26

HEADQUARTERS FOURTH SERVICE COMMAND<br>Office of the Commanding General

ERC 211 DNJ-Es/fm

Special Orders
No. 26

EXTRACT

Post Office Building
Atlanta, Georgia
15 May 1942

3. Pursuant to telephonic instructions, May 10, 1942, from The Adjutant General, each of the following named Air Corps Enlisted Reservists, having been found qualified for Aviation Cadet appointment, is ordered to active duty, in grade of private, effective June 10, 1942, and will proceed from the address shown after his name to Army Air Forces Basic Training Center No. 6, Fort Chaf fee, Arkansas, reporting on June 11, 1942, for Pre-Aviation Cadet Basic Training:

| NAME | SERIAL NO. | ADDRESS |
|---|---|---|
| ALDRIDGE,Cyrus B. | 12667080 | 3614 Maple Ave., Knoxville, Tenn. |
| ALLISON, Thomas C. | 12666391 | Route 6, Crossville, Tenn. |
| ATKINS, Butcher N. | 12178664 | 614 Eighth St., Memphis, Tenn. |
| BALZ, Lawrence M. | 12664589 | 711 East 51st St., Savannah, Ga. |
| BEATTY, Roy S. | 12636914 | 416 South Crost Rd., Athens, Tenn. |
| BENNETT, Joseph F. | 12663981 | 4312 Bono Blvd., Chattanooga, Tenn. |
| BLOCK, Marlow P. | 12649366 | 340 West End, McKenzie, Tenn. |
| BOONE, Joe B. | 12176339 | Woodbury, Tenn. |
| BRANDON, Vincent R. | 12636412 | 1506 Laurel Ave., Knoxville, Tenn. |

```
BRYAN, Charles H.          12199437    166 Spence Place, Knoxville, Tenn.

BUNTIN, Robert A.          12463916    1018 Gale Lane, Nashville, Tenn.

HAAS, Justus C.            12621987    RFD, Baxter, Ky.

HANSON, Robert N.III       12669384    Song Hill Road, Lexington, Ky.

HARCOURT, Lyle A.          12653217    503 Forrest Ave., Mayfield, Ky.

HOLLEY, James C.           12688549    1716 White Ave., Louisville, Ky.

HUNPHREY, Lawrence L.       12818976    12 Power Line Hill, Elkton, Ky.

INGLEWOOD, Thomas A.       12643211    Park Place, Bearden, Ky.

JAMES, Allen S.            12626148    Route 1, Finchton, Ky.

JONES, Frederick P.        12549174    1613 W. Fargo Ave., Lexington, Ky.
```

TCT. TDN. Mon alw in lieu of rat in accord with AR 35-4520 will be pd in adv for periods indicated. FD 34 P 434-02 A 0425-23 (AG 342.1 Aviation Cadets)

By Command of Major General BRIXTON:

W. R. NIXON

Colonel, General Staff

Corps Chief of Staff

OFFICIAL:

  GEO. N. HODGESON

          Colonel

Chief, Adjutant General Branch

-2-

RESTRICTED

When Bob had finished reading, he folded the letter and returned it to the envelope.

"Well?" his mother asked.

"I leave for basic training on the tenth."

There was a moment of silence.

"So little time," his mother said sadly. "Why, that would give you less than a week at home."

"I know," Bob agreed, "but since I'm going, I guess the sooner I get on with it, the better."

**THE THREE OF** them strove earnestly to keep up each other's spirit for the next two days but were only partially successful. His own mood received a boost at the news of the great victory by U.S. carriers at the

Battle of Midway, but his parents could not share his elation. Some relief was obtained by Bob's showing them around Atlanta and the surrounding countryside the next day, and a lively break in the gloom occurred when he took them by the Varsity to introduce them to Doodlebug and to say good-bye to his friend. But all relief was short-lived. Even the graduation ceremonies that year had a somber cast to them.

Bob's mother chose to ride back to Lexington with him in his Buick, so some of his belongings were transferred to the other car. During the trip he sought to ease some of his mother's pain by discussing his views of the war and of his perceived duty, but everything he said seemed to make things worse. Finally he found that the only effective means of distracting her was to encourage her to reminisce about family scenes and events when he was a little boy.

**THE FEW DAYS** he had at home were little better for the parents. Bob's usual pattern of following his own routines and activities was disrupted by an attempt on the part of his mother and father to spend as much time with him as possible. His mother made a point of being downstairs each day to sit with him at breakfast no matter how early he got up. His father wanted him along on walks with the farm director back through the fields of the estate to discuss the various issues relating to planting, fertilizing and harvesting. It was as though he had a vain but subconscious hope that somehow it might change his son's resolve.

Bob felt considerable frustration because of this attention, for he would dearly have liked to have had more time to himself, but nonetheless he understood and was touched. At dinner on the night of the sixth he suggested that all three of them should take a horseback ride together the next day as they used to do when he was a boy. He could tell that his father was enthused at the idea, and even his mother, who had ridden less and less in the intervening years, agreed to get her old habit out of storage. During dessert his father broached the possibility that they follow the old pattern of Sunday communal rides and invite the Garners to join them. His mother assented readily, and Bob also agreed. The rush of pleasure he felt at the possibility of seeing Nancy produced in him astonishment that he had not really thought of her for weeks. He was strongly inclined to call her after dinner but thought it prudent to let his mother call and extend the invitation. The Garners were equally enthusiastic, and plans were made for a rendezvous on horseback at the head of Coy's Lane and an early buffet supper at the Hansons' after the ride.

Bob's parents had gaited horses saddled for their use, but he chose a hunter, for the planned ride at several places would cross one of the better hunt courses that had some challenging timber and stone fence jumps that he had not enjoyed in years. He was pleased and not too surprised to notice at the rendezvous that the Garners had selected the same choice of mounts—the parents were on three-gaited horses, and Nancy was astride a long-legged spirited young gelding fitted with a hunt saddle and bridle.

When Bob saw her approaching in her smart attire of red jacket and black boots and hat, he was chagrined that he had not called her since his return three days earlier. During the winter and spring their correspondence had tapered off to one letter every few weeks and finally had stopped altogether, but the sight of her again on this spring day recast over him her former spell. Her greeting was relaxed and warm, and as they rode side by side behind their parents, her chatter was as usual interesting and frequently amusing.

As they crossed the Burton's Mill hunt course, they asked their elders if they could meet them on the other side of the hill and took off at a gallop across a lush green pasture. The dictates of Bob's gentlemanly code required that he let Nancy take the jumps first, but there was a good chance that her frisky mount would not have tolerated any other arrangement anyway. Following behind gave him the compensatory advantage of being able to watch her superb horsemanship and admire the grace and skill with which she seemed literally to fuse with her saddle as she invariably chose the more difficult of the jumps.

As the course turned and led up over a rise, she glanced back at him with a laugh.

"Come on, slowpoke. We don't have all day."

Bob grinned but then saw that a low-hanging branch was directly in their path.

"Watch out!" he shouted.

She turned just in time and partially ducked, but the end of the branch caught the top of her cap and knocked it off. Seeing that she was unhurt, Bob reined in his horse and dismounted to retrieve the hat.

"Let's give them a little breather," he suggested as he walked up to her to return the cap. "Besides, it will give me a chance to feast my eyes on you."

It was intended as a compliment but also accurately mirrored reality. Her auburn hair, which had been tucked up under her hat, now cascaded to her shoulders; and as Bob looked up at her lovely face against the backdrop of the foliage of a large oak tree, it flashed through his mind that she would have been a perfect model for Titian. She looked him steadily in the eye as she accepted the cap.

"You know, I love to hear your flattery," she said, "even though I know it's cynically insincere. It could be habit-forming. In fact I'm afraid if I were given a chance, *you* could become habit-forming. Hold the reins for me, please."

Bob took hold of her reins near the bit and watched as she wound her tresses onto the top of her head and secured the hat back in place.

"Tell me, Bobby," she added, as she finished the task, "am I going to have to humble myself in order to see you, as I did six months ago?"

"Not at all," Bob laughed. "I promise I'll do the humbling this time. You see—I'm already groveling at your feet."

"You won't have to grovel *every* time," she said with that infectious wrinkling of her nose, "but I warn you that I'm expecting us to have a long and busy summer together."

"I'm afraid our summer is going to be very short," Bob said soberly. "I leave for the Army on Wednesday."

Nancy's face fell.

"You're kidding me, aren't you?"

"No, I'm not kidding. I'll have to be with my folks Tuesday night; I can't leave them. But that gives us an eternity of thirty-six hours. Can I see you tomorrow and tomorrow night?"

"Oh, darn!" Nancy said, frowning. "Sally Ridenour is getting married, and we're giving her a shower tomorrow. There's a party for her and Kim tomorrow night at Idle Hour. I'm going with Ted Schorner. Aren't you invited?"

"No, I'm afraid not," Bob said, very subdued. "I haven't seen her or Kim in years. Well, I guess we'll have to wait until I win the war. That should give me more incentive."

"I tell you what," she countered. "Come out to the Club after supper. I'll meet you at 'our' water fountain at ten o'clock sharp. Maybe I can sneak off for a little while. Okay?"

Bob's face brightened at the suggestion.

"I guess that's better than nothing," he said. "I'll be there at ten."

"Then come on," Nancy said with a lilt in her voice. "Mount up, or the worry-warts will think we've both taken a fall."


**THE SUSTAINED MOROSENESS** of his parents at dinner the following night failed to dampen Bob's elation at the prospect of seeing Nancy again later in the evening. In fact his up-beat mood even helped cheer them somewhat. He kissed his mother good-night and left early for the Club, arriving soon after nine-thirty. It was a warm, lovely spring evening, so he passed the time sitting on a bench by the first tee and listening to the music inside. At five before ten he entered the club-house through the men's locker room entrance and climbed the stairs to the hallway with the cooler. At the top of the stairs he had not even turned left before he heard a "Pssst!" and saw Nancy beckoning to him from a side corridor leading to a terrace. She took him by the hand and led him out through the door, past several couples enjoying the balmy night and down some brick steps toward the rear of the Club.

"I have only a few minutes. Let's sit in your car. Where are you parked?" she asked.

"Around the side by the golf shop. That was the only space I could find."

"That's perfect. There shouldn't be a lot of traffic out there."

When they had climbed in the Buick, Bob asked if she would like for him to put the top back, since it was such a pretty night.

"Mr. Hanson, sometimes you surprise me," she chided. "Why would you want us to be visible?"

Without waiting for a reply she slid across the seat toward him and murmured, "I took my lipstick off in the little girls' room, so kiss me."

Bob was caught slightly off guard by the suddenness of this development but wasted little time in acceding to her request. Immediately the kisses became prolonged and intense, as they had been six months earlier. Recollections of that evening by the quarry came back to Bob with sharp clarity: the feel of her in his arms, the fragrance of her breath and perfume, the very taste of her. Quickly he was carried to the limits of self-control. She had on a light silk dress, and the feel of it as his left hand glided down her side and past her hip was electrifying to him. When his hand slipped off her skirt onto the silk stocking on her right leg, it virtually took on a life of its own and reversed direction, moving hungrily up her leg and under her skirt. Nancy had been emitting barely audible moans, but when his fingers had progressed only halfway to the ultimate goal, they met firm resistance from her right hand. She broke off the passionate kiss that was in progress and said firmly, "Whoa now, Bobby. Not pass the G-line."

His mind more than a little clouded by desire, frustration and confusion, Bob stammered, "Wh . . . what?"

"Not past Mama's G-line."

He sat back and tried to take a deep breath.

"What in hell is 'Mama's G-line'?"

"The garter, silly. Mama told me never let a boy get above the garter, so I call it the G-line."

"You're kidding me, aren't you? You're putting me on."

"No, I'm not putting you on. What makes you think I'm kidding?"

"Well, if you're not kidding," Bob grinned, "why don't we move the garters up another eight inches?"

Even Nancy had to laugh.

"That would be cheating."

"Well, your mother's not here. She would never know."

"But I would, and that's what's important."

"Nancy, that's the most absurd thing I've ever heard. I can't get you pregnant with my hand, for crying out loud! And I promise I won't hurt you."

"I know that," she said with another lilting laugh, "but I won't break the G-rule."

"Never?"

"Not until I'm married. But why the big pout? Don't you enjoy kissing me?"

"You know I do. It's just that when we get that close, you literally set me on fire."

"Well, I've only got a minute left, so let's not waste it. That's not enough time to set you on fire, but I would like for you to smolder a little bit."

Even in the dim light thrown by the lone bulb next to the golf shop door Bob could see the fetching wrinkling of her nose. He took her in his arms and hungrily kissed her again until finally she pushed away from him and moved toward the right-hand door of the car.

"I told my date I was going to the loo," she said. "By now he probably thinks I've fallen in."

Bob walked around and opened the door for her. At the bottom of the steps she stopped.

"I think it best if I go up alone. I have some repairs to make before I re-enter the real world."

She took him by the hand.

"I don't want you to go, Bobby, but I know it's what you want. I'm going to miss you. Will you write to me?"

"We tried that before," he answered, "and it's tough, because we end up in different worlds. I'll give it a try even though I'm a terrible correspondent. But I promise you I'll be thinking about you a hell of a lot more than will be good for me. You won't forget me?"

"I'll be here when you get back," she said warmly. Then she kissed him quickly and ran up the stairs.

* * *

**ON THE SURFACE** Bob succeeded in projecting an air of normalcy on Wednesday morning as his mother drove him to the train station. She showed remarkably more control than he would have anticipated. In fact she gave the false impression of having made a more successful accommodation than had his father, who probably intentionally devised some pressing duty that morning to avoid having to accompany them and whose gruff voice broke on two occasions at breakfast. Bob appreciated the intensity of effort he knew his mother must be making to attain that uncharacteristic degree of control, for his own internal equilibrium was a little shaky.

An anxiousness over the uncertainty of the future coupled with a mild premature surge of homesickness were to some extent offset by an excitement over the expectation of imminent adventures associated with the new direction of his life. But the very strong regret he felt over the prospect of a long separation from Nancy remained without compensation, and it was the very strength of this feeling that made him realize that he had indeed fallen in love.

The train had already arrived as they entered the station, so the awkward period of standing on the platform waiting for its departure was fortuitously foreshortened. The soft sighing of the steam engine up front could be heard above his mother's running instructions about the importance of wearing clean underwear, not getting too tired, and writing postcards to Grandma. The conductor's "All *aboard*" came as a mild relief to Bob and a form of death sentence to the mother. With a quick final hug and assurances that he would indeed be careful and take care of himself, he bounded up the steps of the Pullman car and stood in the vestibule watching as the train pulled out of the station. His mother didn't move. She stood motionless in the same spot as the station receded. As he was growing up, he had always thought of her as being remarkably young-looking and of relatively sturdy stature, but on this day his throat constricted at how old and frail she seemed.

Bob continued to stand on the metal platform for a while, watching the outskirts of Lexington slip by—the switching yard, the factory buildings, the poor shanties built near the tracks. The homesickness he felt on leaving his home town was both strong and sweet, and he hungrily drank in the sights of the farms and gently rolling hills as the tracks wound through the countryside. It was only when the conductor came through and insisted on closing the upper door that Bob went into the car and settled onto his seat.

Almost immediately a change came over him. Not only the home-sickness but the restlessness and disquietude that had plagued him for weeks and even months vanished completely. Once again he felt purposeful and whole. He was on his way.

## CHAPTER SIX

**BOB SLID INTO** military life with ease. It had been four years since he had left Culver Military Academy, but the old attitudes, reflexes and habits returned naturally and unbidden. In fact he found basic training to be less demanding because academic requirements were not piled on top of the military training, drill and physical conditioning. Although he came from a family of considerably greater means than the majority of his fellow trainees, his prior experience made it much easier for him to adjust to and tolerate the burden of strict discipline than it was for them. All in all he was one of the very few prospective cadets actually to enjoy the four weeks spent at Fort Chaffee.

This enjoyment was on several occasions put to a severe test by the abusive proclivities of Sergeant Stan Vronsky, who was in charge of the unit's overall training and indoctrination. Severity of routines and measures were a given for basic training almost anywhere, but this man from the Bronx carried the policy to unreasonable extremes. After a hard day the recruits at times would be called out even in the middle of the night to run obstacle courses, although the usual time was in the stifling heat of mid-day, when the slip of just one man would result in the whole unit having to repeat the entire course. Several wound up in the infirmary with heat exhaustion.

Bob suspected that the sergeant, whose speech and mannerisms betrayed the modesty of his background and education, was acting out a deep resentment against these soft and spoiled young men who were potentially to be officers within a mere eight months. This was very possibly true, but Bob also discovered near the end of basic training that Vronsky was a Regular Army man, who had been placed in this job because of a medical disability after having been pulled from his unit just before its departure for England. The sergeant gained a modicum of sympathy from Bob because of this and even a measure of respect due to the fact that he never gave an order for any exercise in which he himself did not lead the way, raising wonderment as to exactly what his disability was. With Bob probably the sole exception, the recruits developed an almost palpable hatred of the man.

As severe as this abuse was, it never seemed to dim the resolve or patriotic fervor of the inductees. Their determination was strengthened by the daily briefings on the ominous news from the war fronts, and in the closing days of June Allied fortunes stood at a low ebb. The Japanese had landed eighteen hundred men on Attu and Kiska in the Aleutians, had completed the conquest of the Philippines and were only a few miles from Port Moresby in New Guinea. In American coastal waters shipping was being lost to German U-boats at an alarming rate. German troops were advancing rapidly toward Sevastopol, and Russia seemed ready to collapse. In North Africa Tobruk fell to Rommel, who was poised to strike for the Suez Canal. A somber mood contributed to a sense of urgency at the conclusion of basic training.


**BOB HAD BEEN** impressed when his induction voucher had included Pullman accommodations for the trip from Lexington to Arkansas. He did not realize at the time that that would be the last such luxury until after he was commissioned. The railroad cars in which the unit was transported from Fort Chaffee to Randolph Field in San Antonio, Texas, were of antique vintage, rickety and with no amenities. Many of the casement windows, once lowered, could not be raised again—a matter of not-too-great importance, because during the two-day trip no rain was encountered and the oppressive heat required as much ventilation as could be found. More troubling was the fact that all meals consisted of K-rations and there was no water on board for drinking or washing. After every one of the fortunately frequent stops on side tracks to allow passage of higher-priority transportation, a corporal would pass through the cars with a bucket of water and a dipper. On the long stretches across Oklahoma and Texas the soot and smoke from the coal-burning engine swirled freely through the windows and covered everything. By the end of twenty-four hours they all resembled a traveling minstrel show.

Sleep was virtually impossible. Although there was perhaps a half-inch of padding under the cracked leather of the seats, the seat backs were nothing but wood, and there were two passengers to every seat. They would take turns with one standing in the aisle or sitting on the floor while the other semi-reclined, but any attempt at rest proved to be an exercise in futility. One of the recruits once paused in the aisle and asked with as much bitterness as humor, "Have you seen the sign in the john that says 'Shooting buffalo while train is in motion is forbidden'?"

After Fort Chaffee and the ride on the train, Randolph Field was a country club. The barracks and the other buildings on the field pre-dated the war and were clean and substantial. The grounds of the base were immaculately tailored and maintained, and all the personnel from top to bottom were efficient and professional. Its most exciting feature to the weary arrivals, however, was the ordered array of aircraft on the flight line. Although they knew that these were not destined for their use, nonetheless they were a hopeful harbinger of things to come.

No time was lost. Although daily calisthenics and volleyball were mandatory, the rest of the working day was given over to batteries of tests of all kinds: IQ, psychological, visual acuity, depth perception, coordination, physical and psychological stress, high altitude pressure chamber sessions, and on and on. Nervous tension ran high, for each knew that one slip, one bad report, could result in being disqualified, "washed out" of the program. It was a highly competitive situation. No one divulged any of his responses or results for fear of giving someone else an advantage. One exception was made by Ron Hughes, the unit's comic from Jacksonville, Florida. Question 28 on one of the battery of psychological tests read: *Have you ever participated in any unusual sexual activity?* When the monitoring officer left the room for a few minutes, the endemic tension was momentarily relieved when Ron's voice carried forth from the back of the room, "On number 28, do you think fucking a duck would count?"

After the laughter had died down and just before the officer re-entered, Ron offered a soft-spoken qualifier, "It was a big duck."

**ANXIETY AND NERVOUS** tension built steadily during the two-week classification period. A certain percentage would be eliminated entirely from the program, a certain percentage would be assigned to training programs for navigators, bombardiers and even gunners, and of those receiving pilot classification, many would be sent to multi-engine training schools as bomber pilots. Only a fraction of the total would gain assignment to single-engine fighter pilot schools, Bob's first choice.

Monday, July 26, was the fateful day on which the assignments were posted on the bulletin board outside training detachment headquarters. In a ritualistic effort to seduce Fortune, Bob started with the rejections and then read through each of the lists, saving the one for single-engine fighters until last. When he had not encountered the name Hanson among the multi-engine assignees, his heart leaped and he went immediately to the H's on the last list. There it was, between Haggard and Harwood.

Barracks assignments at Randolph had been made alphabetically, so the original basic training units had been broken up. Sidney Haggard occupied the bunk above Bob, and Bill Harwood the lower bunk next to his. The three of them had a boisterous session of mutual congratulations when they got back to the barracks and agreed on celebrating together with a beer or two at the PX after finishing packing for the next day's departure. The mutual friendships initiated that night proved beneficial to them all, for they would be thrown together from that time straight through until graduation from "advanced."

Bob liked them both but was drawn more strongly to Bill Harwood. From Los Angeles, Bill had given up a lucrative defense industry job to join the Air Corps. He had completed two years of mechanical engineering at Cal Tech before dropping out in disgust at the pedantic approach to subjects in which he felt he had a greater personal knowledge that the professors. He became chief mechanic to one of California's top race-car drivers and rebuilt sport cars as a part-time hobby. At the outbreak of the war he had drifted naturally into a good position in a factory producing aircraft engines but fell prey to another attack of restlessness and quit to enlist.

He epitomized what Bob thought a Southern Californian should be. They had roughly the same build but otherwise were totally different. Bill was very blonde with light blue eyes, could probably not have identified a horse from a cow but was an excellent swimmer, surfer and motorcycle racer. Anything mechanical became merely another living limb for him, and he had a sixth sense about the workings of any machine. It was his basic personality, however, that set him apart. Aloof and self-assured, he observed the world and interacted with it with an air of coolness, of detachment. Through the months they were friends Bob never once saw him become upset, rattled or off-balance.

So different in their natures and backgrounds, their friendship would probably not have developed were it not for the intense competitiveness that grew up between them as pilots. Bill was a natural. Everything dealing with the control of an airplane came as easily to him as breathing, whereas Bob attained the same level of skill by dint of focused dedication and hard work. During their primary training at Corsicana, Texas, this competitiveness had not fully developed, for the two of them never flew together, most of the training being either one-on-one with student and instructor or the student doing solo work. It did get its start there, however. They both had the same civilian instructor, who made a point of complimenting each in the presence of the other.

But during basic training at Enid, Oklahoma, this competition came to full bloom. After learning to solo the much larger BT-15 with its four-hundred-horsepower Wright engine, the cadets often flew together in a buddy system. This was especially the case after the onset of instrument flying, during which one cadet would be piloting the plane "under the hood" with no outside visual reference while the other would be in the front seat acting as observer to prevent possible collision with other aircraft. Bob and Bill would have missions wherein they would alternate and trade places, each striving especially hard to outdo the other in accuracy in holding altitude or heading, in speed of recovery from unusual attitudes or in instrument landing approach patterns using the tricky low-frequency radio ranges.

It was during one such latter exercise that Bob came to appreciate Bill's cool-headedness. Bob was acting as look-out pilot, while Bill was "under the hood" practicing an orientation procedure on the radio range. Such a procedure required the pilot correctly to identify in which of the four quadrants around the station the plane had been placed by his look-out, a procedure usually performed by holding a certain heading and listening for a fade or a build-up of either the Morse code signal dot-dash for "A" or the dash-dot for "N." When these two transmitted signals became fused, then a solid tone was heard, and the pilot knew he was "on the beam." The trouble was that frequently there were anomalies in the system that would result in temporary false signals. Such an anomaly occurred with Bill this day and completely threw him off. He picked up his microphone to inform Bob, thinking that the transmitter switch was on "intercom" and that his message would go only to his observer. Unfortunately, the selector switch was on "com" and his message was broadcast on one of the control tower frequencies.

"Bob, I've got to start over. Those signals are lousy, and I'm all fucked up."

In their headphones they heard the crisp voice of one of the female Air Corps control tower operators: "Aircraft just transmitting, give your identification number. Repeat: give your identification number."

Without a second's pause Bill's cool voice was again transmitted, "Listen, lady, I'm not *that* fucked up."

* * *

**THEIR SUPERIOR PILOTAGE** had its disadvantages. They were assigned one instructor for acrobatics and general airmanship and another for instrument training. Both instructors bragged about them to the other commissioned instructors on the base, and as their notoriety spread they were assigned to more and more "check-rides" given by the other officers to verify their reputed skills. During Basic they were also introduced to formation flying. Ron Haggard was not as proficient in overall pilotage as they but due to their example and influence came close to their level of skill in this one aspect of flying. They were dubbed "The Three Musketeers" by their instructor.

On November 24 there were posted on the bulletin board the following orders, a copy of which was sent to each cadet:

```
           HEADQUARTERS AAF PILOT SCHOOL (BASIC)
            ENID ARMY AIR FIELD, ENID, OKLAHOMA
                      Office of the
                    Commanding Officer
SPECIAL ORDERS)                             24 November 1942
NO. - 74
                         EXTRACT
9. Having completed the prescribed Basic Flying Tng
Course, the following named Avn Cadets are reid from atchd unasgd,
Hg & Hq Sq, 48th Basic Flying Tng Gp, and are trfd as atchd unasgd
for further course of instruction to the AAAFS, Moore Fld, Mis-
sion, Tex, reporting to the Comdt thereat not later than 1 Dec 42,
for asgmt to Ci 43-B Advanced Flying Tng Course of ten(10) weeks
duration, beginning 2 Dec 42. WP TDN 1-5168 P436-02 A0426-24.
(Auth: Ltr, file 186.3 (AC)-P, HQ, AAFCFTC, Randolph Fld, Tex,
Subj: Assignment of Students, 16 Nov 42):
```

There followed a two-page list of one hundred fourteen cadets.

On Thanksgiving Day as a salute to the graduating cadets the officers of the base put on an air show open to the public. Although technically against regulations, the "Three Musketeers" participated— the only aviation cadets invited to do so. They passed over the field twice in a tight V formation at one thousand feet in BT-15's. Haggard flew the lead plane, and Bob and Bill flew the wing positions.

* * *

THE ASSIGNMENT TO southern Texas was a pleasant surprise to Bob. At Randolph Field and at Corsicana he had come to like the state and its people very much, and he was happy to be going back. He found this latest assignment to be quite different from the others and in many ways even more pleasant.

One factor was the airplane they used in Advanced—the North American AT-6. Bob liked each aircraft flown in training, but he developed a true love for this one. With its five hundred fifty horsepower Pratt and Whitney engine, retractable landing gear and variable pitch propeller it was a joy to fly. Some countries even used it as a combat aircraft at the time.

He and Bill continued their interpersonal competition to some extent but at a much reduced level of intensity. When four students were assigned to each instructor, the split fell right between Hanson and Harwood, so they ended up with different instructors in Advanced. They did a lot of "hangar flying" at night, however, comparing notes and trying to size up the other's skill. There was one other area wherein they began to spend more time together.

Starting in Primary and continuing into Basic and Advanced, Bob had been almost obsessed with trying to learn as much as he could about the airplane he was flying. On free evenings he would spend the time in the maintenance hangars, watching the mechanics in their never-ending task of servicing, inspecting, repairing and maintaining the airplanes in good flying condition. As he got to know them on a first-name basis, some would relax the rules and let him help in such relatively simple routines as changing oil, sparkplugs or tires. Once in both Primary and Basic he had prevailed on Bill to accompany him with unhappy results. Bill's knowledge of engines and machines in general was much broader than that of the maintenance crews, and he was not at all reluctant to let that fact be known.

At Moore Field, however, he became equally as fond of the AT-6 as Bob and sufficiently impressed with its radial engine to begin to join him in his puttering during off hours. So on weekends, when the other cadets were dating the pretty girls of McAllen or succumbing to the enticements of Mexico across the border, the two of them happily spent hours covered with grease and oil. Bob learned more from Bill in five weeks than he had in the preceding twelve from the mechanics.

Although they could be classified as friends and had been living in close proximity for months, except for discussion of airplanes, the war and flying, there was little mutual intercommunication between them. Neither felt inclined to mention his own past or personal life or inquire of the other's. It was this one similarity that perhaps influenced Bill to draw at least relatively close to Bob, for there was no one else in the squadron that he chose to approach at all. Bob readily accepted the other's aloofness and had come to expect nothing else. Therefore he was caught by surprise one evening in the PX, where they had stopped for a bite to eat on the way back to the barracks.

"Bob, graduation is coming up in a couple of weeks, as you know. I want to ask a favor. I'm getting married the next day, and I wonder if you would stand in as my best man."

At first Bob thought he might be kidding. He knew that the name Harwood came up fairly frequently during mail call but never had a clue as to the nature of the correspondence. Even more responsible for his surprise was an occurrence going all the way back to Primary.

**ALTHOUGH THE INSTRUCTORS** at Corsicana had been civilian, the two examining pilots were commissioned officers. One, First Lieutenant Osborne, had earned a certain notoriety based on two considerations. First, he was admittedly the toughest and most demanding examiner; second, he had a wife that was as sexy a woman as anyone on the base had ever seen. Wherever the lieutenant passed with her on his arm, every activity within visual range—whether work or play—came to a standstill.

At a welcoming reception given by the Commanding Officer for the new 43-B class soon after their arrival, Bill and Mrs. Osborne happened to meet at the punch bowl and struck up a conversation, which continued throughout the entire evening. Although Bill maintained his traditional detached coolness, to all of the numerous observers it was obvious that the lieutenant's wife quickly developed an intense interest in the young Californian. Much to the fascination and burning envy of the other cadets, in the subsequent weeks there developed a sizzling liaison between the two, neither of them making the slightest effort to conceal the fact. Frequently in the middle of the afternoon the Osbornes' red Plymouth would pull up by the side of the PX, Bill would nonchalantly climb into the front seat next to the stunning woman, and the pair would drive off, to return an hour later.

Speculation reached a fever pitch when it was posted that for the final pass/fail check-ride at the end of Primary, Bill drew First Lieutenant Mark Osborne. Considering the modest income level of aviation cadets, relatively large sums of money were bet on whether Bill would end up in the infantry or artillery. Bob had faith in Bill's piloting and took all bets, being the only one wagering that his friend would make it to Basic. When the airplane had returned from the check-ride and parked on the flight line, all eyes were fixed on the pair as they stood several minutes on the tarmac talking. The two saluted, and Bill shouldered his parachute and walked toward the briefing room. As he entered the door, he reacted with a mixture of mild surprise and disdain at the press of cadets waiting inside. As he made his way through the throng, only one cadet summoned the nerve to ask:

"Well, what did he say?"

Bill paused briefly but didn't even glance at the questioner.

"He's a damn good pilot and taught me some things."

Then he walked on to turn in his parachute and post his time. Subsequently it was learned that Osborne had given him the highest test score he had ever awarded.

Frustration for his fellow cadets was compounded by the fact that Bill never once mentioned his relationship with the woman and discouraged by his icy aloofness any discussion of it in his presence. Only once did a partially inebriated fellow cadet inquire with a suggestive leer.

"Hey, Bill, what's the lieutenant's wife like?"

Harwood fixed him with an icy stare.

"I think she's a very nice lady, don't you?"

Although the questioner outweighed Bill by at least twenty pounds, he backed away, mumbling, "Yeah . . . yeah . . . sure."

**BOB HAD NEVER** brought up with his friend the liaison or the gossip relating to it and would not have been disposed to do so, but nevertheless he accepted the speculation as being valid and was surprised suddenly to learn that Bill was involved in another relationship close enough to involve marriage.

When no response was immediately forthcoming, Bill glanced up and then grinned, intuitively guessing the cause of the look on the other's face.

"I'm almost as surprised as you. That's why I haven't mentioned it before. I met Lori at the war plant where I worked, and we started dating steadily. When I decided to leave to join the Air Corps, I asked her to marry me, but she said it wouldn't make sense, because we couldn't be together during my enlisted days. I felt it wouldn't be fair to marry her once I was commissioned, because I hoped to be going overseas, so we gave up the idea entirely. Then, just two weeks ago, she called me and said flatly that she was coming here and that we were going to be married after graduation and that she didn't give a damn about what I thought about it. So I said okay. Well, what do you say? Will you be an accessory to the crime?"

"You know I will," Bob answered. "I'm flattered to be asked, but I have to admit it caught me off guard."

Bill pushed away the plate with the last remains of his cheese sandwich and took a sip of coffee.

"I think I know why you're surprised. It's because of Corsicana, right? But don't judge me too harshly. When we fell in love in L.A., I was in pain I wanted Lori so badly, but she'd never go to bed with me. You see, she's Catholic and has very strict views. I was upfront with her and told her that I considered us married in a way and would be faithful to her if we'd have sex but couldn't promise a thing if she wouldn't. She knew what I meant but still said no dice. But I've been honest with her and told her all about Margie Osborne. Even though it hurt her at the time, she knew she couldn't complain. She's a great gal. You'll like her."

And like her, Bob did—from the moment he first met her. She and her sister arrived in McAllen two days before graduation, having driven all the way from L.A. in a black vintage LaSalle. Lori was by no means beautiful and couldn't begin to match Bill's natural good looks, but Bob soon saw the virtues that appealed to his friend. She was warm and open and solid as a rock—a perfect complement to his introverted restlessness. Around her he took on a different personality, exhibiting a relaxed casualness previously never manifested, and through tact and firmness she exercised an amazing control over his moods and behavior.

There was a striking dissimilarity between her and her sister. Lori was rather short and of slight build, whereas her sister, Martha, almost as tall as Bob, was much stouter with heavy frame and broad hips. She had relatively pleasant features but an almost nondescript personality, seeming constantly to defer to her younger and smaller sister.

**NEAR THE END** of January there had been posted Personnel Orders No. 13 from Headquarters Army Air Forces Central Flying Training Command, Randolph Field:

EXTRACT

15. The following named 2nd Lts, AC, flight officers, AC, and student officers, Class 43-B, having completed the required course of instruction at the AAFPS (Adv Single-Eng), Moore Fld, Tex, are, under the provisions of AR95-60, 20 Aug 42, and AAF Regulation 41-7, 1 Oct 42, rated pilot, effective 9 Feb 43:

Then on February 8 there were issued Special Orders No. 104 from Headquarters, AAF Pilot School (Advanced- Single Engine), Moore Field, Mission, Texas:

EXTRACT

1. Following named Avn Cadets and/or Avn Students, as indicated, atchd unasgd to 2529th AAF Base Unit (Pilot School ASE), Sec "H", Class 43-B, this sta, are dischd from mil sv, effective 8 Feb 43, to enable them to accept commissions and/or apmts as 2D Lts AUS, and/or Flt Officers AUS, as indicated.

```
By DP, each of the following named Officers, having completed the
prescribed course in advanced single engine pilot tng at this sta,
with the rating of Pilot is ordered to AD at this sta as 2D Lt AUS,
or Flt Officer AUS, as indicated, effective 9 Feb 43, and is asgd
to dy with the AC, and pending issuance of further asgmt orders is
atchd unasgd to 2529th AAF Base Unit (Pilot School A-SE), Sec "A",
this sta. Each Officer will rank from 9 Feb 43.
```

Bob and Bill were designated to be appointed Second Lieutenants, but Sidney was to be ranked as Flight Officer, the Air Corps
equivalent of Army Warrant Officer.

On the evening of February 8, the day before graduation, with
the last training flight and exercise completed, excitement among the
cadets was at fever pitch. Exhilaration at having completed the arduous training program was coupled with intense speculation concerning
"further assignment." Large clusters of the prospective graduates gathered in the PX, and rumors and scuttlebutt were rampant.

They had been informed by the CO that temporarily the class
would transition immediately to training in combat fighters, P-40
"Warhawks," a squadron of which were located on another part of
the field. (During their ten weeks there the cadets had watched with
mouths drooling as these fighters, some with the traditional Flying Tiger shark's teeth painted on the cowl, would take off and land,
piloted by graduates of the preceding class.) A period of thorough
familiarization with the aircraft was to be followed by temporary
assignment to Brownsville, Texas, for two weeks of air-to-air gunnery
and air-to-ground bombing training off Matagorda Island. However,
there were not enough of the fighters efficiently to accommodate
all the trainees for this phase, so half the class would be granted two
weeks of furlough while the other half was in Brownsville. Then the
two groups would switch places, and the ones having completed gunnery would be granted their post-graduation leaves.

Bob opted to volunteer for the first group to go to gunnery,
but Bill chose to take his two-week furlough at that time so that he
and Lori could have their honeymoon earlier. The respective decisions caused some hesitation on both their parts, for they had become

conditioned to being together and goading each other on, and this would represent the first hiatus in seven months. This separation was eased, however, by their resolve to try to stick together and fly together later in combat if at all possible.

**THE NINTH OF** February dawned as a perfect spring-like day in south Texas, ideal for the graduation exercises. The former cadets had the thrill of donning their commissioned officer's uniform for the first time for the march to the outdoor ceremonies. Tradition was scrupulously followed, from the congratulatory and exhortatory address by the Commanding Officer, to the tossing of the hats in the air, to the paying of one dollar by each new officer to the first enlisted man to salute him. No one could ever figure out how Master Sergeant Brasher was able to pre-empt from all the other enlisted men on the field this right, but every month he would station himself where the new graduates would have to file by and return his salute. He even had to secure the aid of a private to help cart off all the dollar bills he had thus acquired.

Bill took advantage of his newly attained rights as a commissioned officer to reserve a table at the base Officers Club for the dinner following their late-afternoon rehearsal in the small Catholic church in McAllen. In line with Bill's restricted sociability and circle of friends, the party was small, limited to Bill and Lori; Bob as Best Man; Lori's sister, Martha, as Maid of Honor; Father Mahaffey, who was to conduct the ceremony; and finally Sidney Haggard. The presence of Father Mahaffey, from whom Bill had received two weeks of tutoring and instruction in Catholicism, imposed a certain constraint on the celebratory inclinations of the group, which was probably just as well since all three of the pilots were to report to the flightline at six o'clock the next morning.

The next day Bill and Bob requested and received permission to leave at four p.m. in order to shower, dress and get to the church before the scheduled five-thirty wedding. Even so, they were barely on time, for, since neither of them had a car, they had to arrange for a taxi, which was late in arriving at the base to pick them up. As they got out of the cab, they could hear the organ music already playing, so they went straight into the church and took their positions near the altar.

If Lori the rest of her life could be described as relatively plain, at least this day she radiated a serene beauty as she came down the aisle to the strains of the wedding march. Dressed in a simple white wedding gown with an organdy veil, she smiled and kept her eyes riveted on Bill as she approached the altar on the arm of Sidney, who was standing in for the deceased father. Bob was moved by the beauty of the ceremony and had anticipated that it would last longer than it did. However, after the wedding proper Lori and Bill retired to a tiny chapel for additional instruction and blessing from Mahaffey.

Bob had insisted on hosting the reception at the Casa de Palmas Hotel in McAllen, having reserved a small private dining room and having ordered four bottles of champagne. He was somewhat disappointed when Father Mahaffey declined to join them, for he had developed a definite respect and liking for the priest. The cleric's absence, however, did facilitate the unleashing of the pent-up urge by the members of the wedding party to celebrate the double festive occasions of graduation and marriage, and everyone did justice to the opportunity. The kitchen staff at the hotel had prepared a delicious feast and had even baked a small wedding cake in spite of sugar rationing. The champagne received due attention and appreciation and was buttressed by additional supplies of tequila and rum, so that by ten o'clock no one even made a pretense at sobriety, not even Bob, traditionally a teetotaler.

As they all exited the dining room, Sidney bade them all a good-night and caught a cab back to the base. Bob had wanted to go along with him, since he was to fly a P-40 for the first time the next day, but the other three, feeling he was the least inebriated, prevailed upon him to drive the newlyweds back to the tiny little house Bill had managed to find on the western outskirts of town. Having parked the LaSalle in the gravel driveway next to the bungalow, Bob helped get Bill out of the car and into the unlocked side door. Seeing that Lori was able to get her tipsy new husband to the sofa in the modest living room and had begun removing his tie and shoes, he backed out of the door and closed it behind him. As he was passing the car to head for the street and the long walk back into town, the right front door opened and Martha got out and stood unsteadily holding onto the frame.

"You aren't going to leave me here by myself, are you?" she asked with a noticeable slurring of her speech.

Bob was a little embarrassed. He had forgotten all about the fact that she had been in the front seat next to him.

"Oh, I'm sorry. I thought you had followed us in. Come on, I'll help you inside."

"I can't go in there," she protested. "This is their wedding night, and there's only one bedroom."

"But can't you sleep on the sofa in the living room?" Bob asked, trying to be helpful.

"The bedroom door is missing," she responded, "and that place is so small, if you swung a cat around by the tail, you'd knock over every lamp in the place. Whoooeee! I'm dizzy."

With some effort she got the rear door of the car open and half-fell inside.

"Then let me drive you back to town. We'll get you a room at the hotel."

"With all the families here there's not a room to be had in town. Bill tried everywhere yesterday. C'mon sit in here a while with me."

She reached out, took him by the hand and pulled him inside. Bob was unhappy over this development. He had been up since five o'clock in the morning, had spent a long day studying the operating manual and systems and procedures of the new fighter, and was unused to the enervating effects of alcohol. He needed sleep far more than he did the boredom of trying to carry on a conversation with a tipsy woman.

Conversation proved to be no problem. He had barely settled on the seat after having closed the door when Martha moved over and began kissing him with almost a frenzy. He was caught totally by surprise. The woman had projected, if anything, an aura of asexuality, and never once in their contacts during the preceding two days had there been an inkling or suggestion of attraction between the two of them, in either direction. It was a painfully awkward situation for him. He was not the least interested in "smooching" with a woman who did not appeal to him, and yet his traditionally gentlemanly inclinations precluded a brusque rejection of her overtures. During the protracted first osculation the best response he could come up with was a condescending patting of her arm. When she finally broke away to come up for air, he tried to sit up straight.

"Martha, I think that . . ."

"Shhhh," she broke in, placing her finger on his lips and breathing heavily in the crook of his neck, "don't say it. Just think of what's going on in there. Doesn't that get you excited?"

"Martha, really . . ."

Before he could continue, her full mouth was planted on his again, and her tongue began to dart in and out. Deftly her left hand unbuttoned his shirt, passed underneath his dog tags and started caressing his chest. Even Bob had to admit that the unpleasantness of the situation was rapidly being ameliorated. His hand passed up her arm to the back of her neck and then slowly down the front of her dress toward her breast. Abruptly the kiss was terminated, and she said, "Watch your hands!"

Bob recoiled with astonishment, suddenly struck by the incongruity of the whole experience. Lori, by Bill's description, was devoutly abstinent and chaste, and yet her sister, presumably also Catholic, had unexpectedly metamorphosed into a vehicle of passion, had initiated an apparently experienced sensual activity, and then rejected his first attempt at response. But his surprise was immediately compounded. As he started to move away, Martha began another intense kiss, seized his formerly offending hand and guided it underneath her skirt and between her thighs. While he hesitated briefly in indecision, she proceeded to unfasten the front of his trousers and adroitly extract his equally surprised but rapidly responding member. By the time his hand had caught up with the level of the rest of the activity and reached her panties, it was obvious that she was in a state of dire excitation.

Development continued apace. Martha slid down on the seat and pulled Bob over on top of her between her legs. Even to approximate an efficient position, he had to open the car door with his heel in order to let his legs protrude.

"Wait," he said, "I don't have. . ."

"It's okay; don't worry," she panted. "Go ahead. It's safe."

Coupling was not easy, for in their haste her panties had not been removed. However, she reached down with both hands and effected some adjustments that worked. It might have been due to the dearth of sexual activity on his part for so long, but in spite of her lack of physical attractiveness her vagina was extraordinarily delicious to him. A temporary ebb to his passion occurred when once again he moved his hand up to caress her breast, and she seized it and deflected it. But when it occurred to him that she probably had on falsies and didn't want him to be aware of the fact, he felt a wave of compassion for her, and his erection returned full force. The strenuous rocking to and fro of her legs initially caused his head rhythmically to impact the interior of the car above the armrest, but once he solved this problem by shifting his position somewhat, he was content to let her orchestrate the intensity.

He was gratified to note that his method of mental control was still operative, and he settled onto an extremely pleasant level of awareness and arousal. As an automatic brake, there was no need for recourse to memories of walking in a cold rain across a cornfield, as was required many months before in Atlanta. This time, when necessary, it needed only a realization that their activity was transpiring less than twelve feet from the southeast window of the small house next door. His opening of the car door had automatically turned on the interior light, so any alert and curious inhabitant glancing out the window would be granted a ludicrous but perhaps entertaining spectacle.

Bob didn't know exactly how long this exercise had been going on, for he allowed himself languidly to slip from arousal to drowsiness and back again many times, but at one point he sensed that Martha had sobered from her exertions enough finally to approach orgasm. He fine-tuned his responses and succeeded in timing his own climax to occur simultaneously with hers. He lay inert on top of her for a protracted period and didn't bestir himself until startled when she began to snore. Slowly he extricated himself from her leaden arms and legs and the cramped quarters of the car, positioned her as comfortably as possible on the car seat and quietly closed the door. When he addressed the task of re-ordering his own clothing, he saw why she had felt free to tell him "it's safe." Even in the dim light he saw with some consternation that the entire front of his trousers was crimson from menstrual flow induced by, or at least accompanying, their activities. This indelicate condition would create some problems for his getting back on the base, so on his walk in toward the center of town he picked up from the side of the road the first discarded newspaper he found and held it in front of him.

Although it was only a little past midnight, the town was virtually deserted, so he was lucky to be able to flag a taxicab at the corner of Mesa and Plum streets. Two men and a woman, all of whom had obviously almost emptied the bottle they were passing among them, were sitting in the front seat of the old Dodge. On the drive out to the field they conversed with each other in Spanish, and the blowsy woman winked at Bob twice in the rearview mirror. In the light at the main gate to the base Bob was standing by the cab and reaching into his pocket to get the five-dollar bill demanded by the driver when his newspaper slipped and fell to the ground. Before he could retrieve it, the driver and the woman next to him had noticed the unusual condition of his uniform.

"Haw! Haw!" bellowed the driver. "Looka there! Thees soldier has been wounded in the war."

"He's a pretty one," giggled the woman slurringly. "I wish I'd been the one woundin' 'im."

After the taxicab had left with sounds of hilarity, the soldier on duty at the post saluted and tried hard not to grin as Bob walked through the gate behind his opened newspaper.

## CHAPTER SEVEN

**THE FOLLOWING WEEK** was so busy with the intense transition training that Bob had no opportunity to spend any time with the newlyweds. The residential move to a private room in the Bachelor Officers Quarters was a radical departure from the communal cadet barracks, so he had no chance to miss the daily contact with Bill. With some relief he did learn from him on the fourth day that Lori's sister had returned the day after the wedding to Los Angeles. At the end of the first training period the three of them had dinner together at the Officers Club the night before Bob was to leave for Brownsville and Lori and Bill were to leave on furlough. As they said good-bye after dinner, both pilots were acutely aware of this first break in their common careers since the initial day of Primary at Corsicana. Little did either of them realize how radical this break would prove to be.

The training at Matagorda Island off the coast of Texas fell principally into two parts—dive-bombing at marked targets on the bombing range, and firing machine guns at metal-mesh targets towed behind an old B-26 out over the Gulf. It was at this second exercise that Bob was especially good. The sleeves would be dropped back at Brownsville and suspended on a rack. The ammunition supplied to each P-40 had a distinctive color paint on the tip of the rounds, so that the pilots could count the number of their hits. Invariably Bob outscored all the others.

However, he did notice a strange inconsistency in his scores: They varied according to the airplane he was flying. Consistent with his thoroughness, he determined to find out why. He had been following the training directive of commencing firing at an estimated range of four hundred yards and breaking away at approximately one hundred and fifty yards. To maximize the number of rounds he could get off on any one pass, he would always reduce his power and consequently air speed just before firing in order to remain longer on the curved path necessary to maintain the proper lead on the target. On each return to Brownsville for refueling and reloading he began making simulated passes to check out any differences in the airplanes. The standard pattern was to approach at a higher altitude and on an opposite heading from the target and execute a diving one-hundred-eighty degree turn to make the pass. The effectiveness of the firing pattern was critically dependent upon the perfectly coordinated trim of the fighter during the time of firing, for any skid or slip would spray the bullets off to the side, causing them to miss the target. The sudden decrease in engine torque at Bob's habitual power reduction had to be compensated for by definite left-rudder pressure in order to keep the slip-indicator ball centered in the instrument. What Bob noticed during his checks was that each airplane had a slightly different inherent rigging trim, and therefore the same customary left-rudder pressure at power reduction was correct for some planes but not for others. Therefore he began to compile a list indicating the different characteristics of the various fighters being flown.

In the evening, instead of accompanying his fellow officers across the border to Matamoros, he would continue the habit developed during his cadet days, don fatigues and go down to the maintenance hangars. From the P-40 manual he was unable to find reference to the exact distance of fire-power convergence for the machine guns on each wing. One of the mechanics told him that it was approximately three hundred yards, but when Bob asked if the distance for each plane had been checked and computed, the only response from the mechanics was a blank stare or a shrug. With a metal rod, a sensitive pocket compass and a level Bob made an apparatus with which he checked every gun on every airplane. Using trigonometry from his Georgia Tech days, he found and recorded significant differences in this convergence distance.

He also removed the "ball" portion from a surplus turn and bank indicator and modified it so that he could clamp it securely on the top of the firewall of whatever airplane he was flying, in a manner allowing him to see it out of the corner of his eye while using the gun-sight. His making use of this information and these innovations elevated his already high scores considerably.

On Saturday morning, the last day of the gunnery session, Bob was packing his bag in the BOQ at Brownsville when the Officer of the Day knocked at his door.

"Colonel Sanders wants to see you, Hanson. As soon as you get your flight suit on, report to his office."

Fifteen minutes later Bob reported to the colonel.

"Hanson," the senior officer began, leaning back in his chair and resting the fingers of each hand against the corresponding ones of the other (a mannerism Bob had noticed during briefings), "I don't know how you've done it, but in gunnery scores you've blown away everybody. Yours are running thirty to forty percent above what our best instructors can do. That might be due to luck or natural talent, but I have a suspicion you can teach others to do whatever you're doing. I'm thinking of asking Central Command to transfer you to my unit as a gunnery instructor. What would you think of that? We lead a pretty good life here in Brownsville."

The suggestion was so unexpected that it caught Bob by surprise, but his reaction was immediate.

"With all due respect to the Colonel, sir, and the quality of your operation, I would prefer to stay in the pipeline for assignment to an operational unit overseas."

The colonel reached for a smoldering cigar butt in an ash tray.

"If I show your hit averages to the Commanding General, my recommendation could easily override your personal preferences," he said, squinting his eyes half-testily and half-good-naturedly at Bob.

"Yes, sir," Bob responded, "but today's scores will be averaged in.

If I miss the sleeve entirely all day, then my averages will drop down close to everyone else's, and the general won't be so impressed. And think of the weight on your conscience for all those porpoises in the Gulf I will have shot up . . . sir."

The colonel let out a loud guffaw.

"Okay, Hanson, you win. But I am impressed with your performance, and I'm going to award you the prize Kewpie Doll by exempting you from the ride back to Moore Field this afternoon in that old Gooney Bird. Your CO wants the P-40 you're assigned to today back at Mission. So after your last gunnery run don't come back here but go directly to Moore Field. We'll forward your score today. Give your gear to the BOQ orderly, and he'll see that it gets on the C-47. Any questions?"

"No, sir; thank you, sir," Bob replied, truly appreciative of the opportunity of delivering the plane back to his home field. He was even more pleased when he reported to the flight line and saw that his assigned aircraft was 2369, the P-40N that was his favorite.

The day went smoothly. The towplanes were more on time over the target range than usual, and the crew chiefs were more conscientious and expeditious in servicing the fighters and reloading the guns. The only non-positive factor was the weather. A large static high-pressure dome over the Gulf was pumping unseasonably hot air into the area from the south, resulting in haze in the late morning and the build-up of cumulus clouds in the afternoon. By two o'clock, however, Bob had made his last run, during which he concentrated on trying literally to pulverize the tow-target as a last salute to the colonel.

Instead of returning to the field at Brownsville, he started a cruise climb westward over the water between Matagorda Island and the mainland, setting a course for Moore Field. He was in high spirits: He was pleased with his performance during the gunnery phase, the long training period was drawing to a close, he had a ten-day furlough coming up, and he was certain that transfer to a combat unit in some war zone was imminent.

As he approached the mainland, he saw ahead of him at his altitude a line of cumulonimbus forming along the coast. Rather than descend into the hot turbulent air and under-fly the line in the gloom of the obviously heavy rain below, he chose to climb on top and stay in the clear air. Checking his oxygen reserve, he saw that he had at least an hour and a half supply at high altitude so advanced the engine controls to climb power. He estimated that the saddles between the thunderstorms were probably around fifteen thousand feet, so he turned the oxygen adjustment knob to give him the proper flow for that pressure altitude and settled back to enjoy the beauty around him.

Leveling off in smooth air at fifteen thousand, seven hundred feet, he passed between two large cells and in a few minutes saw in the distance the flat and hazy but sun-lit prairies of south Texas. Immediately behind the initial squall-line, to the southwest of his course, he spotted two giant cumulonimbuses in the process of formation. Inordinately large for this early in the year, their tops were already towering at least thirty thousand feet above Bob's cruising altitude. They were merging into a compound, multi-columned monster with forbidding dark aisles of clear air between the cells. The threat of the awesome power of this leviathan posed a temptation that Bob was powerless to resist. Banking sharply to the left, he headed for the open area between the two main segments of the storm.

Once on a cross-country flight in Primary, he had strayed slightly from his course in order to play with a cumulus cloud and remembered the exhilaration he had felt. True, comparatively that cloud had been merely a puff of cotton and the one hundred seventy-five horsepower of his Fairchild had given him limited options for the game, but it had still been great fun. Now the stakes were increased a hundred- or a thousand-fold. The forces within the storm in front of him could strip the wings from an airplane in a fraction of a second. They could alternately catapult it upwards at thousands of feet per minute or dash it downward at the same velocity, all within a blink of an eye. The challenge was to stay just clear of the jaws of the beast, to taunt it, to mock it. And Bob felt he had the steed under him to do just that. The N-model was a pilot's airplane, clean and responsive, and he felt it was almost an extension of his own body. The thirteen-hundred-horsepower of the Allison engine gave the plane a performance edge that Bob had learned to utilize and had come to appreciate.

As he approached the brooding wall ahead of him, he tightened his shoulder-harness, lowered the long nose of the aircraft and with a muffled shout of joy in his face-mask dove into the area between the two main columns. In pass after pass he steered the sleek fighter through the cavernous canyon, skimming along next to the towering sides, which were formed from boiling updrafts of dark clouds. As the heady game went on, he noticed that the opening was growing narrower and narrower and on one pass finally closed about two miles ahead of him. On reaching the end of the cul-de-sac, he racked the plane into a steep bank in order to execute a one-hundred-eighty degree turn and head out into the open again. He had to lean forward and yell to tense all the muscles in his diaphragm to keep from blacking out from the extreme G-forces. But as he burst forth into the sunlight again, like an addict he was compelled to turn back for yet one last pass. As he guided the P-40 into what was now merely a narrow alley of blue-gray light, he knew there would be no room this time in which to make a lateral turn. The challenge of the situation gave him a sense of exuberance, for he determined to reverse his direction at the last moment by executing an Immelmann—a half-loop with a roll-out at the top. As he entered the gloom of the narrow canyon, he caged his gyros—the directional compass and the artificial horizon—to keep them from tumbling and possibly being damaged during the acrobatic maneuver and leaned slightly forward to squint into the half-light.

Smooth, ordered rows of black cloud just off each wing tip were telling signs of extreme turbulence. Abruptly ahead of him lay the end of the corridor and a pitch-dark wall. He lowered the nose and glanced at his air speed indicator. At two hundred ninety-five knots he knew he had sufficient airspeed to complete the Immelmann so pulled back sharply on the stick. As the nose of the plane reached the vertical, he fed in full throttle, relishing the almost sensuous sound and feel of the power of the Allison. Just for the exhilaration of it he eased forward on the stick and for a few seconds held the fighter in a vertical climb. The altimeter was winding up rapidly, and Bob was having to feed in ever-stronger right rudder pressure to counteract the torque of the engine as his air speed bled off. At one hundred eighty knots he came back on the stick again to complete the half-loop, but just as he was beginning his roll-out to the reciprocal heading, the plane was engulfed in dark cloud, and he lost all visual orientation. In the poor light he had not noticed that the corridor had been growing not only narrower but lower.

Estimating the time of his roll-out, Bob immediately went on "partial panel" to control the airplane. Stabilizing the air speed and altimeter and ensuring that the airplane was not in a turn, he reached up and uncaged his gyros to facilitate the fine-tuning of his instrument flying. Although the magnetic compass was still swinging erratically and heavy rain had begun to pummel the canopy, Bob began to relax. He knew he must be within a few degrees of the reciprocal heading he needed and would soon be in the clear again.

Suddenly the plane was bathed in an eerie pale green light, and the side of the canopy struck his head a stunning blow. As he fought to try to regain the control stick, which had been wrenched from his hand, he was alternately pressed down almost to the point of blackout and then jerked against the restraint of his seat belt by vacillating G-forces. He had no idea of the attitude of the airplane. None of his instruments made consistent sense. The gyros were tumbling wildly, the turn and bank indicators were on opposite ends of the dial and the air speed, rate of climb and altimeter were erratic. The severity of the turbulence let up briefly, and Bob was able to regain a grasp on the control stick. The tightness of the controls and the sound of the air rushing past the canopy let him know that he was probably in a steep dive. A glance at the air speed indicator confirmed this impression; it had settled down and was passing through an indication of four hundred sixty miles per hour. He eased the throttle back with his left hand and tried to center the ball in the turn and bank indicator, but even with his pushing on the left rudder with all his weight, it would not center. He did manage to center the needle with left aileron and began slowly easing back on the stick. The rapid unwinding of the altimeter began to slow and eventually stopped at seven thousand feet. Gradually left rudder control became available as the airspeed bled off until it fell below one hundred fifty miles per hour.

Bob then dropped the landing gear and flaps to help prevent airspeed build-up and fed in partial power with the throttle. Blinding flashes of lightning made it difficult to see the instruments, but he was able to attain a modicum of stabilization in spite of the continued turbulence. He caged and then uncaged the gyros and was relieved to see that they were probably reliable once again. Holding as steady a heading as he could with the directional gyro, he fought to stay level and within an air speed between one hundred and one hundred fifty miles per hour. Gradually the lightning began to flash more to the rear, and, after he had penetrated a zone of very heavy rain and hail, the darkness began to give way to gray, then light gray and finally blue.

Having broken out into the brilliant afternoon sunshine, gingerly and methodically Bob began to check out all the systems in the airplane. The landing gear and flaps retracted normally, the engine instruments were indicating in the green, and control responses were as good as ever. As he verified his position just north of the Rio Grande River and set a course for home, he felt a deep gratitude for the strength and integrity of this fine machine. Approaching Moore Field with a sense of relief and exultation at his survival, he made an especially low and fast pass over the approach end of the runway, cut his power and pulled up steeply to the left, dropping his gear and flaps at the top of the arc to settle in for a smooth landing.

However, his euphoria, which had continued as he taxied onto the ramp and shut down the engine, came to an abrupt end. Two officers walked up to the airplane, and as Bob climbed down from the cockpit, he noticed that one, a large man whose face was obscured by the bill of his hat, was writing on a clipboard. Both he and the other officer, a stocky man with a mustache, wore the insignia of captain.

"Ten-*shun!*" barked the tall officer in a commanding voice.

Bob was startled by the abruptness of the command but, having tucked his flying helmet under his left arm, snapped to attention. The captain continued to make notes on the clipboard as he walked around the left wing of the aircraft and stopped a few steps behind Bob's left shoulder.

Bob's mind was racing. How could anyone have witnessed his violation of regulations by buzzing the thunderstorm and endangering himself and the aircraft? And even if it had been witnessed, how could the information have beat him back to his base? A tinge of guilt convinced him that he was somehow in trouble, but he could not imagine what sequence of events had transpired.

"Lieutenant, were you operating under official orders?"

"Yes, sir."

"Do you feel you carried out your assignment satisfactorily?"

"Yes, sir. I do."

"What kind of approach and landing would you call the one you just made?"

"It was standard, sir," Bob answered but then suddenly became suspicious. The tone of the captain's voice was gruff and commanding but betrayed a certain familiar ring. The next question removed all doubt.

"Lieutenant, there's a rumor you consider yourself the world's second-best pilot. Is that true?"

"No, sir. That's not true. I consider myself the world's best pilot. I have a tall-ass friend somewhere who is the world's second-best pilot."

Bob was almost knocked off his feet by the thump of the hand on his shoulder. When he turned with a laugh, he was lifted bodily off the ground in a huge bear-hug by his friend.

"Hot dam,' li'l Robbie, it's good to see you!" Knute bellowed, pushing his hat onto the back of his head and putting his hands on his hips. "Man, I mean this ol' Air Corps can teach *anyone* to fly, can't it?"

"They gave you wings, so that must have proven it," Bob retorted with a grin.

"Robbie, this here is a friend of mine, Charlie Fedders. Charlie, meet my old roommate, Bob Hanson, the pride and joy of Georgia Tech and Lexington, Kentucky. Charlie's assistant dispatcher up at Kelly Field. I heard through the grapevine that you were stationed here, so when he said he was comin' this way on official business, I hitched a ride down."

"Pleased to meet you, Captain," Bob said, shaking hands. "How long will you fellows be able to stay? I'll cover dinner for us tonight at the Officers Club."

"Thanks for the offer," Fedders responded, "but I have to fly on to the coast this afternoon. I'll stop and pick up Captain McCutcheon on the way back to San Antonio in the morning. How about nine o'clock, Knute? Would that be too early for you?"

"No problem," Knute answered. "Robbie here is pure as th' driven snow. If I follow his example, I'll probably be in bed by eight o'clock."

"Don't over-do it," Fedders smiled. "You might break out in a rash."

Then, having saluted the other two officers, the captain turned and walked toward a B-25 sitting on the ramp.

Bob retrieved his parachute from the cockpit of the P-40 and slung it over his shoulder.

"Come on, Knute. As soon as I report in and get a shower, let's go over to the Club for a beer. Do you realize I haven't heard a word from you in fifteen months? You're a fine friend."

"Now, hol' on, li'l buddy. You gotta admit I answered every one of your letters; now, didn't I?"

Bob had to laugh as they set out across the ramp.


**AN HOUR LATER** as they made their way to the bar in the Officers Club, there was frenetic activity everywhere. The dance floor and tables were being readied for the usual Saturday night dance.

"Robbie," Knute said in a low voice, "I'm a little tired of the food in officers' messes, and these stuffy base parties bore me. Let's go over across th' river and have a few drinks and a coupla steaks. How 'bout it?"

"That's okay by me," Bob answered, "but I'll agree only if you let me pick up all the tabs."

They took a taxi across the bridge into Reynosa, got out just inside the city limits and started walking along the dusty streets, looking in the shops along the way. The town was beginning to shift into high gear after dusk, and there was great hustle and bustle. The sights, sounds and odors of a Mexican border town were everywhere. From every window and doorway came music—some soft and some loud. There were rows and rows of stores selling everything imaginable— pottery, wicker, hats, boots, liquor, leather jackets, perfumes, knives. Whatever could be thought of could be found. And the vendors were anything but passive; they were actively aggressive in hawking their wares—especially those marketing the services of a female member of their family.

During his months in Mission, Texas, Bob had been disinclined to visit Mexico. In fact he had been into Reynosa only twice before. The meat shops with their wares hanging in the heat and dust and covered with flies had discouraged him from eating there on his previous visits, but Knute just laughed at his voiced reservations.

"Aw, hell, Robbie. There's nothin' wrong with it. It's prob'bly good for ya. Now tell me: on which side of the river do ya see th' most people, huh?"

Knute chose a steak house, bought a "Pinch Bottle" of Scotch at a store next door and ordered a table. After some difficulties they managed to get a bucket of ice and some seltzer water and then ordered two T-bones.

"Here's to ya, li'l buddy," Knute said, touching his glass to Bob's and taking a hefty drink. "Ya know, I gotta confess somethin.' I had th' tower alert me when you were comin' in today, so I was watchin.' I hate to admit it, but you were flyin' that thing pretty dam' good. But why in hell did ya choose those li'l pea-shooters? Why didn't ya pick a man's airplane to fly?"

Bob laughed.

"Oh, oh! I guess I must be talking to a bomber pilot. What have they got you in?"

"B-17's," Knute answered, pouring another drink and staring into the glass.

Bob waited for a moment, but his friend was silent.

"Well, come on, old man, and fill me in on what you've been doing. You sure as hell didn't get all that fruit salad at a pawn shop," he said, pointing at the ribbons above the left pocket of Knute's uniform.

Knute glanced down at his decorations and then looked up with a grin.

"Aw, hell, they give ya one of these over there just for pickin' your nose."

"Where have you been?"

"England."

"How many missions?"

"Thirty-seven or thirty-eight. I can't remember."

There was another pause. Bob was having to pull everything out of him.

"Pretty rough, huh?"

Knute didn't answer. He just shrugged and took a drink. Bob noticed that one of the ribbons represented the Purple Heart.

"How did you get that little beauty—fall off a bar stool?" he asked, trying to lighten the mood. Knute managed a grin.

"Naw. One of my li'l English gals agreed to go to bed with me, and I unzipped my fly so fast I got a hangnail."

"Well," Bob laughed, "I'm glad to hear that there's one thing that this war has not changed."

Knute's expression became serious.

"Robbie, ya know, there's somethin' I've thought about a lot. Wouldn't it be great if we could fly together? Man, we could make a real team. When I got back, I was assigned to a trainin' base, but I can't stand sittin' aroun.' My request for another tour of duty has been accepted, but I've made a lot of influential friends, and I could wait around for a while for ya. Get operational for bombers, an' I'll have ya assigned as my co-pilot. What d'ya say?"

Bob looked at the earnest expression on his friend's rough-hewn face and had to fight a temptation to accept the offer.

"Yeah, that would be great. But, old friend, I'm not cut out for bombers. I've always wanted to fly fighters. I'm expecting an assignment soon."

Knute's face mirrored his disappointment, and he reacted with resentment.

"You guys who fly those little shit-cans call yourselves pilots.

You don't know what 'toughin' it out' means. I've seen those dandies criss-crossin' back an' forth way up above us playin' with their cocks while we're down there gettin' th' job done an' gettin' our asses shot off."

There was an awkward silence for a moment, and then Knute grinned sheepishly.

"Aw, hell, that ain't right. I was kiddin.' Those guys've got balls of steel. When they get after a Jerry, they'll barrel-ass after him right down through our formations, through crossfire, ack-ack—anything. In fact I owe my life to one."

There was another pause as Knute took a drink.

"Tell me about it," Bob said, genuinely interested.

"It was on a raid over Hamburg. A Focke-Wulf 190 killed my tail gunner on a pass and settled in right behind us. He was chewing us up really bad and knocked out our number three engine. I caught a piece of steel in my shoulder (that's how I got this li'l thankee note from Uncle Sam). I thought we were goners, but this dude in a P-51 jumped the 190 and cut off a third of his left wing. The Kraut dropped by my window spinning like a top, and that Mustang was rollin' right with 'im, guns blazin' all th' way."

The waiter arrived at this point and placed the huge steaks in front of them.

"Man, these look great, an' I'm hungry as a bear," Knute added. "Think about it, Robbie. If ya ever change your mind, let me know. Say, I tell ya what. When we finish, let's take in an *exhibicion*. I hear they got a gal here who does a nude dance, ya see. Halfway through she puts a shot glass on a table, puts a dime in it and then a quarter and sits down on it. She sashays aroun' th' room again, holdin' the glass in her snatch. After a while she gets some buck on the front row to hold out his hand, spreads her legs an' drops th' dime in his palm. Splat! Just like that. How does she do that? Huh? How?"

"I don't know," Bob laughed. "I can't imagine."

"Well, let's go see for ourselves. Maybe we can figure it out," Knute suggested with a wink.

"I'm afraid that doesn't appeal to me," Bob said. "You take it in some other time. Okay?"

Knute looked at him reproachfully.

"Robbie, ya still never let ya'self have any fun, do ya?"

**AFTER DINNER THE** two friends wandered again up and down the crowded streets, joking and talking about old times in Atlanta.

"Hey, Let's duck in here an' have a li'l fun," Knute said, jerking his head in the direction of a dance hall called La Paloma. Bob only reluctantly followed. Four steps led up to a brightly-lit room with wooden floor and high ceiling. At one end there was a bar, to the side of which was located an ancient Nickelodeon grinding out equally ancient and scratchy music. Along one wall were ranged twenty to thirty chairs in which were seated girls of every conceivable height, weight and appearance. Just inside the door at the opposite end of the room from the bar was a counter, behind which sat the proprietress, a plump coarse woman, whose ample breasts could not have been contained within her low-cut faded blue dress were they not resting on an even more extremely protruding abdomen. She was counting through a stack of bills.

Knute addressed her with mock deference.

"Ah, señora, how much for your lovely ladies?"

The woman turned and looked at him and smiled, revealing a gaping hole where one tooth was missing and severe stains on the other teeth from some mixture she was chewing.

"For you fly-boys," she said with a thick accent, "I always gives a special deal: twenty-five cents for each dance."

"What if I'm not much of a dancer," Knute countered, winking at Bob.

"You wanna fuck her, it cost you ten dollar," the woman answered, returning to her counting.

Knute jabbed Bob in the ribs with his elbow.

"Let's go check out th' merchandise."

He led Bob to the middle of the room, where they stood surveying the line of girls. Many of them smiled and tried to act coquettish, crossing and re-crossing their legs and fluffing up their hair. A few even stood up and initiated pitifully inept undulatory movements. All of them except one had on high heels and a short tight skirt. The exception was a little girl sitting almost exactly halfway down the line. She sat quietly in a white cotton dress with her head lowered and her hands folded in her lap. Her hair was gathered at the back in a pony-tail and, although only a part of her face was visible, she was apparently quite pretty.

After they had scrutinized the line-up for several minutes, Knute whispered to Bob, "I might give that lanky redhead on th' end a try. She looks like she might know a thing or two about fun an' games. But let's go haggle a li'l over price with th' boss lady. That should give us some laughs."

"What's your pleasure, gents?" the proprietress asked as they walked back up to the counter.

"Well, I kinda thought I might try that li'l redhead on this end," Knute answered with a wink at the woman.

"Her name's Rita. That'll be two bits," came the quick response.

"I'm not exactly th' dancin' type," Knute said suggestively.

"Then that'll be ten bucks. There're rooms out back. She'll show you the way," the woman said matter-of-factly.

Knute leaned across the counter and said in a low voice, "But, señora, there's a little problem. I'm low on coin of the realm this month. I'll offer two bucks for 'er and promise not to be rough on 'er. How about it?"

The woman stopped what she was doing and looked up at Knute with obvious scorn.

"Back home you must be a ver-ree funny man. Why don't you go back there where you're appreciated?" Then she turned her head and looked at Bob.

"What about you, sonny? See anything you like, or are you a cheapskate too?"

Bob was caught a little off guard, for this was the first time he had ever seen anyone, especially a woman, stand Knute down so forcefully. But he did manage to stutter, "Well, I . . . I . . . was wondering about the girl in the white dress."

"Maria? Two bits a dance—just like everybody else. But you wanna fuck 'er, it cost you hunnert dollar."

"A hundred dollars?!" Knute exploded. "I thought you said ten."

"Ten for the others. This is Maria's first day. She's brand new."

"Oh, sure," Knute snorted. "Over here everybody's a virgin. Why, I bet you're a virgin too, aren't ya, big momma?"

"You better believe it, fly-boy. Pure an' innocent."

Bob was not too comfortable with the conversation. He pulled a dollar bill out of his pocket and handed it to the woman.

"I'll buy four dances with Maria, then. Do I wait for the beginning of the next record?"

"Na. Go ahead. That one's almost over. We won't count it."

Bob left his hat on the counter and walked over and stopped in front of the little girl. She kept her eyes lowered and did not look up.

"Señorita?" Bob said questioningly.

Only then did she raise her head and look at him. He was startled at the soft beauty of her child-like face, which had been hidden before.

"Dance?" he asked, motioning to the dance floor with his arm.

"*Sí,*" she answered softly and stood up.

"Do you speak English?"

"*Sí,* I mean yes," she answered, putting her hand on the left arm that he had offered her.

The dance floor was beginning to get crowded with cadets and their dance partners, so Bob had to steer her past several couples to find an open space. They had taken only a few dance steps when the record came to an end. They both stood self-consciously while the bartender struggled to change the record on the old machine.

"Your name is Maria, isn't it?"

"Yes."

"Maria is a pretty name. I like it. Maria what? What's your last name?"

"Rodriguez."

"Rodriguez," Bob said with English pronunciation.

Maria shook her head.

"Rodriguez," she said, emphasizing the r's.

"R-r-r-rodr-r-r-riguez," Bob repeated, substituting long trills for the r's.

This struck the girl as being humorous, for she smiled quickly, revealing beautifully even teeth, startlingly white against the golden tan of her face. The interchange broke the ice between them, and during the playing of the four records they chatted fairly easily, communicating verbally much more successfully than with their dancing, which never developed a smooth coordination. Bob found her shy reserve and childish directness appealing and was surprised at how quickly it seemed the four records had come to an end.

"Could we have something to drink and talk a while?" he asked as they started off the floor.

"That's against the rules," Maria advised. "The señora doesn't allow that."

"Then suppose I buy some more dances. Couldn't we just sit or stand and talk instead?"

The girl hesitated.

"I . . . I don't know," she said.

"Then let's go ask," Bob insisted. "If not, then we'll just dance some more."

As they walked over to the proprietress's station, Bob saw that Knute was still in heated bargaining with the woman. His voice carried to them.

". . . you know as well as I do that she isn't what you claim, but I'll give you half—fifty dollars. That's a fair offer, an' it'll make ya a good profit."

"Listen, mister, will you stop wasting my time. I've told you I don' bargain with my girls' services—for their sake as well as mine. Now go away an' leave us alone."

"Well, how about sixty? That's as high as I'm willin' to go."

Bob grabbed his friend by the arm and pulled him aside.

"Knute, what the hell are you doing? She told you only ten dollars for the redhead."

Knute grinned.

"Hell, I decided the risk would be a li'l high with that gal. If I get back to London with a case a' clap, my English chippies would never forgive me."

"Then what the hell are you arguing about?"

"Look," Knute said, glancing over at the counter, "I'm not at all sure that that li'l Maria is what she claims to be, but just in case she is, I'm gonna go th' full hundred for 'er if I have to. But I think th' ol' sow'll let 'er go for eighty. It's worth a try."

Bob was stunned. He turned hot all over.

"You can't be serious!"

"Why th' hell not? Look, li'l Robbie, I've never had a bran' new one before. I might not get many more chances."

"Goddamn it, Knute!" Bob almost shouted, "she's just a child!"

Knute looked at him with mild derision.

"For Christ's sake, when they reach ten years old over here, they're already women, or dam' well better be. Look, li'l buddy, if I don' get that li'l cherry, some other stud will. It might as well be me." With that he walked back to the counter.

"Big momma, I've got eighty smackers here for the' li'l gal. Now let's make a deal."

The proprietress glowered at him with exasperation, but before she could voice a new rejection, Bob stepped up and laid a wad of bills on the counter.

"Here's one hundred dollars, señora. I'll pay the full price."

He had started the evening with a hundred and twenty-six dollars in his pocket. After having paid for the dinner and the four dances, he luckily had one hundred and six dollars left.

"Hey, wait a minute. What th' hell ya doin'?" Knute objected. "I was here makin' th' deal first. Right? Here, big momma," he added, fumbling in his pocket, "I'll give ya th' dam' hundred."

"You're too late, friend," Bob said with more firmness than he usually employed with the big Texan. "I was dancing with her. She was my date already, and I was the first to agree to the contract. Am I not right, señora?"

The woman looked first at Bob and then at Knute, mirroring on her face some of the distaste she had been feeling for the latter.

"The lieutenant is right. I'd say it's his play. But I think Maria should be the one to decide. What do you say, girl? Did the lieutenant win the toss?"

The little girl had been standing by the counter, trembling all over. Her fists were clenched tightly by her sides, and she was staring out the doorway into the street. She started to say something and then bit her lower lip.

"Maria?" the woman repeated, looking at her sternly, "do you agree with me that the lieutenant is the one?"

Maria didn't answer. She just nodded her head.

The proprietress's expression softened. She came around the counter and patted the girl on the shoulder.

"Then that settles it. Deane, lead the gentleman out back and take the first room available."

There was an awkward moment of silence as the girl just stood there.

"All right," Knute broke in, turning to address the proprietress again, "I tell ya what I'm gonna do. I'm gonna give ya fifty dollars for second crack at 'er. When she an' my li'l buddy come outta there, she'll still be half a virgin. But when I get through with 'er, she'll dam' well know she's a woman."

Bob's face flushed with anger. With only six dollars in his pocket there was no way to counter Knute's offer this time. He turned and looked at the woman, whose blackened teeth were again showing in a smile as she snatched the money from Knute's hand.

"Well now, it seems the captain has suddenly come into some coin of the realm, as he calls it."

"Surely you aren't going to take it!" Bob said stridently.

"Fly-boy," the woman said, walking around behind the counter again, "money is money. It don't matter to me where it comes from, and from now on it won't matter to th' girl. Now you two go on. I can't spend my whole evening on this business."

Bob was seething with anger but grabbed his hat and reached over and took the girl by the arm. She started hesitantly and then led him out into the back alley. Some planks had been laid to serve as a make-shift walkway to keep the customers' feet out of the mud and refuse that littered the area. The air was heavy with the odor of garbage and urine, and an emaciated dog was scavenging in some boxes on the other side of the alley. On the right were three cubicles that served as quarters for use by the girls in carrying out their contractual duties. All three doors were latched, so the two of them had to stand on the rough-hewn planks and wait. From the left wafted the sounds of a mariachi band. After a painfully awkward period, the latch on one of the doors clicked and the door swung open. One of the girls came out, chewing gum and replacing hairpins in the bun on top of her head. She was followed by an extremely young-looking cadet, who blushed and saluted when he saw Bob's uniform.

"Good evening, sir," he said, stepping out into the mud to pass.

"Good evening, mister," Bob replied, returning the salute and then following Maria into the dingy little stall.

It was composed of four plank walls and a plank floor with no ceiling. Visible above was the tarpaper of the roof, from which was suspended an electrical cord with a single bulb of no more than twenty-five watts. A wooden bench was standing next to the outside wall and on the opposite side leaned a rickety iron bed, the holes in the mattress of which were only partially obscured by the skimpy bedspread with its patchwork of stains clearly visible in spite of the dim light.

Bob hung his hat on a nail protruding from a wall stud and sank onto the bench, intently observing the girl, who had sat down on the bed. She sat with her dusty little shoes side by side and both hands clasping the small silver cross suspended from her neck. They sat for a long time thus, the only sounds being the mariachi band down the way and the occasional yowl of a cat outside. Finally the girl raised her head slightly and barely audibly said, "I'm sorry, but you must tell me what to do."

There was a long pause.

"Tell me the truth, Maria. Are you still a virgin?'"

"Yes."

Another pause.

"How old are you?"

"Sixteen."

Bob struck his knees with his hands, got to his feet and started pacing back and forth in the short distance allotted by the small room. He felt a deep sense of frustration and agitation at the outrageous situation.

"You are a sweet, lovely girl, Maria," he almost shouted. "I know this is a corny question, but what in hell are you doing in a place like this?"

There was another pause.

"I must earn some money."

"There are other ways to earn money, for God's sake."

"But not here. Not as much as I must make."

"What about your family. Can't they help you? Do they know what you're thinking of doing?"

The girl was silent.

"Maria?"

"I . . . I'm doing it to help my family. My brother is very ill. The doctors say he must go to a sanitarium up in the mountains near Guadalajara, and my mother will have to be with him."

"But what about your father?"

"We haven't seen my father in eight years. My mother has been working in a laundry to support us but will have to quit her job to go with my brother. They will need the money that I can make. The hospital will be expensive."

"How much do you think you will make here in this hole?"

"*La señora* tells me that I can make a hundred dollars a month, maybe more if I try to learn and get to be good at it."

Bob stopped pacing. He sat down on the bench again and took her hands in his.

"Now listen to me carefully. We don't have much time. I want you to leave here for good and go home. Then. . ."

"No, no, I can't do that," the girl said frantically. "I would lose this job. The señora is good to the girls here. The other halls are run by men; things are much worse there."

"Don't interrupt," Bob said sternly. "Now you listen to what I have to say. Tomorrow I want you to cross over the bridge and meet me in McAllen. I gave almost all the money I had to the señora, but tomorrow I will have more for you. Let me think it over tonight. We'll work something out where you won't have to do this to make money."

The girl was shaking her head and trying to pull her hands free.

"No. Please. I mustn't lose my job. If you don't want me, I'll get your money back and . . ."

"Maria!" Bob shouted at her, squeezing her hands tightly.

She fell silent and looked up at him with tears in her dark brown eyes.

"We are not going to argue about it. You're going to do as I tell you to. Understand? Tomorrow afternoon at two o'clock you are going to meet me in the courtyard of the Casa de Palmas. *You are going to meet me there.* Do you understand?"

She nodded weakly. Bob stood up and pulled her to her feet.

"Now I want you to leave, and tell your mother not to worry."

"I must first go see the señora and tell her and try to get your money back," Maria objected.

"No! You mustn't go back in there—ever."

"But. . ."

"Maria! The captain is still there. We are close friends. I know him well, and he will insist on getting what he paid for. You will ruin everything I'm trying to do for you. I don't give a damn about the money."

Bob unlatched the hook on the door and pushed it open, "Go down the alley and straight home. And don't worry. Everything will be all right."

The girl stood in indecision for a moment and then slowly stepped out into the dark alley.

"Maria!" he called after her. When she turned to look at him, he said, "Trust me. *Hasta mañana.*"

He watched the girl until she turned the corner at the end of the alley and then went back into the dance hall. The proprietress was not in evidence, but Knute was leaning back with both elbows on the counter, watching the couples dancing. His face lit up when he saw Bob approaching.

"Hey, li'l buddy, what th' hell took ya so long? What's th' matter—couldn't ya get it up?"

"Come on, let's get out of here," Bob said.

"Now hol' on, buddy. I've got comin' to me a session with your li'l bride. Where is she—waitin' for me in th' room out there?"

"She's not here. She's not feeling well and had to leave. Now, let's go."

"Dam' if that's so! I've paid fifty smackers for a roll with 'er. Nobody screws ol' Knute outta fifty bucks. Lemme find that ol' sow, and she'll get 'er back for me, or else I'll take this place apart."

"Knute!" Bob said forcefully as his friend started off in search of the proprietress, "that's a waste of time. Maria's gone for good. I'll give you your money back. Now let's get out of here," he insisted and stepped out into the street.

In a moment he was followed by the big Texan. But when Bob started to move off, Knute grabbed him by the arm.

"Not so fast, buddy, not so fast. I'm not leavin' this spot 'til I get some answers as to what th' hell is goin' on aroun' here."

Bob looked up at him and finally smiled.

"I'm sorry, old friend. I didn't mean to double-cross you. Come on; let's find a bar and have a drink, and I'll explain everything to you."

They chose a bar on the road back to the border, settled at a rickety wooden table in the rear corner and ordered two beers.

After a couple of false starts Bob detailed everything that had happened after he and the girl had left the room and then tried to explain his own feelings about the whole episode, having virtually no confidence that his friend would or even could understand. During the whole discourse Knute sipped slowly on his beer, rolling the liquid around in his mouth before swallowing.

He didn't look directly at Bob but watched the comings and goings of the men in the bar or gazed up at the ceiling.

When Bob had finished, Knute turned his head and looked at him with a crooked smile that was always a sign of condescension with him.

"Li'l Robbie, I hope ya realize that you've been made a jackass of. You are without a doubt the dumbest, most naive sonovabitch in th' whole Army Air Corps. You've been had, sonny boy. That ol' whore an' that li'l trick spotted you for a sucker from a mile away. They've pulled that routine on a hundred dumbasses before you came along. Why, I bet they're back there at th' Paloma right now laughin' their heads off and splittin' up our dough."

"You may be right," Bob responded, "but I don't think so. I had to act on my own instincts. But I'll know one way or the other tomorrow."

"What d'ya mean?" Knute asked.

"Maria's meeting me in McAllen tomorrow afternoon. I want to help the poor girl if I can. I'm going to see if I can't get her into a school or something over in the States. She'll go down the drain if she stays here."

Knute leaned back and stared penetratingly at his friend.

"You are not only dumb; you are also crazy. If you think that li'l gal is goin' to cross over to Texas to meet ya, ya better have a good book with ya, 'cause you're gonna have a long, long wait."

"We'll see," Bob responded. "But anyway, I hope you're not mad at me for spoiling your plans tonight. I'll make it up to you some day."

"Aw hell, li'l Robbie, I couldn't stay mad at you. Besides, you may have kept me outta trouble. Come on, let's get back to th' base. I've had a long day, and Charlie's gonna pick me up at nine in th' mornin'."

Bob accompanied Knute to the flight-line at eight forty-five the next morning. Since the PX wasn't open yet, he couldn't cash a check and had to borrow from a fellow officer in his BOQ the fifty dollars to cover his friend's loss the night before. When he handed him the money, they were standing outside the operations office, squinting at the B-25 coming in on final approach.

"Robbie, my orders are gonna be cut in th' next coupla days. My friends up at Kelly are givin' me a farewell bash tonight. Come on an' go up with us. I'd like to have ya there. I'll call th' CO and fix it up for ya and arrange a ride back for ya tomorrow. If ya come, ya can keep this money. How 'bout it?"

"Thanks, Knute, I appreciate the thought," Bob answered. "Give me a raincheck—in London maybe. I'm afraid I can't make this one."

They watched as the bomber taxied up and its engines were shut down.

"You still gonna go to that meetin'?" Knute asked, turning to face his friend.

"Yep."

Knute shook his head and grinned. They shook hands firmly, and the big Texan walked off toward the waiting plane. Pausing underneath the belly, he turned and called back, "Robbie, I wanta pass on to ya somethin' my daddy once toll me. He said, 'Son, don' never trust a circus barker nor a whore.'"

Bob grinned and gave him a salute, and his friend, in spite of his large size, swung easily and lithely up into the hatch.

## CHAPTER EIGHT

**BOB CAUGHT A** ride into McAllen with the base Maintenance Officer, whom he had come to know well. It was a beautiful warm day, so he walked on foot to the little Catholic church, arriving in plenty of time for the morning service. Afterwards, he stood around just outside the entrance until the last of the congregation had paid their respects to Reverend Mahaffey and left. When the priest saw Bob approaching, he smiled and came to meet him.

"Ah, Lieutenant, it's nice to see you again. How are you? I haven't seen you since the day of the wedding. In fact I haven't seen Bill or Lori lately either. Are they all right?"

"Yes, they're fine," Bob answered. "When I left for gunnery over at Brownsville, they went to Los Angeles on furlough. But I think they'll be back today or tomorrow. Father, I wonder if I may take up a bit of your time?"

"Why, of course, my son," the priest answered. "Would you like to come inside?"

"It's so pretty out here, why don't we sit on the bench over there under the tree," Bob suggested. "I'll try to be as brief as I can."

"One should never treat problems superficially," Mahaffey smiled. "And besides, I very seldom have a Protestant come to me for advice."

"Episcopalian," Bob countered.

"Ah yes, Episcopalian. Even rarer."

After they had taken a seat, Bob had difficulty trying to decide how to begin. Finally he chose to start from the beginning of Knute's visit and describe in relatively accurate detail the sequence of the events of the preceding evening, omitting only those details he thought the priest might find offensive.

"Father, I want to help this girl and her family if I can. I will arrange to pay for her support and that of her mother and brother. I would like to solicit your help in finding a Catholic school for her here in the States where she can get a good education and . . ."

"My son," Mahaffey interrupted, placing his hand on Bob's arm and smiling at him indulgently, "I hope you realize that the Church can never be a partner in such an arrangement."

Bob stared at the priest uncomprehendingly for a moment and suddenly realized what was troubling him. He had to laugh out loud.

"No, Father, no. You have it all wrong. There will be absolutely no impropriety. I am leaving for overseas any day now, and, after I bring her here to you this afternoon, I shall never lay eyes on her again. Everything will be in your hands. You will choose the school and keep that a secret. I won't need or want to know where she is. You will handle all contacts with her and her family. All money will come to you, and you will dispense it."

Father Mahaffey was thoughtful for a moment, struggling with his own skepticism.

"What money? From where will it come?"

"The money will come from a bank in Lexington, Kentucky, from a trust account that I have there. I will leave you the name and address of the trust officer whom I shall write and instruct to forward funds to cover all of Maria's tuition and expenses with a little extra for spending money, plus the costs of her brother's hospitalization. I don't know how much that would run, but she seemed to imply that it might be one hundred dollars a month. But I will instruct Mr. Arnold, the trust officer, to forward to you whatever amount per month you tell him you need. That is a decision obviously he wouldn't be in a position to make."

Bob paused and looked inquisitively at the priest.

"So you see, Father," he added, "I am going to trust you, so you must trust me."

Mahaffey was silent for a few moments. With a stick he drew a cross in the dust on the ground in front of them.

"Son, why are you doing this?"

Bob looked up at the palm fronds rattling above them.

"I haven't even had time to examine my motives," he answered honestly. "The whole world now seems to be an evil, violent place. I guess in some sense I want to try to counter a tiny little bit of that evil, if I can. I am applying for combat status, and there's always a fair chance that I won't be coming back. That's as good a legacy as I can think to leave."

Bob fell silent for a minute and then continued.

"And, Father, I'm also going to trust your judgment with respect to the girl. I honestly believe she's a good girl, but—as I mentioned—my friend tends to be cynical and thinks I'm being a fool. If she doesn't meet me today, then I have been a fool. If she does, I will bring her here, and you will make the final judgment. I haven't mentioned to her any explicit details with respect to helping her, so if you decide that she's unworthy and that it's best not to proceed, I will just give her a little money, and there will be no harm done."

Mahaffey took the stick and enlarged the sign of the cross.

"All right, my son, if she meets you, bring her here. I will be waiting."


**BOB TOOK A** cab back to the base. After eating lunch in the Officers Mess, he cashed a check for three hundred dollars at the PX and rode back into McAllen. He walked through the gate of the Casa de Palmas Hotel at one fifty and immediately spotted Maria. There was a fountain in the middle of the courtyard, and she was sitting on a high bench in front of it with her hands underneath her, swinging her feet back and forth and intently watching the goldfish in the little pool. Rather than sixteen, she looked like eight or nine years old. He stood observing her for a moment, and the doubts which had been growing concerning his decision evaporated.

As he came up to the bench, she looked up at him and smiled.

"You came," he said.

"Yes," she answered. "You told me to."

*What a lovely child!* he thought. How could she have emerged from the background and environment that he imagined in his mind?

"How about a walk?" Bob suggested. "There's someone I want you to meet."

"All right," she responded brightly, pushing off of the bench. "I always take a long walk every Sunday after church. I got in the habit when we lived on a farm near Sonora when I was little. We had to walk to church, which was three miles away. At the time I thought it was more like a hundred."

Bob smiled and led her out onto the street.

"Well, that is a funny coincidence," he said, "because we are now going to walk to church, and even though it's not three miles, we can pretend it is."

For the most part they walked in silence. Maria at one point retrieved a stick from somewhere and would at times take a swing at the tops of tall weeds on the side of the road. The breeze had shifted to the southwest and brought with it the almost intoxicating fragrance of orange blossoms from the groves but also a rise in temperature. Heat was shimmering up from the macadam road, and occasionally a loud grasshopper would buzz in front of them.

Father Mahaffey was waiting for them at the door of the church. He led them out to the same bench under the palm tree. He had placed a small table next to the bench, and on it was a pitcher of lemonade and a plate with two pieces of cake.

"My parishioners always keep me well stocked in things that are not necessarily good for the waistline. These were left over from my lunch. Please help yourself."

Bob declined, but Maria gratefully accepted a piece.

"I'm going to take a stroll around the church grounds," Bob said. "I'll be back in a few minutes. Why don't you two get acquainted?"

As he wandered through the various fruit trees that were randomly planted in the garden, which Father Mahaffey kept in immaculate order, he stayed close enough to observe the two of them talking earnestly under the palm tree. Finally, during one circuit of the path he saw the priest motion to him, so he walked over to the bench.

Mahaffey winked at him and nodded his head subtly.

"I have discussed your very kind offer with Maria, but she is not sure she can accept."

"But why in the world would you be reluctant to accept it, Maria?" Bob asked. "Is there something that I don't know about?"

The girl shook her head, which she kept lowered. She was looking intently at a flower she was holding in her hand and the petals of which she was nervously and gently caressing.

"It's just that it doesn't seem right. Why would you offer to do this?"

Bob laughed and sat down on the ground in front of them so that he could see her face.

"You know, that's the second time today I've had to answer that question. Does it seem so strange to you?"

"Yes, I think it is very strange."

"Well, let's just say in a way I'm being selfish. I would like to do what your father would be doing if he were around. This is going to be a long war, and I may not live to have a daughter of my own someday. So you see—you're the one doing me a favor."

The girl looked up at the priest.

"Father, what should I do?"

"You are the one who must decide that, my child. But I think you are being presented a marvelous opportunity. I know of an excellent school not too far away where the sisters, although very strict, are also kind and very good teachers. You will be separated from your mother and your brother anyway, won't you? So why don't you give it a try? You can always change your mind."

Maria looked at Bob with tears in her eyes. After a long pause she almost whispered, "I . . . I . . . don't know how to say thank you."

"Great!" Bob said, jumping to his feet and taking out his billfold.

"Then it's all settled. Father, here's a little money to get things started. I'm going home in a few days and will talk to Mr. Arnold right away. You'll be hearing from him within two weeks. Give me your exact address so that I can pass it on to him. I'll head back to town. There are a lot of things you two will have to go over. When you have finished your discussion, call a cab to take Maria home."

"Let me call a cab for you too, son," Mahaffey said.

"No, thank you, sir," Bob responded. "I'd rather walk. The perfume from the orange groves makes it worth it."

While the priest was writing his address down on the back of a copy of the church program, Bob reached down and took the girl's right hand.

"Good-bye, Maria, and the best of luck to you."

She looked up at him and smiled.

"When will I see you again?" she asked.

"I don't know. We may not meet again. From now on Father Mahaffey is the one you should see and talk to. Let him know whenever there's something you need. Good-bye, Father, and thank you for your help. I will send you my home address so that you will be able to reach me if there is anything you need to contact me about. Any letter would be forwarded and get to me sooner or later."

Bob put the folded paper in his pocket and shook hands with the priest. Then he walked down to the road. Before starting out for town, he turned and looked back. The two of them were still sitting under the tree. They both waved.


**AS HE WALKED** along the hot road, he felt an almost giddy sense of satisfaction. He was even nagged by a tinge of guilt at the strength of a feeling of righteousness and nobleness that he realized diluted the full Christian impact of what he had done, but it was too sweet for him to forego. Just before he reached the town proper, he was jarred from his self-serving reflections by the blaring of a horn. Turning, he saw the venerable old LaSalle pull to a stop on the other side of the road. Bill leaned out of the window and grinned at him.

"Wouldn't you know you'd be the first person I'd run into when we got back!" his friend said.

"Well, I'll be damned," Bob exclaimed, letting a bus pass and then crossing the road to shake Bill's hand and say hello to Lori, who was sitting on the passenger side. "When did you all get in?"

"This is it," Bill replied. "We haven't even been to the house yet. Hop in. You can help us unload."

Bob opened the rear door, moved a number of items over to make room and settled on the back seat.

"Well, how was the honeymoon?" he asked.

"With Lori as my bride, you know damn well it was paradise," his friend answered. "In fact the last couple of days I've been considering deserting, but she talked me out of it."

"Don't let him kid you," Lori broke in with a laugh. "I couldn't pry him away from those airplanes with a ton of dynamite."

Bill glanced at Bob in the rearview mirror.

"What in hell were doing walking along out at the edge of town?"

"Oh, I thought I'd walk out to the church and visit the scene of the crime again," Bob grinned. "No, I wanted to go out and talk to Father Mahaffey."

"*You*, talking to Mahaffey?" Bill said with mock surprise. "Aha! Getting nervous about combat and trying to hedge your bets, I guess."

"Well," Bob responded with a grin, "since we've been talking since Primary about one of us being the other's wingman, I figured either way I need all the help I can get. By the way, Mahaffey asked about you two. You should go out and see him soon."

"We are," Bill answered as he pulled into the graveled driveway of the little hut they called home. "We were on the road, and Lori missed Mass this morning, so we'll drive out this evening."

The three of them piled out of the car, and Bob helped them carry all the baggage and articles into the house. Then he walked to the front door.

"It's good to have you all back. I'll go and let you all get unpacked. Let's have dinner together before I leave on Tuesday. How about tomorrow night at the Officers Club?"

"That sounds like fun," Lori said. "It'll give me a chance to wear a new dress I bought."

"Hey, hold on, and I'll drive you out to the base," Bill broke in. "I've got to report in and check on the mail, anyway."

**MONDAY PASSED RAPIDLY** in spite of the fact that Bob had completed all of the required missions in that training phase and didn't have to fly again. He had had in the back of his mind a nagging concern about P-40 2369 after his little adventure on Saturday, so after breakfast, having donned a pair of coveralls, he sought out the aircraft and found it in the maintenance hangar undergoing a one-hundred-hour inspection. Telling the crew chiefs that he had pulled exceptionally heavy G's during some gunnery runs, he borrowed a flashlight and spent several hours going over every inch of the airplane, looking for any popped rivet or slight wrinkle in the aluminum skin that would signal structural stress. Finding none and finally convinced that it had come through the pounding unscathed, he returned to the BOQ, once again impressed by the integrity of that fine machine.

The dinner at the Club that night was relaxed and pleasant. The newlyweds carried on a running account of the humorous and touching events that had happened on their honeymoon, and Bob was in high spirits over his departure the next morning for Lexington.

"What are they giving you to fly home in?" Bill asked.

"An AT-6."

"An AT-6? That'll take you a while. Why don't you ask for a P-40?"

"I did, but they need all of them for you lumberheads to finish up your hours. When do you leave for gunnery?"

"Wednesday morning. I get to copilot the C-47."

"Is Lori going to be over in Brownsville with you? It's a nice town."

"Bill has located a rooming house where I can stay," Lori broke in, "because there are no quarters for transient marrieds on the base. He'll have to stay in the BOQ, but at least I'll be able to see him every day."

"By all means go out to the flight-line," Bob advised. "While I was there, there were a couple of wives arguing like fishmongers over the color of some of the hits on the tow-sleeve, each pulling for her own husband.

"Incidentally," Bill said, "the scuttlebutt around here is that you creamed those sleeves and outscored everybody. I've known you are a good pilot, but I didn't think you were that damn good. You must have cheated. Come on, 'fess up: how'd you do it?"

Bob laughed.

"Well it wasn't exactly cheating, but I did have a gimmick. Here, to show you what a good friend I am, I'll pass it on to you."

Having taken out his wallet, he extracted the sheet of paper with the figures on each of the P-40's used in the gunnery.

"Here are the figures on the range to the firing convergence point for each of the planes," he said, handing the sheet to Bill. "As you can see, they are by no means identical."

"How did you get them?" Bill asked, glancing over the numbers.

"I couldn't find them in any of the tech manuals or individual aircraft logs, so I measured them and made up my own. It took me three days to come up with them, so that means you'll probably better my score. Lori, I want you to tell me if he ever does any bragging about it."

"Is that all there is to it?" Bill asked skeptically. "You mean I just sit there relaxed until I hit these ranges?"

"Not quite all," Bob responded. "You've got to fly the plane damn well also. And most important, keep your ball centered when you're firing."

"Hell," Bill grinned, "in this war it's hard enough just keeping your balls at all, much less keeping them centered."

"All right, you two," Lori interrupted. "When Bill starts talking dirty, I know he's had enough to drink. Come on, honey; I think it's time we go home. Bob should get to bed early anyway."

# CHAPTER NINE

**THE LONG FLIGHT** home was a welcome form of healing for Bob, a type of psychic convalescence. The pace in the AT-6 was again leisurely, almost languid compared to that of the fighters he had been flying, and as the hours slipped by, almost imperceptibly he felt tension begin to drain from his body. So totally preoccupied and immersed had he been in the intensity he demanded of himself with respect to his training that he had been unaware that mentally, physically and emotionally he had become like a coiled spring. Memories and reflections of home, his parents and Nancy had proven to be potentially disruptive to the task at hand, so soon after his induction they had been relegated to a remote corner of his mind. Now that his re-contact with them was imminent, the cupboard doors were forced open and these thoughts were allowed to surge back into his consciousness.

This unwinding was facilitated by the beauty that hour after hour slowly passed beneath the wings of the airplane. Bob had always unabashedly considered himself an ardent patriot, but never before had he been so acutely aware of the magnificence of his country. His course carried him from the expanses of the south Texas prairies northward and eastward across Arkansas and Tennessee, unrolling before him the breathtaking panorama of America in the spring. A ridge of high pressure lay across his entire route, ensuring crystal-clear weather, and, as dusk was falling, he saw below the wide sinewy meanderings of the Mississippi. Since no government fuel would be available at the airport in Lexington, he thought it prudent to land and refuel at Standiford Field in Louisville. The service crews had closed up for the night, creating some difficulties and delay, but by eleven o'clock the AT-6 lifted off on the final short leg of the trip.

Bob had of course informed his parents of his upcoming furlough but had refrained from being specific on the date or time in case there should develop some delay that would cause them disappointment. Therefore, when the taxicab pulled up in front of the stately colonial mansion after midnight, there was not a light to be seen. Repeated ringing of the door bell finally produced a cautious from-behind-the-door query by Lillian, the downstairs maid, as to the identity of the intruder. A moment later the door was flung open, and throughout the house could be heard the woman's clarion shrieks as she announced to one and all the locally blessed event.

During the ensuing hubbub Bob was moved by the touching and spontaneous reactions of his parents, particularly of his mother, who, alternately laughing and crying and wringing her hands, desperately was trying to devise ways to smother her son immediately in the amenities of home.

"Have you had anything to eat? Aren't you hungry?" she asked in a typically maternal response.

"I'm famished!" Bob answered to the delight of the kitchen staff. "I haven't had a bite since a cold sandwich in Little Rock."

Within an hour he was enthroned like a king in the dining room with a veritable feast spread before him. All the staff had been awakened and informed—housekeepers, chauffeurs, stableboys, farmhands—and the walls of the room were ringed by people in half-uniforms, bath robes and overalls. Each bite of roast chicken, turnip greens or hot Southern biscuits was approvingly witnessed by over twenty spectators. To the varied solicitous questions—from what he wanted for lunch that day to what horse should be saddled for him by eight o'clock—Bob finally had to laugh.

"Whoa! Hold on. I haven't won the war yet."

During the next three days the trickle of relaxation of tension begun on his flight developed into a flood, and Bob underwent a curious transformation. When he arose the first morning, he carefully hung his uniform and flight suit in the very back of his closet, removing them from his sight and from his consciousness. He donned old, familiar clothes and spent hours riding along the lanes, chopping wood, splitting logs or walking through the freshly plowed fields, inhaling the aroma of the spring earth. He came to look on this furlough as a needed period of healing and rebuilding, and the contemplation of having ten days to himself induced an almost giddy intoxication.

His father was genuinely interested in hearing about his training, and Bob used the evenings to fill him in. When he mentioned at dinner on the fourth day his experiences at gunnery and his conversation with the colonel in Brownsville, he immediately realized he had made a mistake, for he heard the sharp intake of breath by his mother.

"Oh, son, take it, take it!" she pleaded. "You could give so much more as an instructor, and I could sleep so much better. Why don't you marry some nice girl like Nancy and stay here in the States? It would be marvelous for all of us."

Bob looked at her with compassion and regretted having uncorked her pent-up anxiety. He thought it best to give a noncommittal response and change the subject.

"Well, that's certainly something to consider," he said. "Say, how is Nancy getting along? She should be near the end of her sophomore year."

"She's fine. I talked to her mother just last week. You know, you all are good friends. You really should call her over in Charlottesville. I know she'd appreciate it."

"By George, you're right. I think I'll do that right after dinner," Bob said, not totally unmindful of the slight deviousness in his mother's suggestion. Actually, the prospect of talking to Nancy had a definite appeal and fit smoothly into the process of his renewed contact with the past.

The call lasted over an hour. Once again he was caught off guard by the strength of his response to the sound of her voice, which excited echoes of feelings and emotions that he had suppressed for nine months. He had almost forgotten the frothy pleasantness of her superficial banter.

"Look," she finally said, "why don't you come over here to see me? You could leave your horses for a couple of days, couldn't you? We could have a great time. I'd love to show you the University."

"By George, I will!" Bob said, himself surprised at the immediacy of his response. "When do you want me to come?"

"How about day after tomorrow? Let me know when you'll arrive, and I can meet the train."

"I won't be coming by train. I'll fly my plane over."

"Your plane?! Fabulous! A handsome Air Force officer coming over to see little me in his own airplane! The girls in the sorority will be absolutely pea-green with envy!"

Bob laughed. "I have serious doubts about your memory if you remember me as handsome. Besides, I've aged a lot since you last saw me. In fact, I've lost all my teeth and hair."

"Pshaw! I don't believe a word of it. You're just trying to hide the fact that you've had dozens of those Texas girls swooning."

Suddenly for some reason the levity of their conversation soured for Bob, and it became tedious. "Since we'll see each other in two days, we'd better hang up now," he said. "I'll give you a call and let you know my estimated time of arrival."

Before retiring, he recounted to his mother most of the details of their conversation and told of his tentative promise to visit Charlottesville. Although normally his mother would have been reluctant to give him up even for two of his limited number of days, she was in a way glad to do so, for she was hopeful of thereby gaining the aid of a potential accomplice.

Later Bob was awakened by a soft but persistent knocking on his door. Turning on the bedside lamp and glancing at the clock, he saw that it was three o'clock in the morning. "Yes?" he called, putting on his robe and crossing to open the door.

"Son," came his mother's strained voice, "you have a long-distance call. You can take it in our sitting room."

"Bob," came Bill's voice over the line, "I'm sorry it's so late. I've been trying to get a call through to you for hours."

"Where are you? In Brownsville?" Bob asked, struggling to sweep the cobwebs from his mind and deal with a strange feeling of dislocation.

"No, I'm in Mission. I got back this morning. Our outfit is being cleared out completely by a series of rush orders based on volunteers. There were sixty-four slots for immediate assignment to fighter units, and the rest are to go to multi-engine transition."

Bob's stomach tensed. "Did you put me down for fighter assignment?"

"I tried to," Bill answered, "but that group is all filled. When we got back from the coast, Sidney and I got the last two slots."

"Damn!" Bob almost shouted. "The reason I called," Bill continued, "is that an order has been cut for three pilots to go to recon school. They'll go from multi-engine transition to train in P-38's. I've got them holding one of those slots for you if you want it."

Bob's deep disappointment was eased slightly by this news. "I want it. Have them hold it for me."

"There's only one problem," Bill added. "You have to be back here by tomorrow night, for departure is scheduled for the following morning. If you change your mind or can't make it, call Colonel Hodges. There are a bunch of guys waiting in line."

"I'll be there," Bob said firmly. "Let's you and me and Lori have dinner together."

"I won't be here," came the response. "We leave this afternoon for a POE. But give Lori a call, if you get a chance. Good luck, friend. I'll see you around."

Bob hung up the phone and stared at the floor, stunned by this sudden development. The sound of his mother's clearing her throat made him reaware of her presence, and he looked up at her. She was standing in front of him in robe and tiny slippers, her face appearing ashen in the light of the small lamp.

"I've got to leave."

She said nothing, just nodded her head slowly.

"I need to get to the airport as soon as possible. I think it'll be best if Leslie drive me out . . . And, mother," he added as she turned to go, "do me a favor and call Nancy later on today. Tell her I won't be able to make it this time."

Weariness and worry were etched in her face as she looked at him, and she appeared ten years older than she had at dinner. He felt a wave of pity and regret, but there was nothing he could do or say now to help her. Once again she nodded slowly and turned and left the room.

**DAWN WAS BREAKING** as the AT-6 droned across the flat landscape of west Tennessee, and a lowering overcast was forcing Bob gradually to decrease his altitude as he was flying southwestward. At the early hour of departure he had been unable to get a line through to the weather service and the control tower was not yet manned, so he decided to land at Memphis to top off his tanks and check the weather ahead.

The picture was not good; in fact it was grim. The former high-pressure ridge had moved off the coast, and the briefer informed him that a massive slow-moving system was stretching all the way from Mexico up into the Mississippi Valley, bringing with it low ceilings, rain and fog. Bob's request for a clearance to Houston was denied; the best he could do was file an instrument flight plan to New Orleans, where the airport was forecast to remain open for a few more hours.

Within minutes after take-off he was flying in dense dark clouds as he climbed to his assigned altitude and began the tedious hours-long flight along airways to New Orleans. Occasionally heavy rain would pummel the canopy and seep through the cracks, and persistent static in his headset at times almost drowned out the signals he needed for navigation and the infrequent voice communications. Abeam of central Louisiana he was able to contact the control tower at Baton Rouge, report his position and request the current weather at his destination.

"Army Baker Five Three Six, this is Harding Tower. New Orleans is closed. Weather reported zero-zero. What are your intentions?"

"Harding Tower, from Army Baker Five Three Six, what do you have there?"

"Ceiling and visibility zero. Light rain; fog. Wind calm. Temperature sixty-seven, dew-point sixty-seven. What are your intentions?"

"What about Beaumont and Houston? Any better?"

"Negative. Everything west socked in. You must fly east to find minimum ceilings. I suggest Biloxi or Mobile."

Bob swore to himself. What rotten luck! If he were forced east, his chances would be nil of penetrating this virtually stationary system and making it back to Moore Field by the following evening. Yet his options were few. He had limited fuel remaining, and a cold front inching down from the northwest across Oklahoma and north Texas was spawning a squall line with severe thunderstorms, so deviation to the north was ruled out. His thoughts were interrupted by the voice of the controller again breaking through the crackling static.

"Army Baker Five Three Six, do you read me? What are your intentions?"

"Harding Tower, I have your figures. Will proceed to New Orleans and then east if necessary. Army Baker Five Three Six, out."

Bob did not respond to several subsequent urgent attempts by the tower to reach him again, wanting to avoid any direct orders to change course. He had declared an end to the communication and could pretend to have changed frequencies. When he contacted the New Orleans tower thirty minutes later, however, it was obvious the information regarding his situation had been forwarded.

"Army Baker Five Three Six, amended routing. Maintain four thousand feet. You are cleared from over the beacon to Biloxi via . . ."

"Negative, tower; unable," Bob interrupted. "Fuel reserves for deviation marginal. I will make a couple of attempts—your station. State present conditions."

There was a long pause between transmissions as Bob began setting up for an attempted approach. He felt that his hunch had been right: due to the miserable weather and lack of traffic there was no commissioned officer on duty in the tower—only a relatively inexperienced non-commissioned controller, whose unsteady voice again broke through the static.

"Present weather: ceiling less than one hundred feet; visibility one-half mile; wind calm; light rain; fog; altimeter setting two-nine-eight-four."

"Thank you," Bob responded, wanting to sound conciliatory, "I'll report over the cone for final."

Since there was no wind to cause drift, with the exception of a signal glitch in the northwest quadrant the approach was fairly easy. However, when his timing and altitude had come down to the legal limits, Bob could see no break in the clouds. Advancing the throttle and retracting his gear, he executed a "missed approach" while informing the tower of his intention of making one more try.

"Really, sir, I think that . . ." The young voice of the controller trailed off.

Bob intercepted the beam, flew outbound from the station, executed a procedure turn and came back for one more attempt. He reported crossing the cone of silence to the tower, glanced at the clock, lowered his gear and began a controlled, timed descent, trying to stay centered on the beam. He was still in the clouds when he leveled off at his minimum altitude but encountered heavier rain, a possibly encouraging sign. As his time limit came up on the clock and he was about to advance the throttle to climb power, he suddenly saw the dim outline of dark trees streaking by underneath his wing, and a narrow break in the clouds occurred straight ahead, affording the welcome sight of the edge of the field and a moment later the end of the runway.

He guessed that he would have no hassle from the tower, so after shut-down he went straight to the weather office, where a graying but no-nonsense master sergeant dashed any hopes Bob may have had for continuing on that day. Downing a few crackers and a soft drink, he stood around the office for a couple of hours, hoping against hope for a break in the weather. Finally, exhausted and discouraged, at five o'clock he gave up and accepted a bunk assignment in the BOQ, leaving instructions with the orderly to be awakened at four in the morning.

At four-thirty the following morning the field seemed deserted. Line crews were nowhere to be seen, and the fuel trucks were parked behind the operations hangar, whose corner light shone dimly through the light drizzle that was falling. There did seem to be a definite, although low, ceiling, for the rotating beacon on the field was clearly visible. The master sergeant in the weather office had been replaced by a corporal, who sat slumped over with his head on his desk, sound asleep. Bob flipped through and scanned the stack of midnight sequence weather reports, all of which monotonously reported no change, and projected forecasts for his route for the rest of the day gave no room for encouragement.

Bob walked outside and stood brooding with his hands jammed into the pockets of his flight jacket. He felt frustrated and trapped. Turning abruptly on his heel, he headed for his airplane, parked on the ramp. He had signed for his fuel the afternoon before, there was nothing to be gained by waiting, and he had full tanks. Damn it! One way or the other he was going to be at Moore Field before nightfall. He fired up the engine and taxied to the end of the runway. As he was checking his magnetos, a voice crackled in his earphones.

"Aircraft at end of runway, this is ground control. State your identification."

Bob's heart sank. He had hoped that either there would be no controller in the tower or that he would not be noticed.

"Tower, this is Army Baker Five Three Six, over," Bob responded, trying to sound as calm and matter-of-fact as possible.

"Army Baker Five Three Six from tower. Are you aware that the field is closed?"

Bob's only hope was that this was another inexperienced, non-assertive controller on duty at that hour.

"Roger, affirmative," he answered in a casual, condescending tone of voice. "This is a weather survey flight. I'm to check out a development southwest of the field. I'll report back any changes. Stand by to copy if I do."

"Er . . . er . . . roger. Wilco."

Bob eased the throttle forward and rolled down the runway. Having taken off to the south, he turned right to a heading of two hundred and seventy degrees to traverse the low, flat terrain of Louisiana and eastern Texas. For the first twenty minutes, by staying at an altitude of only one hundred fifty feet he was able to skim along just below the low overcast, but soon he was in and out of scud and then in solid clouds. On instruments he climbed to and maintained an altitude of five hundred feet, occasionally dropping down cautiously to see if the ceiling had again risen. Eventually he could make dim contact with the ground, but visibility remained less than a mile. The reduced visibility and the monotonous drone of the engine had a hypnotic effect on him as over two hours slipped by. He was sitting in almost a trance, when suddenly adrenaline aided his taking a violent evasive maneuver. Out of the gloom dead ahead rushed a tall white obelisk or monument reaching from the ground up into the clouds above. Bob executed a hard ninety-degree bank to the left, and the glistening marble of the structure flashed by a few feet from his canopy.

With his pulse pounding wildly at this near miss, Bob realized that he must be approaching Houston, a grave danger under these conditions. Turning to a heading of one hundred eighty degrees, he flew due south toward the Gulf, straining his eyes to peer ahead. When eventually he saw with relief whitecaps and striations of waves below, he continued for a while on this same heading and then swung gradually to a heading of two hundred forty degrees, determined to remain over the open water and attempt to intercept the coast again near Corpus Christi. For the next hour and a half he felt as though trapped in a gray cocoon of fog and mist. Only an occasional thunderous pummeling of heavy rain on the leaky canopy broke the monotony and brought him alert to monitor his engine instruments and switch fuel tanks. The static in his earphones eventually began to give way to at first faint and then ever-stronger signals from the Corpus Christi radio range, and Bob soon determined that his course was correct and that he would pass south of the Naval Air station and be in position to proceed directly to his home base. As he crossed the coast, the ceiling began to rise slowly, and he could remain several hundred feet above the mesquite and vast expanse of the immense King Ranch. Bob felt only slightly more secure than he had over the Gulf of Mexico, for there were many stories about this nation within a nation, this empire with its own absolute ruler and its own set of laws. There were rumors of aircraft having gone down within it, never to have been heard of again. So it was with a sense of relief that eventually he spotted below a configuration of arroyos and a cattle-watering tank that he had learned to identify as a cadet on cross-country flights. He altered course slightly and in less than twenty minutes entered the landing pattern at Moore Field.

Bob proceeded immediately to Headquarters and checked in. Captain Crawford looked up and grinned when he saw him.

"You just won me a five-dollar bet," he said. "No one else thought you'd get through all that slop and make it back in time. I figure you busted some rules to do it."

"What do you mean?" Bob responded with a smile. "I was in bright sunshine all the way."

"Sure, sure. At forty thousand feet, I guess," the captain said. "Hell, you can go back out and sunbathe a little longer, if you like. There're still two hours to go before I would have had to give your slot to somebody else. Congratulations. The orders are being cut now. You're being transferred to the Second Air Force for recon training. You leave at six in the morning for Lubbock. Hanson, we're going to miss you around here. Will you come back to see us sometime?"

"I promise," Bob laughed. "As soon as I win the war."

Bob chose to walk to the BOQ. He wanted the leisure to observe for the last time this place where he had come of age as a pilot and which he had come to regard as an alter-home. But it had already changed. Most of his class had already left, and the faces he saw, those of the most recently graduated class, were unfamiliar to him. Packing was not much of a chore. All he had to do was add a few things to his already packed B-4 bag. At five o'clock he showered and dressed and walked to the Officers' Club. He placed a call to his mother, as per her request, to assure her of his safe arrival and then called Lori to invite her to have dinner with him.

When she walked through the Club door at six-thirty, she rushed over and gave Bob a hug. Once more he was struck by how pretty this ordinarily plain girl seemed at times. She appeared to be not in the least saddened by the forced separation from Bill, who had left that morning, and all during dinner Bob was again impressed by the extent of her maturity and stability and the depth of her faith.

"I'll make out," she said as they were saying good-bye. "I talked to my boss this afternoon, and he has promised me my job back at Lockheed. Sure, I'll miss Bill horribly, and naturally I'll be concerned. But I won't let myself worry. After all, I feel that, wherever he is, he's in the hands of God."

# CHAPTER TEN

**AFTER HAVING BADE** farewell to that "fledgling" portion of his Air Corps career, Bob found out that up to that point he had never undergone really intensive training. The next few weeks in the Second Air Force made his prior training seem to be a stroll. He and Lieutenants Wilson and Woodard were assigned for only a few days to a multi-engine advanced training unit in Lubbock and after a mere ten hours in twin-engine trainers were sent to P-38 training at Colorado Springs. Less than an hour after their arrival they were already being briefed by the officer assigned to them.

"Gentlemen, I hope that you talked to your families last night, for from now on you are to communicate with no one outside this base. Much of what you hear from me now and in the coming days will be classified information and will be for your ears only. I demand and expect strict silence. Your lives and those of others may depend on it.

"I hope that you volunteered for recon duty and weren't coerced. There is a widespread misconception concerning photo reconnaissance and the pilots that carry it out. It's tough, complicated and exacting. No two missions are ever alike. It is dangerous and demanding work, and there is no more important a contribution within a military operation. One important fact gleaned from an intelligence photo can determine the outcome of a whole battle. The conception, planning and carrying out of an entire campaign or of a single mission—today, tomorrow, next week or next month—is heavily dependent for its success on the quality and timing of the pictures obtained and the intuition and interpretive observations of the pilots. The enemy has hundreds of ways to conceal his movements, but a well-timed photograph, taken by skilled hands, can reveal plenty to the practiced eye of the photo interpreter. In addition to getting the pictures, you will have to observe clearly, quickly and intelligently. Gentlemen, you will carry a heavy responsibility.

"I'm sure that since there are only three of you, you realize that this is a special crash program. For the sake of speed we have limited your number to that of new F-4B's that will be available in your theater given the compressed time frame within which we are working. You would surely be able to guess during the next few days, so I may as well tell you now: you will be heading for the Southwest Pacific theater. Your aircraft are already being assembled in Australia. We can hope that they will be ready by the time you get there. I can tell you only that there will be increasingly intensive military operations in your theater, and your services will be sorely needed. Any questions?"

The captain paused and looked at each of the three.

"Sir, how will we get to Australia and how long before we get there?" Lieutenant Wilson asked.

"Not even I know the precise answers to those questions," the captain answered, "but we are going to work each day as though it's the last day of your training. You will be up at six every morning, and classes will run until noon. After lunch you will have only two hours per day to accustom yourself to the P-38. We don't have any F-4B's on base, but the aircraft are basically the same with the exception that the recons are stripped down. The P-38 comes with four fifty-caliber machine guns and two twenty-millimeter cannon in the nose and the ability to carry bombs. The F-4B's carry three cameras instead of ordnance—no bombs and no guns.

"Your planes are capable of flying higher and faster than any aircraft the Japanese have and—also important—above the reach of their anti-aircraft fire. Classes will start again at three and last until eight. These classes will exhaustively cover photography, map-reading, photo interpretation, camera installation, assembly, disassembly and emergency repair, navigation and the latest updates on enemy military, logistic and camouflage techniques. After you arrive in Australia, you will also receive an intensive briefing course on southwest Pacific meteorology and geography.

"Now down to business. Basically there are two main types of air recon—tactical and photo, both important. Although each of you will receive basic training in both types and be able to switch if necessary, I expect you to specialize in one. The photo recon pilot is the lone eagle of the Air Force. He will fly missions all alone over long distances and at extreme altitudes, and his photos will be largely straight down. The tac reco pilots usually fly in pairs and at lower altitudes, for often oblique pictures give us important information on elevation of terrain and enemy structures, critically important in the planning of low-level, on-the-deck missions for bombers. Two of your planes are being equipped for tactical work and one for strategic. There are three of you. How do you want to be assigned?"

There was a brief pause. Finally Wilson raised his hand. "Sir, Lieutenant Woodard and I have been flying together since primary training. If it's all right with you, we'll take the tactical assignment."

The captain turned to Bob. "How about you, Hanson? Do you feel like an eagle?"

"Not exactly, sir, but I'll take any assignment and do the best that I can."

The captain looked at Bob penetratingly. "I sense a certain tentativeness in your reply. Am I wrong, or do you not have some reservations?"

"Not exactly, sir. It's just that I've heard of problems in the P-38 between the turbochargers and engines at very high altitudes. That could be dicey a thousand miles from home."

The captain again regarded him intently.

"And where did you get that information, Lieutenant?"

"I spend a considerable amount of time with maintenance personnel, and there's always a fair amount of scuttlebutt," Bob answered.

"Well," the captain responded with a smile, "what you heard has been true. There have been problems in Europe. But your planes will have specially redesigned turbos. There shouldn't be that problem."

"Sir," Bob continued in this same vein, "will I have a chance to spend time with the maintenance men? I like to learn as much as I can about any airplane I'm flying."

"That's highly commendable, Lieutenant," the captain responded, "but you won't have time for that here. Now, gentlemen, as soon as you've unpacked, go to Operations and pick up the pilot's manual for the Lightning. You have only the rest of the afternoon to memorize it and familiarize yourself with the cockpit. At eight p.m. you will be given a blind-fold cockpit check, and I expect each of you to make a hundred on the test. I'll see you in class at seven in the morning, and after lunch you'll fly the bird for the first time. Any questions?"

**ON THE NIGHT** of May thirteenth a heavily loaded troop ship eased out of San Francisco harbor and passed slowly beneath the Golden Gate Bridge, bearing elements of a Marine division and two U.S. Army infantry battalions. On an upper deck, leaning on the rail, stood three Army Air Corps officers, watching silently as the silhouette of the darkened city and blacked-out port facilities receded into the distance. Neither of the three spoke, for each was immersed in his own private thoughts.

Bob's mood was characterized by an inner calm. There was no tension, no apprehension, no regrets and no homesickness. Just as he had completely and successfully pushed from his mind all thoughts of things military during his extremely brief leave at home, so now his consciousness refused to allow the intrusion of any reflections or reminiscences of home. In a striking parallel to his departure for basic training a mere eleven months earlier, once again he felt he was on his way.

Two days out of San Francisco the troop ship joined up with a convoy and began the long and tedious crossing of the Pacific. The three Air Corps officers shared a tiny cabin with a Marine lieutenant, there being not enough room for more than two at a time to be out of his bunk and standing erect. They bore this sardine environment with relative good humor; but as bad as it was, it was luxurious compared to that endured by the enlisted men packed in the hold below. Bob could not but wonder at the stoicism and forbearance of these men, who would be helpless and powerless to avoid a fiery or watery death in the event of a successful attack by a Japanese submarine. It's true that the danger in the Pacific was less than that from German U-boats in the Atlantic, but nonetheless it did exist and lurked in the back of the mind of each person on board.

More troubling than the fear of attack was the sheer boredom induced by the monotony as the convoy zigzagged at a seemingly snail's pace across the vast Pacific. The men below sang, argued and gambled to pass the time away, while most of the officers on the upper levels of the ship at least had the luxury of access to open decks. Bob preferred to be out on the deck and spent as much time there as the usually benign climate allowed, watching the flying fish and the waves and the ponderous wake of the ship during daylight hours and the brilliant firmament of stars and occasional flash of a semaphore signal in the dark of night. He often chose to sleep on deck. The soft, gentle rustle of the sea during those nights belied the mortal danger that potentially lay below.

The tedium for all on board was eased briefly as the convoy crossed the equator. The officers lined the upper rails overlooking the broad deck over the hold and cheered as King Neptune held court below and each serviceman crossing the equator for the first time had good-naturedly to endure the hazing and indignities associated with the ceremonies of initiation into the mysteries of the Realm. Several of the officers, Bob among them, volunteered to join the ceremony and suffer even added humiliations at the hand of non-commissioned Neptune himself, a hardened Marine sergeant, who relished his role.

When stormy weather or squalls would drive Bob back into the cramped confines of the shared cabin, he spent most of his time lying on his bunk and poring over the P-38 maintenance manual, a copy of which he had wheedled from the maintenance officer in Colorado—in defiance of regulations, since the manual was classified. So thorough and meticulous was Bob's coverage of this information that he had virtually committed it to memory by the second of June, when the transport broke off from the convoy and docked in the port of Darwin, Australia, on a cloudy, blustery day.

The three Air Corps officers were given little time to regain their land legs. Fifth Air Force personnel met them at the dock and carried them by Jeep to their quarters on an air base, where they were immediately plunged into two weeks of further intensive training, indoctrination and briefing sessions. At the first break in the schedule they had an opportunity to visit the hangar where their aircraft were undergoing the final stages of assembly and to meet the crew chiefs assigned to them. As Bob approached his aircraft, number 73, he saw only the lower half of a body standing at the nose, the upper half buried in the camera bay forward of the nose wheelwell. He had slowly circled the plane twice, scrutinizing as many surface details as he could, when the upper portion of the body appeared. It belonged to a tall, lanky Oklahoma boy by the name of Sergeant Stewart "Stew" Ramsey, who squinted testily at Bob, trying to appraise this man who was going to abuse and perhaps damage or destroy his beautiful masterpiece. Bob walked up, shook the mechanic's greasy hand and introduced himself, but Stew maintained his aloof reserve, not beginning to unbend until later that evening when the pilot returned in coveralls and worked alongside him, displaying a knowledge of and reverence for the machine that, although not equaling his own, still tended to reassure him.

For his part Bob liked Stew immediately, finding objectionable only his habit of chewing tobacco. The crew chief's compulsively meticulous attention to detail coupled with his slow rate of speech and movement rendered surprising his ability to complete a task in a normal span of time. Bob eventually realized that this was possible because with Stew there was never any wasted or superfluous motion. Having worked on tractors, mowers and combines in his home town of Ardmore, Oklahoma, he had grown up totally in synch with machines, a trait that reminded Bob of Bill Harwood. Within one week's time there developed between them a sense of team and a bond of confidence that would come to serve Bob well in the trying months ahead.

* * *

**BY LATE SPRING** of 1943 the war in the Pacific was entering a new phase. Through a determined and desperate holding action the advance of Japanese military power to the south had been slowed and finally stopped. In southern New Guinea, exhibiting extraordinary courage and undergoing indescribable hardships, Australian troops, after having halted the enemy advance only fifty miles from Port Moresby by September 27, 1942, had even succeeded in pushing Japanese ground forces northward back across the Owen Stanley range of mountains, removing the immediate threat to Australia. From a tattered remnant of obsolete bombers that had escaped from the Philippines the Fifth Air Force had been rebuilt into an effective military outfit, and a new Air Force—the Thirteenth—had been formed in New Caledonia. But the task that lay ahead was awesome.

The lines of Japanese military power, like the legs of a huge tarantula, bestrode the Pacific, reaching from the home islands downward to Malay, the Philippines, the Dutch East Indies and New Guinea, embracing the Marianas, the Marshalls, the Carolines, the Admiralties and most of the Solomons. A vast interlocking network of lines of naval, ground and air power, anchored on linchpins such as Truk and Rabaul, extended east and west across the Pacific and south to the shores of New Guinea.

At Casablanca in January 1942 President Franklin D. Roosevelt and Prime Minister Winston Churchill had agreed to assign top priority to the war in Europe, leaving the Pacific Command to fight a "backwater" war as best it could with limited resources and personnel. In spite of this inferior status, Allied forces in the Pacific had begun to secure the first tenuous footholds for the long drive back north. In June 1942 General Douglas MacArthur had announced his plans, code-named Tulsa II, for the recapture of New Britain, New Ireland and the Admiralty Islands. On August 7, 1942, there had begun the first successful American attacks in the Solomons—Tulagi, Gavatu, Tanambogo and Guadalcanal. The following day the U.S. First Marine

Division and elements of the Second captured the airfield on Guadalcanal and renamed it Henderson Field, but although the first American plane landed there four days later and the field became fully operational on the seventeenth, the bloody campaign for the island ground on for months. After the loss of two thousand Americans killed, it was only at 4:25 P.M. on February ninth, the day of Bob's graduation, that all organized Japanese resistance ceased on the island. In response to the American thrust in the Solomons, on November 24, 1942, the Japanese had landed special units at Munda in New Georgia west of Guadalcanal and had proceeded to build in the general area a complex of seven major airfields, from which they could attack and harass American forces. The main threats to Guadalcanal and Allied operations were the bases at Munda and on Kolombangara.

On June 3, the day after Bob's arrival in Darwin, Admiral Halsey's headquarters had issued general instructions for the invasion of New Georgia, with the main objective the Munda airfield. It was to be the first joint operation since that of Guadalcanal almost a year earlier. General Douglas MacArthur was to be in over-all command, General Nathan Twining was to command the Army Air Force units, and Admiral Halsey those of the U.S. Navy. News of the planned operation must have leaked to Japanese intelligence, for on June 7 there began a series of heavy air raids on Guadalcanal, the assembly and communications center of the American forces preparing for the offensive. These raids continued in spite of disproportionate enemy losses: during the June 7 raid the Japanese lost twenty-three planes to nine for the Allies, and on June 12 the imbalance in the score was even greater—thirty-one to six.

When Bob and Lieutenants Wilson and Woodard were briefed on this engagement, they also received orders transferring them to Henderson Field and assigning them to "Photo Recon Eight," administratively attached to the Thirteenth Air Force.

"Gentlemen," the briefing officer concluded, "don't be put off by the number of your Air Force. It was intentionally activated on the thirteenth day of a month, and its pilots will always light three cigarettes on one match, go out of their way to walk under a ladder and try to encourage a black cat to cross their path. They are confident that any attendant bad luck will be for the enemy."

**BOB HAD STILL** not fully flight-tested the airplane when they were issued rush orders to proceed to Henderson Field. Two C-46's left on June 15 carrying a maintenance officer, the crew chiefs and tools, spare parts and replacements. On the sixteenth Bob took off with Wilson and Woodard and flew left-wing position in formation toward the Solomons. In case any mechanical problem should show up in one of the new airplanes they were routed to the northeast to pass fifty miles south of Port Moresby and then direct to Guadalcanal. As they approached within sixty miles of Henderson, however, the flight leader was unable to make contact with the control tower, for the assigned frequency was jammed with urgent messages. It was soon apparent that Guadalcanal was under heavy air attack by Japanese aircraft. Since the F-4B's had no guns or armament, they circled in a holding pattern fifty miles to the southwest, and the three pilots listened in fascination to the radio communications. From the shouts and whoops it was apparent that the Army, Navy and Marine fighters swarming over the area were decimating the enemy formations. Bob marveled at the apparent close coordination and cooperation among the pilots of the three separate services in covering defensive sectors and lending supporting fire and wished fervently he had even one puny thirty-caliber machine gun with which he could join the fray. Within forty-five minutes the main action was over, and the F4B's were sequenced for landing behind Navy and Marine fighters and Army P-38's, P-39's and P-40's.

"Catbird Two, Catbird Two, you are cleared to land on runway one. Land long. There is a bomb crater in the first two hundred feet. Be prepared to follow Jeep with yellow flag."

Bob's head was swiveling continuously as they fanned out over the bay to enter the landing pattern, for it was his first view of a combat zone. Of the many ships in the harbor, there were at least two landing craft, a freighter and a light tender ablaze. Huge columns of smoke were rising from a fuel storage area, and in the surrounding jungle and on beaches for miles around there were smaller plumes of smoke marking downed aircraft.

On the base there was controlled pandemonium. Fire trucks, bulldozers and ambulances were crisscrossing the field, dodging taxiing aircraft. Crew chiefs were scurrying to check out their bombers parked behind revetments or their fighters as they pulled up and shut down their engines. There were visible the bright flames of welding torches as the Seabees were already busy repairing bomb damage to runways and ramps.

The F-4B pilots were understandably treated as orphans. The Jeep had led them to a parking area next to two other tired-looking recon aircraft and then sped off on some other mission. Walking on foot, they found their way into the main operations master sergeant addressed them.

"Sirs, I don't have time to help you now. See that Quonset over on the end of that row? That's the operation center for the Eighth Photo Recon. I suggest you go over there. I'm sure they're expecting you."

As they were filing out the door against in-coming traffic, the sergeant called after them, "And welcome to the Cactus Air Force!"

They were later to learn that this was the name unofficially adopted by all pilots flying out of Guadalcanal irrespective of their official unit or branch of service and was a title worn with pride.

When they checked in at the Quonset hut, a major with exhaustion etched in his face came out of an office and greeted them.

"Man, am I ever glad to see you fellows! We have two planes down for maintenance and a mile-long list of requested missions. Corporal Lance here will show you to your quarters. We're debriefing today's mission now. Be back here for briefing at seven o'clock, right after supper. You should get to bed early. Two of you will have a take-off time of six a.m., and the other, five."

"Where can we find our crew chiefs?" Bob asked. "I'd like to go over my airplane."

"I would imagine they're already on the line," the major answered. "See you at seven sharp."

The major was right. Wilson and Woodard began unpacking

their gear in the crude barracks assigned to them, but Bob left his on his bunk and had the corporal drop him back at the flight line. Stew already had the cowls removed and was going over the engines.

"How did she do, sir?" he asked as Bob walked up.

"Everything went pretty well," Bob answered. "One of the air vents stuck, and it got pretty cool at twenty thousand feet. Also at altitude the throttle on the right engine was a full inch ahead of the left to maintain equal manifold pressure."

"The waste-gate on the right turbo must be sluggish or sticking," Stew said after a brief moment of reflection. "I'll get on those tonight after I finish installing your three hundred gallon aux fuel tank. We've had orders to have 'er ready by three a.m., so you must be going all the way to Tokyo," he added with a grin.

"Could be," Bob responded, beginning a visual inspection of the camera compartment. "I don't know what the target will be. We don't get briefed until seven o'clock."

The briefing of the six recon pilots started at precisely the scheduled time. The major walked in with a clipboard and a wooden pointer under his arm. He pulled down two large maps suspended above a blackboard, one of the northeastern New Guinea coast and the other of New Georgia, New Britain and New Ireland.

Although Bob had exhaustively studied charts of these areas while still in Darwin, in the coming weeks he was to come to know every detail of them by heart.

"Gentlemen, before I start the mission briefing, let me repeat a few bits of advice to the three newcomers. If you are shot down or forced down by mechanical or any other reasons in this theater, make every possible effort not to be captured. I can't recommend taking your own life as a last resort, but after some of the things we've heard, I can't sincerely argue against it either. Apparently the enemy couldn't care less about the Geneva Accords. If you go down in an area near U.S. naval operations and can make radio contact, ditch in the sea. The Navy boys in those PBY's will land right in the mouth of hell to get you out if they can. If not, try to set down on a beach or ditch in shallow water right off of it. But by all means work back from the beach and into the mountains. Travel only at night. Always carry your compass, matches and Army .45 with you. If you link up with the natives, don't trust them. Most of them think the Japs are going to win and figure that's the side of their bread that's buttered. However, carry a bunch of silver dollars with you; it might help. They won't recognize paper money.

"Now for a quick report on today. Some of our shipping took a pounding. We're still fighting the fires at the fuel depo, and the Thirteenth took some heavy damage to their maintenance facility, but it could have been a lot worse. Of the one hundred twenty Jap planes counted in the attack, our Army, Navy and Marine pilots knocked down ninety-six, and we lost only six planes. So the enemy took a beating. I don't think they'll be back soon.

"Okay. Down to business. You'll each compute your own nav routes, distances to targets, fuel requirements and ETA's. Communication frequencies will be assigned and set just prior to departure. But here are your mission targets and take-off times . . ."

# CHAPTER ELEVEN

**FOR BOB THIS** was the beginning of weeks and months of long reconnaissance flights, day after day after day. It was not unusual for him to be in the air for seven or more hours at a stretch, often taking off before dawn and not returning until late afternoon. The F-4B's and their P-38 fighter counterparts were superb aircraft, but they required almost three times as much maintenance and "down time" as the other fighters. However, Bob and Stew were so conscientious that their plane was kept flying more reliably than some of the other recon aircraft, requiring Bob at times to fly fill-in missions in addition to his own. Exhausted after a long day, he would work into the night with his good-natured and easy-going crew chief, grab a few hours of fitful sleep and then be off on another mission early the next morning.

Conditions were deplorable. The pilots were never far from their planes—prisoners within the confines of Henderson Field and their cockpits with no let-up from the stress and the monotony. To get away even briefly was impossible. There were no luxuries. The food was bad. Fungus, infections and diseases were rampant. From the long, uninterrupted hours in the cramped cockpit Bob's body frequently ached as though he had been beaten with a club. Constant care was required to prevent the formation of bruise-like sores. He knew that exercise on off hours would help, but the will was difficult to muster and the opportunities were difficult to find. Just a few hundred feet from the edges of the base towered a jungle of huge hardwood trees. Between their giant roots and trunks stretched a virtually impenetrable wall of underbrush and tangled vines, harboring a variety of rats and other vermin as well as scorpions and boa constrictors. The climate of the Solomons, a volcanic archipelago, was oppressively hot and humid, and the weather unpredictable and at times severe. Pilots frequently had to contend with haze and fog in the mornings and violent thunderstorms in the afternoons when returning from missions. Sleep was hard to come by at night. Everything— clothes, hammocks, bunks, bedding—was permeated by dampness and mildew. The thick mists wafting out of the jungle carried the odor of rotting vegetation, the stench of decomposition and putrefaction, and noxious insects, including malaria-bearing mosquitoes. Bob often reflected in awe on the hardiness, courage and dedication of the Marine, and later Army, foot soldiers who for six months had lived, fought and often died in that veritable hell to evict a cunning, tenacious and fanatical enemy.

The only occasional respite for Bob would come during a mission. To and from a target area he would have to cruise at relatively low-power settings and altitudes to conserve oxygen and fuel but would be at altitudes of over twenty thousand feet over the targets. Here, high above the humidity and haze layer, the air would be cool and smooth and the sky brilliant. The light green of the lagoons and the white beaches of the islands shone like gems against the rich blue of the deep sea, projecting a deceptive aura of peace and serenity and belying the conflict and violence represented by the tiny ships and planes scattered like toys on the scene below.

Bob's first few days were filled with photographic missions along the length and breadth of New Georgia Island and parts of Bougainville as the campaign to take Munda moved into high gear. It was essential that the U.S. command have as accurate information as possible on the fleet of aircraft available to the Japanese, estimated at one hundred ninety fighters, one hundred forty-four medium and dive bombers as well as ninety-eight combat planes from New Guinea. Bob's sorties included reports on most of the major enemy airfields, including Vila on Kolombangara, Ballele, Kahili and Buka Passage.

Hammer strokes by U.S. naval and ground forces began to fall. A forward party was put ashore on Segi Point on June 20 and was reinforced the next day by a battalion of American Raiders from Guadalcanal, followed the day after by the First Battalion of the 103rd Infantry Regiment. An airstrip was begun on June 30 by those magicians, the Navy Seabees, and was operational ten days later. June 30 also saw the landing of the Second Battalion of the 103rd Infantry Regiment at Oleana Bay on Vanganu and the main operation of the Western Landing Force under General Hester, commanding the 43rd Infantry Division and other units in an invasion of Rendova Island across the straits from Munda. On July second and third parts of the 172nd and 169th Infantry Regiments continued the pressure on Munda by a landing on the beach at Zanana (six miles to the east), and on July 4 and 5 the second prong of the pincer was in place with the landing of parts of the First Marine Raider Regiment and the 145th and 148th Infantry Regiments at Rice Anchorage on the northwest coast across the Kula Gulf from Kolombangara.

The assault on Rendova Harbor on June 30 was carried out under cloudy, stormy skies with bad visibility—ideal weather for an invasion—and Japanese resistance was unexpectedly light, the island being fully occupied after only eight hours. However, when the weather cleared, the enemy responded in force. During heavy air raids by one hundred thirty Japanese aircraft, twenty-five fighters of the Fifth Air Force were lost, but one hundred twenty-one of the enemy planes were shot down. To provide a protective umbrella for U.S. forces the Fifth Air Force set up a dawn-to-dusk patrol with thirty-two fighters always on station, an operation requiring the constant rotation of ninety-six aircraft. Heavy bombers of the Thirteenth Air Force also provided important support in the general campaign, bombing Kahili, Ballale, Buka Passage and Rekata Bay.

On the night of July 23 Bob was briefed for a reconnaissance mission for the following day. The targets were already thoroughly familiar to him but had to be kept under constant surveillance to keep watch on enemy troop movements and reinforcements. Stew worked through the night to have the airplane ready, and Bob lifted off from Henderson Field at six a.m. on the twenty-fourth, climbing out in heavy haze and through low scud clouds signaling the approach of a slow-moving frontal system. The long flight, a circuitous route over Vila, Ballale, Buka Passage and Kahili, was routine and went without incident until his approach to Guadalcanal in the afternoon. Between him and Henderson Field lay an apparently solid squall line of thunderstorms, stretching from horizon to horizon and from the rolling swells of the sea up to forty thousand feet. Attempting to go over the storms was impossible, under them inadvisable, and around them precluded by a severe limitation in his fuel supply. Efforts to contact the field by radio were blocked by severe static on all frequencies.

Bob reduced power and circled in a holding pattern while reviewing his options. With less than two hours of fuel remaining he had to try to land at one of the six air bases in the area. Henderson Field might well remain socked in for hours, and the same could probably be said of Carney Field to the east, a base for medium and heavy bombers. There were two fighter strips nearby: Fighter One, the main base for Marine and Navy escort aircraft, and Fighter Two, used by U.S. Army Air Corps and New Zealand pilots. But they both were apparently also covered by the storm system. That left only two possible alternatives, both located in the Russell Islands sixty miles to the northwest. North Field served as a forward staging area for fighters and light bombers, and South Field for fighters only.

Bob set a course for the Russells and started descending to stay under the lowering ceiling. Skimming over the water at only one hundred feet of altitude, he began passing through intermittent scud clouds and areas of heavy rain. Transmissions detailing his plight on the available emergency frequency at first brought only deafening static, then faint garbled responses and finally an intelligible message.

"Albatross Two, Albatross Two, this is Cornbread. Sorry, no room at the inn. Suggest you try Yankee."

"Cornbread from Albatross Two. Negative. Impossible. Must land. Low fuel. Request steer."

At this moment out of the mist ahead loomed the coastline of an island. Bob turned sharply to the left and continued on a southwest heading, paralleling the white beach and the dark tree line.

"Albatross Two from Cornbread," came the exasperated voice of the controller. "We are full up. Have you enough fuel to make Yankee?"

"Cornbread from Albatross. Ceiling is at one hundred feet," Bob responded, beginning to feel a little anxiety mixed with irritation. "Cannot retain contact if I overfly the island."

"Roger. Understand," came the response with a note of resignation. "What can you see? Give us a mark."

Bob remembered that as he encountered the coast, he had passed over the wreckage of two ships a half-mile off the beach.

"Cornbread, I'm just southwest of what I think were two submerged Jap barges, one vertical to beach, one parallel. Over."

There was a short pause that seemed interminable to Bob.

"Albatross Two from Cornbread. Reverse course. Follow coast for twenty miles and then key your mic intermittently. I'll call you. Over."

Bob swung around and headed northeast. After six minutes he began with a slow rhythm to depress his transmitter button. Suddenly the strong voice of the controller came through his earphones.

"Albatross Two. Steer zero seven zero for two minutes, then two seven zero. You will be four miles out. You are cleared to land."

The first heading took Bob out over the open sea, but after he had turned west and approached the coast again, in the gloom ahead he saw a break in the mantle of the jungle and then the end of the coral and steel mesh runway. He had barely finished shutting down his engines and opening his canopy when he heard a tow-bar being fastened to his nose gear. When he stood up in the cockpit to stretch his legs, he saw why the controller had been less than hospitable. Every possible available space on the field was taken by one of dozens of fighter aircraft—P-38's, P-39's and P-40's. As he swung down the ladder to the ground and with great relief began urinating, his F-4B was already being towed unceremoniously off to be stowed behind a battered P-39 in the maintenance area.

The rain had stopped, but the humidity was on hundred percent and large puddles remained from the recent deluge. Bob picked his way through the slush to what he assumed was the operations hut. His request for fuel was met with impatience and derision by the officer on duty.

"I have no fuel to spare, Lieutenant. By tomorrow afternoon I'll be cutting dangerously into my own reserves. Maybe day after tomorrow."

"But I have film that has to be back at Henderson tonight," Bob objected.

A moment earlier a door had opened and a major with short-cropped hair and a mustache had come out of what was obviously a large briefing room filled with pilots. Having overheard Bob's statement, he stopped and looked at him directly.

"Did you just land in that recon?"

"Yes, sir."

The major thought for a moment and then turned to the duty officer.

"Inform Henderson that he's here. If they want the films, send them along with our dispatcher flight tonight."

Then he addressed Bob.

"Lieutenant, check with the sergeant over there. As you can see, we have the Kiwanis Convention here, but with luck he may find you a dry place to sleep."

The sergeant was friendly but not too helpful. "Lieutenant, I'm afraid the best I can do for you is a hammock under a tarp in that grove behind the mess hall. Sorry."

"Well, it's not the Ritz," Bob admitted, "but I guess it'll have to do. I haven't eaten since five this morning. What time is chow?"

"Mess opens at five, sir; but here the enlisted men eat first," the sergeant answered with a grin. "You officers can start at six-thirty. I fear we're not doing much to make you want to drop in and visit us again."

"Not unless the floor show turns out to be awfully good," Bob conceded, picking up the note with his assigned quarters and heading for the door. As he was picking his way back to his plane to secure it for the night and fill out the logs, he walked past lines of P-40's parked three deep. He slowed his gait and affectionately and nostalgically patted on the engine cowl those along his path. Several had small rising suns painted on the side, signifying aerial victories. One had four such emblems, and Bob glanced up at the stenciled name of the pilot: First Lieutenant William S. Harwood! In disbelief bordering on mild shock Bob stood and stared. Surely that couldn't be Bill Harwood from Class 43-B!

Turning on his heel, he walked quickly back to the quonset hut and took a seat in the front room, waiting for the briefing to end. In less than twenty minutes out came the major followed by a long line of pilots. From within that group there soon appeared the composite image of the hackneyed concept of fighter pilot. With his grommet-less hat pushed on the back of his head and his blonde hair framing the young face, Bill sauntered out with an assured air of nonchalance. His blue-gray eyes widened with surprise when he spotted Bob, and he rushed over to grab his hand.

"Bob! Son of a gun! I don't believe this! How in hell did you get to this armpit of the universe? What a break! Have you been assigned to our Fifteenth Fighter Group?"

"No," Bob laughed, clapping him on the shoulder, "I'm still flying an F-4B with the Eighth Photo Recon out of Henderson. The weather forced me in here, and your friends won't sell me any gas to get out. Have you got any pull with the supply officer?"

"Ordinarily I would have," Bill answered seriously, "but tomorrow we really have a big one. We're throwing everything we've got at Munda. But come on. Let's go someplace and talk. My suite isn't palatial, but we can sit on my bunk and chew the fat."

"I've got to go and remove my film canisters from the plane first," Bob said. "They're going to be flown to Henderson tonight. I'll meet you afterwards."

"Okay," Bill responded, opening the door for him and glancing instinctively up at the sky, which was beginning to clear. "My bunk is over in hut thirteen. I'll see you there."

\* \* \*

**THE TWO FRIENDS** sat and talked for over two hours, reminiscing and filling each other in on the happenings of the months since their separation. Bill reported that Lori was five months pregnant but back at work at her job in Southern California and that her sister Martha had married a chiropractor in Carmel. For both the preferred topics dealt with the past and with things back in the States, but eventually these were exhausted and the subject of the war intruded into their conversation.

"Well, you outrank me now," Bob said with a grin. "I really should be calling you sir."

"The squadron had an across-the-board promotion right after I joined, so I didn't do anything to deserve it."

"I don't know about that," Bob objected. "I saw the four kills on the side of your plane. That's pretty good for three months' work. Tell me about them."

"There's not much to tell," Bill responded modestly. "I got a Zeke over Rendova, a Betty off the coast of New Guinea and two Zeros over Guadalcanal."

"Could those Zeros have been on the sixteenth of last month?" Bob asked.

"How the hell did you know?"

Bob grinned.

"That's the day I first flew into Henderson from Australia. I think that subconsciously I knew you were in on that scrap. Damn, I wish I could have been on your wing that day!"

Suddenly Bill's eyes widened and he stared at Bob for a few seconds.

"Son of a bitch! I wonder if it'd work."

"What the hell are you talking about?" Bob asked.

Bill slapped his knees and stood up, beginning to pace back and forth. In a moment he stopped and looked at Bob.

"My wing man, Fred Booker, came down with the local crud yesterday. He's really got the trots and is scratched at least for the morning mission. Fred's a good pilot, but they've assigned me some weak-eyed Flight Officer I don't know anything about. Major Zack owes me one. If I can talk him into letting you fill in, would you do it?"

"Would I do it?" Bob responded with a laugh. "You know damn well I would."

"Okay. Let's go give it a try," Bill said exuberantly, motioning for his friend to follow him.

Major Zachary Wilson was less than enthusiastic about the idea.

"I admit I owe you one, Harwood, but I can't put him down for a mission without official orders assigning him to the Fifteenth Fighter Group or at least to the Fifth Air Force. If he got himself killed, my ass would be in a sling and I'd face court-martial. Besides, he might bend that P-40, and we need every aircraft we can get our hands on."

"You don't have to worry about that," Bill rejoined. "Bob can fly a P-40 as well as I can—well, *almost* as well as I can. Come on, Major. I'd feel a lot better having him on my wing. What if you didn't know about it? He looks a little like Booker, doesn't he?"

Major Wilson looked at Bill with good-natured weariness draped over his entire frame.

"Look, all I'm saying is that I'm not signing him on the mission, and I would not approve of his flying with you. But I promise you that I won't be on the flight-line at four-thirty in the morning."

"Thanks, Major," Bill grinned, "I appreciate it. I'll clean out the stables for you again for this."

In spite of his own considerable fatigue Bob felt a subdued excitement as he and Bill stepped out the door and down the steps of the hut.

"What kind of favor did you ever do for him to 'owe you one'?"

"A week ago his two maintenance officers were both laid low with the bleeding gut, and our group was having to keep one-third of our planes in the air at all times during daylight hours."

"Over Rendova?"

"Right. So I filled in as best I could whenever I wasn't on patrol with the squadron. It was tough work, but we kept them up there, and the record logs made Zack look pretty good up at headquarters. Come on, let's head for the mess hall and then hit the sack as soon as we can. We have to be up at four, and it's going to be a long, tough day. Where are you bunking?"

"I've been assigned a hammock over in the grove behind the mess, so I may just sleep in my cockpit."

"That's not necessary," Bill said as they pushed their way into the mess hall. "Fred's in the infirmary and you can crash on his bunk next to mine. It'll be like old times. We can pretend we're back at Randolph."

"I'm afraid I prefer the weather of South Texas," Bob grinned. "By the way, there's a problem with my going along tomorrow. I wasn't in on the mission briefing."

"No problem," Bill objected. "Grab a plate. I'll fill you in while we're eating, and we can go over the fine details later."

While they sat on the rough bench before the crude table and ate the less than delectable fare before them, Bill described the outline of the massive raid against Munda airfield and harbor by heavy and medium bombers. There were to be eighty-six B-24's and a hundred and fourteen B-25's covered by over a hundred fighters.

"We've got to cover the bombers during their runs and handle any fighters that come up; but once the big boys are through and safely on their way home we can drop down and have a little fun ourselves," Bill added. "I hope you haven't forgotten all your gunnery skills."

He took a piece of paper out of his pocket, jotted down a number on it and handed it to Bob.

"What's this?" Bob asked.

"That's the range to the point of fire convergence for Fred's plane. I assume I don't have to explain what that's all about," Bill answered with a grin.

"Not unless you want to be accused of being a smart-ass," Bob laughed. "I've enjoyed about as much of this ambrosia and nectar as I can stand. Come on. I want to go down to the line. I want to pre-flight while there's still daylight."

"To the line? Hell, let's turn in. We'll be on the line soon enough. Fred and I have a damn good crew chief. He'll have the planes in great shape and all ready to go."

"I'll be along in a while," Bob insisted. "I'm assuming we'll be taking off close to dawn, and it's been months since I flew a P-40. I want to get in some cockpit review and go over the controls, switches and systems."

"You'll find them pretty much the same as at Moore Field," Bill said as he started to move off. "The radios are a little fancier. I'll go over them and the frequencies just before takeoff. Okay, go ahead, but don't stay out too late, son, and be sure and pull the garage door down when you get home."

Bob laughed and gave a wave as he moved off.

**THE MUNDA CAMPAIGN** was a massive undertaking under the direct command of Admiral "Bull" Halsey. Under Halsey, General Millard F. Harmon commanded the ground forces, and General Nathan Twining the air forces. The pre-invasion air strike of July 25 was to be the largest assemblage of air power in the Southwest Pacific for a single mission.

As he sat in the dark cockpit that morning, Bob was impressed by the clock-like precision involved in the efficient launching of all those closely packed fighters from a single runway. Even engine start-ups had to be co-ordinated by Ground Control to avert overheating by the liquid-cooled engines. These were sequenced in the same time intervals in which earlier aircraft were lifting off two at a time.

"Eight One Six: three—two—one—start!"

A moment later: "Six Two Five: three—two—one—start!"

Bob heard the whine of Bill's energizer and two seconds later saw the flames of exhaust along the left side of his engine.

"Niner Four Two: three—two—one—start!"

Bob energized his starter and then changed to taxi frequency, moving out slowly behind the dark outline of Bill's plane. Having received clearance after a brief run-up and magneto check, Bill pulled out onto the runway, and the burst of exhaust flames signaled his full power for takeoff. Bob tucked his plane in close behind and to the side of the other, for the narrowness of the runway gave little lateral leeway. He had to keep his eyes riveted on the dark silhouette ahead and to his right, but out of the corner of his eye he noticed the first faint blush of dawn breaking in the east as they climbed out over the sea to four thousand feet and headed northeast for the rendezvous with the bombers, which would be coming up from the south on the deck, in hopes of catching the Japanese by surprise. The fighters were cleared to this higher altitude, for they could protect the bombers better from there, and it was hoped that in spite of their numbers the enemy spotters would assume that they were merely the first fighter patrol of the day over Rendova Island.

As the light increased, Bob eased off a greater distance from the lead plane. This gave him intermittent opportunities of a few seconds' duration to trim and fine-tune his own plane for maximum performance and even to glance around. This was a sight he had never before had an opportunity to witness. All around him—right, left, above and below—the air seemed full of fighters, two hundred seventeen in all—P-38's, P-39's, P40's and Navy F-4F's. As impressive as it was, however, it was almost overshadowed by the appearance of the bombers a few minutes later. Flying four, and sometimes eight, abreast only a few feet above the water, this superimposed wave of aircraft stretched to the horizon as far as the eye could see. There were one hundred seventy light bombers—mostly Army B-25's and Navy SBD's and PBF's—and seventy-two heavy bombers, B-17's and B-24's.

When they finally approached the target, it was obvious the weather was co-operating, for it was unusually favorable for that area—scattered to broken clouds with a high overcast. A naval task force of seven ships standing off shore had lobbed smoke shells into Munda to mark the target. Some of the fighters from Guadalcanal had been fitted with bombs and went in first to drop their load. Next came the medium bombers at tree top level and then the heavies at higher altitude to drop tons of high-explosive bombs and hundreds of parachute fragmentation clusters ("para-frags," an innovation credited to General Kinney), while the fighter cover zig-zagged thousands of feet above, keeping watch for enemy fighters. From communications over the common frequency it was obvious that some did show up from outlying fields, but with Bob in hot pursuit Bill would race off on one vector after another at each sighting, only to be disappointed when the "bandit" would have already been shot down or chased off. The bulk of the local enemy aircraft had been caught on the ground, so the desired element of surprise had been achieved. The raid was so sudden, swift and brief that the one hundred Japanese fighters known to be based at Kahili did not have time to intercede. By 6:55 A.M. the last of the bombers had dropped their loads and turned back to base.

"Switch to frequency four," came Bill's voice through the headset, so Bob punched in the discrete frequency.

"Our cover duties are over. Let's not haul all this ammo back home with us. I've spotted several ack-acks still operating. Stay up here and cover me. I'm going down and work them over."

Bill's plane peeled off into a steep dive to the southeast, heading for the dense jungle a few miles from the smoking harbor. Bob had to switch his attention rapidly back and forth from scanning the skies for enemy fighters to keeping sight of Bill's P-40 as it grew smaller and smaller in the distance. Leveling off at low altitude and turning sharply to the northwest, it came over the rise east of the harbor at tree-top level. Small puffs of white smoke betrayed the positions of three anti-aircraft batteries as they opened fire, and Bob saw tracers from Bill's guns seem to curve unerringly into one of the emplacements. Passing over the ragged palms at the edge of the harbor, Bill pulled up slightly and then banked steeply to turn back for another pass, during which only two of the batteries were still firing. After his third attack Bill climbed out to the northwest, gaining altitude to regroup with his wingman. The batteries he had attacked were silent as the P-40 pulled up and away, but Bob saw puffs of smoke from two others north and west of the battered airfield and tried to pinpoint their locations in his mind. He circled while Bill climbed to rejoin him at altitude and returned the thumbs-up sign his friend gave as he pulled alongside.

"Sorry I didn't leave you any clay pigeons," came Bill's voice over the frequency. "Let's go home."

"You missed two at the edge of the airfield, smart-ass."

"Where do you think that garbage over there was coming from?" Bob responded, jerking his head off to the side at puffs of "black cotton" anti-aircraft fire.

"Hooo-boy!" Bill shouted. "You're right. Do you have them spotted?"

"I sure do."

"Okay, I'll stay up here and cover. Go get 'em! And Bob," he added as his wingman peeled off, "this ain't Almagorda. Don't throttle back. Go balls out and take evasive action when you aren't firing."

Bob trimmed his elevator forward, switched on his gunsight and armed his guns. He had decided to attack the position on the west side first, so he streaked over the tops of the trees at the east edge of the field and dropped down to a few feet above the deck. Telltale smoke was not needed to spot the anti-aircraft gun. Its camouflage had apparently been partially blown away by an earlier bomb blast, and he could clearly see the enemy gunners swinging their weapon in his direction. His aiming and firing came totally spontaneously and automatically. It was as though he did that every day of his life. He saw his tracers ricocheting off the emplacement, and out of the dust the enemy gun rose almost in slow motion and began to fall off to one side. Taking violent evasive action, Bob banked and passed out over the harbor, circling to the left to make his next pass to the north. With no palm trees on the south side of the field, he had a longer time to fire on the north emplacement, and his guns raised such a cloud of dust that he could not witness whatever destruction they were wreaking.

Even during his first pass Bob was aware of a strange phenomenon taking place within himself. Through the screen of intense concentration and preoccupation there began to seep a heretofore never experienced savage exhilaration, a brutal, primordial elan totally alien to his normal character and personality. By the time he pulled up from his second pass, although his movements and reactions were coldly efficient, he was almost consumed by this primitive fire.

"Tally-ho!" came Bill's voice through the earphones. "Good job! Join up to the south at three thousand."

"One more," Bob rasped, barely recognizing his own voice. "One more pass. I spotted an undamaged hut on the field. I'm going to get it."

He banked to the right and circled to approach the field again from the east. He pulled his power way back to reduce his air speed to grant him longer firing time and came across the tops of the palm trees at almost a leisurely pace. As his eyes scanned for the hut he had spied on his first run, he suddenly caught sight of a lone Japanese soldier racing frantically to cross the crater-scarred field. Looking back over his shoulder, the man tripped and fell, desperately struggled to his feet again and turned to face the oncoming fighter. Bob tightened his trigger finger and pressed his eye against the gun sight. As he approached the optimal convergence range that would ensure that his guns could cut the enemy in half, even the most minute detail of the man became visible with startling clarity. Like a photographic plate Bob's mind recorded it all in a flash.

Cloth leggings extended from the tops of his shoes to below the knees, where they joined the baggy trousers covered with dust and grime from his fall. His arms hung limply by his sides as he stood like a little boy in a school yard, looking up in terror at the snarling approach of death. Bob saw the open mouth, the wide eyes and even the glistening perspiration on his forehead. As he sought to squeeze the trigger, his hand froze. Before him stood no longer an abstract foe, a fanatical demon. In his sights stood perhaps a brother, a father, a son, a friend. In his sights stood, like himself, simply a man. A shiver passed through him as he saw the soldier fall to the ground again just as the fighter passed only inches above him.

Bob pulled up sharply, fighting the confusion caused by a rush of conflicting emotions—a residue from the excitement of the hunt and a sense of relief mixed with disappointment in himself. With defensive anger he fed in full power and guided the P-40 out over the harbor, lining up for a strafing run on a still undamaged barge anchored near the far shore. His first tracers ricocheted off the water, so Bob eased back on the stick and saw the full force of his bullets slam into the side of the target. A massive explosion gave evidence that it had been an ammunition barge, and Bob had to take violent action to avoid the debris.

"I've got you in sight," Bill radioed. "Head southeast and stay on the deck for five miles. Then climb to two thousand, and I'll join up."

As they passed over Rendova Island, two Fifth Air Force fighters from the patrol dropped down to confirm their identification, waggled their wings and then turned back to their sector. After they had passed out over open water again, Bill issued some cryptic commands.

"Spread out. Don't make small power adjustments to stay in formation. Reduce power to twenty-six inches and eighteen hundred rpm. Go to manual lean and come back four notches on your mixture."

A few minutes later Bob had to report, "I've got to go richer. My coolant temp is above red-line."

"Negative," came Bill's immediate response. "Come back two notches more. It should stabilize."

"But Bill . . ."

"Don't argue. Do as I say."

Bob complied reluctantly, fearing overheating and detonation, but in a few minutes the temperature dropped slightly below redline, and the over-heat warning light blinked off.

He was feeling the weight of fatigue, for he had slept only fitfully the night before, and the long hours of this mission were taking a toll on him. The heat and humidity at this altitude were added debilitating factors, and Bob sank into a sort of torpor, from which he was shaken a little later when he noticed that Bill's plane was several hundred feet lower than his, although his own altimeter still registered two thousand feet.

"You're losing altitude," he transmitted briefly.

"Follow me down," came Bill's response. "Move out two miles from me and return to this heading."

Bob suspected his friend had been overcome by the heat but followed the instructions. As he returned to the original heading, in an automatic fighter pilot response he scanned the skies in all directions. It was then that he spotted them—the Zeros.

"Two bogies at five o'clock high," he snapped excitedly.

"I've had them since way back," Bill replied calmly. "Do you still have ammo?"

"Yeah, I should have some. Come on, Bill, let's get the hell out of here and go get them."

"Stay on course," Bill intoned. "Do not change power settings. Stay off of this frequency and obey instantly every instruction I give you." His voice sounded as matter-of-fact as though he were telling him to meet him at two o'clock on the first tee at the golf club.

Bob was frustrated and angry, thinking it insane that they should remain at these reduced power settings. The seconds dragged by as their altitude bled off and the Japanese fighters drew ever closer. Bill had timed their descent to put them just over the water as the enemy fighters would start their run.

"Gun switch on," Bill said in almost a drawl. "They'll split up to attack. When I say 'now,' turn ninety degrees into me and pass on the right. If the bastard is still on my tail, take him head on. I'll do the same. I don't think they'll trade firepower with us."

Bob's hands were trembling. It was all he could do to keep from going to full power and turning to meet the foe.

"Now!" came the call, and as he banked almost vertically to the right, he saw small waterspouts kicked up by the bullets of the Zero behind him. As he and Bill passed a few feet apart and just above the water, Bob spotted the oncoming pursuing fighter and centered the round, radial engine of the Zero in his gunsight. But Bill's prediction had been right: just before he was to fire, the enemy broke off and turned back to the north.

"Back to one hundred fifty degrees," Bill commanded. "I think we'll have to go through that little dance again. He almost got you that time, my friend. When you're shot at, kick in a little rudder. If he's a good pilot, it'll throw off his lead."

*Son of a bitch!* Bob thought to himself. *How can Bill sit there and talk like a professor at a time like this?*

Two similar sequences had to transpire before the Japanese fighters gave up and turned back north, disappearing into the haze. Ever so slowly Bill nursed them back up to two thousand feet and then transmitted again.

"You can talk now, fellow. Give me a read-out on your fuel."

Bob glanced at his gauges and felt a sense of consternation—first at what he saw, and—second at his apparent ineptitude. On his recon missions he had always prided himself on his superior ability to monitor and manage fuel, but that had always been under relatively no-stress conditions. Today, in the excitement of actual combat and having to fly wing position, he had been inattentive and his fuel monitoring haphazard. He now knew why Bill had been so unyielding in refusing to abandon maximum-range power settings.

"Thirty-two gallons. It's going to be close. What do you have?" he asked.

"Forty-one. Relax. Stay loose. I'll drop back behind you."

The next hour seemed an eternity. First Bob flew on each auxiliary tank until power loss indicated it was empty and then switched back to the main tank, whose gauge continued its ominous and inexorable drop. Forty miles out Bill ordered a frequency change and radioed the tower.

"Cornbread from Six Two Five. Forty north with two very thirsty birds. Request priority sequence."

"Six Two Five. I'm taking in three other flights. Would you rather try Yankee?"

"Negative. I'll call from mid-island. Get those sightseers on the ground in a hurry. Six Two Five, out."

A few minutes later as they were crossing the island, Bob's heart skipped a beat as his engine began to cut out intermittently.

"I'm losing it, Bill—getting power loss here," he radioed on the open frequency.

"The field's dead ahead," Bill answered. "Rock your wings. You might have a cupful somewhere. Cornbread from Six Two Five, clear the pattern. You've got a dodo on your hands. Bob, I'm right behind you. Turn right fifteen degrees. Hold your altitude as long as you can."

The wing-rocking had fed some fuel into the intake lines, for Bob's engine came to life again. He reduced power as much as he dared and began a slight turn to bring him directly over the runway at fifteen hundred feet. Entering a circling pattern to the left, he dropped his gear and then his flaps, settling in for a smooth landing as Bill's plane roared past overhead and entered a steep landing pattern of its own. Bob turned off at the end of the runway and swung into a parking space in response to the flagged instructions of a lineman. Before he could reach down to shut off his engine, it died completely. For a few seconds he sat immobile, drenched in perspiration. The crew chief helped him out of his shoulder harness and parachute and began directing the immediate refueling and re-arming of the aircraft as Bob climbed down from the cockpit somewhat unsteadily.

Bill had come sauntering up and stood in front of Bob's plane as cool as a cucumber, waiting to lead his wingman in for debriefing.

"Okay, okay. I admit it," Bob said with a weak grin. "You are the best. You did a fantastic job."

Bill stopped and looked at him thoughtfully for a moment.

"No, I fouled up. I was so stupid it worries me."

"What do you mean? You got us back against pretty tough odds," Bob objected.

Bill set out again for the briefing hut.

"I stretched it too thin. I should have landed at Segi Point."

They walked in silence for a moment. Then Bob grabbed him by the arm and stopped him.

"If Segi Point was available, we could have gone to full power and taken on those Zeros. You could have had your number five today. Why didn't you do it?"

"They needed our planes here. If we had landed at Segi, we couldn't have made it back in time, and I would have missed the afternoon mission back to Munda."

"Hey, Bill!" came a shout as an officer in a flying suit approached from a grove of palm trees.

"Fred, come over here. I want you to meet your alter ego. Fred Booker, meet Bob Hanson. Bob here took your mission this morning, and as far as operations is concerned, he was you. Come to think of it, I'll tell them you got the trots again, and I'll give the briefing for Bob. How are you feeling?"

"Weak as puppy pee but a lot better," Fred answered. "Doc has cleared me for the afternoon mission if it's okay with you."

"Hell, I'm not the one with the G.I.'s. You are. It's a long way up and back. What happens if the crud grabs you halfway?"

"That shouldn't be a problem. Blood and bone is all I've got left to give, and I don't want to miss the Big One."

Fred was a pleasantly good-looking boy of about twenty-two with a sturdy build, and Bob liked him immediately. He could tell from the short interchange that Bill and his wingman got along well together, an important asset for fighter pilots. Booker turned to Bob.

"How did you like my little chariot? She's a sweetheart, isn't she?"

"I fell in love with her," Bob laughed. "When you get ready to sell, let me know."

"Did he ding her any?" Fred asked Bill.

Just a little shrapnel and a couple of bullet holes. That's all. Nothing serious," Bill joked.

"Should I be jealous? Is he a better pilot than I?" Fred asked, fluttering his eyelids and pressing his heart with his hand.

"Nah. He had a bad day," Bill assured him. "He shot down eighteen enemy aircraft and scared the shit out of the Emperor, but otherwise he was pretty lethargic."

"Hanson!" came a shout from the line officer, who came running up. "Where the hell have you been? We received orders to refuel you and get you back to Henderson immediately, but I haven't been able to find you. Somebody's gonna be steaming mad."

"That's the way he is," Bill said to the officer, winking at Bob. "Always goofing off."

"I'll be ready to go as soon as I take a leak and grab a bite of food," Bob said, trying to be conciliatory. "Have I been topped off?"

"Two hours ago," the line officer said angrily, "but the runway's going to be tied up now. You'll have to wait until we get the afternoon mission off."

Booker shook Bob's hand and walked off toward the palm grove. Bill started off toward the briefing hut but stopped and looked at Bob.

"I guess this is it, friend. I've got to get to Operations. I'll try to do your debriefing for you. I think I can report everything pretty accurately. There's only one thing that puzzles me. On your third pass to take out that hut, you didn't fire a shot. You didn't hit it or an enemy soldier right in front of you. What the hell happened?"

Bob felt his face flush.

"It's kind of stupid to admit," he lied, "but in the excitement I pressed the flap switch on the stick instead of the gun switch."

Bill stared at him a moment and then reached out and shook his hand.

"So long, fellow. Why don't you take some dirty movies with those cameras of yours and send me a copy?"

He turned and started off, then stopped and glanced back.

"*You? You* got confused and pressed the wrong switch?"

He stared at Bob for another minute and then with a half-smile and shake of his head walked away.

An hour later Bob stood by his F-4B waiting for clearance as the fighter pilots all returned to their planes. He watched as Bill climbed into his cockpit and buckled up his chute and harness. Just before he pulled his helmet down over his blonde hair, the Californian glanced over, grinned and gave him a thumbs-up sign. A few minutes later Harwood and Booker roared off in a formation take-off, bound for Munda.

# CHAPTER TWELVE

**THE PRIMARY FOCUS** of photo recon missions shifted in early August to Bougainville, which was kept under almost constant surveillance. The F-4B wheels would barely have stopped rolling when the cameras would be carefully removed and the film rushed to the laboratory for immediate processing. As always, Bob would proceed directly to intelligence debriefing to provide visual accounts as accurate as possible to add to the detailed information being channeled to Intelligence, S-2. Sometimes only two hours after the photo recon planes had landed, bombers and fighters would be taking off to attack.

After the interrogation Bob would frequently stop and leaf through the stacks of intelligence reports on the long assembly table. Usually he felt an objective detachment from the sometimes terse, sometimes lengthy, accounts, but there were a few in these first weeks of August that held special meaning for him. On August 5 Munda had fallen to U.S. forces. Photos showed a scene of stark desolation. During thirty raids, although seventy-one American fighters and twenty-two bombers had been lost, nine hundred fifty tons of bombs had been dropped, three hundred fifty-eight Japanese aircraft had been destroyed and 1,674 enemy soldiers killed. U.S. forces immediately began work to increase the size of the runways to accommodate heavy bombers, and within a short time Munda became the most advanced Allied base at the time.

Reconnaissance concentration on Bougainville was occasionally interrupted by missions to other targets—to the important Japanese stronghold of Rabaul on the northeast tip of New Britain and to enemy air bases along the northern coast of New Guinea. In August Bob flew several missions over Wewak, which had been developed by the enemy into a major staging base for their New Guinea air fleet. There were indications that on August 14 Japanese naval air service units began to replace their army air service units in the New Britain area, relieving the latter for operations in New Guinea.

Recon photos showed eighty-five fighters at Wewak on August 3 and one hundred fifteen on August 13, an ominous build-up that would threaten planned Allied operations against Lae—a combination air and shipping base with two good air fields—and Salamaua on the strategic Huon Gulf. Wewak thus became a prime target but nonetheless a difficult one. Previously it could not be hit during daylight hours because of a lack of Allied air cover at that distance, an enemy advantage that led to their complacency. However, on August 17 eighty-three P-38 fighters operating out of a secret advance fighter base supplied cover for an attack by B-24's and B-25's on Wewak proper and three related air fields, catching the Japanese offguard with their planes lined up like sitting ducks. The B-24's came over at six to eight thousand feet to drop their bombs, followed by twenty-six B-25's at low level, strafing and dropping "frags." Another squadron attacked Boram to the south, and during the next two days B-24's continued the pounding. In three days the U.S. had lost ten aircraft, but the Japanese three hundred and nine, relieving enemy pressure against Allied air operations farther to the south.

On the evening of the fourth of September Bob was ordered to report to his squadron commander, Major Brent Farrell, a deceptively soft-spoken man from Minnesota with an affable face but steel insides.

"Hanson," he said, "you've been on the line here for over three months and are due for a break. You've got ten days of leave coming, and I want you to get away completely and put all this out of your mind. What do you say?"

"You won't get an argument out of me about that, sir," Bob

replied with a genuine feeling of relief. "I have to admit I could stand a change of scene."

"Good," the major said. "I'll put you down for leave from the sixth to the sixteenth. The Fifth Air Force has a C-47 transport coming in to take some of our bomber pilots to Australia on furlough. They'll bring all of you back on the sixteenth. I'll have your orders cut tomorrow. You won't be put on a mission, so spend the day packing and taking it easy."

Bob's packing took up a very short time on the fifth, and he had anticipated spending the balance of the day enjoying the process of mentally shifting gears. But the intensity of the conditioning of the preceding months made this transition difficult. Out of habit, after noon chow he wandered down to the line and sat on a crate talking to Stew.

"Well, sir, I'm glad to see you going," Stew remarked, pulling his head down out of the nose wheel well. "How many hours do you think you've put in in the air these last three months?"

"Lord, I hate to think," Bob said with a shake of his head. "I haven't kept count. All I know is my backside is damn near paralyzed. What about you? Will you get time off while I'm in Australia?"

"Hell, no," Stew grinned. "Those of us without commissions are never supposed to get tired. Don't you know that, sir? I've got a week's work to put in on your bird anyway. After that I may get a chance to spend a little time on my bunk. It'll seem strange not standing down there sweating out your return each day. I won't know what to do without that nail-biting every time you're overdue."

Bob grinned at this frank confession on the part of his likable crew chief.

"Those sweats of yours may have pulled me through on one or two occasions, so don't you get out of the habit. I'll be back on the sixteenth."

On his way back to the barracks late in the afternoon Bob dropped by the S-2 building to look over the day's reports. Among the usual accounts of perceived enemy troop and naval dispersals there were two items of interest to him. On the preceding day there had been an infantry assault landing at Bulu Plantation at the mouth of the Busu River, cutting off Lae from the east. It was hoped these troops would be able to link up with the Australian Sixth Division, which was pushing northward by land. Then all day on the fifth, in a massive operation Fifth Air Force C-47's had been crossing the Owen Stanley Range of mountains to the broad Markham Valley and transported an entire Australian paratroop battalion of seventeen hundred men to drop on Nazdeb, located only sixteen miles west of Lae.

The frantic activity associated with this huge operation was evident on the sixth when the transport carrying Bob and the thirty-six bomber pilots touched down at Port Moresby for refueling. Huge quantities of supplies and ordnance were being unloaded from trucks onto transfer points on the field. As the officers were finishing up a spartan lunch and preparing to return to their airplane, a Fifth Air Force operations officer entered the transient mess hall and announced that their continued trip to Darwin would be delayed until the following day. A chorus of groans and protests greeted the news.

"I'm sorry, gentlemen," the harassed officer said, "but we need every available transport plane we can lay our hands on for the next several days in order to carry out our assignment. There will be a Lancaster leaving for Australia tomorrow afternoon. It'll be a little crowded, but I've got you all booked on it. In the meantime Corporal Felsen outside will take you to get your gear and show you where you'll bunk tonight. To make up for this inconvenience the CO has authorized me to reserve a table for all of you to have dinner on us tonight at the Boolawong Club, located off-base. It's run by an old Aussie and his wife, and the food is a lot better than what we could offer you in the mess hall."

The amenities of the Club, although rustic, did go a long way toward soothing the resentment of the pilots over their delay. The meal consisted of barbecued meat of some kind, tasting like pork and garnished with navy beans and a type of breadfruit. Although it could not be rated as gourmet, it was nonetheless a welcome relief from the usual fare on Guadalcanal and was washed down by a generous quantity of an Australian brew that was sharp-tasting and strong. Most of the officers in the group used the onset of their leave and frustration at its delay as a double excuse to over-indulge with respect to the liquid and, by the time they had returned to the transient barracks, represented a raucous and boisterous crowd. They were sitting on their bunks laughing and talking loudly when the operations officer entered the building and asked for their attention.

"Gentlemen," he began, "we have a sizable problem. As you may know, a battalion of Aussie paratroopers have seized Nazdeb. We have air-dropped miniature graders and caterpillars, and by tomorrow an airstrip will be ready for use. Within the next few days our Air Transport must ferry in the entire Australian Seventh Division and hundreds of tons of supplies. All our planes will be in service every daylight hour. We are putting every transport we have in the air and are stretched paper thin on pilots."

He glanced at the officers, many half-dressed and bleary-eyed.

"I'm asking," he continued, "no, I'm pleading, for volunteers to help us out. You may help save lives. By flying co-pilot you would allow us to rotate our pilots enough to perhaps prevent casualties due to fatigue. I need as many of you as I can get. Any volunteers?"

His plea was met by stony silence. Wearily he leaned back against a table.

"Goddamn it, fellows, don't make me pull out all the stops on patriotism and service to your country; but I will if I have to. The missions are not dangerous. We have a hundred and forty-seven fighters operating out of eight different fields to provide constant air cover. No enemy fighters will get through. Now come on. How about it?"

Again there was silence. He began to scan the barracks, and his gaze fell on Bob, who was lying back on a bunk.

"What about you, Lieutenant? Won't you give us a hand?"

"There are two problems, sir," Bob responded. "I'm officially attached to the Thirteenth Air Force, and I'm not qualified for the C-47."

"We have already cleared the first problem through channels," the officer said firmly. "We are authorized to cut temporary orders. Are you rated for multi-engine?"

"Yes, sir, but I fly an F-4B. That and a Cessna Bamboo Bomber are the only multi-engine planes I've ever flown."

"That won't be a problem," the operations officer persisted. "You'll be sitting in the right seat anyway. Will you help us out, Lieutenant?"

Bob glanced around. He felt the fixed stare of the other officers, several of whom were pointedly shaking their head. He looked back at the insistent recruiter and slowly nodded his head.

"Okay," he said with a sigh, "I'll help out."

An immediate regret concerning his decision caused a sinking in the pit of his stomach, a feeling that was scarcely ameliorated by the subsequent volunteering of four of the other officers.

**BRIEFING FOR THE** mission was at four a.m. the next morning, for the first planes were to be airborne in time for them to be over the prepared airstrip at Nazdeb with the first full light of dawn. Bob had been awakened by an orderly and trudged to the briefing room in a half-stupor. He listened with less than full attention to the officer in charge, for he was to be merely the copilot, letting the First Lieutenant who was the pilot of the ship to which he had been assigned copy the necessary information and data.

Two cups of black coffee just before leaving for the flight line helped sweep away the cobwebs in his mind, so he was fully alert by the time the two pilots were dropped off at their waiting aircraft. If he had not been fully awake by then, he would have been as they climbed in the loading bay and moved forward to the cockpit . The inside of the C-47 was so densely packed that they had to turn sideways and squeeze down a narrow aisle between the sacks and crates.

"Hey, Walsh," Bob called out, "have you run a weights and balance check on this thing? It will never get off the ground with this load."

Lieutenant Walsh looked at him briefly and then climbed into the left seat.

"It'll get off the ground," he said simply and then started going through his pre-start-up check-list.

And indeed it did get off the ground. In fact the faithful "Gooney Bird" did not even use up all of the available runway before it lifted off and climbed docilely into the night sky. The stars of the Southern Hemisphere were shining brightly as they droned on at a pace so much more leisurely than the one to which Bob was accustomed in his F-4B that they seemed to be suspended in space within a noisy cocoon. One could have assumed they were all alone in this dark vault of sky except for the numerous faint glowings of exhaust stacks of other aircraft strung out to the right, left, front and back. Soon the ridges of the Owen Stanley Range began to be visible against the dawn breaking in the eastern sky, and twenty minutes later they began a steep descent toward the floor of the Markham Valley.

Given the inevitable extreme congestion this first day with an endless stream of aircraft all landing, unloading and then taking off from one airstrip, there was amazing coordination and efficiency. Within an hour Bob and Lieutenant Walsh were ready for the return flight to pick up another load. In the dark at Port Moresby Bob had not been able to observe the cockpit layout or watch the pilot's procedures for start-up, take-off and flight operation, so this time in the daylight he watched closely. As they climbed to gain the altitude necessary to cross the range, Bob looked up and noted with reassurance the graceful flight of formations of fighters—some P-38's and even a few Spitfires but mostly P-40's—as they crisscrossed back and forth several thousand feet above them. He couldn't help but idly wonder if Bill Harwood wasn't leading one of those formations of Warhawks.

Back at Port Moresby, while the C-47 was being refueled and reloaded, Bob and Walsh ducked into the mess hall for a quick meal, since they had not had time for breakfast that day. As they were walking back to the flight line they were hailed by an Australian major wearing ankle-top boots, thick brown socks and droopy khaki shorts. He was bare-chested, having removed his shirt in the stifling heat and tied it around his waist. His rank would not have been obvious except for the fact that he had removed one of his insignia from the shirt and affixed it to the cap set on the back of his head.

"I say, lads, which of the two of you is the copilot," he asked.

"I am, sir," Bob answered.

"Good! Then your friend there will have to fly this jaunt by himself. We need you to fly the second craft in that line over there. She's loaded and ready to go."

"I'm afraid I can't do that, sir. I'm assigned only in a back-up role as a copilot. I've never been checked out in the C-47."

The major stared at Bob for a minute, the twig he was chewing on protruding comically from out of his beard and rocking up and down.

"Didn't you get out of that plane a little while ago?"

"Yes, sir. I rode over and back for one trip in the right seat."

The major's ruddy face broke into a smile.

"Son, I figure that's as much of a check-out as you need. That little scat-about is now yours for the duration."

"But, sir . . ."

"Not to worry, mate," the major interrupted, grasping Bob's left shoulder and gripping it almost painfully tight. "You'll be the only one in the office. If you prang the bird, you won't kill anybody but yourself. Now hop to it, lads. We don't have time to waste."

The officer was gone before Bob could voice another objection. Lieutenant Walsh seemed to appreciate Bob's predicament.

"I'll call operations control and tell them you have to fly with me. You take off first, and I'll get on your wing. After you're comfortable, I'll take the lead and do the navigating so you can concentrate on flying the airplane. You worried?"

"No, not really," Bob answered truthfully.

"Good. Get the tail up as soon as you can, and don't rotate until you have to."


BY THE NINTH, after only two days of flying the shuttle missions back and forth, Bob already felt perfectly at home in the C-47. He could easily understand why this patient, forgiving workhorse of an airplane had gained the admiration and affection of pilots throughout the world. Although this bizarre assignment had robbed him of his leave in Australia, it was nevertheless a marked change from the past few months and was in a way a form of vacation. These missions were much shorter than those in his recon work and therefore less arduous, and monotony was relieved by the variety of activities associated with this massive operation. Bob became proficient in the techniques of rapid loading and unloading of the transport and on two separate occasions was assigned to air-drop missions to supply units of the Australian Sixth Infantry Division and the American troops moving up to relieve them. All in all Bob would have found this period almost pleasant were it not for the frequent later requirement of transporting the Australian wounded on the return trips to Port Moresby.

After four days Bob was re-assigned to a troop carrier transport, flying in infantrymen of units of the Australian Seventh Division. Stretchers anchored in tiers along the walls could be lowered and secured with straps to convert the aircraft quickly into a flying hospital. Some leaven to the grimness of this at times heart-rending task was partially affected by contact with female Australian nurses, the first women Bob had seen in months. Although they were obviously the cream of the crop in order to be chosen for this demanding and hazardous duty, Bob was still deeply impressed by their compassion, strength, tenderness and courage. There was one in particular that Bob came to admire, Betty Linden, a robust, efficient girl from Melbourne. By chance she ended up on two separate missions of his over and back. On the second there were only a handful of superficially wounded soldiers ferried back to base, so after they had landed at Port Moresby, Bob summoned enough courage to ask Betty if she would have dinner with him that night at the Boolawong Club. To his surprise she accepted.

Bob had become a regular customer at the Club. His usual habit of unwinding at the end of the day by participating in maintenance chores was denied him here. He was unknown to the maintenance crews, and they soon made it clear to him that his presence on the scaffolding necessary for servicing the engines on the tall C-47's was both intrusive and unwelcome. So he had taken up having dinner every night at the Club. Two advantages accrued to him from this decision: one—the food was much better than on base, and two—it gave him an opportunity to get to know some of the Australian service-men, who made up the vast majority of the customers. Bob's inherent reserve would probably have precluded his ever getting to know any of them were it not for the Aussies' brash aggressiveness and his hav-ing been spotted on the second night by the burly major with the red beard. Coming over to greet Bob, he virtually dragged him back to his group of about a dozen officers seated around a table.

"Mates, I want you to meet a brave Yank and obviously a good pilot, since he's still alive. Never having flown a Gooney in his life, he got in one a few days ago and took off all by himself. And he's been fer-rying to Nazdeb ever since."

Bob shook hands with each of the members of the group, and they began plying him with questions. When they found out that he was a "shutterbug," a reconnaissance pilot from Guadalcanal who had given up his earned leave to help in their operation and that he had even flown "biscuit bombers"—their term of endearment for the air-drop planes used to resupply with ammunition, food and medical supplies the ground troops slogging through the dense jungle—he was immediately and enthusiastically welcomed. He thought it prudent not to mention that his volunteering had been somewhat less than sponta-neous and chose to affect the un-Australian characteristic of modesty.

After his inclusion Bob found this group met regularly almost every night to eat, drink and swap stories, and he found he began to look forward to this nightly ritual. He related easily and well to the Australians and found them without exception amiable and outgoing. Several of them had been in New Guinea for twenty months and could tell harrowing tales of the days when Japanese forces were only a few miles from Port Moresby Their usually jocular voices would become subdued with respect whenever they recounted the prodigious feats of stamina and courage performed by the Papuan natives, who were undaunted by the enemy and the almost impassable terrain and cheer-fully carried in supplies to the Australian troops. Frequently there had been no other means of getting out the wounded except on litters borne by the natives or at times literally on their backs Many an Aussie soldier owed his life to the loyalty of these nut-brown benefactors, who deservedly and reverentially had gained the appellation "angels with the fuzzy, wuzzy hair," memorialized by a ballad of the same name.

When Bob walked into the Club with Betty, there were hoots and cat-calls from the assemblage of his friends. On this and the two subsequent evenings when she accompanied him, Bob yielded to the Aussies' invitation to join them for a drink but insisted that the two of them dine alone. As much as he enjoyed the rowdy officers, he enjoyed her company more. She was not actually pretty, but there was an engaging openness and honesty to her robust looks that made observing her a pleasure. When they were alone, they spent hours talking about their pasts and despite the disparity in their backgrounds marveled at the common threads of experiences and influences in their lives. Bob felt no reluctance in opening up to her and was brought to realize how truly lonely he had been for so many weeks. Betty spoke at length about her home, her childhood and her fiancé, who had fought in the North African campaign and from whom she had not heard in over two months.

The association with her and with his newfound friends were unexpected bonuses from this bizarre episode in his military life and were two of several reasons that he approached the end of the ten days with regret. This feeling, however, was mitigated by a feeling of accomplishment. Within this short period the Fifth Air Force Troop Carrier Command had ferried in six thousand men and over two million pounds of equipment, and on the sixteenth—the day of Bob's departure for Henderson Field—Lae and its two airfields fell to victorious Australian troops.

# CHAPTER THIRTEEN

**THE ALLIED PRESSURE** on the Japanese military infrastructure continued unabated. On September 21 the enemy abandoned Arundel Island north of Munda, on the twenty-second a joint naval and Air Force operation captured Finschhafen, and by the second of October the Japanese were forced to evacuate 9,400 men from Kolombangara. As he read the reports on these operations, Bob became aware of the fact that he had participated in one of the most pivotal eight-week periods of the Pacific war. Within that short span of time, as a result of the Munda campaign Allied forward bases had been advanced hundreds of miles and the enemy had lost more than one thousand aircraft, valuable territory, control of the Huon Gulf, air supremacy over New Guinea and the military initiative in the area.

Further Allied progress depended on reducing the effectiveness of the powerful Japanese naval and air base at Rabaul, (40°10" south latitude, 152°18" east longitude), located on the northeast tip of New Britain five hundred miles from Port Moresby. It was the strongest enemy base in the southwest Pacific and a vital hub for their military operations. Simpson Harbor at Rabaul was a trans-shipment point for more than two hundred fifty thousand tons of arms and supplies per year, and from Rapopo Field and Buna Canal enemy aircraft could attack Allied shipping and naval, air and land forces.

A recon mission over Rabaul soon after Bob's return to Henderson in September had revealed one hundred ninety-four aircraft on the airstrip, including fighters, light bombers and medium bombers and only a moderate number of ships in the harbor. A photo mission on October 11 showed ninety-three heavy ack-ack positions and sixty thousand troops and indicated a significant build-up. One hundred fighters had been added, and twenty additional vessels had recently entered the harbor, including warships, merchant vessels and other smaller craft. As a result of these revelations the first major air strike against Rabaul, long in the planning stage, was moved forward in timing.

The next day, October 12, 1943, shortly after ten hundred hours, three hundred twenty-six Allied aircraft—including one hundred fourteen B-25's, eighty-six B-24's and one hundred twenty-five P-38's—took off on the long mission. The weather was very warm, the sea blue-green and the sky brilliantly clear. The heat in the cockpits was oppressive, for the planes approached the target area at only one hundred feet above the water to avoid enemy radar. Buna Canal was hit first, then Rapopo Field and finally Rabaul and the harbor. While the P-38's dueled with the sixty Zeros that came up to meet them and attacked their airfields, the low-level B-25's split into two groups. One went in at minimum altitude to strafe and bomb the ack-ack positions and drop para-frags, while the other attacked shipping in the harbor. The B-24's then came across to bomb the docks, the staging areas, the barracks, and the supply and ammunition dumps. Rabaul was left in flames. Intelligence reports the next day tallied up the figures: twenty-four enemy surface vessels hit, seventeen sunk, one hundred enemy aircraft destroyed on the ground, fifty-one damaged, and twenty-six shot down out of the sky. U.S. losses: seventeen planes and fifty-four crewmen.

**EVEN WHILE AT** Georgia Tech Bob had avidly followed military operations throughout the world and had kept meticulous maps of the various theaters of action. He had continued this practice during his training and after his transfer to a war zone, but during the fall of 1943 his enthusiasm began to lag. The European theater seemed so terribly remote from his daily reality as to be almost irrelevant. He still followed developments in the Pacific, such as the long campaign in November to take Bougainville and the bloody battle at Tarawa, but his interest was beginning to be sapped by a deep physical and psychological fatigue.

As interesting and edifying as had been his participation in the airlift operation to Nazdeb, the resultant loss of a break, a rest, had begun to take its toll. Weariness was beginning to compromise his skills and efficiency, resulting in occasional operational slips or oversights that potentially could be dangerous or even fatal. He was aware of this tendency but powerless to overcome it. He had come to hate the cockpit of his airplane, regarding it as a stifling and perhaps deadly prison. Physical problems increased the unpleasantness. On his right buttock and left thigh there were sores that had begun as insect bites but which had become infected and painful. Treatment was largely ineffectual, because the pressure on them during hours and hours of the long missions coupled with the heat and humidity interfered with the healing process.

More taxing than the physical malaise was the—for him—uncharacteristic tendency toward moroseness. The unrelenting monotony, the at-times seemingly senseless dedication to destruction and death on both sides weighed heavily on his spirits. The increasingly despondent mood was deepened near the middle of November by an item in an intelligence report. Bob's perusal of these sheaves usually was limited to the main paragraphs, which he would glance through rapidly. On this one day he just happened to scan past the main headings through the lists of those killed in action to the bottom of page five, where one line-item caught his eye:

"Missing in action: William P. Harwood, 1st Lt. AUS 12864532"

The change within Bob from an even, balanced confidence to a somber moodiness accompanied by a deterioration in his professional performance did not go unnoticed. Stew became worried enough to request to see Major Farrell to express his concern. The squadron commander had already noticed the problem, but the crew chief's remarks spurred him to try to deal with it as soon as the tactical situation would permit. Near the middle of December he called Bob in for a conference.

"Lieutenant, I don't know why you didn't tell me yourself, but I have found out that you gave up your leave back in September to fly extra missions for the Troop Carrier Command. That was very commendable of you but also self-defeating. We don't grant furloughs here out of the goodness of our hearts. They are necessary to prevent burnout and keep our pilots operating at a high level of proficiency. I have discussed your case with Colonel Fairfax, and he has approved my request to send you on a three-week leave to Darwin, starting four days from now."

The major paused to light a huge Meerschaum pipe.

"Thank you, sir," Bob said to relieve the silence. "I hate to admit it, but I am badly in need of a rest. But three weeks is a long time. Do you have someone to fill in for me while I'm gone?"

"That's my problem, not yours," the major said curtly, squinting at Bob over the flame of the match. "Cut loose, Lieutenant. You've got to cut your mind completely loose from this war until you get back. Understand?"

"Yes, sir," Bob responded, feeling he had been chided.

The major stared at him for a minute and then shuffled through some papers, finally pushing one toward Bob along with a small cardboard box.

"And, Lieutenant, I want you to take those bars off your shirt."

"Sir?"

"With your coloring I think these silver ones will look better on you," the CO said with a grin. "I recommended you for promotion, and the order came through today. I would have called you in earlier, but I wanted to wait until it was official."

"Thank you, sir," Bob said, reaching for the box and the copy of the order, for the first time in weeks feeling a slight lifting of the gloom that had been afflicting him. "I hope that I can prove worthy of your confidence."

The major gave a snort and sucked loudly on his pipe.

"What kind of crap is that? You know damn well you're good. Now get the hell out of here and go and have a good rest so you can come back talking like a pilot and not like some . . . some . . ." His voice trailed off as he had to re-light his pipe.

"Yes, sir. I will, sir," Bob said, saluting and backing toward the door.

"And *First* Lieutenant Hanson . . ."

"Sir?"

"Don't go flying for somebody else, or I'll bust your ass. I'm the jealous type."

"I promise I won't, sir," Bob responded with a grin, feeling his spirits rise even more.


**THE C-46 TRANSPORT** had stopped at Port Moresby to pick up additional passengers for the flight to Australia. The group from Guadalcanal had to wait in the transient operations hut for the passage of a violent spring storm. When the announcement for boarding finally came, Bob noticed a female officer struggling with a heavy B-4 bag and volunteered to carry it for her. When she looked up from underneath her rain hat to thank him, he was surprised to recognize Betty Linden. They both burst out laughing.

"Don't tell me you're going to Darwin too," she said.

"Well, originally I was just coming up here to take you to dinner at the Boolawong," Bob joked, "but when I heard you were leaving, I had to book passage too."

Her company shortened the long flight to Australia considerably. They sat side by side in the bucket seats along the left wall of the transport and talked all the way. They slipped easily back into the relaxed openness of their earlier acquaintance and filled each other in on the three months since their parting. Bob spoke at length of the impact on him from the loss of his friend, whom he had subconsciously assumed to be indestructible. Betty reported that she had finally received a letter from her fiancé from Tobruk and that his unit was probably in England by the time she received the letter.

"Will you make it home to Melbourne for Christmas?" Bob asked.

"No, I have only ten days," Betty answered, "so I won't have time to travel that far. Australia is a big country, you know. One of the nurses at the hospital, a good friend of mine, has a little flat in Darwin and told me that I can use it, and I'm looking forward to sleeping for a whole week. How long do you have?"

"I have almost three weeks," Bob said, "and I'm going to enjoy every hour of it."

"Will you be doing any traveling?" she asked. "Ours is a great country. If you aren't familiar with it, I can recommend some places for you to visit."

"Right now I don't have any plans. All I know is I don't want to do any flying. I suppose I'll be in the tender hands of the Fifth Air Force. I'm sure they have quarters and amenities for us shell-shocked characters. If the Boolawong has a branch over there," he added with a grin, "I'll take you to dinner after your week-long nap."

Betty smiled up at him.

"With an invitation like that in front of me, just give me eight hours' sleep, and I'll be ready."

She continued to look at him for a few moments.

"Bob, you'll probably think I'm either fresh or crazy, but from your description the last few months have been rather dicey for you. It occurs to me that it would do you good to get completely away from the military. I've never seen my friend's flat, but if there's room, you're welcome to stay there. What do you say? You can come and go as you please, and I'll leave you completely to your own devices."

Bob looked at her in astonishment.

"Why, that's the most incredibly generous offer I've ever heard. For God's sake withdraw it if you're not serious, because you know I couldn't turn it down."

"Good!" she said with finality. "Then it's all settled."


**DUE TO THE** delay caused by the storm in New Guinea it was dark when the C-46 landed at Darwin. By the time Bob had reported in, presented a copy of his orders and left information as to where he could be reached, it was already very late. Betty had somehow rounded up a rickety taxicab, and the two of them rode through the dark, blacked-out streets of the city to the small apartment building in the northwest sector. While Bob settled up with the driver, Betty awakened the resident landlady with persistent knocking and secured a key to the third floor flat. By the time Bob had struggled up the three flights of stairs with the bags, Betty had opened the door and stood looking around in dismay. The "flat" consisted of one single room with a bureau, table and double bed, a bathroom and a small hallway that tripled as a closet and what passed for a kitchenette. It had a tiny "fridge" and a bottled-gas two-eye burner.

Bob had to laugh in spite of his weariness.

"Well, you still get an A-plus for the thought. I have the telephone number of your landlady. I'll let you get some rest and then call you day after tomorrow. Okay?" he said, picking up his B-4 bag and heading for the door.

"Wait. Where are you going?" Betty asked, looking at him with distress.

"Back to the base, I guess," Bob answered. "If I move from there, I'll get in touch and let you know."

"But you'll never get a cabbie at this time of night," she said reflectively. "Look, stay here until morning, and then we'll work something out."

"I can't do that," Bob said with a shake of his head. "There's not even enough room for me to sleep on the floor."

"You don't have to," Betty answered with a weary smile. "As tired as we both are, I don't think I have to worry about you any more than you have to worry about me. Now don't be stubborn. I can't stay awake much longer."

"There you go with another of your offers I can't turn down," Bob yawned. "But if I fall asleep while I'm brushing my teeth, just leave me in the bathroom. That would solve the whole problem."

* * *

**WHEN BOB AWOKE,** there was sunshine streaming through the window. At first he felt confused; he couldn't remember where he was. Then he turned and saw Betty still sleeping soundly on the other side of the bed. Moving slowly to avoid waking her, he rose and went into the bathroom, throwing open the small window to let in the warm sea breeze. Having shaved and washed, he went back into the bedroom and retrieved his clothes from the floor, where he had unceremoniously deposited them the night before. He dressed as quietly as he could and opened the door leading to the stairwell. He felt a mild surge of joy as he stepped outside and observed the tidy streets of Darwin again. There was nothing special about this actually rather drab little neighborhood, but the contrast with his surroundings of the previous six months was palpably sweet, and his impression of the city totally different from what it had been back in June.

There was a little teahouse around the corner, where he was served a boiled egg, some "biscuits" with marmalade, and a cup of quite bad coffee. When he had ordered the biscuits, he had hungrily envisioned versions similar to the ones back in Kentucky, but these Aussie products were more like hardened wafers.

After breakfast he strolled down to the waterfront and sat on a wall for a while, breathing deeply the sea air and watching the boats and sea gulls. Over an hour had passed by the time he returned to the apartment. Betty was sitting with the landlady in a small garden in front of the building, sipping tea.

"Bob, I want you to meet Mrs. Effie MacDonald. She has been generous enough to forgive us for waking her in the middle of the night."

"How do you do, Mrs. MacDonald?" Bob said, extending his hand. "I must say, that is a display of real charity."

"Not at all," she answered graciously. "We have to do what we can for you Yanks, who are so far from home. Miss Linden tells me that you've had a bit of a rough time of it and need some good food and rest. I've told her I want to cook dinner for you two tonight. The grocer is a friend of mine, and I think I can count on him to come up with something special."

"That's very thoughtful of you," Bob responded warmly, "but I can't impose on you like that. Besides, I have to find myself some lodging today."

"No excuses!" Mrs. MacDonald protested, shaking her head back and forth. "I have a son who's in the India-China-Burma theater, and I would like to think that some nice woman would do the same for him. I'll expect you children at seven o'clock, and don't be late."

"No, ma'am. I promise we'll be on time."

He and Betty spent the early afternoon walking along the waterfront and through the town. In spite of the austerity of wartime, it seemed like a paradise to them. The shop windows were mostly bare, but the shopkeepers were invariably friendly and hospitable. It was a pleasure to talk to them and listen to their dialect. Bob had sought in vain to find some soap powders, but due to rationing none were available in the stores.

"I have a bar of soap back in the room," Betty confided. "I can wash out any laundry you have."

"No, no," Bob protested, "I can do it myself. It's just that I need something a little stronger."

When they returned to the apartment, Betty procured from the landlady a precious cup of soap powders and brought it upstairs.

"Now give me your stuff," she ordered, "and I'll show you I'm a good laundress."

"Thank you," Bob said. "I appreciate the offer, but I'd rather do it myself."

He was holding wadded up in his hand his socks and the pair of shorts he had removed that morning. He was trying to conceal the stains of blood and pus on his shorts from his still-festering buttock wound.

"You are undoubtedly the shyest or most stubborn man I've ever known," Betty scolded. "Now give them to me. That's woman's work."

As she reached for the laundry items, Bob put them behind him, but she playfully darted around his side, snatched them from him and bolted into the bathroom, locking the door. Bob stood in the bedroom, mortified. Very quickly the bathroom door opened.

"What in hell is this?" Betty demanded, holding up the stained shorts.

"That's a mess, isn't it?" Bob said. "That's why I wanted to do it myself. Now give it to me."

"Don't be ridiculous," she answered. "I'll do it. But what is it from? You didn't tell me you had a bullet wound."

"I don't. It's a festering sore that I haven't been able to clear up. I'm going to stay off of it a few days and give it a chance to heal."

"I'd better take a look at that. Okay, Lieutenant, off with your pants!" she commanded.

"Oh, no!" Bob laughed, backing away. "Not on your life."

"Come on, Bob," she said seriously. "Have you forgotten I'm a nurse? I'll bet I've seen more arses and shillelaghs than you have. Now take them off."

Bob's protests were ineffectual against her determination, and soon he was lying on his stomach on the bed, nude from the waist down. Betty examined his problem closely and then said, "Now you lie here, and I'll be right back."

She returned soon with some alcohol and medicated powder, which she applied diligently.

"We won't put a dressing on it. It needs to be exposed to the air as much as possible. Why don't you stay on the bed and try to take a nap?"

Having said this, she began giving him an alcohol back-rub. The feel of her sturdy hands and the distant sound of an occasional horn coming through the open window benumbed his mind, and soon he was fast asleep.

She had difficulty rousing him at six-fifteen.

"Come on, laddie. It's time to get ready for our dinner date," she said, checking on the laundry items that she had washed and hung on the window sill to dry.

"My God, what time is it?" Bob said, squinting at the darkening sky. "I've slept the whole afternoon away and still haven't found a place to stay."

"Now come off that, Robert," Betty responded, "or you're going to hurt my feelings. Did I snore too much for you last night?"

"Of course not. You were quiet as a mouse. It's just that I can't go on imposing like this. What will the landlady think?"

"I promise she won't think a thing about it. We're not as Puritanical as you Yanks. And even if she did, why should we care?"

**THE NEXT DAY** they rented two bicycles and rode to a secluded spot along the coast out west of town, beginning a ritual that was repeated almost every day that Betty was in Darwin. They usually carried along a small picnic lunch, and Bob soon became accustomed to acquiescing to her insistence that he expose his backside to the sun and air, a regimen that worked miracles with his medical problem.

The compatibility of which they had been aware from their first meeting deepened during those days. Frequently there would be long, relaxed periods wherein neither would speak a word, so comfortable and at ease was each in the company of the other. They didn't have sex until the fourth night, and its inception resulted from neither forethought nor planning but occurred perfectly spontaneously and naturally—characteristic of all the frequent repetitions within the following days. To each it was simply a logical adjunct to their friendship, and neither was inclined toward a troubling depth of emotional involvement. Betty continued to speak frequently and warmly of her relationship with her fiancé and her love for him.

To Bob the sex was a magic elixir, a soothing salve for the turbulent thoughts and moods that had come to harass him inwardly. To each it was an antidote to the spectre of death with which they had been faced day after day, since sex is the flipside of death. With his natural inclination toward respect and tenderness for women, Bob was probably more inclined to slip into a detrimental emotional closeness than was Betty. Whether or not she sensed this in him, she always managed to encourage a relaxed and at times jocular approach to their unions.

"Come now, laddie. Since you have to keep your pants off so much, we might as well take advantage of it."

\* \* \*

**WHEN BETTY LEFT** to return to New Guinea, it was agreed that Bob could stay on in the flat for his extra ten days. This was a definite convenience for him, but it had its drawbacks. It left him with a frequent awareness of the void caused by her leaving. He continued to ride out to the coast to swim and sun, but he missed her presence and found himself thinking of her more than he would have liked. Although their paths never crossed again, she always held a special place in his memory.

## CHAPTER FOURTEEN

**BOB FELT TO** some degree rejuvenated. The three weeks had passed in the blink of an eye but had been beneficial to his spirits. His sores had healed, he had regained some of the weight he had lost, and he approached his work once again with enthusiasm. Stew was also more rested and in good humor and had used the extra time to hang two new engines on old "73" giving it even more impressive performance.

Demand for photo reconnaissance had not slackened but if anything had increased. In early 1944 plans to take New Britain, New Ireland and ultimately all of New Guinea were already being put into play. The first step was to seize the Admiralties, concentrating on Lorengau on Manus Island and Los Negros, while the Pacific Fleet harassed Truk to interdict support and supplies. Tac reco pilots flying low over Los Negros had encountered no ack-ack or enemy air cover, and a six-man squad was secretly sent ashore to scout. They found a large force of Japanese marines but discovered that the defenses were lax. On February 29 with an air cover of Spitfires, eight hundred men of the U.S. First Cavalry Division, having disembarked from a small naval fleet, invaded Los Negros, captured the airstrip within forty-eight hours and braced for subsequent waves of enemy suicide attacks, during which sixty-one American soldiers were killed but over three thousand Japanese died. The rest of the U.S. First Cavalry Division took

Manus Island, and units of the First Marine Division took Talasea—
one hundred and sixty miles from Rabaul—while another Marine unit
captured two islands north of Kavieng. Coupled with the February sei-
zure of Green Island by U.S. forces, these brilliant flanking maneuvers
obviated the necessity of long bloody campaigns to seize New Ireland
and New Britain and invade Kavieng. The Japanese Seventeenth Army
was surrounded and, due to control of the sea by U.S. naval forces, rendered impotent.

In the following two months concentration could shift to New
Guinea. Supported by heavy Fifth Air Force bombing of Aitape and
Wewak, Australian troops struck by land toward Madang. A large naval
armada was formed and then broken up into smaller groups to trick
the Japanese into thinking they were supply convoys. Instead they set
out for the northern coast of New Guinea, and on April 22 U.S. troops
landed simultaneously at Aitape and at Hollandia. By the fourth day
the main Hollandia airfield had fallen, and on the fifth day the last of
its four airstrips was seized. Wewak was thus isolated.

Most of the personnel of the Allied forces in the southwest Pacific
sensed this shift in the military momentum and experienced a lift in
their spirits. Bob was no exception and was gratified to be playing a
role in this far-flung and intricate operation, but the daily physical and
psychological drain of long, dangerous missions once again was taking
a heavy toll on his nerves and morale. But just before this deterioration had reached a stage of compromising his professional acuity, there
occurred a confluence of two welcome events.

On May 10 Bob received official notification that he was being
promoted to the rank of Captain and being awarded the Air Medal for
the scope and quality of his contributions. A week later the almost as
gratifying and definitely more welcome news came that after a year
in a combat theater he was being transferred back to the States for a
sixty-day furlough.

"Captain," Major Farrell said as he was giving Bob the good tid-
ings, "you will be released from the Thirteenth and attached loosely to
the Second Air Force during your leave. You will be formally assigned
to Wright Field in Ohio but will of course have no duties during your

sixty days. Before your leave is up you will be contacted concerning future duty. I'm sure that your input on that decision will be invited, but I want you to know that your return to the Eighth Photo Recon Squadron would be most welcome. Your competence and breadth of experience in this theater would be important to us in the coming months. We are entering a new phase of the war, and although many of our operations will be more demanding and more hazardous, they will also be more important. I hope you have a great leave and get a well-earned rest. You should try to put the war out of your mind during those few weeks, but every now and then think about us back here. Okay?"

"1 promise that I'll do that, sir, and thank you for the kind words. As for the future, my mind goes blank when I try to think past the next eight weeks. I'm like a kid coming up on Christmas."


**THERE WAS A** stark contrast between the monthlong troopship crossing in 1943 and the return in an Air Transport Command C-54 across the central Pacific in May 1944. Even with a day-and-a-half layover in Hawaii for medical screening and uniform reissue, barely a week had passed before Bob was dropped off at the Lexington airport by an accommodating Headquarters Command courier plane enroute to Washington, D.C.

Bob had informed no one at home of his impending leave. A form of superstition had played a role, for subconsciously he was afraid that if he were expected, something might come up to delay or cancel his coming home—a horror he didn't want even to risk. Although he had passed several days at air bases first in Hawaii and then in California, the full impact of the shock of returning to American culture didn't hit him fully until the transport had departed and left him standing on the quiet ramp of the Lexington airport. He stood for a few minutes just drinking in the fragrance of Kentucky in the spring and the sight of the familiar buildings before slowly walking to the terminal.

When the taxi pulled up in front of the house, no one was in sight except for a yardman, whom Bob did not recognize. The front door was not closed, so he opened the screen and stepped into the coolness of the front hall. He put his B-4 bag down and walked quietly into the breakfast room. He heard his mother's voice in the kitchen giving instructions to Fanny the cook concerning dinner, so he took a seat in an upholstered chair in a corner and waited, fairly certain that she would come through from the pantry when she had finished. His guess was right, but he quickly regretted his well-intentioned "surprise party." When she caught sight of him, she let out a gasp and had to cling to the door to steady herself. Her face was pale as Bob rushed over to support her and help her to a chair at the head of the table.

"Oh, my son!' she exclaimed weakly. "My Lord! My son! My son! I can't believe my eyes. Is it really you? Are you really here?"

**BOB'S RETURN HOME** was a replay of what it had been fourteen months earlier—only multiplied several times over. Everyone strove to the utmost to fold him back into the warp and woof of life on the farm and at home, and he tried equally as hard to accommodate to that very process. He initially even begrudged himself sleep, for he was driven by a hunger and thirst to absorb as much of this environment as he could. He could turn down nothing that was passed to him at the table, he wandered around observing the lovely land, breathing deeply and listening to the sounds of spring, and he would delay falling asleep at night in order to stretch and luxuriate in the cool smoothness of the clean sheets. On occasion he had to resist wild impulses, such as to strip off all his clothes and roll naked in the lush bluegrass on the back lawn.

But as intoxicating as it was, there were changes. The farm had been altered radically, and the atmosphere was decidedly different. Most of the former farmhands and stable boys had gone off to the services or to some other job, and their replacements were strangers to Bob. The foaling pens, the riding rings, the tracks—all had given way to fields for agricultural use. Bob's favorite hunter had died, there were only a few other horses in the barns, and when he took his first ride, he found many of the trails overgrown and blocked by fallen trees and branches.

But the changes were two-sided. He realized that in many ways he himself also was a different person. During the preceding year the last vestiges of his childhood and youthful outlook had vanished. He had always had a tendency toward a reserved cheerfulness, but now this inclination had been subdued and he felt old beyond his years. In spite of his efforts to project his former attitudes to those around him, his parents could not help but notice. His father invited him on a walking tour of the farm on the morning of the fourth day and took advantage of the opportunity to have a talk with him.

"Son, you haven't talked to me at all about what you've been through this past year, but I can tell it was really tough on you," he said.

"Dad, what I've been through has been a cakewalk compared to what combat pilots go through. I'm just a little tired. That's all."

"I think it's more than just physical fatigue, Robert. Look, you've done more than your share of heavy-duty stuff. I've got a good friend at Headquarters up in Washington, General Mark Westover. You're due for a States-side assignment now; you've earned a break. Would you go and talk to him? It wouldn't be improper, and he might be able to help or at least give you some good advice."

Bob was silent as he opened a gate for them and then re-closed it after they had passed through. It was an indication of the degree of change in him that the automatic rejection that would have been elicited a year earlier was replaced instead by a serious consideration of his father's suggestion.

"Let me give that some thought, Dad. It might be something that I would consider. But I feel I need to put all of that out of my mind right now and unwind a bit."

"Well, would you mind if I at least give the general a call and see if we could set up a meeting? It'd probably be weeks before he'd have an opening anyway. Whatever you decide, it wouldn't hurt to talk to him."

"Okay, Dad—whatever you say—as long as I'm not committing myself to anything and don't have to make up my mind right away."

\* \* \*

**THAT AFTERNOON BOB** wanted to take his convertible in for some service. He dropped his mother off at the Red Cross Center for her usual voluntary weekly activity of wrapping bandages.

"What time should I pick you up?" he asked as he opened the car door for her.

"We quit at four, but it usually takes a few minutes for us to put everything away and get ready to leave."

"Okay, I'll be back at ten after four. A couple of hours on the car should do it."

He was parked outside the Red Cross building when the doors opened and out came a dozen or so of the woman volunteers. His mother came down the steps and approached the car accompanied by Mrs. Garner, whose inappropriately elegant blue linen suit made her conspicuous in the crowd.

"Mrs. Garner, how nice to see you again," he said, stepping forward to shake her hand.

"Hello, Robert. Welcome home. Your mother told me yesterday that you were here on leave. I'll bet it's good to be home again, isn't it? I'm surprised to see you in civilian clothes. I didn't think you could do that in the Army. But do promise you'll let me see you in your uniform while you're here, will you? I talked to Nancy last night and told her, and she's dying to talk to you. You simply must give her a call. Will you do that? I'm going to check up on you through your mother."

Bob was waiting until he sensed she was pausing briefly to take a breath and then boldly broke in.

"I give you my word that I will call her this very night. She must be getting near the end of exams. What does she plan to do this summer—go to summer school or come back here?"

"Why, she'll be coming back here, of course. She's going to dedicate herself to working all summer in the Veterans Hospital as a gray lady—you know, cheering up the patients, talking to them, writing letters for them and so forth. Have you heard of them?"

"Oh yes. That's very commendable work, and I admire her for volunteering to do it. You and Mr. Garner must be very proud of her."

"Yes, we always manage to be proud of her," Mrs. Garner

answered with a transparently smug expression on her face. "I'll have you know that she has had a straight B average at the University this year."

"That *is* impressive. I'll have to compliment her on her scholarship when I talk to her tonight. Please give Mr. Garner my regards, and I hope to see you again while I'm here."

On the drive home Bob's mother none-too-subtly brought the conversation around to the Garners and asked if he and Nancy had been corresponding while he was overseas.

"I wrote her just before I left Colorado," Bob answered, "but that was the last letter, and I didn't give her my APO number. By the way, why in the world was Mrs. Garner dressed to the nines like that just for the Red Cross?"

"I think she feels it's only proper for her to reflect her husband's business success. It's kind of a way of supporting him."

"Business success? Does wholesale hardware warrant those kinds of fancy feathers?"

"Oh, that's only a small sideline for him now. He has a huge construction company with lucrative contracts for building military installations. He has branches in Maryland, New Jersey, Ohio—all over. They are now what you'd have to call real money."

"Boy, things sure *have* changed in the two years I've been gone," Bob observed as they turned into the driveway.

**AFTER DINNER HE** placed a long-distance telephone call to Nancy at the Delta Delta Delta house.

"Robert Hanson! Gosh! It's good to hear your voice. It's been so long I had just about given up hope of ever hearing from you again."

"Did you get my letter?"

"Well, I received a short note over a year ago, but you said you were leaving that address and I couldn't write you there. All the other long, passionate ones you must have written—those containing your professions of undying love—must have been intercepted by the Germans."

"That's not very likely," Bob laughed. "I haven't been within ten thousand miles of a German for the last year. By the way, I saw your mother today, and she looks great."

"She does look well, doesn't she? They both seem to be doing famously. But I've been worried about *your* mother since I saw her during Christmas vacation. She's really taking your absence pretty hard. I think it's about time you start thinking about us back here. Can't you stay in the States now?"

"Well, that is possibly one of my options, but I won't make that decision for a while yet."

"Why don't you come over here to see me? I'd love a chance to try to sway your decision, and I'm still smarting from your standing me up and breaking our date last time."

"I apologize," Bob replied. "I'm afraid that was unavoidable. But if you're serious about my coming over, I promise to make it this time. I've built up a sizable supply of gas coupons, and I can't think of a way I'd rather use them up. I'll bring my car."

"Oh, Bobby, that's super! Could you make it this weekend? The junior prom is on Saturday night."

"Sure, why not? I'll call the Sigma Chi house and see if they can put me up for a couple of nights. Should I come on Friday?"

"Well . . . sure . . . if you like. But I'm afraid we couldn't have dinner that night. You see . . . Bobby, damn it, you never let anybody know when you're coming, and . . . I've asked Ted Schorner to be my date for the dance. He's up at the Naval Academy now, and he'll be on his way through from Annapolis to Norfolk for some kind of training program. His folks are coming over here to see him and are going to take us out to dinner Friday. But you and Ted and I could do something together on Saturday, and you and I have Sunday night, for he has to catch a train Sunday morning."

"Maybe that's not such a good idea after all," Bob said after a brief pause. "Three's a crowd, they say, and I don't want to intrude into your plans."

"Now don't be a silly, jealous goose! How was I to know you were coming home? You didn't even tell your mother and father. And why are you jealous of Ted? Remember, he was my date at the Idle Hour Club when I sneaked out to be with you."

"I'll admit I have pretty warm memories of that night," Bob responded, "but I still think that I should wait and see you when you get back here."

"But how long is your leave? I won't be back in Lexington until the end of July."

"The end of July?" Bob repeated. "Your mother told me you were going to volunteer as a gray lady at the hospital this summer."

"Oh, Mom's incorrigible! That's an idea she's gotten in her head, and she tells it as though it's true. She was sitting right there in the room when Dad and I were discussing my plans."

"What plans?"

"Dad's bought me a fabulous horse. Wait 'til you see him—really National Show caliber. And I've been accepted for two months coaching up in Middleburg by Ferenc Korda."

"Who in hell is Ferenc Korda?"

"You've never heard of Korda?! He's probably *the* top equestrian coach in the world. He's coached a lot of Olympians."

"Well, bully for you," Bob replied in a sober tone of voice. "I guess that does sound like a lot more fun than nursing wounded soldiers."

"Oh, don't be such a grouch! You'll be proud of me when I make the National team in the next few years. But will you still be there when I get home?"

"No, I won't. My leave is up on the twentieth of July."

"Then you've got to come over this weekend. I will absolutely not take no for an answer. I'm going to call you every hour on the hour until you agree to come."

"All right," Bob said with a lack of any enthusiasm, "I'll come over for the dance, and I would like to see the campus. I hear it's beautiful. But there's no sense in my twiddling my thumbs on Friday night. I'll drive over on Saturday. If I leave very early, I should be there by the middle of the afternoon. Do I need a tux for the dance?"

"Don't you have to wear your uniform?"

"I don't *have* to. Since I'm on leave, I can go either way. Which would you prefer?"

"You've just *got* to wear your uniform. Ted will have his on, and when I walk in there on the arms of two—count them!—*two* military men, the heads will really be turning."

"Whatever you say," he said with a feeling of mild irritation. "I'll come to your place as soon as I check in at the fraternity house."

Bob had no sooner hung up when he immediately regretted having agreed to make the trip. It would be a very long drive for such a short time, and there was actually nothing at all enticing about the weekend. In fact it sounded as though it would be awkward at best. He didn't have quite enough resolve to call back and cancel, so he decided just to make the best of a bad situation but consciously wondered why this girl had such a hold on him.

AS IT TURNED out, the drive over was worth the entire trip.

He left Lexington at dawn, but by the time he gassed up the first time the sun was well up in the clear sky, so he put the convertible top down for the rest of the way. The passage past White Sulphur Springs and through the Blue Ridge Mountains on this early June day was breathtakingly beautiful. This salve to his spirits had worked wonders by the time he reached Charlottesville, and he felt that nothing coming up during the weekend could sully his almost-buoyant mood. Circumstances conspired to prove this confidence to be fragile and unrealistic.

Nancy was more stunning than ever. The two preceding years had enhanced every facet of her beauty, and her confidence, never in short supply, had kept pace. She came down the steps as Bob drove up and was effusively warm in her greetings in spite of the fact that Ted was standing on the porch. Bob, although a little older, assumed he had known Schorner at some time back in his childhood but could not recall ever having met him. Ted was not at all the nondescript, colorless young man he had expected. Somewhat taller than Bob, he was ramrod straight in his Midshipman's uniform with handsome features and piercing eyes. He followed Nancy down the steps, saluted and then shook hands.

"I'm pleased to meet you, Captain," he said.

"Hey now, come off of that," Bob laughed. "We'll look like a couple of idiots around here, saluting every time we pass. From now on you're Ted and I'm Bob. Okay?"

"Well, I'll try, but I don't know, sir," Ted responded and then laughed at his own slip-up. "That conditioning has been pounded in me so hard all year that every time I see your uniform—particularly with all those ribbons—I'll probably have a reflex action and can't keep my arm down."

"Why don't you all come up on the porch," Nancy suggested, "and I'll go get us some iced tea."

"That sounds great. I could use something cool," Bob said, "and that'll give me a chance to pump Ted on the Academy. I had a shot at an appointment after my first year at Tech and almost took it."

**THE DANCE WAS** a disappointment to Bob. The music was good and the scene lovely, but he came to realize how much he had indeed changed. He felt more akin to the chaperones than to the students and could not share or participate in the gaiety. He felt that he was permanently alienated from this type of mood and environment and that he would never be able to go back. The situation was not helped by the fact that for three-quarters of the evening he was able to dance with Nancy only four times—each a brief interlude before being broken on. Standing in a stag line was now irritating to him and no longer placidly acceptable.

Since he had risen early and driven many miles that day, fatigue easily reinforced boredom in impelling him to leave before the dance was over. He had no difficulty in finding in the crowd Ted's brilliantly white uniform. He handed him the keys to the car and told him to tell Nancy good-night for him and that he was too bushed to stay until the end.

"Well, at least let me drive you to the fraternity house," Ted suggested. "It won't take but a few minutes, and I can come right back."

"No thanks," Bob responded. "The house isn't too far away, and the walk will do me good. Nancy said something about our meeting at the Tri-Delt house at ten o'clock in the morning, so I'll pick up the car then. You all have a good time. Good night."

Tired as he was, Bob still could not fall asleep. He tossed and turned for almost an hour before giving up the effort and deciding to take a walk. As he crossed the living room on the way to the front door, he passed a running post-dance bull-session going on. There was braggadocio, laughter, much exaggeration and then a brief hush until he reached the sidewalk outside. He turned right and set out on a four-block circuit of the neighborhood, walking leisurely but steadily and admiring the handsome houses along fraternity row. As he turned down Franklin Street to return more directly to the Sigma Chi house, he was pleasantly surprised to notice something he seldom had a chance to see—parked halfway down the block was a Buick convertible just like his own. A corner street lamp provided backlighting for the silhouettes of a couple inside, and as Bob approached, he smiled as he saw through the rear Plexiglas window the torrid necking of the two actors in this little vignette. But only a few feet from the rear of the car he stopped abruptly, turned on his heel and began retracing his steps. In the dim light he had noticed first the Kentucky license plate and immediately afterward his own registration number.

**NANCY AND TED** were sitting on the porch waiting when Bob walked up to the Delta Delta Delta house at ten-thirty the next morning. There were two Navy duffel bags sitting on the sidewalk next to his Buick.

"Ted's train leaves at 11:15," Nancy volunteered. "He wants to call a cab to take him to the station, but I've insisted that we take him. Don't you agree?"

"Of course," Bob answered. "It would be stupid to waste the money. Come on; you all pile in. I think I know where the station is, because I passed it yesterday."

Bob sat in the car by the curb while Nancy accompanied Ted to the platform to see him off. Fifteen minutes later she returned and got in.

"Well, anchors are a-weigh," she said. "He's gone. Now, how about some lunch? I didn't have any breakfast, and I'm famished. There's a real cute little restaurant about halfway between here and the campus. We're early enough to beat the church crowd, so we should be able to get a table."

During the lunch Nancy babbled away gaily, covering a wide range of subjects and on the surface at least apparently not noticing Bob's taciturnity. But suddenly she broke off almost in mid-sentence, pushed her dessert plate away and looked up at him.

"Bobby, I've read all the horror stories about soldiers returning with their psychological problems and everything, but I never thought that would happen to Mr. Strong Man here. You weren't exactly champagne-bubbly yesterday and last night, but at least you said two or three words—more than you've uttered today. What is it? Do I bore you so? Are you sorry you came?"

"No, you know you don't bore me," Bob answered, "but, yes, I am sorry I came."

"But why? That doesn't make sense."

"I started to call you back right after I agreed to come, and I should have. I've been the odd man over here, and that hasn't been fair to anyone."

Nancy looked at him intently and began to smile.

"Well, I declare! The Green Monster raises its ugly head. Now don't go getting your feathers ruffled. I had asked Ted to come months ago. You know darned well I couldn't disinvite him on the spur of the moment, and I couldn't ignore him. But if you feel neglected, I'll make it up to you tonight. I promise. I'm going to fawn all over you, sit at your feet and bat my long eyelashes at you."

Bob didn't raise his eyes. He had them fixed on the spoon he was rotating in his fingers.

"I'm driving back to Lexington this afternoon, Nancy."

There was a long pause.

"Bobby, I can't imagine what I've said or done to make you this way, but don't be like that. Stay until tomorrow. Let's take a drive tonight and put the top back and look at the stars. It's been a long time.

We can talk or maybe even indulge in our favorite sport à la Cooper Quarry or Idle Hour parking lot."

"I should think you'd be a bit over-trained in that sport," he responded and then immediately regretted having said what he said. "Nancy, I'm sorry. I apologize. I didn't mean that."

"Yes, you did," she said, obviously having recoiled. "But I feel at least you owe me an explanation why."

Bob felt uncomfortable with the situation and disappointed in himself but added lamely,

"I couldn't sleep last night and took a walk down Franklin Street. That's all. I shouldn't have said anything, for it's none of my business."

Abruptly he reached for the check, pushed his chair back and rose. Nancy followed him to the cashier's and then out to the car. They drove in silence until he stopped in front of the sorority house. Then she turned to face him.

"Is this the way you think we should part? Do you think you're being fair? Do you think that you can disappear for two years and my life should remain in a state of suspended animation? Do you mean that in those two years you haven't kissed or necked with another girl? Don't you realize you're being unreasonable?"

"Yes, I am being unreasonable," Bob answered, staring straight ahead, "and I'm very sorry. But I can't help this mood. Considering the small amount of time we've had together and the lack of contact in two years, I know it sounds crazy, but you mean a lot to me. I'm not the strong man you mentioned at the table. I'm struggling now trying to get a lot of things in focus, so I should go and not get more confused and not burden you with my problem."

There was a moment of silence.

"All right," Nancy said, "if that's the way you want it. But I don't think we should split up like this. How can I write to you?"

"I don't know where I'll be going when I leave Lexington. My last address was APO 9416, San Francisco. I guess you can still use that. I'll try to answer if you write, but I can't promise."

He got out of the car and came around to open the door for her.

She stood holding his hand for a few moments, looking up at him. Then she stood on tiptoe, kissed him on the cheek and ran up the steps.

**THE BEAUTY OF** the Virginia and West Virginia countrysides passed largely unnoticed on Bob's return drive to Lexington, so preoccupied was he with the churning within him. Since his return from the Pacific he had been seeking to subdue a general feeling of alienation and dislocation between himself and the relative warm security of America, to come to peace with the distancing of himself from the war as he knew it in order to accept an assignment to a post in the continental U.S.— a hunger deep within a certain segment of his psyche. He thought he had been making some progress in this respect, but the trip to reestablish contact with Nancy had been a setback. He had never been able to explain to himself the strength of the psychological and emotional hold this girl had come to have on him. Their contacts had been few, and there was little obvious evidence of compatibility, but the magnetism was undeniably there and always left him with a vague feeling of yearning and dissatisfaction. The shock of coming upon her in an intimate embrace with another man undoubtedly played a large role in his feeling of agitation, but it was not the only factor. Almost as weighty was his realization of the unbridgeable chasm between him and the attitudes and lives of these other young people. He didn't know how to deal with being a stranger in his own country.

The most effective remedy he could devise was to surround himself as much as possible with the accouterments and activities of his childhood, and he re-doubled his efforts in this regard.

Occasionally he yielded to somewhat more violent methods, such as heading into the woods with an axe to clear the bridle paths or carrying out target practice with his Army .45 automatic. But during the week two unsettling bits of news disturbed somewhat this healing regimen. His father informed him that he had talked with General Westover on the telephone and arranged for Bob an appointment in Washington for Monday, June 26—giving Bob only three weeks in which to resolve his own feelings with regard to his next military assignment.

The second irritant came from a request by his mother that he couldn't refuse: she wanted him to be her proud center display at a large cocktail party she was going to give for their friends on Saturday night. She had been planning it all week but delayed informing Bob, sensing the distaste with which she knew her son would receive the news. She had to tip her hand by Thursday, however, when she asked if she could have his dress uniform dry-cleaned.

By Saturday morning Bob had good-naturedly resigned himself to the ordeal and had even come downstairs to breakfast with the intention of volunteering his help in preparing for the party. But as he pulled up his chair to the breakfast table and put his napkin in his lap, the large headlines of the morning newspaper by his plate caught his eye: ALLIED FORCES LAND IN NORMANDY. The rest of the day was given over by him to sitting by the radio and trying to follow the news of the invasion. Accustomed to his usual ready access to battle intelligence reports, he now felt a maddening frustration at not being able to know what was really going on.

He resented having to abandon the news reports that evening but tried to be as accommodating as possible in carrying out his duty at the party. His mother stood proudly by his side and introduced him to everyone, even to those he already knew. He managed to make it through most of the evening without experiencing too much distaste, but near the end he was approached by a friend of his father's, a heavy-set man for whom he had always felt an aversion. The fellow had an annoying habit of always standing too close to the person to whom he was talking, a special irritant this night due to his strong odor of Scotch and garlic.

"Well, son, how have you been? I was stationed in Scotland and England in World War I—down in Sussex. Are you familiar with it?" the man asked.

"No, sir. I have been in the Pacific."

"Oh . . . well, too bad. I guess the Big One is on today, eh? I see you're a pilot. Do you fly one of those big bombers?"

"No, sir. I fly a reconnaissance aircraft."

The burly drunk swayed slightly and stared blearily at Bob, trying to think of something to say to ease the embarrassment he felt his friend's son must be feeling.

"Yeah . . . We had those in France during 'our' war too. We called them artillery spotters. Well, son, a job's a job. Somebody's gotta do it. Besides, it must be kind of dangerous flying one of those little puddle-jumpers. Right?"

"No, sir, it's not dangerous," Bob said, turning to walk away. "It's a lot of fun. Just a piece of cake."


**THE PROCESS OF** cultural reconciliation that he had been able to initiate in the preceding ten days slowed to a halt in the following weeks and even began to be undone. His repetitive daily routines on the farm lost their rejuvenative effect and began to induce a tinge of boredom aggravated by a sense of frustration in his being totally removed from the epic struggle transpiring along the coast of France. As usual Bob devoured every bit of news that he could come by and, although preoccupied himself with the events in Europe, could not help but be aware of the fact that accounts of the "other war," the "poor man's war" in the Pacific had been pushed to the back pages of the newspaper or displaced altogether.

In Washington on the twenty-sixth General Westover could not have been more cordial or fatherly within the limits of his official responsibility.

"Captain, you father and I have been friends for many years. I wish I could have back just half of the money he's taken from me on the golf course since I've known him. He tells me that you are gung-ho in everything you do in life, and your military record bears that out. I've looked it over, and it's pretty impressive. Let me trot something by you," he said, getting up from behind his desk and walking over to the window.

"Up here we have the responsibility of looking down the road and trying to be ready for what's coming. We anticipate that within a year we'll have air and staging bases close enough to the Japanese home islands to begin to plan for an invasion. It's going to be a long, bloody struggle, but there's no other way to defeat those people. We feel that Okinawa will be the logical primary base for us, but providing air cover for all our operations will be a demanding task. We have to start thinking now about modifying and equipping our fighters and training our pilots for very long missions. They're going to have to be able to escort high-altitude bombers to targets hundreds of miles away, successfully engage in air duels with enemy fighters or deliver support ground strikes, and still make it back to base. It's a tough assignment, and the plane we're looking at right now to carry out the job is the Republic P-47. If anyone in the Air Corps has more long-range experience than you, I don't know who it is, and I see a note on your records that you're pretty good at maintenance and engineering jobs. I feel that with your experience and background, you could be a big help to us in an advisory role. I'm prepared to offer you an assignment as a training and research consultant to help in this program we have under way at Wright-Patterson. I should imagine that being stationed in Ohio close to home wouldn't be too hard to take either. What do you say? Does that appeal to you, or would you like to have some time to think it over? You've still got several weeks in which to make a decision."

"No, sir, I don't need any time in which to think it over," Bob responded. "I've already made my decision. I would appreciate your help in getting me reassigned to the Eighth Photo Recon Squadron in the southwest Pacific."

## CHAPTER FIFTEEN

**WHEN BOB ARRIVED** back at Henderson at the end of July, there were obvious changes. Many of the units had been transferred to bases farther north, and even a large part of reconnaissance operations had been moved. Of more immediate impact on Bob was the loss of his former crew chief and aircraft. Stew had suffered compound fractures of both legs when a Jeep in which he was riding overturned, and he had been ferried back to the States. Bob's replacement pilot had totaled old "73" when the gear collapsed on landing, and the aircraft had been scrapped and cannibalized for parts. His new aircraft had some design and equipment improvements over the old, but Bob felt it would be weeks before he could finetune it to the degree he would like, and he and his new crew chief, Ricky Jordan, were not as compatible as he and Stew had been.

By early September, overall U.S. strategy was working to perfection. The Gilberts, the Marshalls, the Marianas had been conquered, and the Admiralties were being consolidated. Ground forces under General MacArthur were storming up the New Guinea coastline. The major Japanese strongholds of Truk and Rabaul had been immobilized and bypassed, thus weakening enemy supply lines. The only remaining barrier in the way of a direct assault on the Philippines was the powerful enemy garrison in the Palaus to the east. It was here that the ambitions of General MacArthur, directed northward, and those of Admiral Chester W. Nimitz, pushing westward across the central Pacific, converged.

On September 15 there were simultaneous assaults by U.S. forces on Pelelieu Island in the Palaus, fifteen hundred and eighteen miles northwest of Port Moresby, and on Morotai, eleven miles northeast of Halmahera. The latter was taken without a single American casualty, and work began immediately to finish airstrips from which bombers and fighters could reach the Philippines. Pelelieu was a totally different story. A Marine colonel involved in the mission had predicted victory in four days. It took a month.

General Sadai Inoue had appointed as commanding officer Colonel Kunio Nakagawa, who assured his superiors that the island could never be taken. U.S. intelligence was unaware that engineers had dug five hundred caves in the mountain that dominated the island. These caves were on several different levels and connected by miles of tunnels cut in and completely through the mountain, rendering enemy positions impervious to aerial and naval bombardment. To defend the island Colonel Nakagawa had at his disposal ten thousand crack combat troops, including the proud Japanese 36th Regiment. Under Nimitz's "Operation Stalemate," Admiral "Bull" Halsey's battle group from the Third Fleet for ten days subjected the island so mercilessly to naval and air pounding that observers were certain that few living things could have survived. Special attention was directed to the high ground north of the airstrip, which had to be neutralized and taken. In addition, on D-day plus one two regimental combat units of the U.S. Army 83rd Division landed on Anguara Island, five miles south of Pelelieu, and construction of an airstrip was begun immediately in case the one on Pelelieu should not be captured.

On September 22 Bob and another photo reco pilot, Sandy Wadlington, were called in for a special briefing.

"Gentlemen," the mission officer said, "I'm calling on you old-timers because we have a critically important mission tomorrow. The Old Man is obsessed with landing in the Philippines again as soon as possible. We have to gather as much information as we can in preparation for an invasion. We're going to be running non-stop recon missions for the next couple of weeks. You two gentlemen have the dubious honor of being the first. Wadlington, you are to proceed to Middleburg Island, where you will refuel and RON. Then the next day you are to take off for Mindanao and Luzon—here is a list of the targets to be covered—and proceed to Pelelieu for refueling before returning here. Hanson, you are to proceed directly to Pelelieu to refuel and RON. The next day you are to thoroughly cover Cebu for us—here are your primary and secondary targets—and get to Middleburg for refueling. We are especially interested in troop and naval dispersal. Take-off is scheduled for six hundred hours, and frequency assignments will be handed out prior to engine startup. Any questions?"

Sandy and Bob looked at each other and then shook their heads.

"Good. I suggest you learn to love the Philippines. You'll be seeing a lot of them in the coming weeks. Now get a good night's sleep. That's all."

The next morning at 5:45 Bob was about to initiate engine start-up when Ricky climbed up and handed him a letter.

"Here, sir, you missed mail-call yesterday. This came for you."

Bob glanced at his name and APO number on the envelope and recognized Nancy's handwriting.

"Thank you, Corporal, that'll give me something to do. I'd have time to read *War and Peace* by the time I reach my destination."

An hour into the flight he engaged the autopilot, took out the envelope and opened it, noticing immediately the distinctive and exciting trace of Nancy's perfume—utterly incongruous in this setting. The very short note was dated June 4, 1944.

"My dearest Robert—I cried all afternoon. It was so sad for us to part that way and so stupid. I don't want to talk about the weekend. Let's just forget the damn thing. Let's think instead about the future, for we *are* going to have a future—you and I. Believe me, you mean as much to me as you said I do to you. You are trapped, my dearest; don't try to get away. Our fates and futures are intertwined. I don't know where you'll be when you read this, but do take good care of yourself. For *my* sake. x x x x N."

Bob put the note back in the envelope and shoved it in the chart slot to the left of the pilot seat.

He had to devote special care to fuel management and navigation on his flight to Pelelieu. He had covered over two thousand miles on a single flight before, but if he missed the Palaus even by a few miles, there would be nothing but thousands of square miles of ocean below and no alternate place to land. As meticulous as his navigation had been, he was still quite concerned when, according to his estimates, he was within communication range with the controller at Pelelieu and yet his repeated attempts to establish contact were met by silence. Finally a voice came over the frequency.

"Shortstop King Queen Joker, this is Anguara. What is your problem?"

"Anguara from King Queen Joker. I have been directed to Pelelieu but cannot raise them. Am I on the right frequency?"

"Affirmative. But the field is under mortar attack. They cannot clear you to land."

"Damn it! I'm low on fuel and have no alternate. What the hell am I supposed to do?"

"Shortstop King Queen Joker, stand by."

Bob had climbed to twelve thousand feet a half hour earlier to gain a wider visual sweep of the ocean. Down below dead ahead there began to appear the outlines of small islands, so he started a reduced-power descent.

"King Queen Joker from Anguara. The strip at Pelelieu is cratered. You couldn't make it. We are working on a strip here, but only the first half is matted, and the sand and coral beyond is very soft. What are your intentions?"

"I'll have to give you a try. Clear the strip and keep your fingers crossed," Bob responded and checked his charts to pinpoint the location of the strip at Anguara.

Bob dragged the F-4B in just over the water with full flaps and as low an air speed as possible. He stalled the aircraft onto the first few feet of the runway and stood on the brakes as hard as he dared. He was still rolling when he saw the end of the steel-mesh "Marston mats" flash by, so he released the brakes and hoped the nose-wheel wouldn't sink in the sand and buckle under him. He felt a strong deceleration, and the plane came to a stop.

For a moment there was dead silence, for he had cut his engines and master switch in case there were a crash. With a deep sigh of relief he opened the canopy and began extricating himself from his restraining harness and parachute straps.

"I'd say that was a pretty fair job, Captain," came a voice on the left side.

Bob looked down and saw the grinning face of an Army lieutenant, who didn't look a day older than sixteen.

"No sweat. I land like that all the time," Bob said and prepared to climb down.

Euphoria over his successful landing was soon displaced by concern over his total predicament. The nose-wheel and main gear, which Bob had examined and determined to be undamaged, were mired in the soft sand, and even the full power of the engines would not be sufficient to budge the plane. Members of the engineering battalion huddled and then assured Bob that they could winch the aircraft up improvised ramps back onto the mats.

"Could you take off again in the distance available?" one of the engineers asked.

"It would be awfully close," Bob answered. "Since I would be way under gross weight because of low fuel, I could probably make it if you could give me two more lengths of mat."

The engineers looked at each other.

"Give us two hours, and it'll be done. Come on, boys, hop to it."

This was only one of Bob's problems. There was no aircraft fuel yet at Anguara. Even if there had been, it would have been of no help since he could not have become airborne with a full load off such a short strip. He had to get into Peleliu in order to refuel, but the prospects for this did not seem good. He spent over an hour in the communications hut conferring with a Navy Seabee officer at Peleliu. It was finally decided that if the Seabees could repair the landing strip and there were no other mortar attacks, Bob should proceed to cross the five-mile strait and arrive with the barest minimum of daylight to make a landing.

"You understand," the Seabee said, "that we cannot promise the safety of you or your aircraft. The Japs have howitzers and mortars trained on us from the high ground. We'll do the best we can, but there are no guarantees."

"I understand," Bob said, "but I have no alternative. We'll call from here just before take-off to verify conditions. I will otherwise maintain radio silence in case the Japs are scanning the frequencies. See you in a couple of hours."

The Army engineers met their deadline and had strung together the added lengths of mat. By holding his brakes until his engines had attained full power, Bob was able to become airborne and retract his gear with a few feet of runway to spare. The flight was so short that as he approached the strip at Pelelieu, he realized that he should have delayed longer and used up more of the fading daylight. After shut-down he barely had time to exit the cockpit before the Seabees were swarming over the plane, pulling across camouflage netting and hooking on an improvised tow-bar to move the aircraft behind revetments with the aid of a small grader.

"Captain, follow me on the double," said a Marine private, leading Bob at a trot to the edge of the airfield, where a group of other Marines were arrayed defensively in slit trenches.

"Down!" he yelled as an eerie whine became audible. Bob had no sooner hit the bottom of a trench than an explosion rocked the gaunt scarred remnants of palm trees at the edge of the field. When he raised his head, he saw with horror that a large crater had been opened up only a few yards from the F-4B, and part of the camouflage netting had been shredded.

"Oh, no!" he said in despair and started running toward the airplane. He was vaguely aware of shouts but paid no heed. As he drew near the crater, he was choked by the acrid smoke from the shell and forced to slow his pace. Suddenly someone tackled him from behind and rolled with him into the still-smoking hole. A fraction of a second later another explosion stunned him and he was covered with sand and fragments of coral and hot steel. Before he could dispel a wave of confusion, he was lifted to his feet and literally dragged at a dead run back toward the edge of the field, noticing dimly the stripes of a master sergeant on the arm doing the dragging.

"We have eight seconds before they reload," the Marine said. Before they could reach the trenches, the piercing whistle could be heard again.

"Mortar coming in!" came a shout.

Instinctively Bob hit the ground at the same time as the sergeant and thought he might have heard the whine of shrapnel passing overhead. Leaping to his feet, he glanced back and saw smoke rising from the same crater in which they had been sprawled a few seconds earlier. No other shells followed, but they stayed crouched in their trench during the fading of the last daylight. Bob felt the scrutiny of the eyes of the Marine sergeant, who had undoubtedly saved his life. When the soldier spoke, however, there was no trace of rancor or contempt.

"Those bars don't make you immortal, Captain. Those bastards will kill you soon enough without giving them a clear shot at you."

"I'm sorry, Sergeant, but I have a mission to carry out. I wanted to see what damage was done to the airplane."

"Your running around out there brought in two extra rounds. You endangered the plane all the more. We'll have a three-quarters moon tonight. I'll go out there with you later on. Now let's go. We have to move a hundred yards farther in."

As Bob followed the Marine along a path winding among foxholes, he was unprepared for what he encountered. Behind crudely constructed walls of palm trunks lay rows of dead infantrymen interspersed with wounded, some grievously.

"Keep talking to me, son," a corpsman was urging while hurriedly but efficiently attending to a badly maimed private. "What city are you from? Akron? I know Akron. That's a good town. Do you know Dayton? Come on, son, keep talking to me."

"Help me, Father," came another voice, weak but sharp with fear. "Oh, God, I don't want to die! Don't let me die!"

"*In nomine Patri.* . ." intoned the soft voice of the chaplain as he was making the sign of the cross.

The sergeant was looking back at Bob, who had involuntarily slowed almost to a halt.

"Now that it's dark, the landing craft can come in," he said. "We'll get the dead and the wounded down to the beach so that they can be evacuated. Come on. We don't have much farther to go."

They must have ended up near the Marine defensive perimeter, for every few yards sentries were posted behind downed tree trunks and sand bags. The sergeant extracted from a back-pack two tins of food and tossed one to Bob, who didn't see it coming and had to retrieve it from the bottom of the trench.

"Better eat while we can. The moon will be up soon."

Bob realized that he should eat but wasn't sure that he would be able to swallow. The odor of cordite, mixed with the stench of putrefaction and death, hung like a pall in the still air. Somewhere off to the left could occasionally be heard the crackle of small arms fire. The moon was beginning to creep above the horizon before Bob could summon enough resolve to remove the lid from the tin and explore the contents. As he was trying to force down a few mouthfuls, he noticed for the first time two Japanese prisoners being held at gunpoint by a Marine guard a few yards away. Half-naked, they were squatting on their haunches, immobile except for their eyes, which were impassively observing what was going on about them. The closest one looked gaunt and half-starved, so Bob got up and moved toward him, holding out the half-tin of food he could not finish. Instantly the Marine sergeant brought his rifle to his shoulder and aimed at the head of the prisoner. Bob was stunned and stopped, still extending his hand with the container. The prisoner turned away, rejecting the proffered food, and Bob returned to his place. The sergeant again leaned his rifle against the side of the trench and continued chewing on some dried meat.

"Damn it, Sergeant, we're in a war, but there is such a thing as humaneness," Bob said somewhat shakily.

The Marine didn't speak immediately. Finally he responded.

"Captain, five days ago one of my men offered a wounded

prisoner a cup of water. When he reached out to take it, there was a grenade in his hand with the pin pulled. Score: one Japanese prisoner dead—four good Marines dead."

He fell silent for a few minutes and then stretched.

"Johnson, take the prisoners down to the beach. If one of them even stumbles, shoot him."

"Yes, Sergeant," responded the guard and moved off down the path with the two hapless men.

"The moon won't be high enough to help us for another two hours, Captain. You'd better try to get some sleep," the sergeant said and removed his helmet to serve as a crude pillow.

Bob knew some sleep would be essential to him. He tried to find a comfortable position in the trench, but sleep would not come. Relative quiet had fallen over the area, but off in the dark could be heard the squeaking and chattering of rats as they gnawed on unretrieved corpses, and at first softly and then more plaintively over and over came a plea from no-man's land.

"Corpsman, over here . . . Help me, buddy. . . Don't leave me here."

Bob sat up and then got to his feet.

"Stay where you are, Captain," came a firm order from the sergeant.

"Damn it, there's a wounded man out there," Bob protested. "You can't just leave him. I'll go if no one else will."

"Sit down, Captain. That's an old Japanese trick. My best friend fell for that back on Guadalcanal. We found him the next day with his throat cut. All our dead and wounded are accounted for, so try to get some rest."

Bob sank down and leaned back against the sloping side of the trench.

"I'm sorry," he said. "I guess I seem pretty stupid to you."

The sergeant smiled and closed his eyes.

"I couldn't fly your airplane," he said after a pause. "We're just fighting two different parts of the same war."

For some reason, in spite of the oppressive heat Bob shivered.

"What's your unit, Sergeant?"

"K Company, First Marines."

"How long have you been here?"

"We were in the first wave."

"I hear it's been really rough."

"There were two hundred and thirty-five in our company when we hit the beach. There are only seventy-eight of us still alive. We took a real beating up on 'Bloody-Nose Ridge.'"

"My God," Bob said in a subdued voice. "I thought I knew what war was all about."

There was a protracted silence. A shaft of moonlight was slanting into the trench and giving Bob a chance to observe the Marine's face. Under swarthy skin he had prominent features characterized by high cheekbones and an aquiline nose.

"Sergeant," Bob began anew, "you probably saved my life at least once tonight, and I want to thank you."

The Marine was silent, and Bob couldn't tell if he had dozed off.

"We will probably never meet again, and I guess introductions are stupid out here, but I'm Bob Hanson from Kentucky."

The sergeant opened his eyes and rolled his head to the side to glance at Bob.

"Pleased to meet you, Captain Hanson. I'm Niwot Vasquez from Colorado."

"I'd say I'm very lucky to have met you, Sergeant Vasquez," Bob rejoined. "What did you say your first name is?"

"Niwot."

"I'm no authority, but that sure doesn't sound Spanish to me," Bob said. "Is it?"

"No, it's Indian. My mother was Arapaho, and my father an immigrant Mexican. *Niwot* means 'left hand' in Arapaho and was the name of a great chief. Since I'm left-handed, my mother gave me the name too. I'm afraid I'll never live up to my namesake, however."

"I'm not so sure," Bob said with considerable conviction.

Vasquez closed his eyes again and soon seemed to fall into a deep sleep. Bob continued to observe this remarkable soldier, who exhibited all the characteristics—courage, strength, skill and resourcefulness—that he had always associated with the image of a "good Marine." He was musing over the man's strange name and mixed parentage when he himself slipped into a troubled sleep.

**HE JERKED VIOLENTLY** when awakened by a shake of a shoulder.

The moon was high in the sky and flooded the island in a ghostly light.

"We'd better get with it," Vasquez said. "It's not going to get any brighter. Here, put this lamp-black on your hands and face and anything bright you might have on you. At night enemy snipers climb those palm trunks."

Bob began smearing the black substance on his face and neck and tops of his hands while watching the sergeant, who with precise but unhurried movements checked the ammunition cartridge of his rifle, stuffed two hand-grenades into pouches on the back of his trousers and extracted from a sheath strapped to his leg a vicious-looking double-edged knife with a serrated knuckle-guard. He reached over, took some of the lamp-black and began lightly coating the blade.

"Sergeant," Bob asked, "how much sleep have you had in the last week?"

Vasquez reflected briefly and then said, "In all, maybe twelve hours."

Bob completed his smearing and then wiped the palm of his hand against the right leg of his flight suit.

"You stay here and get some sleep," he said. "You don't need to go with me. I can find the way—especially with the moon up."

"No, Captain," the Marine answered immediately, carefully returning the knife to its sheath, "I'm going with you. They try to infiltrate our lines every night. They don't get through often, but you never know. Don't worry about me. We're being pulled back and relieved tomorrow. Then I'll get a lot of sleep. But what about you? If it's not top secret, where are you heading tomorrow?"

"It'd be ironic if I didn't trust you," Bob replied. "I'm heading for the Philippines and then to an island off the northern New Guinea coast."

Vasquez whistled and then leaned over to pick up his rifle.

"That's quite a jaunt. You've got a long, long day coming up; you need the sleep more than I. Well, what the hell; let's go and check out your airplane."

Bob followed him back along the path they had taken hours earlier. Once out onto the field, it was obvious that the Seabees had wrought their magic: there was not a trace of the previous shell holes. As they drew near to the revetment, a soft liquid sound could be heard. The Seabees had formed a line stretching to the airplane from drums stored in a former grove down near the beach and were passing five-gallon containers of fuel up the line and empty ones down the line. Bob crawled under the camouflage netting and began his inspection, mostly by feel. His first concerns were the landing gear tires, and he was greatly relieved to see that none had been punctured. Next he determined that the cameras had not been damaged, but as he ran his fingers along the belly and over the surfaces of the wings, he felt many dents probably caused by chunks of coral hurled by the explosions. There were only two gashes penetrating the aluminum skin. One was about seven inches long by one and a half inches wide and was located under the right wing. Bob was careful to determine that no auxiliary fuel tank or fuel line had been pierced by the projectile, but there were jagged edges that would protrude into the slipstream. The other gash was a three-square-inch rectangular one on the right side of the nose fuselage. Both of these had probably resulted from pieces of shrapnel or mat. A Seabee officer ducked under the netting, where a small group of sailors were finishing filling the three-hundred-gallon belly auxiliary tank being inspected by Bob.

"We're almost through, Captain. Another twenty minutes should do it. Is there anything else we can do to help?"

"Yes, there is, Lieutenant. I need to borrow some metal shears or a file to smooth out the edges of a rent in the wing surface. Also, although I've looked at the prop blades as well as I can, to feel at all comfortable I need to crank her up to be sure the engines and props are all okay. Could you get your men to peel back the net for a few minutes and let me check them out?"

"No, sir, I can't do that. The enemy gunners up above know you're here; they just don't know where. Once they spotted your exhaust stacks, your plane wouldn't last three minutes. As soon as we finish topping off your tanks, we'll move the plane to the end of the runway and remove the net just before you start your engines. Could you execute a night take-off?"

"No, I wouldn't want to risk that. With no runway lights for orientation, a full gross-weight take-off would be risky. I need to be able to see the end of the strip coming up."

The lieutenant j.g. was thoughtful for a moment. Vasquez, who had been silently circling the airplane since their arrival, ducked under the netting and joined them.

"Okay," the Seabee officer said. "Be in your plane ready to go. At the first light of dawn, you've got to get rolling. I'll have two flares lit at the end of the runway the moment you crank up. You'll have to go for immediate take-off."

"Immediate?!" Bob protested. "I can't take off with cold engines. I could never be sure of getting the full power I'll need with this load off such a short strip. I'll need to warm up at least three minutes."

"Captain, if you aren't in the air thirty seconds after you flare your exhausts, you'll not be going anywhere. I've seen the Jap gunners hit moving LCI's out off the beach. Your plane would be a dead duck."

Bob sank glumly onto his haunches. The situation had no happy resolution; any decision he made could be a deadly one. As a pilot he had a real calculated anxiety concerning a fiery crash following an unsuccessful take-off attempt. And yet the lieutenant j.g. was even more certain of disaster if he didn't attempt it. With a sigh he turned and looked at Vasquez, who had knelt onto one knee in the shadow of the wing and who was intently scanning like a wild animal the line of vegetation at the edge of the field.

"Well, Sergeant, it seems I don't have much of a choice. Either way it looks as though there's a fair chance that I'll get a very long sleep sooner than I had anticipated. All right, Lieutenant, we'll do as you say. What time are we looking at?"

"The sooner the better," the officer replied. "I'd say in an hour and a half. There should be enough light by then for you to see the end of the runway."

"Why don't you try to get some sleep, sir? I'll stand guard and wake you in an hour," Vasquez volunteered.

"Thank you, Sergeant," Bob responded, standing up in front of the wing and stretching his aching back, "but I doubt I could get to sleep again. You go on. I'm going to check the oil and a few other things under the cowls."

As they stepped out from under the netting, the Seabees were already inching the heavy airplane out from behind the revetments toward the end of the runway. Bob held out his hand.

"Good-bye, Sergeant, thank you again, and good luck."

"Good-bye, sir; the same to you," he responded and then turned and vanished silently into the darkness.

With the help of two Seabees Bob climbed into the cockpit twenty minutes before the agreed-upon time for engine start-up. The moon had sunk behind the bloody mountain and deprived him of even its faint light. In the dark he went over his checklist several times by feel, trying to ensure that he could jettison at the last moment the huge auxiliary tank under the plane's belly if he saw that its weight would prevent his lifting off or if he were to lose one engine at that critical moment. He placed the drop-tank switch in the "safety" position and the drop-tank selector on "off" so that the tank could be dropped simply by punching the drop-tank release button.

Ten minutes before the time was up it was still dark, but once dawn began, it came rapidly. At take-off minus one he put the fuel selector on front tank, dropped fifteen degrees of flaps, advanced his mixture controls, activated his magneto switches and sat with one hand on the left engine primer switch and the other on the starter button. Like ants, a swarm of men surrounded the plane and began pulling back the camouflage netting. As soon as the net cleared the propellers and the canopy, Bob engaged the starter and the left engine sprang to life. Immediately he followed the same procedure with the right engine, which caught, then sputtered and died. A new attempt resulted in what seemed an interminable cranking of the engine with no luck. Even as he was struggling to start the second engine, in his peripheral vision he saw in the dim light the Navy personnel scattering in response to fear of incoming mortar rounds. Gambling that he may have over-primed, Bob retarded the mixture control while continuing to crank. The engine gave an encouraging cough and then caught. Bob moved the mixture to full rich, stood on his brakes and pushed the throttles full forward. The airplane shuddered and strained, but Bob was certain he wasn't getting full power. Fearful that he was at the limit of the thirty-second safety allotment predicted by the lieutenant j.g., he had to gamble and so released his brakes.

As the F-4B rolled down the runway, Bob sensed with some relief that the level of power was increasing. Straining his sight forward to try to determine the end of the mesh strip, he put his left thumb on the drop-tank release button and watched for the flares. He had the luxury of neither light nor time to consult his air speed indicator. Only by the seat of his pants did he sense that the airplane would be ready to fly. As the two flares rushed the last few feet toward him, Bob pulled back on the yoke and hit his gear-retraction switch. The plane staggered into the air, mushed for a few seconds out over the water and then rapidly gained air speed. Bob milked the flaps up slowly, switched to aux fuel tank and in a wide arc turned to head westward to the Philippines.

# CHAPTER SIXTEEN

**BOB HAD INITIALLY** intended to stay low to avoid the radar of any chance enemy surface vessel on his approach to the islands, but in less than two hours after sunrise the temperature in the cockpit was already over a hundred degrees; and this, coupled with the fatigue that was beginning to weigh heavily on him, gave him a stifling sense of virtual claustrophobia. He began a cruise climb to ten thousand feet and found slightly more comfortable conditions there, but his physical discomfort was joined by an ill-defined mental anxiety. Despite the dulling effects of heat and weariness, he felt—he vaguely sensed—that something just wasn't right. Try as hard as he might, however, he could not pinpoint where the trouble lay. He had brutally forced his laggard attention to check and double-check his navigation and fuel management and knew them to be correct, but he could not relax even though indications on all engine instruments were within normal ranges and he had jock-eyed the propeller controls several times to assure that the propellers were synchronized. He tried to push the concern out of his mind as he pulled out his charts and began reviewing his target assignments.

As the dim line of the shore of Mindanao came into view on the horizon, Bob hooked on his mask, flipped the oxygen control switch to "auto" and moved the engine controls to climb power. He was starting an ascent to twenty-six thousand feet earlier than he had planned, but his approach at ten thousand feet had most probably been picked up by enemy radar, and soon fighters would be scrambling to intercept him. The superiority of the F-4B in speed and altitude capability gave Bob the needed edge in this competitive situation, and he felt secure in his knowledge that he could cruise high above the Zeros and anti-aircraft fire, as he had done so many countless times before.

But before he was half-way across Bohol, this confidence was tainted by a generalized mild confusion. He was experiencing intermittent waves of vertigo, requiring him to check his gyros frequently to be sure the plane was flying straight and level. After one such attack he almost dreamily realized that his visual scan had fixed on only one instrument and that he was in a diving left turn. A reluctant alarm pierced the murky shroud of his consciousness, and he forced himself to try to react to it. With difficulty he began checking and re-checking all systems. It was testimony to the level of his confusion that the normally most logical culprit was the last he checked. As he flew out over the straits between Leyte and Cebu, his eyes settled at first uncomprehendingly and then with grudging realization on the oxygen supply gauge. It read zero! There was no pressure.

Bob looked down at his fingernails and saw that they were almost blue. He banged his hand violently against the left console, hoping that the pain would help clear away the mist in his mind. How could he have been so stupid? In the graduated tests in the pressure chamber at Randolph Field he thought he had discovered that he had a constant awareness of the degree to which his reactions were hampered by increasing anoxia. Yet here, in a vitally important situation, it had crept up on him from behind. He had checked the gauge before take-off from Henderson and had used no oxygen on the flight to Pelelieu, so the shrapnel that penetrated the nose fuselage must have pierced the reservoir or the line. In the darkness before take-off he could not have visually checked it.

Again he became aware of being in a steep left turn and unsnapped his mask.

"God damn it! You idiot! Fly this damn thing!" he screamed at himself at the top of his voice.

The exertion or sharpened realization helped restore some level of mental control. He righted the plane, fumbled for his charts and, since Cebu was coming up below, began to prepare for his first run across the target. It required an immense effort at concentration to set up and engage the autopilot and operate the camera switches in the proper sequence. The second sweep was even more difficult. Near the end of this run across the island he thought he was beginning to hallucinate: there was an irregular droning in his ears. As he turned to take up a heading for another run, his sluggish consciousness finally admitted that it was not imagined. His propellers must no longer be synchronized. Even with the impairment of his fuzzy eyesight he saw the oscillating needle on the number one tachometer. The left propeller was erratic. By switching to manual control he was able to stabilize the RPMs for brief periods, but very soon the oscillation would begin again, finally becoming so severe that the left engine would occasionally choke down and backfire. Even in his semi-stupor Bob realized he had to shut the engine down. Retarding the throttle, he moved the propeller control to full feather position and the mixture control to "idle cut-off." When the propeller feathered and stopped rotating, he cut all electrical switches and fuel to the left engine, increased power on the right one and started trying to salvage his third photo run over the target. By the end of the sweep the impairment of his judgment had grown worse. It was several minutes before he became aware of the fact that inexplicably the left propeller was beginning to windmill again, slowly moving toward low pitch. Although he had fairly effectively trimmed the plane for single-engine flight, the extra drag of the flattening blades caused increased yaw to the left, and more ominously his air speed began falling off. In a dark recess of his waning consciousness a survival alarm went off and convinced him that he had to get to a lower altitude to clear his mind and deal with the developing emergency. He managed to disengage the autopilot, turn to a general heading of ninety degrees and begin a descent toward the coast of Leyte.

As he descended through sixteen thousand feet, he was aware of a piercing headache, but his mental faculties were returning and it became possible to address his problem more rationally. Continuing flight with only one operative engine would be no problem, but the increased drag of the windmilling propeller would seriously compromise his ability to make it to Middleburg Island with available fuel, for he had jettisoned the auxiliary tank as he began his initial climb to altitude and his gauges indicated that his other tanks had not been completely topped on Pelelieu. He leveled off at fourteen thousand feet and decided to try to restart the left engine. Even with a runaway prop he could utilize partial power to decrease the drag component. He had turned the fuel selector valve to the front tank, advanced his mixture and propeller controls and was reaching for the magneto switch when the aircraft was jolted violently and he had to fight to retrim. At first he thought he might have penetrated an updraft in the unstable air at lower altitude but then saw ominous black puffs of smoke to the sides and ahead of his path. He had descended into the range of Japanese anti-aircraft batteries along the coast.

Going to full power on the right engine, he tried to initiate as effective evasive action as he could, given his single-engine limitations to maneuverability, but the graceful yet dark and deadly mushrooms began to converge on his path. He was diving to increase his air speed and turning sharply left and right, heading toward the ridge running down the middle of Leyte. Just as he thought he might succeed in getting past the range of the enemy batteries, he was thrown against the side of the canopy by another close explosion. He righted the airplane with no difficulty, and control responses seemed to be normal. With relief he saw that there were no more black puffs ahead and to the side of his course.

His relief was not sustained. As he once again initiated his restart procedure for the left engine, the coolant temperature warning light for the right engine flashed on and he saw the reading on the gauge was above redline. He realized that shrapnel must have pierced the coolant housing, that the engine would seize up within a short time and that sustained flight soon would no longer be possible. His altimeter read only eleven thousand feet, and the dark green jungle was clearly visible below. He had been informed during his briefing that U.S. naval forces would be present in at least some strength near the

Gulf of Leyte as a prelude to a much heavier build-up, but he had no information on their present disposition. Nevertheless, he headed for the Gulf in a vain hope of perhaps ditching near a U.S. vessel if one could be found.

Suddenly there was silence, broken only be the rush of wind past the canopy. The right engine had seized up without even a backfire. As Bob began a shallow diving turn, he saw the beaches of the eastern coast of Leyte ahead of him but also small vessels that could be enemy patrol boats. He had to make a quick decision whether to ditch near the beach or bail out inland and almost instantly chose the latter course. With both propellers unfeathered the aircraft's glide angle was excessively steep, but by nursing his air speed carefully Bob was able to recross the mountain ridge with about two thousand feet to spare. He snapped on his oxygen mask, disconnected his oxygen hose and radio lead and pulled his goggles down. Moving the elevator trim full forward as he rolled the airplane inverted, he reached up and activated the canopy release. When the canopy whipped away in the slipstream, he released his seat belt and shoulder harness and dropped free, instantly grabbing for his ripcord. He sensed immediately that he was tumbling but did not have time to correct this before deploying his chute, being unsure as to how much altitude he had left. Luckily he did not foul the shroud lines as the parachute popped open above him and slowed his fall. He had no time to try to pick a landing spot or steer his descent, for the solid blanket of jungle rushed upward and swallowed him as he crashed through the limbs of a tree and was snapped to an abrupt halt.

His helmet, mask and goggles had probably saved his face from lacerations from the branches and vines, but now he felt he was about to suffocate. He unsnapped the mask and ripped off the helmet and goggles and was able to breathe more freely. It took his eyes a minute to adjust from the sunlight above to the gloom under the forest ceiling, but gradually in the subdued light he was able to assess his predicament. He was encased in a chamber of green surrounding him on all sides. His parachute had been snagged by the upper limbs of a tall tree, and he was left dangling high above the jungle floor. He was unable to judge exactly the distance to the ground, but by dropping his helmet and listening for the impact he guessed it must be at least sixty feet, a drop that—if not fatal—would probably result in serious injury. In the surrounding forest the initial dead silence probably occasioned by the sound of his crashing through the limbs of the tree began to give way to the calls, chattering and thumping of birds and other wildlife.

Bob looked up and saw that the canopy of the parachute was supported by a fairly substantial limb. If he were able to climb up the shroud lines and the collapsed chute to get to the limb, he might be able to traverse it and somehow let himself down the sturdy trunk. His physical condition was not propitious for the attempt. He was exhausted, his head was pounding, and he was weak from mild shock, but since a drop to the ground had been ruled out, there was no real alternative. He made three attempts. On the first he had shinnied half-way up the canopy to the limb when the perspiration from his hands caused them to slip uncontrollably on the silk fabric, and he fell back down. If he had worked his way out of his harness first, he would not have had the added weight and cumbersomeness of the harness and shroud lines and probably could have made it all the way. But as a con-cession to caution he had elected not to do this, for in the event of failure there would have remained nothing to impede his fall all the way to the ground. The next two tries were even less successful, his not even reaching the canopy on the last feeble attempt. Limp with fatigue and his stamina sapped by the oppressive heat and humidity, he decided he had to wait until he could rebuild his strength before try-ing again. For a while he vainly sought to fight off a cloud of insects swarming around his head and then fitfully dozed off with his head slumped onto his chest.

**HE WAS JOLTED** awake by a clap of thunder. The gloom under the ceiling of vegetation had deepened due to an approaching storm. The thun-der rumbled and rolled across the mountainside, and faintly at first but then more loudly came the sound of heavy raindrops on the leaves above. For a while the rain did not penetrate to the lower levels, but when it did, it came as a deluge. The parachute shroud lines acted as conduits for the water cascading from the canopy, and Bob was soon totally drenched even through his flight suit.

The storm was violent but brief, and after its passage the normal sounds of the jungle, temporarily silenced, began to return. Bob's physical discomfort tested the limits of endurance, and he realized that he could not for long remain in that state of suspended imprisonment. The thorough soaking of the canopy and shroud lines by the downpour effectively removed the possibility of his again trying to climb up them to the limb, but the only other solution open to him—a free fall into the underbrush way below—was one that he naturally tended to delay in carrying out. A maddening swarm of mosquitoes prodded him to action, however, and he was about to unsnap his harness when he became aware that quiet had once again fallen in the forest. Eerily the only sound that could be heard was the occasional dripping of moisture down through the tiers of leaves. Bob held his breath and tried to pick up any clues as to the cause of this reimposed silence. At first very faintly and then more clearly he heard human voices mixed with the crackling of pedestrian passage through the underbrush. The patterning and intonation of the language alerted Bob to the ominous and almost certain probability that it was Japanese. Slowly and noiselessly he reached down and unfastened the flap on the right-leg compartment of his flight suit that held his .45 Colt automatic. His cramped position impeded his efforts, but he was able to extract the weapon and hold it in both hands.

He did not want to inject a shell into the chamber immediately, for the unavoidable noise would assuredly reveal his presence, so he chose to wait until the very last moment. His every faculty was strained to maximum alertness, but inwardly he was strangely calm. He knew full well that he would be an easy, helpless target and that he would last only a matter of seconds in any firefight. He would choose surrendering if that option were open to him, but if it became apparent that he was to be executed, he was determined to take as many of the enemy soldiers with him as he could with the eight rounds in his cartridge magazine.

Suddenly he made out in the dim light below a dark round face peering up at him from a bank of vegetation. He seized the charging mechanism on the top of the automatic and was about to effect the simultaneous loading of the chamber and cocking of the hammer when he paused. The owner of the face below had placed his finger against his lips, admonishing silence. There was a brief show of teeth and a wave of a hand, and the face disappeared. Soon Bob noticed that the voices began moving off into the distance and eventually faded away.

He remained hanging there for a long time in confused indecision. What the hell was going on? Who was the character down below? What should he himself now do—risk the fall to the ground or wait longer? The necessity of a decision was removed by the sudden appearance of three men below. Bob was startled, for they had come through the jungle so quietly that he had not been aware of their approach. Instinctively he slammed a cartridge into the chamber of his automatic, but a voice called out from below.

"Don't shoot, American. We are friends. Don't shoot."

Bob peered into the gloom but could make out only dimly the outlines of the three apparently native men.

"Drop your gun, American. We can help you."

Bob was leery of this order to divest himself of the only card he had in this grim game.

"Why the hell can't you help me if I keep the gun?" he called down.

"Please. We must talk as little as possible," the man said softly. "We need your gun. We will help you. You will see. Drop it."

At first Bob hesitated in indecision but then reluctantly admitted to himself that he had no real bargaining position. He restrained the head of the hammer with his left hand, applied pressure to the trigger and eased the hammer forward to prevent firing. Then he dropped the weapon to the forest floor below. One of the men picked it up immediately, and the three disappeared.

"God damn it!" Bob said to himself. "They've euchred me out of my gun and then left me here!"

But in a moment they reappeared, bringing ropes and talking

softly in a language that Bob could not identify. He watched as the smallest of the three tied a light line around his waist and approached the trunk of the tree with two approximately eight-foot lengths of rope. He circled the trunk with one, passed it around his body and deftly tied a knot. He held the other short length of rope in his teeth while beginning a remarkably agile ascent of the tree. Bob watched this display of skill in utter amazement. The man would flip the rope up the back of the trunk, lean back against the loop while advancing his bare feet, then lean forward quickly and flip the rope again, repeating the process over and over in a smoothly co-ordinated rhythm. In the dim light he at times resembled a giant woodpecker as he steadily moved up the tree. Whenever he encountered a limb obstructing his progress, he would pause, remove the spare rope from between his teeth, toss one end over the limb and pass the rope under his arms. Knotting this new support and untying the old, he would then continue the same routine.

When he had climbed almost to Bob's elevation, he positioned himself firmly in the crotch of a large limb and dropped the short lengths of rope to the ground. Pulling up a very long length of the light line, he drew up the .45, which had been tied to the end, and began swinging it in a wide arc beneath him, increasing the radius and height with each oscillation. With a final heave he directed the gun up and over the limb that was holding Bob's parachute. Having retrieved the automatic as it came down the other side, with slow, deliberate movements he untied it and pulled on the line, lowering its liberated end to the ground. One of the other men fastened to it a stronger rope, which was then drawn up and over the top limb and to the end of which was secured the .45.

"American, my friend is going to swing the gun over to you," one of the men below said so softly that Bob could barely hear him. "Catch it and untie it. Wind the rope twice around your chest underneath your parachute harness and knot it tightly. When I tell you to, release your harness snaps, and we will lower you to the ground. Okay?"

Bob just nodded his head and waited for the automatic, which was getting nearer to him on each swing. He came close to seizing it once, but the contact with his hand disrupted the arc, and the weapon struck against the tree trunk, necessitating a restart of the whole procedure. On his second try he was more successful and followed the directions he had received. He noticed that the shell had been removed from the automatic chamber and the magazine was missing but slipped the gun back into its pouch in his flight suit.

"We are ready. Release your harness whenever you like, but be careful. You may swing against the tree trunk hard, so have your feet ready."

Reaching up with one hand, Bob raised himself slightly, facilitating the unfastening with the other of the chest snap and then the leg portions of the harness. When he let go, he dropped free of the parachute and was caught by the rope, which swung him toward the tree. The native's warning had been timely, for his feet and legs were required to absorb the impact with the trunk before he was quickly lowered to the ground.

"Say, that was . . ." Bob began with an immense feeling of relief.

"Shhh . . . We must not talk," the English-speaker whispered, again holding his finger in front of his lips. "There are several Japanese patrols in the area. We must move very fast."

Even as he spoke, he and the other man had returned the end of the rope to the tree-sitter and then quickly lowered him to the ground also. With lightning efficiency the ropes were coiled and wrapped, and the three set off quickly through the underbrush with Bob following as quietly as he could. The lead man would halt every hundred yards or so and hold up his hand for the others to do likewise. Then they would listen intently for any human sound before proceeding on. As they were crossing one of the many small rivulets coming off the ridge, Bob asked for a brief break, for his throat was parched from the heat and exertion. As he was about to drink the water he had scooped up in his hands, the guide grabbed his wrist and shook his head, leading him over to a plant with broad fronds slanted upward. Pulling one of the fronds down, he pointed out to Bob the rather considerable reservoir of rainwater trapped near the base, and in a short time his thirst was slated.

After having covered what seemed to Bob to be about two miles, the leader, who was the one who could speak English, signalled a halt and scouted ahead. In a few moments he returned.

"*Peligro*! Danger!" he said. "There are enemy ahead."

He guided them into a dense copse entwined with heavily matted vines and motioned for them all to crawl behind him into a fairly spacious hollow beneath a large tree.

"We will rest here until dark," he whispered to Bob. "In daylight we might be spotted. We know these trails much better than they and can still make good time tonight when the moon is up. It will be dark very soon, Captain. Try to get some sleep. We will not be here long."

Although his wet clothes had still not thoroughly dried on his body, Bob, exhausted, dropped onto a damp but open patch of ground and, using his bent arm as a pillow, almost immediately sank into a deep sleep. When he was awakened, he had no idea how long he had slept, but his fatigue had been eased somewhat and his headache was gone. The moon was already up, and the occasional ray slanting through a hole in the jungle canopy above produced an eerie mottled effect on the forest floor. They set out again in single file with Bob following just behind the leader. In spite of the thick vegetation and almost pitch-darkness the pace was rapid, and not once did they wander from some path which would have been invisible to Bob.

Before long the jungle began to thin out, and apparently they would occasionally pass near settlements, for Bob could hear dogs barking. After about two hours they arrived at what appeared to be their destination, a small village located in a grove of trees on a hillside. Two of the men faded quietly away, presumably to rejoin their families, but the guide led Bob farther up the hill to a primitive hut with a thatched roof and sides made of corrugated tin.

"Captain, this is where you must stay. There is a bed inside. Do not come outside. The Japanese come through here almost every day. My name is Paolo Loro. I will be back in the morning."

"Paolo," Bob said, stooping to avoid hitting his head against the low pole across the top of the door, "how about returning my magazine? If the Japs stumble on me, I want to be able to welcome them hospitably."

Bob could not be certain in the dark but thought he saw the native smile.

"They will not come tonight. Do not worry about that. We will talk again when I come back. Good night, Captain."

Paolo closed the rickety slat door, and Bob heard a slight click. When he was certain that the man had gone, he tentatively tried the door and confirmed his suspicion: there was a padlock on the outside. In the pitch dark by feel he located the "bed," a pile of leaves and dried moss alongside the back wall, and stretched out as best he could. But sleep did not come easily in spite of his fatigue. The relief initially experienced at having survived first the bailing out and then the descent from his lofty perch was gradually being replaced by a growing anxiety. There were ominous signs that his situation was anything but secure, and troubled thoughts persisted. He heard two roosters prematurely heralding the dawn before he fitfully dozed off.

# CHAPTER SEVENTEEN

**BOB WAS AWAKENED** by the stifling heat inside the hut. The angled sun rays against the metal wall on the east side had turned the enclosure into an oven. He rattled the door twice, but it was too securely fastened to be budged. Between the slats he had a wide view of the open area in the middle of the village below and saw Paolo sitting on a bench in an apparently intense conversation with a middle-aged man with deeply lined face and white hair. In a moment Paolo with a nod of his head rose and disappeared into a shack nearby, emerging a few minutes later with a bottle and a plate, which he carried up the hill in Bob's direction.

"Captain," he called from outside the door, "I have brought you some water and food, but when I open the door you must not come out. Do you understand?"

"No, I don't understand. Damn it, man, I'm suffocating in here. It must be a hundred and twenty degrees," Bob protested. "I've got to come out."

"You do not understand. You can come out later but not now. If you do not give me your word, I cannot open the door."

"All right, blast it, I won't come out if you'll open the door wide to let some air in here and promise to give me some answers."

"I will tell you what I can," Paolo said, releasing the padlock and thrusting the plate of food and bottle of water inside the opened door.

"Move back and do not let yourself be visible," he added, taking a seat outside and leaning back against the door jamb.

Bob sank onto his mat and squeamishly examined the contents of the plate—a form of gruel made from millet or rice. He picked up the embedded bent spoon, determined that he could force down the tasteless concoction and proceeded to do so, albeit with total lack of enthusiasm. In between forced swallows he tried to elicit some information from Paolo.

"Listen, Paolo, I can't stay in this sweatbox. For one thing I badly need to go to a latrine."

"I know," the native answered, "but there are some things you must understand. The Japanese have patrols out searching for you. They will be through here every day. There is a reward for your capture. There are two men living in this village from a different tribe. They have worked with the Japanese, and we cannot trust them. Not even Calaban can control them."

"Who the hell is Calaban?"

"He is the chief of our tribe—a very smart man."

"Is he the man I saw you talking with a few minutes ago?"

"Yes. He has put me in charge of you, since I speak English. You must promise to do immediately everything I tell you to, or else you can bring us all much trouble and grief, if not death. Do you understand?"

"Not really," Bob answered, "but right now you're the only game in town. I'll have to go along with you. But how about returning my magazine?"

"Calaban has forbidden that. He is afraid that you might do something foolish. You must understand that this is a very dangerous situation for us. If the Japanese find out that we have been hiding you, they would kill everyone in our village. You should hand your pistol to me, Captain."

"I think I'll hang on to it as a souvenir," Bob said laconically, washing down the last bit of the gruel with a swallow of water from the bottle and sinking into solemn reflection. He had not had a good look at his native contact in broad daylight but was in no way disposed to trust him. Yet for the time being there was no alternative. There were no U.S. forces anywhere within hundreds of miles, and he could not on his own survive for long in the jungle.

"Paolo," he finally said, "if you help me get out of this, as soon as I am back with Americans I will give my gun to you as a present. Now when the hell can I go take a leak?"

"As soon as the two men have left the village. I will go check and come back. I will leave the door open if I can trust you."

"Paolo, for right now I am your man. I will give you advance warning when that is no longer the case."


**DAYS DRAGGED BY** with no change in the routine. Paolo was a paradox. He brought him food and water twice a day but would always secure the padlock at night. On the rare occasions when exercise was afforded by their taking a walk into the edge of the forest, the two of them together, Paolo invariably would carry along an ancient single-load rifle and never turn his back on his charge. And yet when the heat forced Bob to live in only his underwear, Paolo managed somehow to have his flight suit cleaned and ironed.

One night at the beginning of the third week Paolo announced that the two "exotribal" men had gone into Ormoc for two days and invited Bob to join him for a meal around a small fire. This was such a festive holiday for Bob that he even put on his pressed flight suit for the occasion. The only other persons around the fire that evening were the two men who had been with Paolo that first day. One was named Turo, and the other—the agile tree climber—was named Carlo. A frail, shadowy woman was serving them the food, consisting of a "*gabi*"—a yam-like tuber—and some kind of roasted meat that tasted like pork.

"*Mabuti*," Turo said.

"*Mabuti na mabuti*," Carlo agreed, nodding his head.

This was the first time Bob had heard in close proximity a word from either of the two men. He glanced at them and then at Paolo.

"What does '*mabuti*' mean?"

"It means 'good.'"

"Then what about '*mabuti na mabuti*'?"

"That means 'very good,'" Paolo answered, smacking his lips and licking his fingers. Bob continued to nibble on a shank of bone with some meat on it, and although it was admittedly better than the standard gruel and occasional piece of green fruit, he wasn't totally disposed to accept the natives' favorable assessment.

"What's the word for 'bad'?"

"*Masama*."

"Would I be right in assuming that '*masama na masama*' would be 'very bad?'" Bob grinned.

"Ah, very good, Captain," Paolo said. "You are beginning now to speak Bisayan."

"What the hell is Bisayan? I never heard of it before."

"It is the language of my people, and we are a mountain tribe. Bisayan is a dialect of Tagalog, which is spoken by many people here in the Philippines."

"Paolo, if you are a mountain man, where did you learn to speak English so well?"

The native picked up a piece of bone from the wooden platter on the ground in front of them and began to suck on it. "I went to Manila when I was young and worked for the Americans in a Navy supply depot there. When the Japanese came, they were shooting those who had worked for the Americans, so I came back here to my people."

In the flickering light from the small fire Bob watched as the man wiped his mouth on his sleeve and searched the platter for any other morsel that might have been overlooked. Daily contact had engendered a certain liking for his conditional benefactor, but Bob still did not trust him.

**TWO NIGHTS LATER** Bob awoke with a hard chill. His teeth were chattering uncontrollably, and he was shaking so violently that he had difficulty pulling on his flight suit to try to get warm. During the next few days the fever was unrelenting. In spite of the heat the chills would seize him periodically, and by the third day his temperature was so high that he would briefly slip into delirium. Paolo tried hard to be an effective nurse, insisting on liquid intake and bringing steamed palm hearts and an occasional egg, but Bob had difficulty getting food down and rapidly lost weight. The cause of the malady—bad water, bad food, or the thousands of suffered insect bites—was immaterial, for no medicines were available. On the third night Paolo did bring a bitter brew that had been made from roots and bark from a tree. Bob was induced to drink the foul-tasting potion, and within twelve hours, although it might have been coincidental, the fever began to subside, leaving him so weak he could barely rise.

The next afternoon a brief thunderstorm passed, and the reemerging sun brought the heat and humidity to oppressive levels. For some reason Paolo had closed and locked the door to the hut even though it was in the middle of the day. Bob was lying on his back on the mat, rocking his head from side to side and trying to get a breath of air. Hearing voices down the hill, he rolled onto his side and crawled to the door. If one of the speakers was Paolo, he was going to rap on the door and demand that it be opened. Through the slats he did see his caretaker sitting on the ground halfway down the hillside. Bob struggled to a sitting position and raised his fist to pound on the metal wall when he caught sight of four other men in the village "square." Three of them were squatting on their haunches. One was Calaban, another a Japanese officer and the third apparently an interpreter. The fourth, a Japanese soldier, was standing off to the side, cradling a rifle in his arms and intently scrutinizing the shacks in the village.

Bob leaned weakly against an upright support and watched the scene below. Apparently there was an intense conversation going on between the chief and the Japanese officer, each of whom would occasionally gesticulate and nod or shake his head as though bargaining. Bob noticed that Paolo, seated near enough to overhear the interchange, was pretending to be repairing a wicker carrying sling but was obviously listening. When the three men rose to their feet, the officer bowed to Calaban in a ritual salute and then turned and led his group out of the village.

Paolo brought to the hut soon afterwards a bottle of water and a murky broth and sat on the ground just outside. Contrary to his usual routine when restricted to the settlement, this time he brought his ancient firearm, which he kept beside him during the entire time the door was left open while Bob was slowly trying to ingest the nourishment.

"Paolo," Bob said after a moment, "what's going on?"

There was a moment of silence before there was a response.

"Captain Hanson, I think the Japanese are convinced that you are in this area. They are stepping up their search."

Bob put the cup of broth down and looked up.

"I've never told you my name. How did you find out?"

"The Japanese found the wreckage of your airplane," Paolo answered.

Bob was puzzled. He had refused to let Ricky stencil his name on the side of his latest F-4B. Then he realized that Nancy's letter must have survived the crash. He stared at the back of Paolo's head. He somehow sensed on the native's part a certain evasiveness that caused him concern.

"Look," he said, "in the last few weeks I believe we've become friends of a sort. In the name of that friendship why don't you level with me?"

Paolo was obviously uncomfortable and tried to ignore the question.

"Calaban is convinced that the Japanese will come back tomorrow and search the village. I will bring you some meat and *gabi* tonight, and you must try to eat it all and build up your strength. We will move you early in the morning and try to hide you. But it will be difficult, because the Japanese troops are very thorough. They will search the countryside all around."

Bob's uneasiness was in no way diminished by this exchange, but his head had begun to swim, so he crawled back to his pad and collapsed on his side.


AT THE CRACK of dawn the next morning the door was thrown open and Paolo entered with his two former colleagues. They helped get Bob to his feet and support him on the walk to the latrine in the woods. He had tried with great effort and some success to eat the food that had been brought the night before but was plagued now by nausea and abdominal cramps. Half-carrying him back to the village, they took him not to the corrugated metal cell but to one of a group of chicken pens, each covered with a vaulted thatched roof.

"Captain," Paolo said in response to Bob's quizzical stare, "the Japanese will search every building in town. We are hoping to be able to conceal you up under the roof of this larger pen.

"We have placed three boards across the horizontal supports, and there will be just enough room for you to be able to lie there out of sight. We have sentries posted. We will be back when it is time to lift you up. Until then, lie here and rest."

Bob sank limply onto the muddy ground. When the three men moved off, he tried to call out to Paolo to return, but a wave of nausea choked off his voice and he began to gag. As he lay there for almost an hour, he tried hard to suppress the effects of his physical malaise sufficiently to re-order his thoughts. He could not be certain that his debility and illness were not directly responsible for a growing, almost paranoid feeling that something inimical to his welfare was afoot, but by the time Paolo and Turo climbed back up the hill, he was fairly certain he knew what was going on.

"Captain, we must get you into your hiding place, where you must be very still and very quiet. A platoon of soldiers has left Kugara and is heading this way. They will be here soon."

Bob sat up unsteadily and clasped his knees with his arms for support.

"Paolo, I'm not going to move from this spot until you give me some straight answers."

"Please, Captain, we do not have time now. We can talk later."

"No, Paolo, I will not co-operate until you are honest with me. Calaban is selling me to the Japanese, isn't he?"

Paolo was apparently thrown off balance by this remark.

"You are wrong, Captain. Why do you think we are trying to hide you?"

"Because if the Japanese find me here, they will take me for free and probably execute all of you. Isn't that so? Calaban knew that the reward would keep going up, so he held me prisoner until the price was right. Why did he decide to move now? Why didn't he wait longer?"

Paolo was obviously distraught and looked about nervously. Then with an air of resignation he sank onto his haunches not far from Bob.

"All right, Captain, I will be honest with you. But do not think that Calaban is a bad man. He is a very good man. He had thought to keep hiding you, but that will no longer be possible. The Japanese are landing many troops at Ormoc, and soon there will be thousands of them in this area. If it is certain that they will capture you, it will be safer for you that it will be done peacefully. And Calaban reasons that if you are going to have to be a Japanese prisoner, why should his people not get some help that they need so bad. We need to buy food and clothes for our children; we need medicines and tools and almost everything. Calaban's father and grandfathers before him were chiefs when the Spaniards were here and then the Americans. They always thought first of their own people. Calaban is like them; he is only doing the same."

Paolo jumped to his feet.

"But please, we must hurry. Let us help you to climb up to your hiding place. They will be here soon."

"Why should I go to that trouble? What do I have to gain? Why should I not just let them take me here?"

Paolo knelt in front of Bob with a look of desperation on his face.

"Please, Captain. I was honest with you. If you tell them we have been hiding you, all my people—my parents, my wife, my two little babies—could be shot. Calaban told the officer that he is pretty sure he knows where you are. Not here, but up in the mountains. He is to agree today with the Japanese where and when the transfer will be made—you for the money. It will probably be in the mountains in order to protect the village, and it could be two or three days away. Please, Captain, do not cause the death of our children."

Bob was silent for a moment and then struggled to stand up. With the help of the two men he crawled through the narrow door of the chicken coop and with great difficulty climbed on top of the rickety boards. Immediately he was almost overcome by the powerful stench under the hot roof, where the gases from the chicken excrement accumulated and where mites and lice were  clinging to the supports and crawling on every frond. Paolo's appeal was only one factor in determining Bob's decision to comply. If an extra two days were to be available, there would be at least some chance that he might be able to attempt an escape.

He felt that he should be able to break through the thatch roof of his prison and make it into the jungle if only the extra time could grant him a little more strength.

The barking of dogs at the edge of the village led him to believe that the Japanese were approaching. By thrusting the blade of his hand through the fronds of the roof he was able to make an opening through which he, although lying on his side, could view the place where Calaban and four of the tribe's elders were seated awaiting the visitors. He saw Paolo move down the hillside and take up the same position as on the preceding day.

When the Japanese approached, it was obvious they had come in strength with almost a full platoon. The soldiers fanned out and ringed the central circle while the same officer and interpreter as before approached Calaban and took seats in two chairs that had been placed for their benefit. Calaban motioned to some women standing in the doorway of the town's main building, and they came forward with platters of fruit and seven cups containing a liquid. The voices during this ceremony were too low for Bob to hear, especially above the almost incessant clucking and scratching of the fowl in the coop.

Bob was seized by a wave of nausea and began to retch, and it was only with a massive exercise of will that he was able to control the spasm. When he had regained enough composure to peer through the slit again, he saw a young native run into the village, slow to a walk and then climb the slope to squat by Paolo. An animated exchange apparently ensued, and then Paolo rose, approached and knelt behind Calaban, whispering in his ear. There was an impression of general confusion, Calaban said something to the Japanese officer and then summoned the elders to follow him into the main building. Paolo picked up from beside the building a portable cage made from bamboo and climbed slowly and nonchalantly up the hill to the chicken coop. Squatting by the door and pretending to be selecting one of the fowls, he spoke in a very low voice.

"Captain, we have just received news that American troops have landed on Leyte two days ago. There is a beachhead on the eastern coast, and they are advancing inland."

Bob's elation at this news was tempered only by his deplorable physical state and the knowledge that almost insuperable obstacles existed to his being rescued.

"Paolo, what's going to happen now? What's going on down there?"

"I don't know, Captain. I must go now. I'll try to find out."

Before Paolo had descended the hill halfway, Calaban and the elders emerged and approached the seated officer. After the interpreter had communicated to him a statement by the chief, the officer rose abruptly and threw his chair to the side. Turning, he barked a brusque command to his soldiers, who dispersed at a trot throughout the village. They entered and searched every structure in town, by force if necessary. Bob saw a soldier take the butt of his rifle, smash the padlock on his former cell door and enter. While this search of the village was going on, the natives were herded together in the square. The report of a rifle shot gave Bob concern that a massacre might ensue, but the scream of a wounded animal let him know that one of the village dogs had paid a heavy price for trying to defend a household.

Bob was startled by the sound of two enemy voices within a few feet of his precarious perch and heard the cage door just below him being opened and the cackling and scuffling of the chickens below. A cloud of dust and feathers accompanied the seizing by the soldiers of their booty, and, combined with the heat and stench, induced in him an almost uncontrollable wave of nausea. Only willpower aided him in suppressing temporarily a spasm of regurgitation that would have immediately betrayed his presence. This control finally broke down, and he began to gag, but by then the soldiers were carrying the cage with their loot down the hillside, and the attendant noise masked that of Bob's retching.

He lost track of time. He must have passed out, for it seemed only a few minutes before he felt his foot being shaken and heard Paolo's voice.

"Captain, they have gone. You can come down now. Here, let me help you."

Bob was helped back to his mat in the hut and sank weakly onto the straw after having removed his filthy flight suit, which Paolo took to have cleaned again. He returned a little later with a wash cloth, pan of water and a bit of broth and bread.

"Captain, you must try to eat and gain some strength. Calaban says you cannot stay here. He told the Japanese that you had escaped up in the mountains, but he is sure they will be back soon. He has ordered that Carlo and I are to take you across the mountain tomorrow and try to get you in touch with American troops. We must leave before dawn, so try to eat and rest."

Bob had managed to sit up and clean his face and hands, but it required great effort to swallow the food and keep it down.

"Paolo, why did Calaban change his mind? I don't understand why he didn't take the money. Or is this just a ruse, and you still plan to hand me over to the Japanese tomorrow?"

Bob immediately regretted this statement, for the look of hurt on Paolo's face was too graphic to have been feigned and had to be real.

"Captain, I am not lying to you. I have told you that Calaban is a good man. He hopes that by getting you back to your people, when the Americans come they will help his people. He has risked much to protect you."


IT WAS STILL dark when Bob was awakened, helped into his clothes and shoes and encouraged to eat a boiled duck egg and a cup of gruel. Before exiting the hut he retrieved the .45 Colt he had buried under the straw of his mat and brushed off as much of the dirt as he could. As he was unbuttoning the leg flap of his suit, he felt a nudge as Paolo handed him the magazine.

"I hope this will not have to be used today," Paolo said, "but the Japanese are moving up very many troops, and there will be a lot of patrols."

Carlo came hurrying up from the square below and spoke briefly to Paolo in Bisayan.

"Come," the latter said urgently, picking up his ancient rifle, "we must leave immediately. There is a platoon moving up the road toward the village."

When they reached the edge of the forest, the three men set out in single file with Paolo in the lead, picking his way along hunting trails he had known as a boy. The going would have been difficult under any circumstances, but for Bob it was tortuous. The way soon led up steep slopes through jungle underbrush, and, once the sun rose fairly high, the heat and humidity became intense. Weak and debilitated, he stumbled along as best he could behind Paolo but frequently fell and had to be helped to his feet by Carlo, who was bringing up the rear. Paolo would leave them periodically and scout ahead, granting welcome respite to Bob, who would lie on his back gasping for air and fighting dizziness, and there were occasional protracted periods of delay caused by the proximity of enemy troops. As they neared the crest of the mountain ridge in late afternoon, Paolo had to resort to a remote, very steep trail, which Bob was simply too weak to negotiate. With barely a pause in their progress Carlo took him onto his own back and inched his way up the difficult slope in spite of the fact that the wiry little man weighed probably twenty pounds less than his burden.

Just over the crest of the ridge Paolo found a fairly concealed spot under a ledge and instructed the other two to remain there while he reconnoitered the area below, a section of the forest unfamiliar to him. It was almost dark when he returned an hour later to advise that they remain there until morning. The Japanese were bringing up artillery across the passes, and there were many infantrymen preceding the big guns and fanning out across the slopes. When the wind would shift and occasionally blow out of the east, the distant rumble of artillery duels and probable U.S. naval gunfire could be heard.

A temporary camp was set up behind the trunk of a large fallen tree to one side of the ledge, and Paolo doled out to each a meager portion of cold yams, nuts and hard bread. As Bob was chewing thoroughly on his share preparatory to trying to swallow it, in the dim light he noticed Carlo's eyes fixed on him. When Paolo leaned back against the old trunk, he also noticed this scrutiny. Carlo glanced at him and then nodded his head at Bob.

"*Paláran*," he said barely audibly.

"*Paláran*," Paolo repeated, smiling and nodding his head affirmatively.

When night had fallen and each was lying on a crude mat fashioned of fronds and leaves, Bob whispered into the darkness, "Paolo . . ."

"Yes, Captain?"

"What does '*paláran*' mean?"

"*Buláhan*," Paolo replied sleepily.

"Of course," Bob retorted half-sarcastically, "why didn't I think of that?"

"I'm sorry; I forgot," Paolo said with a soft laugh. "They mean 'fortunate.' Carlo says you are a lucky man, and I have to agree with him. Now try to get some sleep, Captain. Tomorrow will be a difficult day. We will have to move fast, and you must be able to keep up."


**THE NEXT DAY** was indeed a trying one, physically and emotionally. Having started their descent before dawn, they would rapidly cover as much ground as they could and then lie motionless in vines and weeds for extended periods during the passage of enemy troops, sometimes so close that Bob could hear a belch or a cough. As the day wore on, increasingly audible were the sounds of mortars and even small-arms fire. In mid-afternoon Paolo returned from one of his extended reconnaissance sorties and announced that the Japanese, in anticipation of an American infantry assault, had dug in defensively on a ridge below them. The only possible passage for them would be down a steep ravine cut by a waterfall, a route so difficult that the Japanese had not bothered to cover it defensively.

"Captain, I know that you are tired and very weak, but I'm afraid we must move immediately. We cannot wait. I'm sorry we didn't bring ropes, but we will have to do the best we can."

Bob raised his head and looked wearily at the earnest face above him.

"Paolo, I can't ask you and Carlo to go on any farther. It is much too dangerous now. Accept my thanks and go back to your families. Tell me how to get to the ravine, and I will go on alone. One person may have a better chance anyway."

"No, Captain, we cannot allow that. We will try to get you close to the American lines and then go back. From now on we must not talk, even in whispers. Now come. Let's go."

The next hour passed in a haze to Bob. He stumbled along with his eyes fixed on the feet of Paolo in front of him. He looked neither left nor right, trusting implicitly in his guide.

Fortunately no enemy troops crossed their path and they were able to move along steadily. The descent down the precipitous wall of the ravine close by the waterfall was a harrowing experience Several times Bob would have plunged to almost certain death had it not been for the solicitous aid of the two natives. Once at the bottom, Paolo refused to allow even a minute of needed rest and insisted that they follow the stream bed and push on for another two miles across this no-man's-land lying between the opposing forces. Finally he signaled a halt and approached a jumble of limbs and brush that had been piled up by previous flood waters. Within a few minutes he had hollowed out a small chamber and stepped back to survey his handiwork.

"Here, Captain, crawl in there, and we'll cover up the entrance. Stay there until you are sure your people have come. This is where we will leave you and go back. Come quickly, for Carlo and I must reach the top of the ridge before it gets dark."

Bob was in a way unprepared for the suddenness of their separation. Silently he shook hands with both men and started to crawl into the narrow opening. Then he paused, unsnapped the leg pouch on his suit and, having extracted his .45 automatic, laid it on the ground.

"Here, Paolo," he said, "this is a very small reward for all you have done for me; but I want you to have it."

Paolo hesitated briefly and then with a wide grin handed his antique firearm to Carlo and picked up the pistol. Bob pulled himself into the hollow, watched as they piled a light layer of branches across the opening and then heard their receding footsteps. Through the heavy veil of his fatigue there intruded a mixture of relief and loneliness. After darkness fell, he tried to sleep, but it proved impossible. Discomfort caused by the rounded, water-washed stones that served as a floor to his cave was acute, and there was a constant assault by crawling insects with painful bites. Daylight had again been showing for perhaps an hour through small chinks in his makeshift abode when he heard indistinct voices in the distance. At first he was afraid that a Japanese patrol might have followed their footprints in the soft loam along the stream bank but then realized that it was definitely English being spoken. Anxious that the soldiers not pass him by, he summoned all his strength and called out while beginning to push out the branches blocking his exit.

"What the shit was that?" he heard one of the soldiers ask.

"Damn if I know," answered another, "but it came from over there by that pile of wood."

"I'll cover you. Toss a grenade over there," came a third voice.

"No, wait! I'm an American," Bob shouted as loudly as he could.

"Hey, you hear that? It's a Yank."

"Don't fall for that old trick. We're the only patrol in this area. You'd better blow that bastard outta there."

"Damn it, I'm an American!" Bob repeated, pushing the last of the wood and leaves out of the way. "For God's sake, come and see for yourself."

"Ya better stay down, Cooper. They pull that all the time. Hey, Sarge, what should we do? We got a Jap over here claimin' he's an American."

The sergeant's answer came from farther off to the left.

"Check him out, Dubinsky, but be careful."

In a moment a different voice sounded closer by.

"Okay, Tojo, if you're American, who pitched the winning game for the Yankees in '40?"

"Dubinsky, you jackass," Bob replied with frustration, "I don't follow baseball. I'll come out with my hands up, and you can see I'm American."

"Cooper. I tell ya that's gotta be a Jap. Toss a coupla grenades over there."

"Take it easy," came the sergeant's voice, a little closer this time. "Let's be sure we know what we're doing. Hey, fellow, what's your outfit?"

"I'm an Army pilot. I was shot down a month ago."

"Where are you from in the States?"

"Lexington, Kentucky."

"Hey, Frank, tell Palmer to come up here on the double."

There was a short pause accompanied by the sound of a soldier moving up at a run.

"Palmer, this bird claims he's from Kentucky. You're from Kentucky. See what you think."

"Hey, mister," Palmer shouted. "I'm from the big city of Bethel. You know where that is?"

"I sure do," Bob answered. "It's up near Moorefield and Sharpsburg. There's good fishing up that way."

"Hey, this guy's legit," Palmer said. "We ain't never had no Jap up that way."

"Okay, birdman," came the sergeant's voice, "come out with your hands reaching for the sky and stand in that clearing by the water, facing the other way."

Bob staggered away from the blind and stood with his arms over his head. Gaunt, dirty and with a five-day beard, he realized that he looked like anything but a commissioned pilot.

"You got any friends in there?"

"No, Sergeant, I'm all alone."

Bob was startled by a sustained burst of automatic fire as his former refuge was riddled.

"Well, if you weren't before, you are now. Now turn around and walk slowly in this direction."

As Bob complied, he tried in vain to spot the men of the patrol, but his vision began to blur and his head to swim.

"Catch him!" barked the sergeant as Bob sank to his knees.

Two figures leaped from behind clumps of vegetation and seized him by the arms to keep him from falling. The sergeant materialized from behind the trunk of a large tree and walked up, saluting.

"I'm sorry if we were rude, Captain, but we don't run into a lot of officers strolling around out here."

"That's all right, Sergeant," Bob replied, beginning to recover from his dizziness. "I'm so glad to see you characters, you can go right on being rude."

"Sir, if you were shot down a month ago, how have you managed to survive out here?"

"I hid in a village on the western side of the mountain. I came over last night."

"You mean you came through the enemy lines?"

"That's right. There's a waterfall near the headwaters of this stream, and the terrain is so steep that the Japanese have left it very lightly defended. They're bringing up a lot of artillery over the pass just to the south of here and are probably expecting a frontal assault. If you have a real good team with mountain training, I'm sure you could scale this ravine and outflank the enemy gun positions."

The sergeant squatted on his haunches and was thoughtful for a moment.

"Thank you, Captain. That may be helpful. Cooper, you and Palmer were in on the patrol briefing and know the way. Take the captain back to Company headquarters and report the information he just gave us. We'll continue on to the base of the gorge and be back by sixteen hundred hours."

"Gotcha, Sarge," Cooper said. "Come on, Captain, let us give you a hand. Do you think you can make it?"

"Yeah, I'll be okay if you don't go too fast. I'd be willing to crawl on my knees if I had to. What's your outfit?"

"The best, sir—Tenth Corps of the Sixth Army."

\* \* \*

**IN HIS EUPHORIA** at being with Americans again Bob's appraisal of his own strength to be able to get back behind U.S. lines under his own power proved to be overly optimistic. For the final two miles he had to be half-carried with an arm draped over Cooper's and Palmer's shoulders. From advance company headquarters he was dispatched by litter-bearers down the tortuous trails toward the coast for transfer to a hospital ship off shore This transfer, however, was delayed for several days.

The American attack had been massive. Over seven hundred ships supported the two amphibious forces of the 10th Corps and the 24th Corps of the U.S. Sixth Army. To counter these American landings on Leyte the Japanese had launched Operation *Ta*, pouring thousands of troops onto the island through Ormoc, and during the last week of October four enemy naval forces—from the Philippines, Borneo, Taiwan and Japan—had converged to clash with the American Second and Seventh Fleets in one of the greatest sea engagements ever fought—the Battle of Leyte Gulf. Involved in this epic struggle were one hundred sixty-six American versus seventy Japanese warships and 1,280 American versus 716 Japanese aircraft.

During these days Bob was confined to a stretcher in a field hospital in a rear staging area near the coast. From his cot, day and night, he could hear the unceasing distant thunder of the huge battle taking place out in the Gulf. Since evacuation had been curtailed and the medical corpsmen were severely taxed to handle the ever-increasing number of wounded infantrymen under their care, scant attention could be paid to him, since his malady—although mysterious—was not critical. He was given intestinal emollients for his nausea and frequent doses of Atabrine for his fever but little else except for whatever nourishment he could tolerate. He did not find this relative neglect objectionable, for in spite of the depressing nature of his surroundings he now experienced, in contrast with the preceding weeks, a sense of almost fetal security and was content to lie there, suffering through the violent chills and slipping in and out of a somnolent state.

* * *

**A THREE-WEEK STAY** in an Army hospital in Australia did much to restore Bob's strength and health. The intestinal malaise was effectively cured, and the Atabrine in combination with other medications largely eliminated the severity and frequency of the chills. However, there was a recurrent low-grade fever that persisted in spite of treatment.

At the end of the third week Bob was visited in the hospital by the Adjutant from the Fifth Air Force Base Headquarters.

"Captain, I came over to visit a friend of mine and thought I'd drop by to see you. We've had some inquiries on your behalf at Headquarters. All of your gear and belongings are being sent here from Guadalcanal. Your outfit is being transferred out of Henderson, so you won't be going back there. But there's a problem with your re-joining the Eighth Photo Recon. The doc here doubts that you can be cleared for flight duty again anytime soon. I've discussed your case with Colonel Brattle, and there are two possibilities. You can be rotated on a medical disability voucher back to the States, or we've got a job you could fill with us in the Fifth. We're going full bore in the Philippines now and need good intelligence work. Although you're not technically trained in intelligence, you've had a lot of experience at photo interpretation. We're developing Tacloban Airfield on Leyte into a forward bomber base, but we'll also have some fighters assigned there for cover and a couple of recon aircraft. Although you won't be flying, we could use you as a kind of liaison with G-2. You're being discharged from the hospital in three days, so you've got a little time to think it over. Will you drop in to see me on Thursday?"

"There's no need for that," Bob replied immediately. "As long as I can help at all, I'd like to do whatever I can. I feel I should do something to pay Uncle Sam back for that aircraft I lost, anyway. I'll take any assignment you've got for me, sir."

**ON DECEMBER 5** Bob landed at Tacloban Airfield, which was already fully operational even though the occupation of Leyte had not been completed. Fighter and light bomber sorties were dispatched daily to support ground troops and harass enemy supply lines. On December 14

Bob was on his way down the ramp to attend debriefing of pilots having participated in an attack on Mactau when he saw a new squadron of P-47's peeling off for landing. He knew they were scheduled to come in to help provide air cover for the invasion of Mindoro, which was to be launched on the fifteenth. At the evening briefing for these fighter pilots Bob was certain he recognized one of them and went up to him after they had been dismissed.

"Aren't you Fred Booker?" he asked.

"Yes, sir, I am. Say, didn't I meet you over a year ago at a field in the Russells during the Munda campaign?"

"That's right. I took your place on the morning mission because you were sick."

"Now I remember you. You're the only fellow I ever heard Bill Harwood brag about. On a couple of occasions he even hinted you might be as good a pilot as he was. And he was the best."

"I read that Bill was lost in November of last year, but I don't know any of the details and have heard nothing since. Were you with him?"

"Yes, I was. It was just a damn fluke!"

"Tell me about it."

"We were flying out of a field on the Kunai Peninsula and had taken part in a heavy raid on Wewak. On the way back we were at four thousand feet above a light undercast about even with Boram when an anti-aircraft battery opened up on us. I don't know how they could direct their fire, for we were above the clouds. Bill made a single transmission. He said: 'Fred, I'm hit.' That's all he said. I saw his plane go into a left turn and then spiral down through the undercast. I followed him down, calling him several times on the frequency, but he never answered. I lost contact below the clouds and circled several times but never saw a trace of him. It was just damn, rotten luck!"

"I've always wondered what happened," Bob said pensively. "That doesn't help me a lot, but thanks for the information anyway. How long have you been in the P-47?"

"About five months now."

"Do you like it?"

"For ground support it can't be beat. But everything's a trade-off. In many ways I miss the old P-40."

"Well, it was good seeing you again," Bob said, holding out his hand. "Good luck tomorrow."

**AMERICAN FORCES CONTINUED** to increase pressure on the Japanese throughout the Philippines. On December 16 Ormoc was captured, on the nineteenth there was a heavy attack on the Leguspi airdrome on Luzon, and on the twentieth Seventh Air Force B24's flying all the way from Anguara attacked Cebu as the last enemy resistance was being mopped up on Leyte.

Bob had been pestering the base Quartermaster Corps officer for over a week and on the twenty-fourth set out on a narrow, treacherous road across the mountains in a requisitioned Jeep loaded down with cartons and canisters of everything he could scrounge—food, medicines, tools, blankets, clothing and (even though it was strictly against regulations) several confiscated Japanese firearms with considerable ammunition. The map he had at his disposal was not too accurate. It took him all day to locate Calaban's village, but a little before dark he pulled up in front of the municipal building. At first he thought the settlement was deserted and feared the Japanese may have resorted to revenge, but then he saw the face of a child peeking out from behind a door. Bob got out to stretch his legs and motioned for the little boy to come out. Before he knew it, he and the Jeep were surrounded by a crowd of curious townspeople, who had emerged from God-knows-where.

He spent all of Christmas Day with these people he had come to regard as his friends. His reunion with Paolo and Carlo was boisterous and moving, at least for him. He had not fully anticipated the depth of pleasure he would experience in distributing the supplies and provisions he had brought and in vain tried to dissuade Calaban from ordering a feast in his honor for later in the day. The chief placed Bob on his right, and he in his turn insisted that Paolo and Carlo take the next two places after his. Tension was obvious when Bob inquired whether the two collaborators from the different tribe were still in the village. At first Paolo tried to be evasive but finally relented in the face of Bob's persistence and confessed that they indeed were but were not at the gathering. Bob insisted that they be summoned and invited to join in, and when the two men arrived and timidly and uncertainly seated themselves at the banquet, there was a spontaneous release of laughter and good will.

Early the next morning after a ceremonial visit to his former cell and a fond farewell with Paolo, Bob left in the Jeep for the drive back to Tacloban. Now that he knew the way, less time was required for the return trip, and he arrived back at the base at mid-afternoon. Although the return had been shorter, he felt a heavy fatigue. The trip had been far more emotionally trying than he had anticipated, and he sensed the on-set of the recurrent fever. He had been absent for over forty-eight hours, so he stopped by intelligence headquarters to catch up on the two days' military action. Having covered the main paragraphs, he was about to leave when he saw an appended item: a translated letter written by an unknown Japanese soldier on December 21 and found by men of the U.S. 32nd Division.

"I am exhausted. We have no food. The enemy are now within 500 meters of us. Mother, my dear wife and son, I am writing this letter to you by dim candlelight. Our end is near . . ."

Bob walked slowly back to his quarters. Mechanically he tossed his helmet into the corner and sat down on his bed. For a long time he stared at the floor in front of him. Then he bent over, placed his face in his hands and began to weep. He was crying for this unknown infantryman, for this mother and wife and son, for the nameless soldier on the airfield at Munda, for Bill and for Lori, for the dead and dying on battlefields throughout the world. He was weeping for all of tortured mankind.

## CHAPTER EIGHTEEN

**BY JANUARY 9** there was already fighting on Luzon. On the 23rd there began repeated attacks on Corregidor, the guardian fortress of Manila Bay, carried out by aircraft from the Fifth and 13th Air Forces and also from the 7th, which was operating out of the Palaus. A month later over two thousand paratroopers of the 503rd Airborne Division jumped onto the tiny island, and by February 27 all organized resistance ended.

Bob was unable to participate in or follow the subsequent thrusts of American military power toward the north. Throughout January and February the recurrences of the fever had become gradually more frequent and more severe, so that by March 1 he was no longer able to carry out his duties effectively. He had no inclination to object to orders he received on the tenth directing his return to the United States for medical care.

So far as Bob knew, the exact nature of his illness was never definitely determined, but after seven weeks' treatment at Walter Reed Hospital he apparently was fully cured, for the symptoms finally ceased and did not reappear. In spite of a natural elation at being back in the States, he was burdened throughout this period by a tendency to lapse occasionally into a mild despondency. Although his mood was buoyed by the surrender of Axis forces in Europe, by conditioning his thoughts were directed to the Pacific, and he knew the horror of the death and suffering that lay behind the cryptic newspaper accounts of the terrible battles for Iwo Jima and Okinawa.

His spirits were lifted, however, by approval of his request for return to flying status. On his release from the hospital on May 1 he was granted a ten-day furlough and received orders to report thereafter to the 249th Air Force Base Unit of the 2nd Air Force at La Junta, Colorado, to serve as one of the instructors for a group of new fighter pilots. They were to be thoroughly trained on a compressed priority schedule for very long range missions, and Bob was certain that they were to be prepared to fly out of Okinawa to cover the invasion of the Japanese home islands.

His parents had been to Washington several times to visit him in the hospital, so by the time he arrived home on leave they had adjusted to his being back and the reception was not as charged and frenetic as it had been in the past. This, and the fact that his next assignment was not overseas, afforded him the luxury of a leisurely, relaxed furlough. The farm had changed so much in those three years that identification with the memories of his childhood was impaired, but he spent many pleasant hours going over with his father the extensive plans already being drawn up for after the war. He talked to Nancy three times by telephone. Since she was preparing for final examinations and graduation and his days at home were so limited, there was no consideration of his going over to Charlottesville to visit.

"Son," his father said at dinner on the night before his departure, "you told me the other day that you're pretty sure this group in La Junta is destined for Okinawa. Does that mean you'll be going with them?"

"No, sir," Bob answered. "At the present time I am assigned only as an instructor. I am not officially a member of their unit."

"Thank God!" his mother said with a deep sigh. "It has taken a long time, but at last my prayers have been answered."


**BOB WAS ELATED** to be back flying again, and La Junta was a very pleasant community in which to be based, but he fretted over the young recently graduated pilots under his charge. Given their limited experience they could fly the airplanes reasonably well but lacked the sharpness of judgment and skills they would need to survive in combat. With only eight weeks in which to prepare them he was constantly trying to devise ways to improve their performance. It required persistent pestering of the CO and training staff officer to gain some easing and flexibility in the normally rigid training rules and regulations. He finally gained permission for his own group always to take off in formation.

"Look, that's what they're going to do over there," he had argued. "Why wait until they have the stress of a real mission coming up and have five-hundred-pound bombs strapped under each wing?"

He also abandoned the usual scheduling of simulated aerial combat on one day and practice on the bombing range the next. He arranged to have "enemy" fighters "bounce" his students as soon as they were departing the range so that they would learn to adjust immediately to a likely real-life scenario.

With their long range auxiliary fuel tanks the late-model P-47N's were capable of flying long hours without refueling, and part of the training program was designed to condition the young pilots to these extended missions. Frequently the training flights would depart at dawn and fly east to Missouri, south to Arkansas, west to Texas and then back north, arriving at home base over seven hours later. Bob would be amused at the occasional inability of the trainees to exit their cockpits without the aid of the crew chiefs and tried to instruct them in exercises he had devised to relieve cramped fatigue during his long flights in the Pacific.

Noticing that the formations would be getting sloppy near the end of these grueling flights, he exercised a little diplomacy and arranged with the training officer at the P-38 training base in Colorado Springs for some of their instructors to pounce on the P-47 formations as they made their turn at Pueblo for the last leg back to La Junta. Bob's suspicion was right. Dulled by fatigue from seven continuous hours in flight and achingly looking forward to the end of the mission, his pilots had lost all attentiveness and alertness. Not a single one noticed the four P-38's coming at them from out of the sun.

"Knuckleheads!" Bob shouted over the radio frequency. "Bandits at six o'clock high! Scramble!"

Precious seconds were lost during the subsequent confusion and disarray following this transmission, and all the training directives were forgotten as the weary pilots scattered in all directions. During the subsequent debriefing of the mission Bob made the exhausted lieutenants stand at attention for a longer than usual time.

"Gentlemen," he said, "I hope you realize that in a real-life replay we would be lucky if even two of you would be alive to be standing here. Harrison, what were you doing in that medium left turn—trying to frighten the enemy pilot by showing that you were crazy? You know this airplane by now. What can it do better than any other?"

"Dive, sir."

"That's right. Point the nose of this flying safe toward the ground and it can outrun anything. That's probably why they call it the 'Thunderbolt.' Now, how many of you went to water-injection?"

Not a single one of them raised his hand.

"All right, gentlemen," Bob said with a sigh, "I want all of you here on the flight-line at five hundred hours tomorrow."

As the weeks passed, gradually he was able to whip them into reasonably good shape. It was a closed circle: the better they became, the more confidence they acquired; the more confident they felt, the better their performance. But he began to fret over them as a mother hen over her brood, and as the date for their combat assignment approached, he had made a decision. After returning from a training mission on Monday, August 6, he requested an appointment with the commanding officer.

"Sir, I'm feeling pretty good about the pilots in my charge. I think they can cut the mustard now. They're a good bunch of kids, but I'm nagged by a feeling that they might backslide if I'm not there to ride their asses all the time. I understand they'll join the 55th Fighter Group of the Fifth Air Force. I wonder if you could get me assigned to go along with them? I started in the southern Pacific; I might as well end up in the northern Pacific."

Colonel Braxton pursed his lips and looked at Bob for a moment.

"Captain, I could get you assigned, all right; there would be no problem. But there's a good chance they'll just be stuck with occupation duty. I don't think that's what you have in mind, is it?"

"I don't understand, sir."

"Have you seen the newspaper today?"

"No, sir."

The colonel opened a paper and tossed it on the desk in front of Bob. There were four-inch headlines: U.S. DROPS ATOMIC BOMB ON JAPAN.

"I still don't understand, sir. What's an atomic bomb?"

"Apparently it's something revolutionary—some kind of new weapon. I talked to Washington today. They think it's going to end the war. Don't you think we'd better hold off on your request until the dust settles? This whole thing could be over in a matter of weeks."

"Yes, sir. I guess that would be a good idea."

The colonel was right. On September 2 Japan surrendered unconditionally. On the field pending overseas assignment orders were put on hold, and training programs were curtailed. Authorization was granted to pilots only for flights to satisfy the monthly minimum number of hours to qualify for flying pay. Bob replied negatively to an official questionnaire asking if he would consider remaining in the Air Corps with a promotion in grade. Instead he asked for immediate relief from duty, and after three and a half years on October 16 he received the following orders:

```
                    RESTRICTED              ROI/v/LP
SPECIAL ORDERS )                        HEADQUARTERS
            :                    LA JUNTA ARMY AIR FIELD
NUMBER 99   )              EXTRACT LA JUNTA, COLORADO
                                           16 Oct 1945
1. The fol-named Offs, Sq as indicated, 249th AAF BU this sta are
reld fr asgmt & dy this Hq O/a 19 Oct 45 & WP home: Addresses as
indicated via AAF Separation Base, Lowry Fld, Denver Cob rptg on
20 Oct 45 for TDY as required for processing & separation fr the
sv under the provisions of RR 1-5. CO Separation Base, will issue
orders specifying amount of terminal lv, date of release fr separa-
tion base and date off reverts to inactive status. Terminal lv & WD
AGO Form 53-98 auth.
```

\* \* \*

**ON THURSDAY THE** eighteenth, Bob checked out a brand new P-47N for four hours and all alone headed west toward the mountains. It was a beautiful crystal-clear day and visibility was so superb that the peaks, capped by early snow, stood out brilliantly from over a hundred miles away. He roamed up and down the range, turning in lazy circles around many of the fourteen-thousand-foot summits along the Continental Divide and then wandered south, moved by the beauty around him and the upwelling of sheer exuberance at flying— a joy he had not experienced for many long months. With the elan of the neophyte of years ago he dove into the western end of the Royal Gorge and roared eastward only a few feet from the towering rock walls. When the frail suspension bridge across the Gorge came into view he momentarily considered passing underneath it but feared that there might be invisible stabilizing cables below. Coming back on the stick, he roared over the top of the bridge while executing a leisurely slow-roll and then headed northeast for La Junta, climbing to fourteen thousand feet.

As he passed south of Colorado Springs, he spotted the two P-38's when they were mere specks several thousand feet above and behind him and kept a casual eye on them as he started a gradual descent. Abeam of Pueblo he grinned as his private prediction came true and they peeled off to make a friendly pass at him. As they came within normal firing range, Bob rolled inverted and executed a "split-S," reversing direction. As he anticipated, the P-38's followed suit, so he immediately performed the maneuver again. Although he had increased the intervening distance, he was familiar enough with the P-38 to know that he would not be able to outrun or out-turn them. He was less than three thousand feet above ground level by now, so he correctly assumed they would be reluctant to follow him through another "split-S." As he rolled again to the left and glanced back out of his bubble canopy, he saw the flight leader start into a left "wing-over" to reverse direction more safely. Bob continued his roll past two hundred seventy degrees and pulled into a tight right turn, rolling out on a westward heading behind the twin-boom fighters and turning on his gunsight and camera switch. He fed in full power and went to water-injection, rapidly closing the distance between them. The other pilots had lost sight of him and were apparently scanning the deck below. Bob alternately centered each fighter in his gunsight and squeezed the camera trigger on his control stick. As he eased up beside the P-38's, he grinningly saluted the startled pilots, reduced power and then broke sharply away to the left. As he entered the traffic pattern at La Junta a few minutes later, he was smugly certain that if there was film in his cameras it would record that on this, his last, final, farewell flight he had scored two "kills."

**ON THE NINETEENTH** Bob checked into the Brown Palace Hotel in Denver. It was a crisp, cool evening, and after dinner he decided to walk around town for a while before turning in. For almost an hour he enjoyed looking in the store windows, savoring every moment of the delicious luxury of contemplating a return to civilian life. On his way back to the Brown Palace he had paused for a traffic light at an intersection in front of the Cosmopolitan Hotel when he heard a voice behind him.

"Captain Hanson!"

When he turned, he saw three men standing under the street light, one of whom looked familiar. As the man walked toward him and saluted, he recognized him even though he was in civilian clothes.

"Well, I'll be damned! Sergeant Vasquez!" Bob exclaimed, returning the salute. "I can't believe I've run into you again. Why, it's been a long time since that dark day on Pelelieu."

"Yes, sir. Over a year now. I heard you take off that morning and was glad you made it. Since you're here, I guess everything went okay."

"Well, things kind of fell apart later that day, but at least I survived. How about you? You look well. Are you on leave?"

"No, sir, I'm a civilian now. I received a medical discharge two months ago, and I'm looking for a job here in Denver."

"Medical discharge? What happened?"

"I was wounded on Iwo Jima. I had planned to stay in the Marines, but they won't take me now. I have a piece of steel lodged near my heart, and the doctors said it's best to leave it there and not mess with it. But it doesn't bother me. I feel okay. In fact I'm getting married tomorrow."

"Married? You?"

"Yes, sir," Vasquez grinned. "That's why we're celebrating. Captain, these are my friends, Pedro Delgado and Juan Chavez. Amigos, this is Air Force Captain Robert Hanson."

"I'm glad to meet you," Bob said and held out his hand. The two other men stepped forward hesitantly and shyly shook his hand.

"Well, congratulations, Sergeant," Bob said, turning back to Vasquez. "I must say, it didn't take you long after you got out."

"No, sir. But Consuela and I have known each other since we were children. We've talked about being married since we were ten years old."

"Then let me buy you a drink. There's a place a little way down Nineteenth Street. How about it? You don't get married every day."

Bob led them into a dimly lit bar and selected a small table just to the right of the entrance. He hung his hat on a peg on the wall and, pulling up a chair to the table, signaled the waitress.

"Were you in the service also?" he asked the other two men and then regretted his question when he saw the embarrassed shake of their heads. "Well, let me tell you about your friend here, for I doubt he has," he added, motioning again for the waitress, who walked on by for the second time. "But first, what would you like to drink?"

All three chose a beer.

"Excuse me a moment," Bob said and rose and walked to the bar. "We'll have four beers," he said to the bartender, who had tried to ignore him.

"I'm sorry, sir. I can serve you, but I can't serve the others."

"And why not?"

"We have a dress code in this establishment. We have rules."

Bob glanced around at all the other customers.

"My companions are dressed no worse than some of the others in here," Bob said. "That'll be four beers, please."

"I don't think you understand, mister," the bartender said.

"Yes, I understand perfectly well," Bob responded, "and I think you need to understand something also." He leaned forward and continued in a low but very firm voice. "See the big fellow on the left? A year ago as a Marine he saved my life in the Pacific and soon afterwards almost lost his own fighting one of this country's bloodiest battles. Now you are going to give me four—not one, but four—beers, or I'm going to take this pretty little bar of yours apart, splinter by splinter."

He straightened up and tossed a ten-dollar bill on the bar counter. "We'll be having only one beer apiece, but make them draught."

He was seething inside and breathing heavily but was himself amazed at this aggressiveness on his own part, so uncharacteristic of him. Nevertheless he was relieved when the bartender stared at him for a moment and then drew the four beers. Having returned to his group and placed the drinks on the table, he pulled up his chair again and glanced up at Vasquez. The face was impassive, but a trace of a smile at the corners of the eyes assured Bob that his friend had guessed what had transpired.

"Here's to the happy couple!" Bob said, raising his mug in a toast. Putting his beer down and wiping the foam from his lips, he looked at Vasquez's friends and smiled.

"I hope the bride realizes what a hell of a man she's getting. Did he tell you that he saved my life at least once last year?"

Both Pedro and Juan glanced briefly at the former Marine and then shook their heads.

"I figured he wouldn't. But he was a terrific soldier. Sergeant," Bob added, looking at Vasquez, "I want to give you my address. If I can ever do anything for you, I want you to let me know."

"That's not necessary, sir," Vasquez answered in almost a drawl but then suddenly looked up. "Well, if you're serious, sir, there is something you can do for me . . ."

"Captain, are you stationed here in Denver?"

"No . . . well, yes, but only until tomorrow. I'm being mustered out of the Air Corps at Lowry Field in the morning. Why?"

Vasquez paused, obviously reluctant to continue.

"Well, sir, Consuela has no parents. We would be very honored if an Air Corps captain stood in for her father to give the bride away. That is, if it would not be trouble for you."

"I am the one that would be honored, Sergeant. I should be all through by early afternoon. What time is the wedding and where?"

"Four o'clock at the Sacred Heart Church in the twenty-seven hundred block on Larimer. But don't worry if you can't make it, sir."

"I promise I'll be there unless at the last minute they decide to throw me in the stockade for losing one of their Lightnings. In case I'll be running close on time, I'll come straight to the church."

Bob alighted from the taxicab at the church at ten after three, placed his B-4 bag in the vestibule of the secretary's office and knocked on the door jamb.

"Yes?" a pretty middle-aged woman responded, glancing up from her paper work at a large desk.

"Excuse me, but I'm supposed to take part in the Vasquez wedding. I'm a little early, but I thought I might check with the priest and get some directions on what I'm supposed to do. Is he busy right now?"

"Father Versavel stepped out for a few minutes," she answered, "but he should be right back. Won't you have a seat?"

"Thank you, but if it will be all right, I think I'll go up and take a look at your church."

"Please do. When Father Versavel gets back, I'll tell him you will be up there."

Bob climbed the narrow steps to the main church and wandered up and down the aisles. The choir loft was above the main entrance, and the altar was at the opposite end. Along both sides lavender, yellow and blue stained-glass windows stood out brilliantly against the stark white walls, on which were ranged depictions of scenes from the life of Christ. Within ten minutes a priest of medium build and gentle but piercing eyes came up the central aisle and held out his hand.

"Ah, Captain, welcome. Niwot told me to expect you. It's very nice of you to come."

"Not at all, Father. I owe a large debt of gratitude to that man, and, besides, it will be a pleasure. I don't want to take up your time, but I thought you should perhaps describe my duties to me."

Father Versavel smiled.

"There are very few duties for you, Captain. The ceremony is going to be very simple. You will wait back there with the bride until you see Mrs. Montero nod to you. She will be at the piano, and as soon as she begins the Wedding March, you and the bride will proceed down the center aisle to the altar, where Niwot and I will be standing. When I ask: 'And who gives this woman to this man?' you just say 'I do' and step back. That's all there is to it. If you don't mind, I may get you to sign the certificate as a witness."

"I'll be glad to, Father. May I ask you a question, sir? I noticed your distinctive raiment, and I'm ill-informed on the Church. What is your order?"

"I am a Jesuit, my son. All of the priests since the founding of this church have been of the Jesuit order."

"That's very interesting. How old is your church?"

"It dates from 1879, but although it was Denver's third Catholic church, it is now the oldest church still using the original structure in the metropolitan area. Father John Baptist Guida, a Jesuit professor of philosophy from Georgetown University, became the first pastor and celebrated the first Mass."

Father Versavel paused and looked around warmly.

"Sacred Heart parishioners have included many famous people. For instance, Mrs. Horace 'Baby Doe' Tabor and her husband used to attend services here."

At this moment the main door opened and three girls entered nervously. They were all dressed in white, but one, carrying a tiny bouquet and a simple tiara with a short veil attached, Bob assumed to be the bride.

"Excuse me, Captain," Father Versavel said, "but I had best go and make the final arrangements. I'll see you in my study after the ceremony."

Bob nodded to the priest and then walked over to the girls, who were whispering and securing the tiara with bobby pins.

"Consuela, I'm Bob Hanson. Your groom has asked me to give you away today. Did he tell you about that?"

Through the veil the girl glanced up at Bob timidly and didn't answer. She just nodded her head. She seemed tiny to Bob, appearing to be not much over five feet tall.

"Are you nervous?" he asked.

Again she didn't answer, just nodded her head, but he thought he saw behind the veil a faint smile.

"That's natural," he said, "but I hope you are also happy, for you are a very lucky girl. I think you are marrying a good man."

Some doors opened down in the front. Mrs. Montero crossed and took a seat at the upright piano, and Father Versavel proceeded to the altar, followed by Vasquez and his two friends, Pedro and Juan. Bob reached down and took Consuela's hand and patted it. Then he looped her arm through his and turned to wait for Mrs. Montero's signal.

After the ceremony the wedding party was to congregate at the groom's house for a celebration. Bob had asked the lady in the church office to call him a taxicab but canceled the request when he realized he would probably hurt his friend's feelings if he did not attend at least briefly. Vasquez lived less than two blocks from the church, so everyone went on foot. There was a brief but heated contention between Pedro and Juan over which was to have the honor of carrying Bob's B-4 bag, and it was not settled until agreement was reached that each would carry it halfway.

Vasquez's home was a tiny little house on Lawrence Street almost directly across from the Sacred Heart School. There was a front porch and on the west side a small immaculately kept yard bordered by lush beds of still-blooming flowers. It was fortunate that the wedding party was not larger, for it would have been difficult to fit any more people into the diminutive living room. Bob retrieved from his B-4 bag the bottle of champagne he had bought for the occasion and stayed as long as he thought expedient to be polite. Vasquez later accompanied him out onto the porch to wait for the cab Pedro had been dispatched to call.

"I wish you could stay for dinner, sir."

"Thank you, Sergeant, but I must catch a transport leaving Buckley Field at seven on a milk-run flight back east. By the way, do you mind if I keep calling you 'Sergeant'? It just seems natural."

"No, sir; call me whatever you like. No one but Father Versavel calls me Niwot anyway. My Mexican friends call me 'Vasqui,' and my gringo friends 'Lefty.' But since this is goodbye, that won't be a problem."

"We never know. I said once before that our paths would never cross again. I'm not going to say that this time. Who would have guessed a year ago that we would be standing here today?"

**CHAPTER NINETEEN**

IT WOULD BE easy to describe Bob's entire former life, even from childhood, as a succession of productive and happy periods, permeated by a deep appreciation of the sheer joy in the process of living. But none could be more aptly titled a truly golden period as the next seven months after his discharge. A combination of factors contributed to the almost-giddy exhilaration he experienced day by day.

The last vestiges of his malady had disappeared, and he felt healthy and sound once again. He was able almost instantly to put the war behind him completely except to use memories of it to enhance the raptures of submerging himself in civilian life once again, to savor the luxury of being free to plan into the future for periods longer than just a day or a week. He shared readily in that mood of euphoric optimism that prevailed at that time in the United States, which had been exempt from the physical ravages of war and which stood now pre-eminent, powerful and secure. Unlike most veterans he was at least temporarily relieved of the need to worry about finding a job or deciding on a profession, for on his last leave he had assured his father that he would take over the task of directing the reconversion of the farm from crop production to horse-breeding.

This enterprise was ideal for the absorption of his pent-up energies; there was so much to be done. The fields had to be harrowed, rolled, sown and fertilized to guarantee optimum utility as pastures. Corrals, riding rings and the race track had to be designed, laid out and properly fenced. The paddocks, barns and stables that were left over from pre-war were in need of extensive repair and refurbishing, and new additions had to be built. The physical and creative demands posed by these activities were a psychological and spiritual balm for Bob, drawing on those proclivities he had enjoyed since childhood. He was impatient to rise and start each satisfying day, being on the job-sites soon after dawn and remaining until dark with a break only for a substantial communal lunch with the work crews, which were composed largely of former stable- and farmhands who had returned after the war—some with wives and children. So engrossed was Bob in these routines that he would take time off only on Sundays to ride or on rainy days to pursue some other interest.

This compulsive preoccupation virtually ruled out any active social life for him but represented no real break with the past. He had no inclination to see anyone outside the family with the exception of Nancy. They had picked up their friendship where they had left off years earlier and had an easy, relaxed relationship, but their time spent together was severely limited by the infrequency of her returns to Lexington from training sessions with various coaches for her and trainers for the two horses she was preparing for international competition. This restriction on opportunities for mutual contact probably served to increase their closeness, for the areas of incompatibility in their natures which were occasionally manifest before but less obvious with the end of the war could remain dormant and unobtrusive.

When in town Nancy would prevail on Bob to escort her to various parties and functions, a duty that would have been onerous for him were it not for the pleasure of watching her operate so scintillatingly in such environments. Ever relaxed and confident, she excelled in the art of "small talk," feigned affection and all the other requisite skills. In any room or assemblage of people she would be conspicuously a center of attention, particularly from men, irresistibly attracted by her beauty and easy charm. This induced no jealousy in Bob, for, although she was openly honest in appreciating the admiration of men and enjoying her obvious effect on them, she was never more than mildly flirtatious with anyone except him. Bob accepted gracefully but with some puzzlement the fact that she had stopped dating everyone else. Only once—in the week she was in Lexington during the Christmas holidays—did she depart from this pattern and have dinner with Ted Schorner, on temporary leave from his last year at Annapolis.

Bob for his part never dated anyone else, but due to Nancy's frequent absences during the winter and early spring the conditions were not propitious for their being able to draw significantly closer to each other. In May, however, there occurred a stretch of several days that provided a break in this pattern. Bob had just finished supervising at the maintenance building the replacement of iron rims on the wheels of a hay wagon when a pick-up truck drove up and Nancy hopped out with a wave of her hand.

"Well, I can't believe the restless world traveler has deigned to grace us with her presence again," Bob called out as he walked over with a grin.

"'Grace' is probably not the right word," Nancy laughed, "for I may overstay my welcome this time. I'll be here for almost two weeks."

"Two weeks? Only a death in the family could slow you down that much," Bob remarked. "Did poor old Uncle Joe pass away?"

"I didn't come over here to listen to your wisecracks, Bobby. I came to ask for your help. Can you spare a few minutes?"

"Sure. I'm just about through for the day anyway. Come on and give me a ride up to the house. I'll get Fanny to fix us some of her fabulous tea punch with mint and pineapple, and we can sit out back and talk."

**"OKAY, PRINCESS," BOB** said after they had settled in white wooden armchairs in the shade of a sycamore tree on the back lawn, "you said you need my help. What evil dragon can I slay for you today?"

"I hate to ask so much time from you," she began, "for I know what a compulsively hard worker you are, but I would really appreciate your acting as my handler for four days. Now don't say anything until I finish and then be honest with me. If you say you can't do it, I'll understand. I'm sure that with all the hoopla going on you are aware that the Association is putting on their first post-war Three Day Event this weekend. I've got two horses entered. Duane Simpson is going to ride Tommy's Frolic for me, and his crew will take care of him. But I'm going to ride Foxhall myself, and I'll need someone I can trust to do all the prepping, warm-ups, cool-downs, and grooming. I've watched you in the past, and I think you are a natural with horses."

"Nancy, you've got one of the best handlers in the State in Ben Starsi. What do you need me for?"

"Ben's got to leave for Indianapolis in the morning—some kind of illness in the family. He offered to stay on until Monday, but I insisted he go on. Look, I know it's dirty work and a long grind, and I can always use one of the younger grooms if I have to."

"Now don't go getting sensitive," Bob countered. "You know I'll be glad to help if I can. But why four days? I assume you'll be riding in the Dressage and Formal Jumping, but that's only two days."

"No, I'm doing the whole event on Foxhall, and it'll take us at least a day to prepare."

"The Cross-Country too? You've got to be kidding. They don't let women compete in that phase."

"They won't let me compete in it, but I am going to ride in it. What status they give me is their problem."

"How in hell did you manage to swing that?"

"They needed a lot of financial support this year to get the course in top shape. Daddy was a big donor, and a precondition was that his little darling be allowed to ride."

"I don't know if I approve of that. The Cross-Country is too damn dangerous for a woman."

"Now, don't you go getting stuffy too. Look, I've been training hard for months, sometimes on Olympic style courses. Someday we women will be competing equally with you men. You just wait and see. Well, whether you approve or not, can I count on you to help?"

Bob looked at her and grinned. "Surely you didn't think you had to ask that question. Of course I'll help."

\* \* \*

**THE INTENSE JOINT** effort of Bob and Nancy during these few days changed his perception of her and enhanced his appreciation of her. For the first time he could observe her working diligently at menial tasks, perspiring from the heat and exertion and covered with dust, dirt and grime as they hooked or unhooked the trailer, exercised the horse or loaded and unloaded gear, tack and equipment. The long continual hours spent together afforded them an opportunity to achieve a heretofore unknown relaxed informality and closeness.

But it was her skill as a rider that came as a true revelation to him. He had considered her an excellent rider almost four years earlier when he had last seen her ride, but the contrast with her current skill was stark. To him she appeared now to be a consummate equestrienne, a real professional. Even though he had groomed, prepped and saddled Foxhall for the first day's event, he was still unprepared for the display of beauty and grace displayed by the horse and rider during their five-minute routine at dressage. Dressed in white riding pants and white scarf and gloves contrasting with her jet-black jacket, boots and hat, Nancy made the traditional salute in front of the judges' stand. She sat ramrod straight, and the horse was as motionless as a marble statue. Once their routine was started, there was never once discernible another motion on her part in the effortless control of her mount. Whatever rein pressures or leg aids she employed—instantly responded to by Foxhall—were invisible to spectators and judges. His walk and trot were characterized by long graceful strides with head line precisely vertical and ears and attention fixed straight ahead. His canter was smooth and fluid, and when at an unseen command of hers he angled across the ring in a "half-pass" (or "two-track," as it was commonly called), there was a murmur of appreciation from the knowledgeable spectators. When she finally halted her mount again in front of the three-member "ground jury" and removed her hat in salute, there was a spontaneous burst of applause in appreciation of this virtually flawless display of precise control, discipline and sheer obedience on the part of horse and rider. It was obvious to all present that they would receive an excellent score, and even some of the other competitors applauded.

Bob tried hard but in vain to talk Nancy out of participating in the long, taxing Cross-Country Phase the following day. She merely laughed at his voiced concern for her safety on this dangerous equine marathon. For fifteen grueling miles it placed severe tests on the stamina, skill and courage of both horse and rider. Before dark the night before, they drove around the entire course and discussed the difficulties and options at the various jumps. Bob finally gave up trying to convince her to take some of the less-demanding but more time-consuming alternate routes through the jump complexes, realizing that he was wasting his breath. He determined, however, that he was going to let one of the grooms help in the final preparations the next day so that he could race by bicycle to be near the two most difficult series of jumps by the time she and Foxhall would arrive.

The course alternated long gallops with easy jumps and then more difficult combinations. The two most demanding complexes were "Maxwell's Maze" and the always-dangerous water complex. Since Nancy was one of the last riders to start, Bob had an opportunity to observe a sufficient number of horses struggling through the "Maze" to feed his anxiety by the time she and Foxhall came galloping over the ridge. He was relieved to know that she had at least survived the fourth jump, a difficult one with a deep ditch in front of the brush barrier, and the infamous "Sink-hole," but he would have been reticent to tackle the "Maze" himself. It represented the first real test by the course designer of all the dressage skills required: Could the rider guide the horse over the expanse of "Lincoln logs," then immediately right up onto a bank, control the length of its stride to turn left abruptly and finally jump a white fence designed to prove the skill and control of the rider but also the courage of the horse, which could not see the point of landing far below until the moment of take-off? Nancy glanced neither right nor left, so concentrated was she on the task at hand, but Bob did notice that she bent slightly more forward momentarily and said something to Foxhall as they approached the expanse of logs. Bob watched with apprehension and admiration as they maneuvered smoothly and without a hitch through the "Maze" and out onto the bluegrass of the open field toward the next series of easy jumps.

Taking off on his bicycle, he pedaled furiously toward the water complex but arrived only in time to see Foxhall bounding for the last time out of the water up onto a bank and over a fence for the long gallop toward the finish.

There was some effort made by the Association officers to hide the fact, but by intermission time at the ball that night it had become common knowledge that, although Nancy could not officially be recognized as having competed in the Cross-Country, her time had been several seconds better than that of the second-place finisher— a male rider by the name of Duane Simpson on Tommy's Folly. Bob was proud of her and did not in the least mind his identity being even more than usual relegated to that of "Nancy Garner's escort." He was also gratified to notice that whenever one from the throng of admiring men usually surrounding her would get too carried away by her attractiveness and tend to become too forward, she would seek Bob out, loop her arm through his and then continue to exude charm, letting his presence hold the rest at bay.

After Nancy's performance the first two days it was almost a foregone conclusion that she and Foxhall would also capture the final Formal Show Jumping Phase, and they lived up to those expectations. Returning to the paddock later in the afternoon after having changed out of her riding habit, she was surrounded by various people, even including reporters from two national magazines, so it fell on Bob's shoulders to cool down, wash and dry Foxhall, assemble all the accoutrements and load the trailer and van for the ride back to the Garners'. Having completed his duties, he was taking a breather and leaning against a fence when Nancy finally was able to break away and approached him. She was such an arresting vision in tight blue jeans, low boots and a checkered light wool shirt with her hair pulled back in a neat ponytail secured with a real sapphire clip that Bob was unaware of the obviousness of his rapt gaze. But she quickly noticed the intensity of his stare.

"Okay, Bobby, what's the problem? In the rush did I put my make-up on wrong?"

"No, you didn't put it on wrong; and even if you had smeared it all over your face, you'd still be beautiful."

"Now I know why I like to keep you around—to lift my sagging spirits and boost my fragile ego."

"Fragile—my foot! You're probably the most irritatingly confident person I know but—damn it—justifiably so. You are truly an extraordinary woman. You're a world-class rider, you are a fabulous dancer and play a good game of golf and tennis. Is there anything you can't do well?"

"That's for you to find out some day," she answered, glancing at him suggestively and wrinkling her nose.

"Well, at least as far as equestrian skills are concerned, I doubt I'll ever see a more impressive display than you put on this weekend."

"You just wait. I've still got a long way to go, and I'm going to get better in the next twelve months," she responded with conviction. "You'll see. But I was able to pull it off this weekend because of some first-class back-up support," she added, giving him a kiss on the cheek. "I had hoped that Foxhall would perform well, but sometimes he tends to be a bit fractious if he's been in a trailer recently. Your even temperament must have rubbed off on him, for he was solid as a rock. I think you and I could work well as a team, Bobby. Now hop in. I'll do the driving. I want to show you something."

Before they reached the road leading to the Garners' stables she turned down a tree-lined lane and after a mile and a half pulled off onto a dirt road. She stopped the van and trailer on a rise, from which an impressive compound of barns, buildings and stables were visible.

"Pretty, isn't it?" she asked, cutting off the engine.

"Of course," Bob answered. "Who wouldn't appreciate Windemere?"

"Will you promise not to breathe a word if I tell you something?"

"Sure. I promise."

"Dad is negotiating to buy it."

"Windemere?! My God, that's twelve hundred acres. He's already got over six hundred. Why would he want to buy this huge showplace?"

"As you know, it adjoins both our place and Faircrest. He envisions a huge spread, and just between us I think he secretly hopes to give Windemere to us as a wedding present. Silly, isn't it?"

Bob was so taken aback by this statement that he didn't know how to respond. They had frequently joked during the last few months about his sitting on the back porch of a shanty in his undershirt drinking beer while she stood in the kitchen with stringy hair surrounded by whining kids and a couple of mangy cats, but they had never talked seriously about marriage. Now he realized that perhaps subconsciously an unspoken assumption had been creeping up on them that they would one day be married. On one or two occasions he had even ruminated that there could well be an important basic compatibility between them based on the proclivity of each to become totally absorbed and involved in individual activities or projects, and they had both been amused at times by their respective parents' none-too-subtle approval of their "getting together." Bob had to admit that he was flattered that Nancy, the "Belle of Lexington," would single him out and that the two of them had come to be regarded as the reigning local "prince and princess," a status enhanced by their necessarily infrequent social appearances.

"I doubt that he would seriously consider me for a son-in-law," Bob finally said. "I would imagine that he has some high-powered Northern socialite in mind. Your folks have been planning and working for a long time for your dazzling debut in New York coming up in a couple of weeks, haven't they?"

"Well, that was Momma's big thing. Dad only went along with her on that. No, I know that he likes you. They both do. But you're using that as a dodge. I think I've made you uncomfortable, and I apologize. Damn it! What's wrong with me? I had to practically beg you for our first date, and now I'm caught trying to wheedle a proposal out of you."

It was obvious she was genuinely upset, and she started the engine again. Bob laughed to ease the tension and reached over and turned off the ignition again.

"Sweetheart, a woman like you would never have to wheedle any man. I'm flattered that you would even consider me as a suitor and a bit puzzled. Why would a sequined dance slipper like you pick out a plain old shoe like me? You love parties and social life and all that attendant glitter, and stodgy old me can barely tolerate them. How could I keep pace or peace with a shooting star?"

Nancy's face relaxed again, and she reached for his hand.

"Well, I'll admit some minor changes will have to be made," she said with a grin, "but you'll love them. We'll break up that stodginess a bit, and you'll be the life of the party. Well, I guess this is as close to a proposal as I'm going to get. There's not enough room on the floor of the van for you to get down on your knee. Are you waiting with bated breath for my answer?"

"Nancy, seriously, how can we even joke about getting married now? You've outlined to me your plans for your big push on the circuit for the next twelve months or so. You know I'm tied up here and couldn't follow you around like a pet dog and would hate it if I could. That's no way to start off a marriage."

"I didn't mean we have to get married right away. Haven't you heard of long engagements? Think of the fun we could have, and it would be a big help to me to be engaged. I would have something to fend off all those conceited Romeos on the circuit, who waste so much of my time. Bobby, let's set a date. Come on. Can we?"

"Well . . . I guess there's no harm in thinking about it. You're the one with the heavy schedule in the coming months, so it seems to me you should be the one to pick the timing. Why don't you think it over and . . . "

"I already have," Nancy said brightly. "The wedding will be on Saturday, May third, next year. We can't make the announcement until after my debut, but we'll do it as soon as I get back from New York. That'll give our friends time to plan and crank up some parties for the rest of June and early July before I head for northern Michigan."

"Maybe we'd better delay a bit longer. June would be okay, but July won't be available," Bob broke in. "I'll be in Europe with Mom and Dad."

"Europe? You didn't tell me about that."

"Dad wasn't too happy with the spring sales here in Lexington. He bought a new stud but felt this year's crop of yearlings wasn't too good. Frankly I think he just got outbid. He thinks with everyone hurting over there he might get some good bargains in England and Ireland, and he wants me to go shopping with him. We're going over on the *Queen Elizabeth* on July second and coming back the first week in August."

Nancy was reflective for a few moments.

"No. We'll go ahead and make the announcement. We'll still have months in which to catch up on the festivities. I'll make dozens of copies of my schedule and hand them out to all our friends so that we can have parties every time I get back in town off the circuit. Oh, Bobby, Bobby! I'm so excited! It's going to be so much fun! We'll have a huge wedding reception on the back lawn at Windemere, and we'll invite everyone—absolutely everyone."

"Whoa!" Bob said. "Slow down. I can't afford Windemere, sweetheart. I don't have that kind of money."

"That doesn't make any difference. We'll be living at Windemere anyway. Daddy will buy it for us. I know you've been on hunts on parts of the estate, but have you ever been inside the house? Fabulous! And wait until you hear what Momma plans to do to it. We'll have teak stables for our children's ponies, and they can just ride next door in either direction to visit their grandparents. Oh Bobby, I can't stand it I'm so excited."

Nancy paused and became reflective in order to indulge her daydreams. Her face was radiant, and she hummed to herself and drummed the fingers of her left hand on the steering wheel. Bob sat observing her with mixed emotions. Her beauty was always compelling, and he had come to accept over the years the inexplicably powerful hold she had over his emotions. But he had been caught off-guard and shaken at how quickly they had apparently backed into this tacit assumption that they would get engaged. It wasn't that he had any active objections and in many ways viewed the prospect with pleasant anticipation. It was just that he was always wont to plan his life in an orderly manner and by nature was suspicious of hasty decisions. Certainly he didn't have to worry about his parents' reaction. Nancy was universally regarded as the prize catch among their circle of acquaintances, and his mother would be delighted at the news.

"Well," Bob added as a mild concession, "I'm glad you're excited, but I suspect that after a little reflection you'll see me a little more realistically and reconsider."

"Ha! That'll be the day," she responded brightly. "Bobby, let's tell our parents right away so that we can start making plans. Why don't the six of us all have dinner together soon, and then we'll spring it on them. Okay?"

"Sure, if you like. I haven't learned how to say no to you yet, have I?"

"That's something I don't want you ever to learn," she laughed, wrinkling her nose at him and starting up the van.

Bob helped Nancy's stablehands back the horses out, unlatch the trailer and unload from the van the saddles, bridles, blankets, brushes, buckets and all the other myriad attendant items Then he and Nancy ducked into the tackroom for a brief but fervent embrace before he walked to his car. There had been a spring shower that morning, so he put the top back for his drive home and relished the buffet of the cool, fresh air on his face. He was aware of an intensified stirring of that happiness and exhilaration that had characterized the past six months. Every facet of his life seemed to be moving toward a near-perfect harmony, an impression reinforced by an item of mail awaiting him in his room—an envelope addressed:

Brigadier General Robert Hanson the Second, Third or Fourth
Somewhere in Lexington (I think)
Kentucky

There was no return address and no letter or note inside—just a picture of a gaunt Bill Harwood seated in a wheel chair. He was flanked by Lori and a little two-and-a-half-year-old girl, and in the background there appeared what seemed to be a military hospital.

This echo from the past was followed almost immediately by yet another. At dinner that evening his mother interrupted a low-key conversation between him and his father.

"Oh, Robert, I forgot to tell you. Right after you left on Friday there was a long-distance call for you from a Catholic priest in Texas. He wanted to talk to you, but when I told him you weren't here and that I was your mother, he asked all about how you were. He went on and on about what a fine person you are and what a generous thing you did to support a Mexican girl and her family while she completed her education. I told him I hadn't heard anything about it. Why didn't you tell us? I think that was a very charitable thing for you to do."

"My Lord!" Bob said, putting his fork down and looking at his mother. "That was over three years ago. I had completely forgotten all about it. Was the priest's name Father Mahaffey?"

"Yes, I believe that was it. He seemed to be an awfully nice man, even if he is Catholic, and I enjoyed talking to him. The girl was there with him and was distressed that she couldn't thank you again personally for your generosity so asked to speak with me. She sounded like a lovely child and insisted we let her know if there is ever anything she could do for us in return. I took her up on it right away and asked if she'd like to come and work for me."

"Here in Lexington?" Bob asked with surprise. "Why, mother, I don't think that would work out. She wouldn't be happy in this part of the country and would probably be homesick or lonely. Besides, what could she do for you? You already have enough menial servants to fill a theater."

"Well, by coincidence your father told me just last week that I could look for someone to help me manage this house and the gardens. It's too big a job now for me all alone. I described the job to the girl, and she said she'd like to try to help. The references I received from a New York employment agency didn't sound too promising anyway. If it doesn't work out, son, she can go back home. Don't you think it's worth a try?"

"Well, I don't know. I can't see her in that kind of role, dealing with servants, making decisions and everything. She's just a little Mexican girl with a thick accent."

"Really? That's not the way she sounded on the phone. The priest told me she is graduating first in her class and is highly thought of by the Catholic sisters at the school. Well, it's too late to back out on it now, because she's on her way. She's getting a ride as far as Kansas City with one of the sisters. What's the girl's name? Maria something, isn't it?"

"Yes. Maria Rodriguez," Bob replied, energetically rolling the r's and smiling at the memory of that evening so long ago.

## CHAPTER TWENTY

**THE CO-FAMILY ANNOUNCEMENT** dinner was a rousing success. The two mothers cried and hugged each other and each of the children, and the fathers—acquaintances but never especially good or compatible friends—attained a degree of uncommon congeniality.

"Why don't we make the public announcement on Monday after the debut?" Mrs. Garner asked giddily. "We'll all be in New York, and I know someone who can get it in the *Times*. Sarah, what do you think?"

"Well, I don't know, Grace," Bob's mother replied. "That might be rushing things a bit. Don't you think it would be in better taste to wait a few weeks?"

"Besides, Mrs. Garner," Bob broke in, "we won't all be in New York, although that's not too important. I'm not sure, but I don't think that Mom and Dad are planning on going up."

"You and Bob won't be there?" Mrs. Garner asked with disappointment in her voice, turning to Mrs. Hanson. "We have a whole bank of rooms reserved at the Pierre for our friends and were counting on you."

"That's sweet of you to ask us," Bob's mother responded, "but I'm afraid we won't be able to make it. That would push us a little. You see, we're going to be in New York in a few weeks to spend a couple of days before we leave for Europe. But I know Nancy will be the most beautiful girl in the city that night. We'll get to see all the pictures, and the rest of you can give us a full report when you get back to Lexington."

**NANCY WAS INDEED** stunning when she was presented at the ball at the Waldorf-Astoria, and there was less of the strained artificiality commonly associated with the immediately post-war debuts in New York of girls from the boondocks. Mrs. Garner had expended large sums of money and immense effort to elicit a favorable response from New York society and had at least partially succeeded, managing to secure the attendance of an impressive although modest number of *grandes dames* from the City and Long Island and even one from Newport. At the earlier parties all week and at the ball Saturday night Bob was once again relegated to the role of consort and attendant. With few acquaintances among the throng, he passed and mingled almost unnoticed and was even amused to hear on several occasions a current rumor linking Nancy romantically with a certain Mr. Fitzhugh M. Ashton III. When his presence was not required at social functions, Bob actually enjoyed being in New York, wandering leisurely from floor to floor at Abercrombie & Fitch or spending hours in the Museum of Natural History, but by week's end he was anxious to get back home. He revealed to Nancy during the ball his intention of returning to Lexington the next day and withstood her strenuous entreaties that he stay with her for several parties the following week.

On the return flight to Lexington in an Eastern Airlines DC-3 he alternated in randomly retrieving certain mental images of Nancy in her dazzling ball gown and allowing himself to be drawn by the drone of the radial engines back to more-distant memories rendered sweet by the passage of time. As much as he had in ways enjoyed New York, he was anxious to settle in once again into his routines on the farm. There occurred on Monday morning, however, a sharp break in the previously smooth, happy progression in the course of his life.

He had set out early in the morning to check the progress made during his absence on two projects that had been underway. He was surprised to note that the track for the bale-loader in the loft of the upper barn had still not been installed, counter to his orders before his departure. He sought out and eventually found the three-man crew to whom he had assigned this task. With a hint of irritation in his voice he called them down from the main stable roof, where they were installing a large new weather vane.

"Alfred, what the hell are you all doing up there?" he asked, addressing the tall, muscular black farmhand, who was the informal leader of the crews and who had always been the most dependable mainstay among the employees. "Before I left town I told you I wanted the upper barn loft finished first in order to be ready for the early hay cutting. Why didn't you follow my orders?"

The huge man shifted his weight from side to side and avoided looking Bob in the eye.

"Well, sir, we worked up there Monday and Tuesday but then were ordered to get onto something else."

"How could that be?" Bob asked, his voice rising. "I told Johnny before I left what I wanted you all to be doing. He knew all about it."

All three of the hands averted their eyes and were obviously uncomfortable.

"Alfred!" Bob repeated sternly. "What the hell is wrong with you all. Out with it!"

"Mister Bob," Alfred began haltingly, shaking his head, "things have changed around here."

"Changed? What do you mean changed? Cut out this double-talk and make some sense."

Alfred was obviously disconcerted and distressed. He looked to the other two for support, but they just looked down and scuffed their shoes in the dirt.

"Mister Bob, the old Master has fired Mr. Wodehouse."

"Dad fired Johnny?!" Bob exclaimed incredulously. "But why— for God's sake?"

"I don't know, sir. We wasn't told nothing about it. 'Parently they had an argument on Wednesday, and Mr. Wodehouse had moved his family and everything out by Thursday night. The new boss was here first thing Friday morning and started changing things around. He's the one told us to work on the vane here."

"New boss? You mean Dad's hired a new foreman already?"

"Yes, sir, I guess so. He's in the office there now."

"Well, I'll see if I can find out what's going on, but in the meantime you all go back up to the hay barn and finish putting up that track."

**"YES, SIR," ALFRED** said with a wide grin, and the three of them set off at a fast pace.

As Bob walked down the long center aisle of the main stable, he heard a voice coming from the central office. Opening the door, he saw a lean, wiry man with a narrow face, sharp features and close-set eyes talking on the telephone with his feet propped up on the desk. A small, compact, muscular white dog lying by the side of the desk had raised her head and curled her lips in a snarl as Bob stepped into the room.

"Shut up, Sassy!" the man shouted, directing a kick in the direction of the animal and glancing up at Bob but making no effort to end the conversation, his portion of which was punctuated with profanities and unpleasantnesses. After a minute Bob turned and was about to leave when he heard the receiver being replaced.

"Can I help you?" the man asked in a reedy voice.

"I came down here looking for Johnny Wodehouse," Bob responded, trying to keep his voice even.

"Mr. Wodehouse doesn't work here anymore," the man said, "but I might be able to find you his forwarding address."

"That's not necessary," Bob countered. "I'm Mr. Hanson's son. I've been reviewing the progress and lack of progress on some of the jobs I had outlined for the crews before I left for New York and wanted to talk to Johnny about some unauthorized changes."

"Oh, you're the *young* Mr. Hanson," the man said, getting to his feet with a cadaverous grin and slowly coming around the desk to extend an almost emaciated-looking hand. "I'm pleased to meet you, Mr. Hanson. My name is Silas Allen. I've heard you were responsible for all the projects around here. I'm very impressed with what I've seen—almost professional. In fact there are only a few changes that I recommended to your father."

"Changes? What changes?"

"I've sketched out a plan that I think you'll agree with. Maybe you and your father and I can go over it at you all's convenience."

"Speaking of changes, I put Alfred and his crew back to work on the upper barn loader track. I want that finished in time to handle the early hay storage."

"Very well, sir. I'll give them two days to finish it. Then I must pull them off and back to putting up the weather vane."

"What's so damn important about a weather vane?"

"It's a new design that directs the exhaust vents for the stable roof, lowering temperatures and improving air circulation. I want it in place by Thursday, for your father has three new horses arriving on Friday, including the new stud."

"A new stallion? I haven't seen Dad since I got back, but he didn't mention anything to me about that before I left."

Silas showed his widely spaced teeth in another skewed grin and leaned back against the desk.

"Well, your daddy's a pretty busy man with a lot of things to worry about other than the farm. But if you ever have any questions, feel free to ask me any time."

An angry response welled up in Bob's throat, but he managed to suppress it. Instead he stared at the semi-leer on Allen's face for a moment and felt a wave of intense dislike for the man. Without uttering a word he turned and opened the door, and the white dog curled her lips and snarled again.

"Shut up, Sassy!" Silas said with an oath, aiming in her direction another kick, this time partially successful.

Bob chose to leave the pick-up truck by the stables and walk the half-mile back to the house, a route so deeply embedded in his childhood memories that he hoped it would help quiet the turbulence of his feelings. The dirt road led from the stable compound gate over a small creek and then up a gentle hill past the fruit orchard and the asparagus beds to the complex of antebellum stone fences encircling the smokehouse, the north garage with its servant quarters and then the main house. Halfway between the stables and the creek was a wrought-iron hand pump, with which one could draw up water from deep in the ground. Bob paused, primed the plunger with the dipper of water always left by the previous user and began moving the long handle up and down vigorously. Fifteen to twenty strokes brought a surging flow of water, and once it tested ice-cold he filled the dipper and began to drink. The strong taste of iron and other minerals was as familiar to him as the gently rolling countryside and carried him back to hundreds of slated thirsts on hot summer days during his boyhood.

Leaving a full dipper on the sideboard for the next user, he continued slowly across the bridge and up the hill with his eyes focused on the path immediately in front of him. Concentration on the placement of each step of his boots and meticulously avoiding crushing the numerous spring beetles that traditionally swarmed at that time every year helped him put aside temporarily the troubled thoughts that were plaguing him. So intense was his preoccupation that he was already at the steps leading over the stone fence before he noticed on his left a woman sitting on the ancient mounting platform, from which the ladies used to be able to slide onto their side-saddles with minimal effort and awkwardness.

"Good morning,Mr. Hanson."

"Oh. Good morning," he responded, glancing up at her. She was sitting on the mount in a short-sleeved cotton dress, the whiteness of which was in stark contrast with the rich tan of her complexion. She was holding an open book on her lap, and her long dark hair was pulled straight back and secured on each side by silver combs.

"You have changed very little, sir," she said. "Perhaps a bit more distinguished. That's all."

"I beg your pardon," Bob said, somewhat surprised at her remark.

"You don't remember me, do you, sir?"

Bob looked at her again and then smiled.

"Why, of course. You must be Maria!"

"Yes, sir, that is correct. I'm happy that you remember me. Have I changed?"

Bob looked at her more intently.

"Yes, my dear, a good bit," he responded. "You've grown taller and more mature than I remember from the past, and you haven't a trace of an accent now. How is that possible?"

Maria looked up at him and laughed.

"*That* had to be changed immediately, sir. The dear sisters insisted on it and pretended they didn't understand me unless I spoke correctly. The only non-standard English pronunciation they allowed me was in Latin class."

"Latin? Did you take Latin?"

"Yes, sir, three years of it, and they felt the Spanish pronunciation was probably no further from the original than the English version."

"*Gallia est omnis divisa in partes tres, quarum unam incolunt Belgae, alium Aquitani . . .*" Bob intoned.

"*. . . tertiam qui ipsorum lingua Celtae, nostra Galli apellantur. Hi omnes lingua, institutis . . .*" she continued.

"Okay, okay, you win," Bob laughed. "That's all I remember. How long have you been here?"

"I left Kansas City by bus Monday morning and arrived here Tuesday night."

"Kansas City?"

"Yes, sir. I rode that far with Sister Denise from the school. She was transferred and appointed as head of an orphanage there. It was very sad to part with her, for she was always one of my favorites."

"Well, it is our good fortune to have you here. I'm sure you'll be a big help to my mother. Thank you for coming."

"Thank me? I am the one who is grateful, sir. It is a gift from God to be able to repay some of the debt that I owe you."

"Maria, you don't owe me anything. That was not a loan to you. I did it for myself."

"I can't accept that, Mr. Hanson. I have sworn to myself to try to pay you back. Your mother is being kind enough to give me three hundred dollars a month. My personal needs are very small, and I have a little saved from my allowance over the years, so I'll be able to give all of the three hundred to you."

"But what about your mother and brother?"

"He is much better now, thank you, and is going to school in Mexico City, where they have moved. Both he and my mother have jobs, so they don't need my help."

Bob glanced down at the book she was holding in her hand.

"Are we reading Latin or Greek today? Ah, *Out of My Life and Thought*. Why Albert Schweitzer?"

Maria blushed and looked down at the book.

"I admire him very much and hope someday in a small way to be able to follow his example. You will probably laugh at me, sir, but I would like to go to Africa eventually and help in his work."

"In Lambarene? How would you help?"

"I would like to become a nurse. In fact your mother has been most helpful in securing permission for me to register for pre-nursing at the University this fall and agreeing to let me adjust my hours so that I can attend classes. She is so kind."

"Yes, she's a pretty nice lady. Well, welcome to Falcrest Acres. I hope you'll be happy here."

"Thank you, sir. I'm sure I shall be."

Bob smiled and shook her hand and walked off toward the house. Their conversation had granted him a brief respite from his troubled thoughts, but now they returned. He was anxious to have a conference with his father but knew he would have to wait until afternoon. There was a standing rule that nothing problematic was ever to be discussed during meal time—only things that were pleasant or interesting.

"Robert," his mother said just before the end of lunch, "what a stroke of luck to have hired that girl. She's everything I had hoped to find—and more. She moved in and took over immediately and has the house running like a Swiss watch. She borrowed all my gardening books from me and two days later gave Leslie a list of fertilizers and sprays to get for Alfred to use on each kind of shrub and plant we have in the garden. I tell you, she's a gem. My mind will be at rest while we're in Europe."

"I'm glad, Mother. I knew she would be conscientious but wasn't sure she'd fit in with the servants. I hope you found her quarters in town, for I think it would be awkward for her in the servants quarters."

"I started to but then thought we'd fix up that small room and bath off the back stair landing we'd been using for storage. It has no air conditioning, but she says she doesn't mind and has the room fixed up real cute. If she's as good as she seems, I'd build her the Taj Mahal to keep her, for she's changed my whole life."

"She's changed all our lives around here," the father laughed. "Your mother hasn't been this pleasant in ten years."

"Robert!" the wife said. "You should be ashamed of yourself for saying that."

"That's great," Bob laughed. "By the way, Dad, could I talk to you for a moment in the library?"

After they had settled in chairs, the father lit up his traditional Corona.

"Well, son, what is it you want to talk about? Are you going to need some money for your honeymoon?"

"No, sir. That's not it. I had a rather unsettling experience this morning when I went back on the farm. Dad, why did you let Johnny Wodehouse go?"

The father took the cigar out of his mouth and squinted at his son.

"He disagreed openly with me on several matters, and I don't want anyone around here who's not happy with his job."

"But, Dad, Johnny is a wonderful man and had been with us since I was a boy."

"I know, son, and I was sorry to see him go too. I offered to let him stay on as an assistant, but he turned it down."

"As an assistant? To that jerk Allen? Where in hell did he come from?"

"Don't prejudge the man, Robert. He was highly recommended by Charlie Garner."

"Mr. Garner?!"

"Yes, Charlie brought his manager and accountant over here, and they spent a whole day with me. They made me realize what a loose ship we've been running around here and how we can make the farm pay its way and pull its own weight."

"Pay its way? After over twenty years why do you now insist it be profitable? We've always had a marvelous sense of family, of community on this place. Don't you realize this fellow Silas can ruin all that?"

"He has good references and an impressive track record. There's no reason not to run a farm as a business."

"Dad, I distinctly dislike the man. I don't think I can work with him."

"Well, son," the elder Hanson said, taking a draw on his cigar, "it seems to me that with your getting married and everything you won't be able to devote full time to the farm for quite a while anyway. This way, I won't have to worry about it. Now just don't go jumping to conclusions, and give it a try. Okay?"

**BOB'S GRIM MOOD** was relieved somewhat by Nancy's return a few days later and the announcement the following week of their engagement. But the rash of parties this engendered was even more burdensome to him than they would have been normally under the best of circumstances. He welcomed the approach of the end of June, when this phase would come to an end. His parents left for New York by train on Wednesday, the twenty-sixth. Nancy had decided that since Bob was to fly up to New York on Monday, the first of July, to meet them, she and Ben Starsi would leave on Sunday with the horse van for northern Michigan to join her mother and father for eight weeks.

Bob adamantly refused to condone another engagement and farewell party for them on the twenty-ninth and insisted the two of them spend the day alone together. He ordered lunch for them at the Idle Hour Club and made arrangements for her favorite horse to be brought to Falcrest for a long afternoon ride. In the evening the cook was to prepare and have served to them on a small table in the library an intimate dinner with formal place settings and candlelight.

The weather could not have been more co-operative. A cold front had moved through and the day was crystal clear and not too warm.

The horses barely worked up a lather on a double circuit of the jump course on the back of the farm, but in order to cool them down Bob decided to slow them to a walk for the long return to the stables. When they approached a fence running along the top of a rise, Bob did not have to dismount to open the gate, for it swung open for them.

"Good evening, Mr. Hanson. Good evening, Miss Garner," Maria said, pulling the gate to after they had passed through.

"Good evening," Bob responded. "Nancy, may I introduce Maria Rodriguez, who has come here to help my mother manage the estate. Apparently she already knows you."

"No, sir, we've not met," Maria responded, "but I recognized her from your pictures in the papers. May I congratulate you both on your engagement."

"Thank you, and please call me Nancy. Isn't this a lovely day?"

"Yes, ma'am, it certainly is. I couldn't help sneaking away for a long walk this afternoon. You won't report my transgression to your mother, will you, Mr. Hanson?"

"I promise to keep your guilty secret and not squeal on you," Bob joked.

A small creek ran along the bottom of the hill, and Bob decided the horses had cooled enough to be watered. They both dismounted and sat on the bank while their mounts drank the clear, cool water and nibbled at the watercress clustered around a small tributary spring. The muffled gurgle of the creek was only occasionally punctuated by the call of a bird or the snort or pawing of one of the horses. Bob was relishing this oasis of peace and quiet within the context of the last two weeks and turned to express this feeling to Nancy. Her face was averted, however, and Bob saw that she was watching Maria descending the hill. Having removed her sandals and hiked her brightly-colored skirt above her knees, the girl waded across the stream a hundred yards to their right and then climbed up the opposite slope. As she disappeared behind the hay barn, Nancy became aware of Bob's scrutiny and laughed self-consciously.

"So that's the drab little Mexican girl your mother was telling me about! Well, she doesn't exactly fit my idea of drab. In fact in a way she's rather pretty, Bobby. Your mother brags that you contributed money to her education. Are you sure your contributions to her . . . er . . . education have been purely of a financial nature?"

Bob laughed and lay back on the soft grass, gazing up at a puffy white cloud suspended in the brilliantly blue sky.

"Now I've heard everything! The sun complaining about the moonlight."

"If you think flattery like that can get you anywhere, mister, you're dead right," Nancy said with a laugh and leaned over to kiss him.

**THE COOK HAD** outdone herself with the dinner that evening. The unusual combination of gourmet and Southern cooking was strangely compatible and delicious.

"I wanted this to be a fitting replay of that night at your house," Bob said. "Remember the dinner in front of the fire? That was the night that you definitely set the hook, and I was a goner after that."

"That's nice to hear," Nancy said, "but, you know, I don't feel at all secure about you. I don't know why; I can't explain it. Maybe it's that damn self-sufficiency you always project. Sometimes I wake up at night kind of in a panic, thinking that I'm going to lose you."

"*You* lose *me?*" Bob said incredulously. "You're the show horse, and I'm the plow horse. I'm the one who's lucky. You won't find anyone in this state who will disagree with me on that. Now finish your wine. I have a tall stack of records on the player in the south parlor, and we're going to dance until you say 'Uncle.'"

The dancing did not last through the stack of records, however. Whereas their deportment on the dance floor had previously always been discreet even during the closeness attendant to the playing of slow music, their privacy in the big house this evening and the awareness of their engagement tended to loosen the bonds of restraint, and passion soon displaced any pretense at dancing. Nancy's kisses as always would increase his appetite rather than assuage it, and his hands roamed along and across her body with more freedom and less resistance on her part. Once they had retired to the long sofa, Bob took advantage of Nancy's supine position to attempt again to caress her. To his joy he found that the "G-line" was no longer inviolable, and the deliciously liquid evidence of her own excitation drove him beyond the limits of self-control. As he sought to roll over on top of her, however, she suddenly became galvanized into action and began to struggle to extricate herself.

"No, Bobby, please. We mustn't."

"Nancy, relax. I won't hurt you. I promise. It's all right. We're engaged now."

"No, we can't. I'm in the middle of my cycle. It would be too dangerous."

"Nancy, please; I'm in pain," he panted. "Okay. Okay. We won't go all the way. Just let me . . ."

"No, Bobby, no!" she pleaded. "I can't trust myself. Let me up. I'd best go home."

"Nancy! For God's sake, don't be this way!"

"Bobby, I'm sorry. I really am sorry, but believe me, I know what's best. Please?"

Bob got to his feet and took a deep breath, but the blood was pounding in his temples and his loins were consumed by fire. He crossed to the record player and abruptly turned it off. There ensued a deep silence broken only by the sound of their breathing and Nancy's efforts to restore order to her clothing. He avoided looking at her, partly out of a feeling of resentment and partly from a lack of confidence in his self-control. "I'll see you home," he said in clipped syllables as they walked toward the front door.

"No, I have my car here," she answered. "There's no need for you to go."

"But I'd better follow you to be sure you get there safely."

"No, sweetheart, with Momma and Daddy gone I don't trust either of us enough to be safe at my house. You stay here, and I promise to call you as soon as I get home. And, Bobby," she added, taking him by the hand and looking up at him earnestly, "don't be angry at me. I wanted to just as badly as you did. We will—just as soon as

I know everything is right. It will be different when we all get back. You'll see. Will you miss me? Are you going to think about me while you're in Europe?"

"I'll be damned lucky if I can think about anything else at all."

"Oh, my love, I said I'm sorry. Are you mad at me?"

"No, I'm not mad," he said, not totally truthfully. "Now you'd better get home, and call me as soon as you get there."

A few minutes later he stood in the doorway and watched the tail lights of her car wind down the long driveway and turn left on the highway.

**WHEN BOB AWOKE** the next morning, his mind was still clouded by the extreme sexual stress of the preceding evening. No erotic dream during sleep had relieved the pressure as it would have in his teens. He even found it difficult to concentrate on the information in the newspaper at breakfast.

"Mister Robert," Fanny said from the kitchen door, "I'm leaving on my vacation this morning, but before I go I'll make up a bit of chicken salad and leave it in the refrigerator for your lunch. You want me to fix anything for your dinner? There's some cold biscuits and country ham in there, and I believe there's a dish of creamed corn too."

"That'll be fine, Fanny. Thank you. I'll make out for supper. Oh, do me a favor, please. Call the stable and have Lightning saddled for me. Tell them I'll be down in an hour. Where are you going on your vacation?"

"I'm going down to Memphis to see my mother and aunt."

"Well, I hope you have a good time and find them well. We'll see you when we get back from Europe."

"Yes, sir. Thank you, sir. And you all take care of yourselves crossing that big water."

**THE LONG RIDE** that morning helped alleviate Bob's problem somewhat. Lightning had not been ridden in three days and had so much ginger in him that Bob had to restrain him from making a headlong rush at each log jump on the trail. Conditions along the shaded pathways were ideal, but when they later made several circuits of the brush jump enclosure out in the open, both horse and rider felt the intensified heat. The high pressure following the cold front had moved off to the east, and a southerly flow was pumping warm, moist air up from the Gulf. By eleven o'clock the horse had worked up a lather, so Bob dismounted and led him leisurely back toward the stable. One of the stable hands came out to meet them and take over the care of the horse.

"Hey, Sam, what's all that racket in the stables?"

"That's Trojan, sir. Mr. Hughes sent a mare over to be bred this morning, and that stallion always knows when there's action coming up. He's a piledriver, that horse."

Bob had to pause in his walk down the long center aisle of the stable, for the stud, being led out to the breeding enclosure, was giving the two men handling him all they could do to maintain control. His nostrils were extended, his eyes were ringed by white, and his massive neck was proudly arched as his hooves sounded a drumbeat on the cedar bark of the floor.

Bob followed them out into the sunlight and stopped by the watering trough. The mare, a beautiful bay horse with fine configuration, was restrained by the narrow sides of the enclosure and by the two-by-sixes affixed behind her rear legs to rule out the possibility of a fractious kick inadvertently emasculating the costly stallion. Padded beams were in place along the top to support the anticipated weight of the stud, and the mare's long silky tail had been wrapped with twine and tautly tied to the side to facilitate access to her vulva, which was already pursing and clenching in anticipation. As Trojan mounted, one of the handlers with a rubber glove seized the end of the phallus and guided it adroitly to the appropriate target. The mare gave out a low squeal as the huge member was driven home, and then a strange semi-quiet settled over the scene, broken only by the grunting and snorting of the stallion and the mare's occasional flatus in response to the brutal pounding. Although accustomed to having witnessed this ritual many times in the past, every one of the six men present watched this raw, violent display of the basic act of mating with fixed, glassy-eyed fascination. From a mutual, unspoken code of self-consciousness not a one glanced at any of the others.

The arching backwards of Trojan's head accompanied by the emission of a loud squeal and the trembling of the posterior muscles of the rear legs gave evidence to ejaculation, and soon thereafter the stallion backed away and withdrew. Almost immediately the quiet was shattered by the voice of Silas Allen.

"Goddamn it! She's a squatter!"

With a foul oath the man grabbed a pail of cold water and ran over to direct the contents at the mare's exposed genitals, but he had acted too late: the mare had already lowered her hindquarters and expelled onto the ground the large mass of equine semen. Within seconds Allen's white dog had dashed over in an attempt to retrieve it.

"Sassy, you slut!" shouted the man in a falsetto voice, delivering a full kick to the side of the dog and sending her reeling. "Son of a bitch! We've wasted a whole day. We'll have to repeat tomorrow."

Bob had turned and walked to the fence gate, trembling inwardly. Not only was the temporary relief he had achieved that morning totally negated, but the tension within him was even further increased by the witnessing of that scene. He stopped at the pump, primed it and, having removed his shirt, bent over to direct the frigid water onto the back of his neck so that it flowed around onto his face and off his nose and chin. The shock of the cold water returned some stability to the outside world, but as he walked slowly up the path toward the house, every one of his senses—visual, olfactory, auditory, kinesthetic—was almost painfully acute. Every input hinted insidiously at sensuousness—the hot sun on his bare back, the shimmer of heat off the graveled path, the fragrance of the honeysuckle along the fence row. The entire external environment seemed permeated by fecundity.

Bob walked past the smoke house to the main garage and knocked at Leslie's door.

"Leslie, I will need you to drive me to the airport early tomorrow morning. We should leave by six-thirty. You might call me at five-thirty to be sure I'm up."

"Yes, sir, Mr. Bob, I'll do that. Do you want to use your car?"

"Yes, I believe so. Did Fanny get away this morning?"

"Yes, sir. I took her to the bus station right after breakfast, but I believe she left you some iced tea and lunch in the kitchen."

"I know. She told me. By the way, I'm going to leave my riding clothes in the laundry room. Have the pants sent to the cleaners and ask Alfred to clean and polish my boots for me. There's no rush on that, for we'll be gone a month. I'll fix my own dinner tonight, so you can have the afternoon and evening off."

"Thank you, sir. I've been recruited to cook the barbecue for my church on the fourth, so I'll use the time to make some preparations. But I'll be back by nine o'clock if you should need me."


BOB SAT AT the table in his shorts and slowly ate his lunch in the coolness of the kitchen. In a way the total quietness of the big house was soothing to him but in a way also provided no distraction from the painful visceral tension within. Many times in the past ten years had he, as most young men, been subjected to the discomfort of such hormonal onslaughts, but never to this intense a degree. Everything disassociated with this central neuro-chemical focus took on an artificiality and superficiality that made it difficult to deal with and relate to in even a moderately normal fashion. Like a robot he placed the dishes and empty glass in the sink and started up the back stairs to the second floor. He was trying to concentrate his attention on the feel of the smooth hardwood of the steps on the bottoms of his bare feet and was suddenly startled on the halfway landing by a hum coming from the right. Glancing to ascertain its source, he was halted in his tracks.

The hum was coming from a small oscillating electric fan on the floor of the small bedroom past an open door. Sheer white curtains were being agitated by a breeze coming through an open window, and between the window and a sturdy wrought-iron bed was the lovely figure of a woman. In a pose straight from a painting by Degas she was bent over from the waist in a graceful arc while brushing her long, freshly washed hair. Every tiny detail of the scene was imprinted indelibly in Bob's mind: the smooth motion of the arms, the perfect curve of the shoulder, back and waist, the absence of a bra or panty line beneath the white cotton slip, the firm muscles of the calves of her legs and even the occasional raising of a toe on each bare foot to maintain balance.

Bob observed the scene in a semi-hypnotic trance. He was unaware of how long he stood thus transfixed or when he involuntarily began to move into the room. So quiet and slow was his pace that he had stopped a few feet in front of her without her noticing his approach. Only when she straightened suddenly and tossed her long tresses over her head onto her back was she aware of his close presence. With a sharp intake of air she took a step backward in fear and without an utterance stared at him with wide eyes and partially opened lips. For a moment he visually devoured every detail of her lovely face—the symmetrical hair line, the arching eyebrows, the slightly flared nostrils and the perfect curve of the lip line. As he stepped forward, she retreated until the bed blocked her path. Placing a hand on each side of her face, he looked deep into the dark frightened eyes.

"Forgive me, Maria. You must help me."

Moving his hands slowly down the sides of her neck, he carried the straps of her slip past her shoulders and down her sides. He touched his lips to the base of her throat and continued the kiss downward past the small silver cross and across her smooth skin as he sank to his knees and forced the garment to the floor. Placing a forearm under each thigh, he lifted her and followed her body onto the bed. Beyond hope of any restraint, he was driven by an irresistible compulsion to possess her, to harvest her like a field of ripe grain. There was not even a remote possibility of recourse to his earlier devised pattern of mental and physical control. Relentless was his drive to enter the divine city. Even the pressure against the initially stubborn resistance of her hymen afforded pleasure of indescribable intensity, and the subsequent tiny incremental yieldings carried him to a frenzy. Suddenly the resistance gave way, the girl gasped, and he was totally ensheathed. A roar filled his ears, his eyes—though open—were blinded by a crimson haze that obliterated the striated pattern of the bedspread, and every cell in his body seemed to scream in an ecstatic, simultaneous paroxysm. The intense spasm was gradually supplanted by a warm, all-encompassing glow that followed him as he slowly withdrew and walked unsteadily toward the door.

A partial return of normal mental functions induced in him a belated concern for the welfare of the girl, and near the door he turned and looked back. She still lay motionless across the bed with her legs suspended from the side and her head turned toward the open window. There was a lovely contrast between the golden hue of her skin against the white of the bedspread, and his eyes were arrested by the soft triangle of her pubic hair. Unexpectedly and inexplicably passion welled up within him anew, and even while aware of his own consternation at his behavior he walked back and stood by the bed to gaze down at her beauty. Her eyes were fixed on some insubstantial point in the sky outside the window, and suddenly his passion was infused and partially supplanted by compassion. He reached down, lifted her in his arms and laid her lengthwise on the bed.

Occasionally the hum of the fan would be joined by the song of a mockingbird in a tree outside as for over an hour he gently and tenderly made love to her.

## CHAPTER TWENTY-ONE

**THE CROSSING OF** the Atlantic on the *Queen Elizabeth* was more than just pleasurable for the Hansons. The relaxation, leisure and unavoidable proximity served to facilitate a substantial amelioration of the rift that had begun to develop during the preceding three weeks between father and son. Part of this success was achieved by an unspoken agreement between the two not to discuss or even mention the replacement of Johnny Wodehouse by Silas Allen. Whatever the causative factors were, the rapprochement was gratefully welcomed by the mother, who had sensed the growing estrangement between the two. She blossomed like a flower in the renewed warmth and appeared happier, prettier and younger than Bob had seen her since before the war.

The re-establishment of his closeness with his father allowed Bob to enjoy the entire trip much more than he would have otherwise, but its structure and nature would have been edifying to him under any circumstances. He loved this first chance to indulge his Anglophilia and took full advantage of it, insisting the three of them visit at some time the locus of the family prior to emigration to America. His spirits were subdued by the still-evident damage and destruction sustained by London and other British cities during the war, but he was gratified by the almost universal civility and cordiality the three of them encountered in the British Isles. He realized that a commercial motivation on the part of their hosts dictated such a response somewhat but still found it impressive.

During their stay of several days at the Dorchester in London soon after their arrival Bob was able to purchase on Saville Row at an amazingly modest price a complete new riding habit, including hat, scarf, "pink" jacket, pants and boots, enabling him later to participate in hunts across the beautiful countryside of Suffolk and Warwickshire. He had a suspicion that these hunts were perhaps organized out of season by the hosts for his benefit, but out of courtesy and appreciation at being included he did not specifically inquire. On more than one occasion he reined in his mount at the top of a rise in order to enjoy the colorful panorama below—the green fields, the hounds, the horses and the riders in their brilliant red coats—an animated reproduction of a work by an eighteenth-century artist.

When the Hansons were due to make a three-day side trip to a breeding farm in Ireland not long before their return to the States, Bob begged off and let his parents go without him, agreeing to meet them in London on their return. He was loath to give up any of his limited time in England and had been invited to an estate in Sussex owned by the father of Andrew Dunsworth, a former RAF pilot with whom he had struck up a conversation in the Dorchester bar. Dunsworth, an extremely personable man, was a barrister in London. He and Bob felt immediately compatible and found they had a great deal in common, not the least of which was a capacity to talk about airplanes for hours on end. Bob's host drove him down to Sussex in a pre-war Bentley with occasional side forays to show him historical sites and also the former aerodrome from which he had flown Hurricanes.

The estate was smaller than the ones Bob had visited to the north and gave evidence to the need for more repair and refurbishing than the apparently constrained means of the owner could afford, but its more modest size and impressiveness were more than offset by its tasteful style and beauty. A gem of an Elizabethan manor house, it was nestled in a setting of gardens overlooking pastures and outbuildings. Andrew's father, the Right Honorable Wyndham Fitzhugh Dunsworth, a former Coldstream Guard under King George, was the prototype of

Bob's image of an English country gentleman—garrulous and charming with bushy eyebrows, moustache, a stentorian laugh and an awesome capacity for stout and brandy.

Andrew, Bob and the father stayed up very late the night of their arrival, drinking, talking and telling war stories that could have described battles on three totally different planets—those of the father from World War I, of the son from the Battle of Britain, and of Bob from the South Pacific. Thus the planned ride the next morning to show Bob the countryside was delayed by several hours—a development that was not too disruptive, for even in July it was a raw, chilly day with fog and light drizzle.

"We're rather accustomed to this sort of thing, you know," Andrew said at the conclusion of a late breakfast, "but would you prefer to scratch our sortie this morning?"

"Not at all," Bob replied. "I don't want to miss a single day. If I can borrow a rainslick from you, I'm game for at least a couple of hours."

"Bully for you," Andrew said. "What kind of horse do you Americans prefer? We can offer you a half-Arabian renegade with a mind of his own or an elderly gray with an ass of lead."

"That's an interesting field of candidates," Bob laughed. I think I'll try the renegade, if it's all right with you. The third time I end up on the ground, we'll swap mounts."

"Andrew," the father said, studiously tamping the tobacco down in his pipe, "why don't you have Top Hat saddled up for Robert?"

The son looked at his father in surprise.

"Sir . . . I . . . I . . ."

"No, I'm serious," the older man added. "If this young man is as good a rider as he is a story-teller, then he'll appreciate quality. I'd like for him to see what kind of horses we can turn out over here."

Andrew turned and looked at Bob as they were walking down the lane toward the stables.

"You must be a sorcerer, my friend. Only three people other than my father have ever been allowed on Top Hat since he bought him years ago. Even I get to exercise him only when the old squire is sick. I would never have believed this if I had not been here."

"Well, I'm quite flattered," Bob responded, "but I don't want to take any chances with something that important to him. Why don't we trade mounts?"

"No. He really wants you to ride him. Besides, this is an opportunity you shouldn't miss."

The groomsman brought out the half-Arabian, tethered him to a cross support and went back into the second stall. In a moment he led out a tall chestnut gelding that made Bob stare in admiration. He had been raised around fine horses all his life, but never had he seen one quite like this. Standing at over seventeen hands, the animal's bone structure and configuration were from an idealized concept in the mind of an artist projected through a nineteenth-century lithograph.

"My God, what a beautiful animal!" Bob said in awe.

"His looks are the least extraordinary thing about him," Dunsworth responded. "Come, my friend, let's mount up."

The following two-hour ride was one Bob would never forget. He could afford little attentiveness to the beauty of the countryside, so fascinated was he by the performance of the horse under him. Whatever the gait chosen, it was smooth and effortless, There was never a hint of hesitation, faltering or awkwardness in the approach to any type of jump—brush, timber, stone or water—and the execution was as close to flying as any thousand-pound animal could achieve. His disposition and nature were as remarkable as his physical prowess. For two hours there was only one position for the ears—straight forward. Well-mannered, patient and forgiving—if ever the appellation of "gentleman" could be applied to an animal, it suited him. Bob felt that if he had never been on a horse before, he could have ridden Top Hat.

After they had dismounted back at the stables, Bob was reluctant to part with the horse. He stood by the side of the head, scratching the nose and behind the ears and looking into the soft, liquid brown eyes until the groomsman came to lead him away.

"Damn!" he said to the grinning Andrew as they walked back toward the house. "You and your father have just ruined all other horses for me."

"I know exactly what you mean. He's really quite a show, isn't he?"

"What's the story on him? Where did your father get him?"

"In 1938 he was one of the most promising steeplechase horses in all of England. Then tragically some infection partially broke his wind. He was still sound enough to finish fourth or fifth in races, but that was never good enough for him. He would never accept any position but first and would have killed himself trying. The breeder retired him and sold him as a hunter to a family living over near the Cotswolds. The owner was killed at Dunkirk, and my father bought the horse in the fall of '41. He'll be pleased that you like him."

Bob and the younger Dunsworth were to leave soon after lunch the next day for the drive back to London. The inclement weather had passed and the sun would occasionally break through the clouds to paint a lovely mottled pattern on the woods and fields. Late in the morning Bob took a walk through the gardens and ended up strolling down the paddock lane. Top Hat interrupted his grazing in a lower meadow and came over to the fence to greet him, so Bob climbed over the rail and stood by the horse for a long time, patting him, scratching his forelock and straightening his mane. As he approached the house a few minutes later, he was a bit embarrassed to notice the older Dunsworth standing at a window on the second floor, watching him.

On the drive back to London at Bob's insistence Andrew described in great detail the long frightening months in the early stages of the war and the dark, desperate weeks of the Battle of Britain. By the time they drove into the city Bob had sunk into a sober, reflective mood, but as the Bentley drew to a stop in front of the Dorchester, Dunsworth turned to Bob abruptly and said, "Robert, would you like to buy Top Hat?"

At first Bob thought he was joking and then realized that perhaps he wasn't.

"Surely you can't be serious!"

"Yes, I'm dead serious. My father and I had a conversation just before lunch, and he suggested I ask you."

"But why would he consider that? He loves that horse."

"I know. It will be like cutting off his left leg. But I've known for several months that he has been forced to consider selling—for financial reasons. He's in quite a bind right now. He's very anxious, as you can understand, that the new owner will appreciate and take care of the horse. You're the first person he has indicated he would be willing to sell to. What do you say?"

"How much is he asking?"

"Three thousand pounds."

"Three thousand pounds!" Bob repeated and whistled. "That's a hell of a lot for a hunter."

"Yes, it's a lot of money, but it's also a lot of horse."

Bob was silent for a moment, but the doorman had opened his door and was standing expectantly.

"All right, it's a deal," Bob said, shaking Andrew's hand.

"Can you take care of the shipping arrangements and let me know the total cost? I'll get the funds to you as soon as I get back to Lexington."

"I'll handle the details. Here's my card. What port do you prefer?"

"Let's try Charleston, South Carolina. If that's not available, let me know. I'll drive over to pick him up, wherever he comes in."

"Good-bye, Robert," his friend said, extending his hand. "It's been a pleasure meeting you, and it will give us comfort to know that you have the fine fellow with you."

"Thank you, Andrew. If you ever get to the States, you must visit us. I might even consider letting you ride him."

As Bob and his parents were on the way to the dining room that evening, Bob paused at the desk of the concierge.

"At what time does the Globe Saddlery Shop open?"

"At ten o'clock, sir."

Bob's father had overheard the exchange.

"What's with the saddlery shop? We leave by train for South-hampton at one o'clock."

"I know. But I want to buy a beautiful hand-made hunt saddle I saw the last time we were here."

"A saddle? We have dozens of them at home. Why do you need another?"

"I want to get this English one to go with the new hunter I just bought."

**THE RETURN CROSSING** on the *Queen Elizabeth* coincided with and contributed to another lofty level for Bob's spirits and mood. Even the small dark cloud of the hiring of Silas Allen by his father was blocked out by the sunny specter of virtually every other area of his life. During his frequent walks around the deck at all times of the day the mental reflection on any aspect of the future invariably yielded the promise of satisfaction and happiness.

He himself had lucked onto the most extraordinary horse with which he had ever been familiar, and his father had purchased three excellent brood mares in England and one in Ireland to add to his stables. His parents were still relatively young and in good health, and within less than ten months he would be married to the most beautiful and talented girl in Kentucky.

His thoughts of Nancy were most satisfactory when confined to her personal charm, beauty and skill as an equestrienne. Whenever his daydreams and memories touched on her physical desirability and their past intimate contacts, invariably the train of thought would be disrupted by intrusions of recollections of his sexual encounter with Maria on that hot afternoon.

Reflex guilt demanded the purging of such thoughts, but memories of the details of their lovemaking were so exquisite that they doomed his efforts in this regard.

The intensity of his pleasure that day had puzzled him whenever subsequently he had recalled it in the ensuing weeks. He was at a loss to explain to himself why it had been qualitatively so different from his other, although admittedly limited, sexual encounters and why, even though Maria had been far more passive and inexperienced than his previous partners, his vaunted former restraints had been swept away by a total emotional as well as physical abandon. The related guilt he felt was not from moral compunction but induced by two other considerations. One was the fact that the event occurred soon after his formal engagement to Nancy, but a more powerful factor was his sense of having done a grievous wrong to Maria. Even after his having left her that afternoon, his sense of elation and exhilaration had been diluted by a realization that his uncontrolled impetuosity had abruptly negated all of the beneficence of his prior influence in her life. He had no hope of being able to rectify the wrong and compensate her for his transgression, but his conscience demanded that he make at least a determined if insufficient apology to her.

**"GOOD AFTERNOON, MR.** Bob," Leslie said, picking up the two valises at baggage claim and heading for the long black family limousine.

"Thank you, Les," Bob responded. "I'm impressed that you remembered when I was due back. I thought I might have to telephone."

"I have to confess, sir, that I wrote it down the day you left. When will the master and mistress be coming in?"

"Unless you hear otherwise, you're to meet them at the train station day after tomorrow at three forty-five."

"All right, sir. It'll be good to have all of you back."

"How did your barbecue turn out on the fourth?"

"It was the best I've ever done, sir. I'll bet there weren't five pounds left."

"You'll have to cook up a batch for us on Labor Day."

"I'll be happy to, Mr. Bob. I can rig up a good pit right next to the smokehouse."

When the chauffeur had pulled up in front of the Falcrest mansion, he got out of the car and came around to open the door for Bob.

"Les, after you carry the bags upstairs, would you wash my car for me? I'm supposed to drop by the Club this evening, and it was pretty dirty when I left."

"Yes, sir, I'll be glad to. I'll get on it as soon as I get back from the bus station."

"The bus station? Is Fanny getting back from Memphis today? I thought her vacation was for only two weeks. I hope her mother and aunt are all right."

"Yes, sir, they're fine. She's been back a couple of weeks. Miss Rodriguez has asked me to take her to the station."

"Maria?" Bob asked in surprise. "Did she say where she's going?"

"Yes, sir. She's leaving for good. Going back west, I guess."

Bob was stunned. He stood inside the front door while the chauffeur brought in the bags.

"Just put them down here, Les, and I'll carry them up myself. By the way, don't worry about going to the bus station. I'll take Miss Rodriguez wherever she might need to go. Go ahead and get onto washing my car."

"Yes, sir. Right away."

Bob set his bags in the vestibule to his small complex of rooms and walked immediately to the back stairs. When he had reached the landing, he knocked lightly on the closed door.

"I'm not quite through packing, Leslie," came Maria's voice. "Please come back in about five minutes."

Bob hesitated for a moment and then opened the door. Maria's back was to him, for she was kneeling on a low stool before a small crucifix she had set up in the corner of the room.

"I'm sorry to intrude," he said. "Forgive me, but Leslie tells me that you are thinking about leaving."

Startled at the sound of his voice, the girl turned abruptly and rose to her feet.

"Yes," she said in a small voice, "I must go."

Bob walked over to a small cane-back chair and sat down, uncertain as to how to begin.

"Maria, this is not easy for me, for I feel very bad about what happened. I want to ask you to forgive me. I don't know what made me behave like that. It's not like me, but I completely lost control that day. I can promise, however, that it will never happen again, so you can stay. Let's try just to put it behind us and start all over. Okay?"

Maria was standing very erect, facing him, but nonetheless seemed small once again, as she had years ago. She lowered her head and spoke in a barely audible voice.

"No, sir, I must leave."

"No, you don't," he responded emphatically. "What can I do or say to convince you that you don't have to be afraid of me? Be reasonable and give me a chance to prove it. I tell you what," he continued, trying to lighten the mood, "I'll give you one of my riding crops, and any time you see me even looking at you, you can hit me with it. How about it?"

The girl remained immobile with her eyes lowered.

"I'm sorry, sir. I cannot stay."

Her obstinacy began to irritate Bob.

"Look, Maria, you are a big help to my mother. She has come to count on you and needs you here. You've talked about how much you feel you owe me. Now this is a chance for you to show it. Let's not hear any more talk about your leaving."

Maria's shoulders sagged, and when she looked up at him there were tears in her eyes.

"Mr. Hanson," she said after taking a deep breath, "I'm going to have a baby."

There was a shocked period of dead silence. Bob had heard the words but for a few moments rejected their meaning. Even after it had begun to sink in, he refused to accept it, and his mind frantically searched for evasion.

"Maria, that's not very likely. Your system suffered a severe shock. It's natural that the trauma could cause you to miss a period, but that doesn't mean . . ."

"I went to the University clinic last Thursday," she interrupted, "and I learned this morning that the tests were positive. So now you understand why I must go. Excuse me, sir, but my bus leaves at four o'clock, and I must finish packing."

Bob's mind was racing.

"Maria, that's not necessary. Listen to me. The fiancée of a friend of mine here in Lexington had an abortion four months ago. It was performed at night by a good doctor in a well-known clinic. I will call and . . ."

"No, Mr. Hanson," she said emphatically, "I would never do that."

"Maria, there's nothing to it—particularly at this early stage. It's a minor procedure and perfectly safe when done properly. No one else would ever need to know, and everything would be like before. Instead of ruining your life you'd be free to go on with it and carry out all your plans."

"No!" she repeated forcefully, tears beginning to stream down her face.

"Damn it, Maria! Why are you being so stubborn?" Bob almost shouted.

"Because that would be a greater sin than the one I have already committed," she responded, her chin trembling, "and . . . and," she continued in a barely audible voice, "I want my baby."

Only now did the full impact of this turn of events hit Bob, and he turned hot all over. He now realized that the ramifications of his precipitate blunder and her unyielding obstinacy were potentially as devastating to his own life as they were to hers, if not more so. Grotesquely, echoes of his mother's long-ago admonitions concerning the dangers of such a situation reverberated at the periphery of his consciousness. He would forever be hostage to this one blunder, never free from its consequences. Even if this girl were not now appreciative or even aware of the power it gave her, could he ever be certain that in the future she or her family would not use it to blackmail him? The threat of revelation of his paternity would be a sword of Damocles eternally suspended above his head.

Neither spoke for a long time. Maria went to the corner of the room, carefully wrapped the crucifix in a small towel and walked over to place it in her suitcase, which was lying open on the bed. Then she closed the top and buckled the two straps securely.

"Where were you going?" Bob asked in a dull voice.

"To Kansas City. I'm not sure where after that. Would you please see if Leslie is out front? I must be going."

Bob started, as though awaking from a dream.

"No," he said, getting to his feet, "that's not necessary. I will take you myself. I'll be back in a moment to get your bag."

He climbed mechanically to his room and picked up the telephone. First he summoned the garage on the intercom and requested Leslie to bring his car to the front door. Then he looked in the telephone directory and dialed the Kentucky State Department of Human Services.

\* \* \*

**NOT A WORD** was exchanged in the car until Maria noticed that they were not headed toward the center of town.

"This isn't the way to the bus station, Mr. Hanson. I remember that it is back that way."

"I know," Bob answered. "We aren't going to the bus station. I'm taking you to Louisville."

"But . . ."

"I'm sorry, but I don't want us to argue about this too. Since you insist on going through with the pregnancy, I must at least be certain that you are safe, comfortable and well cared for medically. I have made a reservation for you at a non-denominational home for unwed mothers recommended by a state social worker."

"Please, Mr. Hanson, just let me get on the bus. I can't continue to be a burden to you."

"No, Maria. For the sake of my own feelings I must be adamant about this. I shall enter you there and pay in advance for your full term. If after I leave, you ever want to get a refund and go off on your own, then that is your business. Now let's not discuss it any more."

The rest of the trip to Louisville was passed in silence. Bob pulled up in front of the Lorna Grey Home, located on a pleasant tree-lined neighborhood street, and carried the bag up the steps and into the front hall. He rang a small bell on a desk and stood with Maria under a slowly revolving ceiling fan until a woman came out from the dining room area. Dressed in a starched blue semi-uniform, she had about her that air of affectedly warm officiousness that Bob always associated with social workers.

"Good evening," she said. "I assume this is Maria."

"That's correct," Bob answered. "Maria Rodriguez."

"My name is Susan Waldron. Please, won't you all step into the office. You can leave the valise there. Maria and I will take it to her room later."

After they were seated, there was an awkward silence while the woman searched for an admittance form, filled in a few of the top spaces and then pushed it toward Maria.

"You may complete this form at your leisure and drop it by this office in the morning. Answer as many of the questions as you can. The more we know about you and your past, the better able we will be to help you. Are you the gentleman who called and talked to me this afternoon?" she asked, glancing at Bob.

"Yes, I'm the one."

"Are you the father?"

Bob bristled at the directness of this question.

"I am the one who will be financially responsible," he countered.

The woman looked back at Maria.

"Is he the father?"

Maria glanced at Bob and then lowered her head.

"Yes.

"Let me begin by describing some of the rules of the Home. First, all rooms must be kept clean and in good order. They are inspected every day. Attendance at meals must be prompt. If a girl knows she will not be here for a meal, she must inform us at least four hours in advance. We encourage all of our boarders to be involved in some kind of work outside the Home—either a paying job or public service. We don't want anyone sitting around on her hands feeling sorry for herself. Do you have an obstetrician that you prefer, or do you want us to choose one?"

"I want the best that is available," Bob suggested, "and I am not familiar with doctors here in Louisville."

"There is one that I can highly recommend. Now, that brings up the question of billing, both for medical and boarding costs. You said you are going to cover these?"

"That's correct," Bob answered.

"Shall we bill you monthly? If you plan to pay by check, I'll need a financial statement or credit references."

"I'll be paying by cash. I have enough here for the first month," he said, tossing an envelope on the desk. "I shall forward to you by mail order in the next few days enough to cover the entire term of Maria's residence and anticipated medical costs. If there is any left over or she decides to leave early, she is to take the balance with her."

Bob sensed the mild scorn in the woman's fixed stare and knew that she was fully aware of the evasiveness of his effort to avoid any possible evidence of his involvement. She continued to observe him for a moment while tapping a pencil on the desk.

"There is one other requirement we make of our girls that I should mention. We require that they mail a letter at least once a month to the father, if his identity and whereabouts are known. Naturally we would like for them to receive return letters, but unfortunately we have no control over that."

Bob felt ill at ease under her gaze and stood up, pushing his chair back.

"Are there any other matters we need to cover?" he asked. "I need to start back for Lexington."

"No, I think Maria and I can cover everything else. My dear, would you like to accompany Mr. . . . . Mr. . . . .?"

"Hanson," Bob said, resentful of the woman's obviously oblique subterfuge in learning his name.

"Yes, Hanson. Would you like to accompany Mr. Hanson to his car? I'll wait here in the office for you."

"Yes, thank you," Maria said, rising and following Bob out the door and down the steps to the car.

Dark was falling, and the warm summer air was permeated by the sweet fragrance of the flowers in the neatly maintained beds on each side of the cement walkway. Bob was intensely uncomfortable as he stood by the curb, not having anything he wanted to say. An awkward silence persisted until Maria spoke.

"Mr. Hanson, I am very sorry that I have in any way been involved in causing you pain or trouble. I appreciate what you have done for me in the past, but there are two things in this world that I simply cannot do for you—take my own life or that of my child. I hope someday you will understand that and forgive me." She was standing in front of him and looking up at him openly. Her expression was remarkably serene, and her voice calm.

Bob was reticent to meet her gaze, and she noticed this.

"And Mr. Hanson, please don't be too hard on yourself. You are a very fine, good man. Just realize that your feelings of guilt . . ."

"Guilt?" Bob interrupted. "What makes you think . . . ?" His voice trailed off.

"I don't mean guilt for what happened that day," she continued. "I mean guilt from hating me. Just realize that that is natural."

Bob reacted instantly to this remark of hers. He looked down at her, then without a word walked around the car and got behind the wheel. He started the engine, put it in gear and drove off without looking back, hounded by a mixture of emotions. He was sickened not only by feelings of anxiousness, guilt and regret but also by resentment at her pious condescension toward him. The nerve of her to lecture him—her, a simple little girl whom a few years earlier he had saved from a degrading life of prostitution! And on the drive back to Lexington it didn't improve his mood any to realize that she was right. All previous positive feelings toward her were now replaced by negative ones.

## CHAPTER TWENTY-TWO

**THE LANDSCAPE OF** Bob's life had been totally altered. The many happy facets of promise in the future were now clouded by the new reality. There was not a single joyous expectation that did not bear the seed of possible contamination and ruin. After he had secured and mailed off the balance of necessary funds to the Home and endured the emotionally charged informing his mother of Maria's sudden need to return to her family in Mexico, he tried desperately to push the whole matter out of his mind and restore some balance to his life, but that proved impossible. He was faced with the necessity of coming to a momentous decision—whether to reveal the truth to Nancy and try to achieve some kind of accommodation with her or to keep his secret to himself. Dealing with this dilemma consumed many hours in the weeks ahead. His role on the farm provided him with scant compensation. If any conflict arose between him and Silas Allen, the reedy little man made an ostentatious show of obsequious deference to Bob's views but would then later subtly subvert the substance of Bob's wishes.

The only temporary break in this grim period occurred when Bob received notice that Top Hat was due to be unloaded at Charleston near the end of August. He had a hitch put on his car, borrowed a trailer from his father and left two days early. He had made a reservation for a week at The Cloisters in Sea Island, Georgia, for he had been there with his parents before the war and knew that there was a good stable and riding rink associated with the hotel and miles of smooth riding trails floored with pine needles.

He was greatly relieved to find the horse in good shape in spite of what had been described as a rough crossing and would have sworn that the animal recognized him when he claimed him at the unloading dock. Informally he decided to call him Topper, and the big chestnut soon learned to respond to the new name. The next five days went a long way toward restoring Bob's sense of balance and stability. They fitted in with his need to be by himself, and he spent a lot of time with the horse during daylight hours and in the evening took long walks alone up and down the beach. By the time of his departure he had at least partially come to peace with what lay ahead and had decided to be open and honest with Nancy, feeling that mendacity and dishonesty were alien to his basic nature. Having made this decision replaced a potentially permanent burden with a short-range dread, and he resolved to make his confession at the very first opportunity offered. This resolution, however, was destined to be thwarted.

Nancy had arrived back in Lexington the day before Bob returned. Having learned from his parents of his purchase and probable time of arrival, she had visited with them for a while until the stable personnel complied with instructions and informed the main house of his arrival. The three of them drove up to the stables just as Bob was backing Topper out of the trailer. Nancy ran up and gave Bob a kiss and then immediately turned her attention to the horse. Walking around and around the handsome animal, she gave out a low whistle of appreciation.

"Bobby, you have pulled off an absolute coup. I am simply pea-green with envy."

"I don't blame you," he replied. "I have to admit I'm pretty proud of myself on that one. Well, what do you think, Dad? You hit the ceiling when I told you how much I had paid for him."

The elder Hanson was also scrutinizing Topper from every angle and walked up and patted him on the neck.

"A handsome horse, son, a handsome horse. I take back what I said about your judgment."

"Really, Bobby," Nancy said teasingly, "you shouldn't have bought me such a fabulous wedding gift. What in the world could I possibly give you to make up for it?"

"Simple," Bob answered with a grin. "All you have to do is just give him back to me."

"Well, you two can argue about the horse over dinner," said the mother. "Nancy has agreed to stay for supper with us. When you get unloaded, son, join us up at the house."

**AFTER DINNER THE** four of them sat in the living room talking about their various activities and experiences since their last meeting, but once the coffee tray had been removed the mother and father excused themselves and retired upstairs to allow the engaged couple some time alone. Bob both welcomed and dreaded this privacy, for while he had been showering and dressing he had resolved to take advantage of any opportunity that very evening to make his fateful revelation to Nancy.

"I'm glad you all had such a successful trip," Nancy said. "It must have done your mother a world of good, for she looks well and seems to be in good spirits, although she told me she was upset over that Mexican girl being ungrateful enough to leave her in the lurch. But *I'm* not at all upset over that," she added, getting up and coming over to sit close to Bob on the sofa.

"Bobby, I have a confession to make," she said, taking his hand.

"You? A confession?"

"Yes. I have to confess that I was very uneasy about that girl being around here. There was something about her that made me think she was dangerous. And there's something about me that I've jokingly tried to hide from you; but you would find out sooner or later, so I might as well tell you. I am terribly, terribly jealous. I will try very hard to be understanding and tolerant if your eye begins to wander, but if anything else ever wanders, I couldn't handle that. In fact, I don't ever even want to hear about your past romances. I know myself well enough to realize that sooner or later I would use the information to torture myself and bludgeon you."

Bob was rendered mute by this statement. Useless now were the well-crafted rationales he had planned to use to soften the impact of his intended revelation. After his decision to reveal the truth to her he had blithely assumed that her hurt and shock would be temporary and that reason and common sense would eventually help her to accept and adjust to the situation. The relative peace of mind that openness and honesty were going to grant to him was now denied. He was faced with only two choices: live with his deception and secret or confess and probably irretrievably destroy another critical segment of his life. The grimness of his thoughts must have been reflected in his face, for when he glanced up he saw that Nancy was observing him with a puzzled expression.

"Whoa, now, fellow!" she said with a laugh. "It's not the end of the world. I'll more than make up for all the other women that you will miss. I promise."

Then she stood up and held out her hand to him.

"Come on, love. Let's go to the back parlor where we were dancing last time."

The door had no sooner closed behind them than she moved in front of him and put her arms around his neck.

"Hold me, Bobby. Real tight."

He complied, but with no passionate inclinations.

"When I was in Michigan I thought many times about our last evening, and it bothered me a lot. It was so terrible for you, and I have felt very guilty about it. I have decided that I can't subject you to that for another six months."

She was speaking very softly, almost breathlessly, with her lips near his ear.

"I want us to start planning a very special evening sometime soon when we can be completely alone together and have a lot of time. I'm keeping a chart with day count and temperature so that we can be certain that it will be safe. After a few times, for your sake I will get fitted for a diaphragm so we won't have to worry about it. So there!" she said brightly, looking up at him and wrinkling her nose. "How's that for an early Christmas present?"

He took both of her hands in his and looked down at her.

"Sweetheart, that's a very kind and charitable thing for you to consider, but I think we should really discuss it fully. I've felt some regret about that evening myself, for I thought I had been unfair to you in light of your feelings about things. We've known each other a long time now, and we've made out okay. It won't hurt either of us to wait a little longer."

The smile on Nancy's face faded, and she looked at him solemnly.

"I can't believe what I'm hearing. Helloooo. Is this Bob Hanson I'm talking to?"

Then she smiled weakly and placed her palm on his forehead.

"Are you sure you feel all right? Well, we won't worry about it. Things will work out. I have a feeling you'll very quickly change your mind. Now, I'd best be leaving. I've still got a lot of unpacking to do."

**AT THE LEAST** propitious time in his life Bob was beset by yet another problem—idleness. This was something new to him, never before encountered. Even in childhood he had never once harassed his mother with the traditional "Momma, what can I do?" For him a wealth of interests and resources had always made of time a valued commodity in short supply and not a cloying burden, but after Nancy's departure for her weeks of dedication to the circuit, even though he was relieved to be freed from the tedious boredom of superficial social functions, he now felt adrift, trapped by circumstances in a cocoon of impotence with no ready channels for the dissipation of his energies.

The constructive phase of work on the farm had been completed, and activity had settled into a set pattern of predictable routines. Bob could have enjoyed participating in these as he had in years past, but there was a palpable difference in the atmosphere on the estate. It was no longer that happy environment that he remembered and had taken for granted. He missed Johnny Wodehouse and resented the changes that had been made since his departure. Admittedly most of them were minor but nevertheless altered the tempo and flavor of the daily life outside of the household itself.

An example of such a change was the prohibition, instituted by Silas Allen, of the farmhands eating their lunch during good weather while seated or lounging on the old stone walls down by the main garage—a practice that extended back as long as Bob could remember. In his youth he frequently chose to have his own lunch there with them, for he loved to listen to the rich voices—sometimes serious but usually jocular—as they talked and joked with one another, told stories or bantered with Fanny when she would bring down for them large pitchers of tea or buttermilk. He had warm recollections of summer days when the talk would taper off after eating and before the hour was up. He would lie on his back on top of the wall and stare up at the leaves of the oak tree above, sometimes dozing off to the sound of the cicadas or the low humming or singing of a spiritual. The new manager, however, felt that this was unseemly for a professional breeding farm and gained the owner's permission to have the "help" eat at an institutional-style wooden table out of sight behind the garage.

Allen was shrewd enough not to contest Bob's wishes or directives head on but was always circling like a jackal at the periphery, deviously and usually successfully biding his time to subvert their intent or spirit. For that reason Bob usually tried to avoid him and spent less and less time on matters relating to the running of the operation, thereby allowing the man to attain the result he was seeking. Soon their only contact would occur when Bob would run into him coming out of his father's study or would see him as he passed by the farm office on the way to Topper's stall.

Initially the horse was Bob's only salvation during this trying period. Not only were the long usually daily rides on him a soothing balm to his troubled spirit, but he relished more the hours spent tending to him—feeding, watering, currying, bathing—than he had to any other horse he had ever owned—even his beloved Tilly of his childhood. But there was a limit to the compensation that even this remarkable animal could provide. More and more Bob felt a pressing need to find some new interest or activity that would help distract him from his somber mood and the ever-present anxiety lurking in the back of his mind. In the last week of September he was spurred to find some answer.

Having returned to his room late one afternoon, he was glancing through his mail, which had as usual been placed on his desk by Leslie, when he noticed a plain envelope addressed to him in a very neat block print. There was no return address, but the postmark indicated Louisville. He hesitated for a moment before breaking the seal, extracting the one folded sheet of paper and beginning to read.

*Dear Mr. Hanson,*

*I am reluctant to intrude again this way into your personal life, but Mrs. Waldron insists on collecting all the letters and mailing them herself. She feels it important that we...*

Bob struck the top of the desk with his fist, crumpled up the letter and envelope and threw them in the wastebasket. A wave of resentment mixed with hopelessness washed over him. The little success he had achieved in pushing this personal nightmare into the back of his consciousness was now voided. He got up and began pacing back and forth in his room, trying to solve in his own mind how to find some mechanism through which he could in the coming months maintain his emotional equilibrium if not his very sanity. No traditional avenue that was open to him held any appeal, but later as he was glancing through the evening newspaper before supper a small article that ordinarily he would have passed over caught his eye.

*A producing well was brought in on Tuesday in western Breckinridge County south of the Cloverport Gas Field near the township of Tar Fork. At a depth of 1,630 feet a steady flow of crude was secured from the Chester SS Formation, and a potentially good flow of natural gas was also encountered in the Warsaw LS. The well is located on the farm of Paul Bosworth in the northeast corner of a lease owned by the driller and producer, Frank A. Rutledge of Hopkinsville.*

Bob closed the paper, stared out the window and sank into deep reflection. Slowly a possible plan of an activity that could lay claim to his time and interest began to emerge. He had a rough familiarity with the oil business in Kentucky. He knew of the maddeningly irregular and unpredictably spotty deposits of petroleum in the very old geological structures of the region and was aware that the major oil companies for the most part were reluctant to invest much effort or expense in exploration, being content to buy up the production resulting from an occasional lucky find by one of the legion of small independent wildcatters. These men could be seen in all parts of the state, driving down country roads in battered trucks towing old drilling rigs. It was a touch-and-go business with a large component of luck to it. A producing well in no way guaranteed that dry holes would not be encountered at the legal separation distance on all sides of it, and returns were usually measured in bare subsistence rather than fortunes.

The more Bob thought about it, the more the idea appealed to him. Even if unsuccessful, it would consume his time and energies and remove him from the irritations of the farm. After the purchase of Top Hat and the covering of all the projected expenses in Louisville, Bob still had a healthy balance in his income account. His own personal needs for money were minimal, and not only had his trust at the bank made steady, albeit modest, deposits throughout the years, but he had funneled into the same account the majority of his Army pay during his years in the service. He figured that if he were prudent in holding down lease costs and selective in hiring crews and rigs, even with no luck his funds could last until the time of the wedding, after which they would have to be devoted to other uses.

After supper Bob excused himself and retired to his room. For the first time in months he felt a sense of purpose and excitement. Rummaging in the back of his closet, he pulled out a box containing some of his books from courses at Georgia Tech and stayed up until the early hours of the morning reading through these texts from years past.


**BOB LEFT IN** his car early the next day and began a weeks-long process of learning some of the rules of a chancy and involved business. He spent a lot of time collecting maps and charts from the University and appropriate state agencies, conferring with engineers, visiting drilling sites and talking at great length with operators and members of the crews. By the middle of October he felt he had prepared himself as well as he could for his venture and had already chosen a rig and crew to hire on a weekly basis. The part of his efforts he enjoyed the most was contacting farmers in the various counties and utilizing friendliness, tact and patience to lease/purchase petroleum and mineral rights to their acreage. His low-key personality and farming background frequently helped him win over their trust, but very early in his campaign he realized that his convertible was by no means an asset in this regard but a hindrance. With pangs of regret, in the first week of October he traded it in for a Pontiac station wagon—a much more utilitarian vehicle for his needs.

This new enterprise served its intended purpose far more than he had hoped. Even if he had not been blessed with beginner's luck and brought in a low-volume but economically viable natural gas well on his third try, the whole effort would have been worth it. He was able to submerge himself completely in his plans and projects and once again enjoy what he was doing. As the weeks and months slipped by, more and more was he able to shed the irritations of the troublesome areas of his personal life. Except for the rewarding hours on Topper during his visits home on the weekends he spent little time on the farm and thus avoided the previous frustration. Whenever there appeared near the middle of each month the envelope with the neatly printed address, he would drop it unopened into the wastebasket, exposing himself only briefly to the pain of reflection.

His improved mood redounded positively on his relationship with Nancy. After her return in the fall she had been annoyed and mystified by his uncharacteristic moroseness and mental preoccupation and was relieved when he seemed almost his old self. One possible point of friction that was carried over and that puzzled her was the apparent reversal in their views regarding sexual intimacy. His mild rejection of her well-intentioned concession at their first meeting at the end of the summer had hurt her and slowly developed into almost an obsession with her. Fortunately, during the frenetic months of the fall there were no opportunities for them to be in situations of sufficient privacy for the conflict to arise. Nancy's infrequent returns to Lexington would usually occur during the week and thus coincide with Bob's absences, and on those occasions when they were in town at the same time, their leisure would be largely pre-empted by social or family functions. The nagging persistence of the problem, however, was evident in Nancy's occasional jokes about it with Bob—frequently more pointed than humorous.

They were both in town for most of the week following Christmas and over New Year's. They left a New Year's Eve party shortly after midnight, and Bob drove them out to park north of the quarry to relive and reminisce over that memorable "date" five years earlier. Although there were noticeable differences—his convertible was gone, there was no moon this night and the cold, damp weather discouraged their getting out of the station wagon—they both welcomed the chance to talk quietly and to be alone together. Their kisses and embraces were initially gentle and affectionate but soon became more heated and passionate. Nancy's occasional hesitant efforts to initiate greater intimacy, however, were met by lack of responsiveness or passive resistance on Bob's part. Abruptly she moved away and stared into the darkness outside the window on her side of the car.

"Bobby, I hope you won't be offended, but there's something that has been nagging in the back of my mind and that for the sake of our marriage I need to ask you about."

"Oh?" he responded, feeling a tensing of his stomach muscles in response to his reflex fear that she might come to suspect or learn of his secret.

"Yes. If there is a problem, we should face it now. Don't be mad at me for asking, but . . . are you impotent?"

Bob was both startled and relieved by her question.

"No," he laughed, playfully grasping the back of her head and shaking it lightly. "You should know better than that."

"Well, I *thought* I did, but you seem to have changed. Then are you punishing me for having turned you down back in June?"

"No, my love, I have no reason ever to want to punish you. Surely you know that. I haven't changed. Maybe my attitude about some things has changed but, if so, I think in the right direction."

Bob was of course not being honest with either Nancy or himself. He had changed. He could not consciously admit it to himself, but the catastrophic consequences to his last sexual union had strongly conditioned him to reject a matter-of-fact, relaxed acceptance of intercourse. Any recognition of its imminence now acted as a brake and inhibited the intensity of his desire.

"Our first lovemaking can be just as beautiful after the wedding," he continued. "Don't you agree?"

"Of course, but that's not the question," she answered. "I think sexual compatibility is critical in a marriage, and it seems to me it would be important to know in advance that it exists rather than finding out too late it's not there."

She fell silent and continued to stare out the window.

"Are you angry with me, sweetheart?" he asked.

"No, I'm not mad," she answered with a sigh, "but I am a little weary. Let's go home. Shall we?"

**DURING A PERIOD** of several months Bob was able to push this sensitive matter out of his mind with an unrealistic conviction that the wedding would initiate a totally new period in their lives and automatically resolve all previous problems, but unfortunately this tension resurfaced soon after the middle of April.

In February Mr. Garner had closed the deal for the purchase of Windemere, and renovations not only of the farm but of the main house had begun immediately. There was frenzied effort to complete all work before the wedding, for Nancy's wish that the reception be held on the back lawn of the mansion was taken by the parents to be written in stone. But the reception was not the only cause for concerted haste. The last two weeks prior to the ceremony were to be crammed with multitudinous social functions, among which were two other events at Windemere—a dinner dance the Saturday night preceding the wedding and the following day a huge hunt breakfast followed by a double drag hunt. Bob anticipated all of this activity with his usual lack of enthusiasm but was anxious for this stage to pass and the wedding finally to arrive. His hunger for this troubled period to be relegated to the past was reinforced on Friday, the eighteenth of April.

In his mail that day there had arrived the eighth plain envelope from Louisville. As with the preceding six, he dropped it unopened into the waste basket, then hesitated and retrieved it. It had felt heavier than the others and somehow different. When he opened it he found a piece of blank paper folded around a snapshot, initially only the back of which was visible. On it was printed: "The first picture of Roberto Rodriguez, born March 20, 1947." After a moment of hesitancy Bob turned it over. Seated in a chair at a forty-five-degree angle from the camera, Maria was gazing serenely at a small baby she was holding on her lap. Her left hand was supporting his back, but even so it was sitting amazingly erect with tiny fists holding onto her right index finger. The small dark eyes seemed to be looking directly at the camera, and it was the eyes that gave Bob a shock. There suddenly flashed through his mind the realization that this was flesh of his flesh gazing out at him, not an abstraction representing a burdensome problem.

With a quick reflex motion he dropped it in the wastebasket again and walked over to the window. He stood there for a long time watching the bobbing and weaving of a robin on the back lawn, aware of a sudden feeling of sadness. Finally he returned to his desk, retrieved the photo from the basket once again and placed it for safekeeping in the thickest of his text books.

In an effort to dispel the remnants of a persistent despondency he planned and arranged for himself and Nancy a pleasant interlude for the following day. After lunch with a few friends at the Club they had gone for a long ride in the afternoon prior to attending a dinner that evening given in their honor. In accordance with the plan they had met on horseback at the main stable at Windemere and conducted a thorough circuit of the extensive estate. Upon its completion Nancy insisted that they tether their horses near the main house and that Bob come inside with her to inspect the new decorations, planned by her mother and completed with, at times, more opulence than good taste. There was still an odor of fresh paint in the house, and since it was Saturday the furniture movers had quit work promptly at noon.

Bob was largely disinterested in the decorations and furnishings but went along with the tour out of deference to Nancy, who was like a child in a toy store. There were exclamations of delight at each room they entered, and her eyes were flashing with excitement. When they entered the room on the second floor that was to be the master bedroom, she was almost beside herself. The carpet had been laid and most of the furniture was in place, but the mattresses to the king-sized bed were still covered with brown paper and had been unceremoniously left by the movers in the middle of the room. Nevertheless, she clapped her hands rapturously, turned to Bob and looked up at him.

"Isn't this going to be *divine*? Tell me, Bobby, don't you like it too?"

He had never before seen her more beautiful than at this moment or with more child-like appeal. He walked over and put his arms around her.

"Yes, my love, I think it's going to be 'simply *divine*' too but nowhere near as divine as you are."

When he bent over to kiss her, she wrapped her arms around his waist and returned his kiss fervently. Somehow the faint odor of horses mixed with the aroma of her perfume and lipstick ignited a flame in him that he had not known for months. Her lithe body was warm and firm against his and reciprocated his movements of passion.

"Oh, yes, darling, yes," she said breathlessly, her arms holding his pelvis against hers. "Now is the time. Oh, yes!"

Releasing her hold, she fell backward onto the covered mattress and raised her right leg.

"Help me get out of my boots, and I can do the rest."

The loud rattling of the wrapping paper on the mattress may have acted as a switch, but for some reason a chill suddenly seized Bob's stomach, his hands became clammy and he lost all trace of sexual desire.

"No . . . no, Nancy . . . Not now . . . Not here," he stammered.

"Bobby!" she almost screamed. "Please! Make love to me! Please!"

"Not this way . . . Not like this," he said lamely.

"Wh . . . what?" she uttered incredulously, her face mirroring deep hurt soon displaced by anger. Leaping to her feet, she glowered at him.

"Just what the hell *is* it with you, Bobby? Are you trying to drive me crazy, or are you a Jekyll and Hyde?"

"Sweetheart, there are only two weeks to go and we will be married," he said, seeking some credible evasion. "I don't feel we need to go rolling in the hay somewhere before the wedding just to prove a point."

Without uttering another word, Nancy walked briskly out of the room and trotted down the long graceful winding staircase. Bob followed her but had difficulty keeping up. He caught up with her just as she had untied her horse and swung quickly into the saddle.

"Wait, darling," he said. "Don't leave angry like this."

"Bobby, you obviously don't want me. I don't turn you on, do I?"

"My love, how can you say that? You are the most beautiful woman I've ever known," he responded.

"That's not what I asked," she said bitterly. "Don't bother to pick me up for the dinner tonight. I'll get there on my own."

With that she turned her horse abruptly and galloped off.

In spite of their efforts that night to conceal the tension between them they did not have much success, and several of the guests overheard her shrill anger when she learned that Bob would be in the southeastern part of the state on Monday and might not make it back for a party to be given for them by her cousin.

"Are you some kind of nut or something? Why are you still pouring money down those stupid holes in the ground, especially right now? Are you doing it to spite me, or are you trying to tell me something?"

"Nancy, I told you about this project a month ago, and I've already contracted the rig and crew. This is my last one—I promise. This is my swan song. I'll try hard to be back, but I sincerely doubt I'll make it in time. The site is in a tough location, and we're going to have to cut our own road. A Cat is being trucked in and should be there by the time I get there, but it'll be slow going."

"I'm not interested in all that," she retorted. "Let's put it this way:

If you ever decide you've got a little time for me and my friends, just let me know." With that she turned on her heel and walked away.

**AT SIX O'CLOCK** on Monday morning Bob was finishing breakfast when Leslie appeared at the breakfast room door.

"Mr. Bob, Miss Nancy wants you on the telephone."

When Bob heard her voice, he knew that she had been crying.

"Bobby," she said, trying to control her sobs, "I was miserable all day yesterday, and I didn't sleep at all last night. What's happening to us? How did all this get started?"

"Sweetheart," Bob answered, "don't worry about it. It's just been a spat, a misunderstanding. People have them all the time. Just keep reminding yourself that we love each other and it will all pass. I'll get back as soon as I can."

"Oh, darling, I'm so sorry," she sniffled. "Sometimes I get so confused. But I didn't want you to leave with us still mad at each other. Drive carefully and take care of yourself. Don't rush by trying to get back tonight. Just call me the first chance you get. Okay?"

"I will, darling. Have a good time at the party, and tell Bernice I'm sorry I couldn't be there. I love you."

## CHAPTER TWENTY-THREE

**BOB'S LAST EFFORT** was to be a test well drilled to eleven hundred eighty-five feet on some very hilly acreage on the line between Knox and Bell counties. He had secured the lease four months earlier, but its low cost and his delay in exploring it were due to the fact that topologically and geologically it held little promise and, according to state records, had not attracted the interest of any other drillers. The owner of the tract of land, a bare subsistence farmer typical of the "hill folk" of the region, was a lean, sparse man named Simpkins, whom Bob had come to like immediately. Taciturn, aloof and fiercely independent, he had nonetheless displayed the typical regional characteristic of warm hospitality. Having opened the door in response to Bob's knocking that raw day back in January, he regarded him guardedly until Bob explained his presence and then ushered him into the tiny board-and-batten cabin. After a tentative agreement had been reached on the terms and conditions of the lease while they were seated around the single coal stove, the farmer and his wife had invited this relative stranger to remain for lunch. As the cold wind sighed through the bare branches of the gaunt trees outside and tried to force its way past the caulking in the warped and weathered sides of the shanty, Bob had sat at the pine table and shared with them the cornbread and white beans with hamhock.

Bob went immediately to the shack when he arrived this morning, for as a point of courtesy he wanted to inform the farmer of their arrival and intentions and, although legally not required, secure a final authorization for their drilling. The wife informed Bob that her husband had gone down into the hollow to help a neighbor clear some stumps but that she was sure it was all right to proceed. When Hank Pilley, the rig owner and foreman, had finished unloading the grader, Bob spread out a map on the ground and sketched in with a red pencil the route for the required access road to the selected drill site, marked with a cross. He had exhaustively studied all the charts on the area that he could find, especially the geological maps of the counties and the topological surveys of the farm and surrounding area, but there were not even subtle clues that could facilitate a professionally based judgment on the possible location or even existence of petroleum deposits. Bob's decision was based purely on a hunch. Three ridges with quite steep slopes converged about a quarter-mile from the farmer's cabin. In one of the valleys to the east of the summit there was a hint of a secondary geological structure that just might indicate the possible existence of a deep-lying granite dome. In a process about as exact as throwing a dart at a map, Bob had marked a cross on the map.

"Why did you pick the location down on the slope of that steep draw?" Pilley asked. "In rainy weather it'll be a mess getting trucks or equipment up and down in the mud. Let's move it up on top of the ridge. It'll be a helluva lot easier to cut the road in and set up the rig. We can drill that much farther down in the time saved."

"No," Bob answered, "I want it where I've marked it. There's probably nothing but junk down there, but if there is a dome I don't want to penetrate the top and blow any head of natural gas. I'd rather come in down the side and maybe be able to retrieve any oil. As for getting up and down, use the Cat if you have to. We've had to lease it for a whole week anyway, haven't we? Now let's get at it. I don't have much time to spend here with you."

The going was slow. Not only were there the usual minor breakdowns and troubles with the equipment, but the steepness of the slope required occasionally the time-consuming anchoring of the grader with steel cables to avoid the risk of having it tumble into the valley. By dark the access road had been completed, but there was not enough daylight left in which to start setting up the drilling platform.

"Okay," Bob called out to the crew, "let's knock off for the day. I'll drive you all into town to the hotel. I ate in the coffee shop a few months back, and the steaks are good. I know that when I leave tomorrow this slave-driver Pilley will starve you all to death, so dinner's on me tonight."

Bob had them at the site by shortly after dawn the next morning, and three hours later the platform had largely been secured. He knew his presence would not be required for the erecting of the rig, so after a final conference with Pilley he set out for the return to Lexington.


**HE STOPPED HIS** station wagon by the steps in front of the house and was requesting Alfred, the gardener, to have Leslie clean all the mud and grime off of it by mid-afternoon when he noticed an unfamiliar car coming up the long driveway. It was a beautiful late-model four-door convertible Buick with the top down. Bob was so engrossed in admiring the car that it had pulled to a stop behind his before he noticed the military hat of the driver.

"Well, I'll be damned!" he laughed.

"Hey, little Robbie!" came the greeting as the door opened and the tall frame of his old friend towered above him. "I always knew you were rich, but I never realized you were *this* rich," he said, with a whistle, looking up at the intricate molding and heavy brass chandelier of the stately columned front entrance. "Damn! It's good to see you again. It must have been at least three weeks since I left you on that ramp in South Texas."

The two friends embraced, and Knute lifted Bob bodily off the ground as he used to do in the past.

"Knute, you son of a gun! When I didn't see your picture at the head of any of those victory parades in Europe, I assumed you had bought the farm. What the hell are you doing in Lexington?"

"I'm just passing through on the way to an assignment in Washington. I've been home on leave. My old man had a heart attack."

"I'm sorry to hear that. Is he doing okay?"

"Not really. He's still alive, but he won't last long. He refuses to leave off the liquor and women."

"Well, come on inside," Bob said, opening the front door. "You're just in time for lunch. Alfred will bring your bags in. You will be able to stay for a visit, won't you?"

"A couple of days maybe, if I won't be in your way."

"In my way? My Lord! It would take us a month to catch up on all the news."

Bob's parents were not at home for lunch, so the former schoolmates had ample opportunity to sit and talk to their hearts' content.

"I should have guessed that you would stay in the Air Corps after the war," Bob said, "but I thought you would be at least a bird colonel by now. You must have made a pass at the CO's wife to be busted back to the rank of major."

"You're partly right, Robbie. I was a bird colonel, but that was wartime rank. My commission is now Regular Army. That's why I was reduced in-grade, so you were wrong about the CO's wife. Besides, I don't chase women anymore."

"You've obviously changed a lot," Bob laughed, "but I seriously doubt you've changed *that* much."

"I've changed?" Knute asked. "You're just like you always were, little buddy. How have I changed?"

"Well, I guess the most noticeable thing is the way you talk. You speak pretty good English, not west Texan. You use a lot more consonants now and actually complete whole syllables. How did that miracle occur?"

"There you go with that highfalutin' intellectual talk of yours," Knute grinned. Then he took a swallow of coffee, put his cup down and looked out the window onto the back lawn with a sober expression on his face and a faraway look in his eye.

"I had some excellent tutoring."

"Oh?" Bob said quizzically, motioning to Lillian that they were through and that the plates could all be removed.

"Robbie, would you believe old Knute tripped up and fell in love?"

"Yeah, I believe. As long as I've known you, you've fallen in love with every woman you've seen on the street."

"Naw, I mean *really* in love."

Knute's continued pensiveness deterred Bob from attempting humor again, so he just waited, sensing that his friend would continue. Knute took another swallow of coffee, cleared his throat and glanced at Bob.

"You're the only person I will ever tell this to, little buddy. The 92nd Bombardment Group was stationed in Bovingdon, not far from London. When I was made exec officer in 'forty-four, I started living off the base, in the gate house to a large estate. The owner, a British naval hero, was captured during a raid on Dieppe, and his wife, Lady Margaret Carrington, was—is—the classiest woman you'll ever see. Really top-drawer stuff in every way. You won't be surprised to hear that I put the move on her right away, but then it began to backfire on me. I thought about her all the time and wanted to be around her all the time—not just when we were in the sack. She launched a one-woman crusade to educate me. She taught me how to use a knife and a fork, how to hold a tea cup—see?" he prompted, holding up his coffee cup, "how to talk and even how to dress. She even had me reading books I didn't understand. I had to do everything she told me to, because I was really clobbered, little friend. I would have walked through fire if she had asked me to. I was ready to quit the Air Corps after the war, marry her and stay in England."

Knute placed his cup in the saucer, pushed it away from him and fell silent. Bob waited for a moment and then asked, "Why didn't you?"

Knute leaned back slightly and looked up at the ceiling. "When her husband, who had been an Olympic middle-distance runner in 1936, got back from a POW hospital in April, she saw that he was in terrible shape—a cripple, an invalid for life. If he had been healthy, I think she could have left him, but, being the kind of woman she is, she decided to stand by him. So, little buddy, I've decided to stay married to the Air Corps. But it's a pretty good mistress. You should have stayed in too. It's a good life. We're being set up as a separate branch, so there'll be Army, Navy and Air Force."

"What will you be doing in Washington?" Bob asked, anxious to change the tone of the conversation.

"Some staff work; but that'll be temporary, I'm glad to say. We are forming a Strategic Air Command, and I'll ultimately probably end up out west with flying duty. At least I've requested it. We've got an airplane on line now—the B-47—that an old barnstormer like you wouldn't believe. I tell you, Robbie, you should have stayed in. But enough about me. When did you get out and what have you been up to?"

"I got out right after VJ Day, and I've been helping my dad with the farm and doing a little drilling here in Kentucky for gas and oil."

"*You*, a wildcatter? Well, I'll be damned," Knute laughed.

"Yeah, but that career is about over for me, because I'm getting married next Saturday."

"Married?! Son of a bitch! I've been sitting here braying like an ass and here you're the one with all the news."

"My Lord!" Bob said, jumping to his feet, "you've made me forget all about the fact that I had promised Nancy I would call her as soon as I got back."

He rang the summons bell, and Lillian appeared again at the door.

"Lillian, would you show Major McCutcheon back to the south guest room? Knute, I'll be with you in a couple of minutes. Change into some comfortable clothes. I've got a horse I want to show you."

When Bob talked to Nancy, he informed her of Knute's arrival and asked if he could bring him along that evening.

"Bobby, cocktails wouldn't be a problem, but this is a seated dinner. It's too late to call and have him included."

"Don't worry about it," Bob advised. "We're old-time friends, and he's a laid-back fellow. When I come to pick you up, he can follow in his car and come on back here when we sit down to dinner. I'll have Fanny fix him a good supper. He's only going to be here two days, so I can't leave him completely."

**BOB'S SUGGESTED ACCOMMODATION** proved to be unnecessary. When they walked into the party, Knute's charm took center stage and he captivated everyone, especially the women. The overbearing physical presence he had always exuded was now enhanced by his military bearing in his dress uniform, and the personal characteristics that had even in his younger years made him engagingly attractive were rendered more effective now by a softening of the rough edges and a suppression of the raw crudeness. The hostess was so breathlessly impressed that she insisted he stay for dinner and had an extra plate set between those of Bob and Nancy. Knute kept both of them highly entertained during dinner, and when he stood up at one point to shake the hand of someone whom the hostess wanted to introduce, Nancy leaned forward and whispered to Bob, "Bobby, I'm so glad you brought him along. He's charming, and he's really made the party. Why don't you bring him over to our place tomorrow afternoon? I'll be working with Ben on my new horse, but I'd love to show him around."

"Well, we'll see," Bob answered. "He doesn't have much time here, but I'll ask him what he'd like to do."

When Knute sat back down, Nancy turned to him.

"Major, that is a perfectly yummy car you have. Where did you get it?"

"I bought it in Dallas a few days ago. I'll tell you a secret. When your friend here and I were at Georgia Tech together, I loved him like a brother in all respects but one. I was so envious I literally hated him for a beige Buick convertible he had at that time, and I swore that one day I was going to have one like it."

"I knew his car very well," Nancy laughed. "He still had it until six months ago. But you've outdone him now, for yours has four doors. Will you all excuse me, please? I have to go to the little girls' room."

When Nancy had left, Bob noticed Knute cutting his eyes at him and grinning. Then with a low whistle he turned and faced him

"Man, little Robbie, where in the world did you find her? Son, I hate to tell you but you are over-horsed, and I do mean *over*-horsed! Whoooeee! You're going to have to live carefully from now on, for you've just used up all your luck in one shot."

"You know something, Knute?" Bob responded with a grin. "I think I have to agree with you on that."

**WHEN THEY DROVE** up to the Garners' "schooling ring" the following afternoon, Nancy was standing by the fence in riding boots and pants and a short-sleeved cotton shirt. Her hair was pulled back in a jaunty ponytail, and although she had on very little make-up, she was as stunning as ever. She was watching as Ben Starsi was taking a gray gelding around the ring and over some jumps. She motioned him over when Bob and Knute got out of the car and approached the gate.

"Ben, this is Major McCutcheon. Knute, this is my right hand man, Ben Starsi."

"Pleased to meet you, Major," Ben said, touching his crop to the bill of his hat. "How are you, Mr. Hanson?"

"I'm fine, Ben, thank you. What have you got there? It's a nice-looking horse."

"This is Bruno's Talent, my latest," Nancy interjected. I bought him a month ago."

"How's he doing?" Bob inquired.

"Oh, he's coming along, but there are a few things we have to work on."

"Like what?"

"He goes along smooth as silk and then will suddenly refuse a jump. Ben, take him around a few times."

Starsi made one perfect trip around the jumps, but on the second circuit the horse refused jump number three. Two of the next circuits were flawless, but on a last one he refused the same jump again.

"Does he give you a hint that he's thinking about refusing?" Bob asked.

"No, sir. None at all."

"Does going to the whip nudge him over?"

"No, sir."

"The mystery is that out on a brush or timber course he's always eager to go—never refuses," Nancy said.

"Would you mind if I give him a try?" Knute drawled.

Bob looked at him and laughed, certain that he was joking.

"That's not a quarter-horse, Knute."

"Well now, little buddy, don't you go putting me down. How about it, Nancy? Can I take a couple?"

"Why . . . sure, Knute. I guess so," she answered uncertainly.

Ben dismounted, and the Texan stepped through the gate and swung easily into the saddle. He trotted the horse for a few minutes in a figure-eight pattern in an open area of the paddock and then completed four leisurely circuits of the jumps. Bruno's Talent didn't refuse a single one.

Nancy and Ben were impressed, and Bob was dumbfounded.

"All right, Major, what's your secret?" Ben asked, pushing his cap on the back of his head.

Knute dismounted and handed him the reins.

"I happened to notice that he likes a right lead when he's jumping slightly to the left on number three," Knute drawled. "The times he refused he had for some reason switched to a left lead just after clearing number two. He's still young and will get over that, but in the meantime hold him in a right lead on that turn and he'll do okay."

"When did you learn so much about jumpers?" Nancy asked, looking up at him with open admiration. "In Texas?"

"No, ma'am. I had a friend in England who had Benson Thomas, one of the best trainers in the country, living on her place. They were badly short of help during the war, so I volunteered to help exercise her stable of horses. Mr. Thomas had to teach me a lot before he'd trust me to hunt on them."

"You mean you've been on fox hunts in England?" Bob asked in amazement. "Well, I'll be damned. I had always imagined that you couldn't stay in a saddle unless it had a horn on it."

"Well, I'll have to confess something to you," Knute grinned. "The first time I got up on an English saddle and looked down I thought I had lost a dear, dear friend and my voice went up two octaves."

Bob laughed, noticed Knute's wink at Nancy and heard her giggle.

"Have you done any hunting over here?" she asked.

"No. Not yet. But while I'm stationed in Washington I hope to do some down in Virginia and Maryland. I've got a batch of fancy duds."

"Knute," Nancy said, grabbing onto his arm, "Bob tells me you plan to leave Thursday. Don't go. Stay for the weekend. There's going to be a great party at the Club on Friday night, my parents are hosting a dinner dance for us on Saturday, and on Sunday we're going to have a hunt over a long beautiful course. I'll even let you ride one of my favorite horses."

"Well, I don't know about that," he answered. "I could check with Headquarters to see if they could do without me for a few days, but I imagine little buddy here will have seen enough of me by in the morning."

"You know that's not true," Bob responded. "I wish you could stay for ten days. Then I'd have Bill Christie kidnapped and make you my Best Man. When we get home, give Washington a call. If they give you a hassle, I think Dad might be able to help out. He's a good friend of General Westover."

**KNUTE'S PRESENCE DURING** the next few days was a boon to Bob. His friend's company eased the tedium he usually experienced at parties, and they had a lot of time to reminisce, talk over old times at Tech and relate war-time experiences. Nancy was enthralled by the big man and stayed in a good mood, there being no opportunity for friction between her and Bob. On Friday night the three of them were standing at the bar at the Club laughing and talking when a waiter approached.

"Mr. Hanson, you have a telephone call. You can take it in the hall."

"Thank you," Bob said. "You kids excuse me. I'll be right back."

"Mr. Hanson, this is Hank Pilley," came the voice over the telephone.

"Yeah, Hank, what's going on?" "We're down to eleven hundred and sixty feet, and I thought I'd get your permission to stop here. Overtime starts tomorrow, and I see no reason to run up the cost on you."

"What do the deepest samples show?"

"Nothing, sir. If you can find a market for limestone and clay, you'll be a rich man."

"Well, you're probably right about pulling out, but we might as well go down to the depth I set. You should be down all the way by noon, and I'll pay the overtime. Okay?"

There was a pause at the other end of the line. "Well, sir, I can't do that. I broke my last bit this evening. Let's just call it quits, and I won't charge you for it."

"You broke your bit? What happened? Did you get it out?"

"Yes, sir, we got it out. I don't know what happened. It had been going real smooth."

Bob thought for a moment. "Listen, Hank, stay put. I'll drive up in the morning and pick up a couple of bits on the way. I'll get a good hard one. I should be there by ten o'clock."

When he walked back to the bar, Nancy and Knute looked at him questioningly. "Is everything all right at home?" Nancy asked.

"That wasn't from home. It was my rig foreman up in Knox County. I've got to run up there for a little while in the morning."

"You've got to *what?*" Nancy asked shrilly.

"Look, sweetheart, I'm just going up to close the operation be back by the middle of the afternoon. I promise."

"You and that stupid drilling," she snorted. "I think it's disgusting. You must have a girl up there, or something."

Having said that, she flounced off in a huff. Knute regarded Bob for a moment with a crooked smile.

"Tell me if I'm wrong, little buddy, but somehow I get the feeling she doesn't want you to be an oil man."

"You know, old friend, now that you mention it, on a couple of occasions I've had the same vague impression."


**BOB WAS AT** the rig by nine-thirty the next morning with two new bits. He told Pilley to resume drilling immediately and continue to the target depth of eleven hundred eighty-five feet, which shouldn't take more than two or three hours at the most. His decision to adhere to his original plan was based almost solely on stubbornness. Certainly he did not need the extra expense of paying the crew overtime wages. Luckily he had put aside the funds he and Nancy would need for their honeymoon in California and Hawaii, for by now his account was exhausted. He had even had to sell at a sacrifice price a month earlier the production from his one gas well.

"Mr. Hanson, this shouldn't take too long," Pilley said, "but if we're not all the way down by one o'clock, we're going to have to pull out. It'll take us over an hour just to plug the hole, and I'm on contract to be at a site over in Muhlenberg County by tomorrow night."

"I understand," Bob said. "That's okay by me, for I have to leave about then myself."

He stayed at the site and watched as the new bit was installed, the shaft again lowered into the bore hole and the drilling continued. Pilley was fuming at the slow rate of progress when he suddenly let out a loud oath.

"What's the problem?" Bob called out.

"I think we just broke another bit," Pilley answered. "How about it, sir? Let's call it a day and go home."

"What was the depth?"

"We're down to seventy-two."

"See if you can get the bit up and let me look at it."

Forty minutes later Bob was inspecting the ruptured tip. He rubbed some of the grit between his fingers and was fairly certain it was granite. He glanced at his watch and saw that it was eleven-fifteen.

"Put on the last bit and go down another ten. Then pull out and plug. I'm going up to the house and tell Simpkins we made a good try. I'll meet you there at one o'clock and give you a final check for what I owe you. I won't be able to give the boys what I had hoped, but I'll make a little gesture anyway."

Simpkins and his wife were sitting on their porch when Bob walked up. The farmer was whittling on a piece of willow with a knife, the blade of which had been worn narrow and almost paper-thin by months and years of whittling and honing, whittling and honing. The wife was sitting in a wooden rocking chair, shelling beans.

"Well, Mr. Simpkins, we'll be wrapping it up today. I'm sorry for the scar on your land there, but it couldn't be helped. Maybe you'll be able to find some use for the road."

"That's all right, son," Simpkins said, leaning over and spitting off the edge of the porch. "Maybe someday I'll just set up a little still down there."

"Not a bad idea," Bob laughed. "You could make some good stuff. There's a spring about fifty feet beyond the drill hole flowing good clear water. If we could just have found some flowing black stuff, then you could have bought all the premium bourbon you could ever drink."

"Well, Mr. Hanson, that don't bother me none. Carrie and I have been all through the Depression and all through the war, and we'll still make out. We won't go hungry. Our two boys have gone off on their own, so our needs are pretty simple. I would've liked to buy Carrie a new stove and maybe one of them fancy clothes-washing machines, but if I had, it probably would've ruined her anyway."

Mrs. Simpkins laughed softly to herself but continued rocking and shelling.

"Well, I'm going down to my car," Bob said and waved. "I've got a lot of paper work to finish for the state. I'll be back up in about an hour."

At twelve-thirty Bob shoved the last report forms into his brief-case, got out of his car and walked up the footpath toward the shanty. Suddenly the ground and the still air reverberated with a deafening low-frequency explosion. Chickens that had been scratching in the front yard squawked and started running for the security of the hen house, and four goats dashed around and around their small pasture with the bells on their collars tinkling. Bob hesitated for a moment and then started running down the muddy road toward the drill site. As he rounded the last curve, he came to an abrupt stop. Members of the crew were whooping and shouting, and sixty feet in the air towered a black geyser, cascading back down onto the platform, the drill shaft that had been blown out of the bore hole and the drilling scaffold that had been toppled by the force of the eruption. Running toward him like a figure from hell came Pilley, covered with oil and with only his eyes and grinning teeth clearly visible.

"We've got a blower, Mr. Hanson!"

"Anybody hurt?"

"No, sir. We were lucky."

Bob's mind was working with feverish speed. Hesitating only seconds, he began barking orders.

"There's a logging road around that side of the ridge. Take the Cat to the end of it and push on as close as you can get to the bottom of the slope below the well. Scoop out a reservoir and pile up a dam on the downside. If I can get in touch with Huggins, I'll have him dispatch some tanker trucks right away. I'll have him bring an auxiliary pump and some extra line to reach the turnaround point. Do you think a thousand feet should do it?"

"Yes, sir, for the time being. But we've got to get that monster capped."

"I'm going to call Thompson up in Ohio. I hear he's the best. If I can locate him, I'll have him rent a plane and pilot and fly down. He should be here by tonight. What will he need that we don't have?"

"Just tell him to get down here. What we don't have we can get from Baxter's in town."

"Okay, hop to it," Bob said and took off at a dead run for the shack.

The farmer was still sitting on his bench going through the motions of whittling, although he was looking down the road and paying no attention to the success of his manual labors. His wife opened the screen door and looked out.

"Poppa, what's going on?"

"Mr. Simpkins," Bob said breathlessly, "we've had a stroke of luck. You can order that washing machine now as soon as I get through using your telephone. May I?"

"Why, sure, Mr. Hanson. Carrie, tell your gossipy friends to get off that party line. Tell 'em you'll call 'em back when we're through."

Bob's luck held. He was able to reach not only Huggins but also Sims Thompson within twenty minutes and get the necessary balls rolling. Pausing to catch his breath, he realized he had best alert Nancy. He was so excited and elated that it did not occur to him that her reaction might be different from his.

"Sweetheart, I have great news!"

"Then that must mean you're back in town. That's the best news you could give me. But you sound funny. We must have a bad connection. Where are you?"

"I'm still up in the country, but listen, love, we've hit oil this morning—a really big one. If I can tie up this area, we'll be on easy street and I might even be able to afford to run Windemere."

"I'm happy for you, Bobby, but you know perfectly well you don't have to worry about money. Now, I've got to run. I'm meeting Sissy at the Club in twenty minutes. Pick up Knute and come straight there. You can tell me all about your little fun games when you get in. About three o'clock, you think?"

"Nancy, you don't understand. I can't leave here now. We have oil flowing onto the open ground. There are a million things I have to take care of. Sweetheart, I hate for you to be disappointed, but I can't make it back by tonight. We'll have to cap the well, and I don't know how long that will take. I'll get back as soon as I can in the morning."

There was stony silence on the other end of the line.

"Nancy?"

"Robert," her voice began, cold as steel, "you're not going to do that to me and my family again. My mother and father have gone to a lot of trouble and expense to give this dance for us, and you're going to be here for it. I don't care what you have to do—strike a match to your little playtoy or whatever . . ."

"But . . ."

"Let me finish," she interrupted. "I want you to pick me up at my house at seven-thirty. If you're not there, as far as I'm concerned, don't come back at all."

There was a loud click as the receiver was slammed down. Bob felt a wave of chagrin at this total lack of understanding on her part but did not have the luxury of time to worry about it. Immediately he dialed home.

"Mrs. Hanson's residence."

"Lillian, is my father there?"

"No, sir. He went to play golf."

"Is Major McCutcheon there?"

"Yes, sir. He's having lunch with your mother in the dining room."

"Call him to the phone, please."

"Hey, little buddy, what's going on?"

"Knute, you've got to do me a big favor."

"You name it. Where are you?"

"I'm over in Knox County. We brought in a well this morning."

"Hot damn! That's good news!"

"Yeah, but I don't have much time to talk right now. It's a big one for around here—a gusher—and we've got to get it under control."

"Listen, old buddy, tell me where you are and I'll be right there. I helped the Old Man cap a few in the old days, and I'll stick with you."

"I appreciate it, Knute, but I've got a fellow coming down from Ohio to cap it for me. That's not why I called you. I need you to help me there. I just talked to Nancy, and she's mad as hops—really furious. There's no way I can make it back tonight. I've got to pick up my capper at the airport forty miles away and get him up here, and then I've got to start beating the bushes and try to pick up as many leases in this area as I can before the vultures start streaming in. I'm sure the news is already out, for I had to call a shipper this morning. I want to ask you to pick up Nancy for me at seven-thirty and look after her during the dinner and the dance. You can't miss her: she'll be the one foaming at the mouth. Man, was she mad! Try to help her understand my situation so that she'll be hunting the fox tomorrow and not me. Will you do that for me?"

"Hey, little Robbie, I won't be doing you a favor. It's the other way around."

"And one other thing. Have someone tell Sam to have Topper saddled and ready to go in the guest corral up near the house at Windemere by nine-thirty in the morning. Okay?"

"Consider it done, little buddy."

"Thanks, old friend. Now I've got to make tracks. Just remember:

Don't stick your little pinky out when you're drinking your coffee tonight."

**THERE WAS NOT** a moment of let-up for the next ten hours. At eleven p.m., not having stopped to eat since an early breakfast at home, Bob had to settle for a cup of coffee and a package of cheese crackers at the bus station before falling bone-tired into bed at the Pineville Hotel. Even though exhausted, he had a feeling of elation at what he had been able to accomplish that day:

Rupert Simpkins had been invaluable to him. He knew almost everyone in that section of both counties and accompanied Bob up the hollows and down the country roads to talk to other farmers and land-owners. Calm and placid in spite of the considerable good fortune that had come that day to himself and his wife, he encouraged his acquaintances to grant Bob leases and exerted the pressure of his own implied disapproval if they sought too high a price. As a result by nine o'clock Bob had succeeded in tying up the bulk of the good acreage within an area of over a hundred square miles. He had picked up Thompson at the airport at three-fifteen, rounded up four extra helpers and helped them get started up at the site. Every time he and Simpkins had passed near the farm on their crisscrossing of the area, he would stop by to see if any progress was being made. Finally, at eight-forty under the glare of bright lights powered by a generator, Thompson, Pilley and their crews succeeded in stemming the flow, capping the well and installing the fittings and valves necessary for controlled production.

**ON THE DRIVE** back to Lexington the next morning Bob could scarcely contain himself. His excitement bordered on giddiness. What a stroke of luck to have attained success on his very last try—and such astounding success! He enjoyed wildcatting and had regretted having by necessity to abandon it. Now he would not only be able to continue what he enjoyed doing but would also be able to make enough money independently to support himself and Nancy in the style that Windemere would demand. This afforded him the sweet luxury of extinguishing his distaste at the prospect of having to rely on hand-outs from his father and father-in-law.

With a few days' effort in the coming week he would be able to tie up all the loose ends in the area and be prepared to start a planned and concerted drilling program when he returned from his honeymoon. For a change there seemed to be few clouds on the sunny horizon.

Bob stopped by the house to shower, shave off a day's growth of beard and don his riding clothes. It was nine-forty-five when he walked into the loggia at Windemere. The riders had departed thirty minutes earlier, but the fabulous array of dishes for the hunt breakfast was still on the sideboard—sliced turkey, country ham, beef, cold lamb, kidneys, sausage, bacon, scrambled eggs, grits, potatoes, biscuits, cakes and many kinds of spiced and fresh fruits and juices as well as coffee and tea. Having paused to eat only a quick bite, he proceeded onto the back lawn and saw Topper tethered to the rope of the temporary corral. Mounting quickly, he set off at a gallop.

He knew well the long course that would be taken by the riders on the double hunt. He felt that if he cut west down Morrow Lane, passing close to Falcrest Acres, with Topper's speed he could intercept the pack at the turn and move easily to join the front runners. The rhythm of the powerful movements of his extraordinary mount added to the exhilaration that Bob was already feeling. He was confident the horse understood his shouted encouragements as he guided him into an oblique jump over a stone fence onto the meadow on the right. The jump was as smooth and virtually effortless as ever, but Bob was almost dislodged from the saddle as Topper began to limp badly after he had landed on the other side. Bob reined him to a halt and dismounted to examine the favored right leg, dreading the possibility that he may have fractured the navicular or sesamoid bone or cracked the lower end of the metacarpal. There was no flinching, however, when he applied pressure all the way down from the shoulder to the hoof, and when he raised the foot he was relieved to see that the trouble was caused by a large stone that had wedged firmly between the sides of the shoe. Having no success in dislodging it with the aid of any of several sticks he found in the area, Bob on foot led Topper through a break in the wall back down the lane and through an east gate into Falcrest Acres.

This further delay ruled out his catching up with the other riders, but Bob was not disappointed. In fact he welcomed the long, leisurely walk through the pastures and up the hill to the maintenance barn. It was a magnificent morning, one of those April days in Kentucky that brings with it the full promise of spring, and the interlude gave him the opportunity to reflect at leisure on the sudden happy turn in the tide of his affairs.

His preoccupation was so intense that when he heard a low whinny from one of the stalls inside the barn, he had to force himself to make a mental note to inform someone on the weekend crew. No horses were to be penned up there on Saturdays and Sundays, for there were no "demand feed" watering troughs in those stalls. Having tied the reins to the half-open gate, he walked down the earthen aisle enjoying a sweet wave of nostalgia.

The sight of a tiny mouse scurrying around a corner and the lush silence broken only by the cooing of pigeons and the occasional chatter of an English sparrow in the loft above brought back memories of countless times he had played in that barn as a boy.

He took down a small crowbar from its rack inside the door of the tool room and had started back toward the gate when he came to a sudden stop.

The door to the feed room was slightly ajar, and in the soft light from a single window he saw a couple making love. The thirty-degree angle of the top of the hinged feed bin made of it a perfect platform for the supine woman, whose empty left riding boot was resting on the plank floor while her right one and bare left leg were waving in the air to the accelerating rhythm of the covering man's energetic movements. Bob had to smile at the fact that the man's swallow-tailed jacket draped itself in such a manner as fastidiously to screen the critical area of their physical union. Not wanting to embarrass the lovers, Bob had started silently and discreetly to move on when the man, apparently in order to secure the pleasure of observing the woman during a final, climactic phase, straightened from the waist, thereby allowing her upper body to become visible. Beneath her still-intact riding hat her features were so distorted by passion that it was a full second before Bob recognized Nancy's face—at almost the exact instant she caught sight of him through the opening in the doorway.

Later Bob could never recall clearly his thoughts or actions in the next few minutes. He didn't know how he had gotten back to his horse, but, after having heard whispers and Knute's "The hell you say!" he dimly remembered forcing the stone from Topper's shoe and dropping the crowbar in the sawdust by the gate. His memory regained lucidity only after he was once again seated in the saddle and he saw Knute come half-trotting toward the gate, trying to rearrange his clothing.

"Hey, Robbie . . . Listen . . . Come on . . . Look . . . we just started joking around a little last night and . . . Aw shit! . . . This doesn't mean anything . . . It's no big deal."

"No big deal?" Bob repeated, his voice deceptively calm and steady. "Why, it's a very big deal, old friend—cause for a huge celebration. You've finally gotten yourself a 'brand new one,' and it didn't even cost you a hundred dollars. The champagne should be on you."

He wheeled Topper around and started off.

"Hey, wait, Robbie. We're still friends, aren't we?"

Bob reined up for just a moment and looked back at the almost-comical figure of the big Texan, resplendent in his red jacket and black hat but standing forlornly by the barn gate.

"Sure, Knute. Sure, we're buddies. We're *good* buddies, you and I."

Then Bob rode down the hill at full gallop.

# CHAPTER TWENTY-FOUR

**BOB DID NOTHING** to check his horse's speed as he rode full-tilt toward the main gate near the stable. But with his ears pointed forward Topper adjusted his stride, cleared the top metal bar by more than a foot and then accelerated again up the gravel road toward the garage. Bob tied the reins to a hitching ring in the stone wall and walked over to the chauffeur, who was polishing the finish on the black sedan with a cloth.

"Les, would you please see that someone gets my horse to the stables and unsaddles him for me?"

"Yes, sir, Mr. Bob. As soon as I've dropped your mother and father off at church, I'll come straight back and take care of that."

"And one other thing. Take someone over to Windemere with you to drive my station wagon back. The key is on the floor. Have it left by the front door. I'm going to need it soon."

Bob walked slowly up to the house, in the recesses of his mind amazed that with the final total collapse of his personal life the world still went on as before, as though nothing had changed. In spite of the agonizing pain in his throat and midriff, the mockingbirds still sang and the warmth of the spring sun brought forth the rich perfume of the boxwoods. The intensity of his anguish, however, carried with it neither confusion nor indecision, and by the time he had walked through the service end of the house and met his parents in the main hall, the path he knew he must take lay clearly in front of him.

"Why, son, I thought you were on the hunt," his mother said as she was adjusting her hat in the tall mirror above a massive mahogany table. "Surely it isn't over yet."

"No, it's not over. Mom, Dad, would you please come into the living room with me. There's something I need to discuss with you."

"Son," the father said, "we're about to leave for church. Let's talk when we get back."

"I won't be here when you get back."

"Well, then later on this afternoon."

"Dad, you don't understand. I'm leaving Lexington. Now, please, come into the living room."

The parents glanced at each other and then followed their son.

"Really, Robert," the father said, "you've been gone from Lexington every week for the last few months, so what's so different? Let's get to the point. We don't want to be late for the service."

"The difference is that I'm not coming back this time," Bob said, walking over to one of the tall French windows and staring out onto the back lawn.

"Not coming back?" his mother asked. "But you have to be back for the wedding."

"There isn't going to be a wedding. Well, that's not totally accurate. There's going to be a wedding, but not in Lexington. And I'll not be marrying Nancy."

"Son, don't be joking with your mother," the father said brusquely. "We don't have time for that."

"I'm not joking, Dad. I wish to hell I were."

"But, Robert, you can't mean what you're saying," his mother insisted. "What about all the plans and the hundreds of wedding presents? If you two have had a fight, don't be upset about it. Engaged couples frequently fight during the last week before a wedding due to natural tensions. You two will make up."

"No, it's not a question of a fight, and there will be no making up."

"Son, you said that there's going to be a wedding, but not here," she persisted. "I don't understand."

Bob came to stand behind her chair and placed his hands on her shoulders to try to soften the blow. "Mother, I'm going to marry Maria."

There was dead silence in the room, finally broken by the father. "Maria? That Mexican girl? Now I know you've lost your mind! I hope to God you're kidding us. That would never be accepted here. Even if you were stupid enough to ignore your own interests, you should think about any children you might have."

"I do have a child, Dad, and you all have a grandchild. And he *is* the one I'm thinking about now."

There was another long period of shocked silence. "Oh, dear God in Heaven!" the mother finally uttered almost inaudibly. "I would never have thought that. She seemed such a nice girl."

"She is a nice girl; it was not her fault," Bob responded drearily. "It was all my doing, and I am going to have to pay the price.

"Damn if that's so!" the father exploded. "Son, I can't let you wreck your life just because of a misguided sense of duty. Okay—you made a big mistake, but you would be making a bigger one if you sacrificed your whole future because of it. There are other ways out of this. We'll buy the girl off. I'll get in touch with my lawyer in the morning and . . ."

"No, Dad, no. I have made a firm decision. I have bungled my own life and hurt people on all sides of me. I have lived with lies, self-interest and deception long enough. I think it's time now that I return to honesty and do whatever I think is right."

"Do you love the girl?" the mother asked plaintively.

"No, but I will sacrifice her no more than I have to. The baby is the innocent one, and I must do right by him. I will make him my legal heir, and after an appropriate period and I feel I've done everything I can, Maria and I will get a divorce."

"Then you will be coming back?" the mother asked with a note of hope in her voice.

"Yes, of course—some day. But I don't know when. It will be a while. Some memories will have to fade. Now, I've got to go pack. Leslie is waiting for you out front. You all go on to church and pray for us all."

"But what about your guest, Major McCutcheon?" the mother inquired.

"I wouldn't worry about him if I were you," Bob said, starting for the door and making no effort to conceal the hardness of his voice. "I have a feeling he'll be leaving before evening."

As they were walking into the hall, the father put his arm around his son's shoulder.

"Son, I still think you're making a mistake, but I understand your wanting to do what you feel you must. It will be very lonely for us here without you. I don't know how we'll be able to get along on the farm."

"Dad, you haven't needed me for almost a year—since you hired Silas Allen. At least he'll be glad I'm gone. But if you ever do really need me, let me know. You know I'll come."

Bob embraced and kissed his weeping mother and started up the stairs. Then he paused and looked back.

"I'll be at the hotel in Pineville tonight if you need to reach me. And, Dad, I'm going to ask a favor of you. I want you to make arrangements for Top Hat to be shipped."

"Of course, son. As soon as you get settled, send me your new address."

"No, not to me. I want you to have him shipped to England, to the Right Honorable Wyndham Fitzhugh Dunsworth—as a gift. I'll leave the address on my desk."


**WHEN BOB ARRIVED** back in Knox County, he drove straight to the Simpkins' farm. The owners were not at home, so he walked down the road to the well site. The well was shut down, and crews that he had hired the night before were busy. One was starting the long process of cleaning up the aftermath of the flow of the black, viscous oil, and another was stringing pipe from the site down the hillside to the loading point for tanker trucks. Having verified the progress of the crews, he walked back up the road toward the station wagon. As he came around the curve, he saw a car pull up to the modest little shack. Simpkins and his wife, dressed in their Sunday best, got out, waved good-bye to the couple in the front seat and started for their porch.

"Good afternoon, Mrs. Simpkins. Good afternoon, Mr. Simpkins," Bob called out. "I was about to leave. I'm glad I didn't miss you after all."

"Evenin,' Mr. Hanson," the farmer answered, stopping at the foot of his porch steps and waiting for Bob to approach. "We ain't seen those folks in over a year, but they called and insisted we have a little lunch with them after church and take a little drive over to Barbourville. I declare—we're finding out we have more friends than we ever figured. It sure is puzzlin', ain't it?"

For the first time Bob thought he saw a trace of a smile on the taciturn face.

"I have a feeling you'll also soon be surprised at how many cousins you have," he responded. "That brings up the main reason I was anxious to talk to you. Every huckster and shyster in this part of the State is going to descend on you with sure-fire schemes to triple or quadruple your money. Don't even let them in your front door. I have two business cards here for you. Take them. One is of a very good lawyer in Lexington and the other of a man whom you can trust to help you safeguard and invest your money. Don't you ever do anything or sign anything unless you talk to them first. I want you to promise me."

"But I don't know those fellows, Mr. Hanson. I'd rather listen to what you have to tell me."

"I appreciate that confidence," Bob said, "but I won't be around to give advice."

Simpkins squinted at him and spit off to the side.

"You won't be around? I figured you'd have a bunch of drilling to do around here."

"No, sir. I'm afraid I've got to move on. I'm going to sell off my interest in the acreage and leases in this area. You tell those gentlemen on the cards that I sent you, and they'll treat you right. You can trust them. My lease with you has been recorded at the county seat, but you hang onto all legal papers and documents. Your first royalty payments will be coming from Crown Oil Company, but if that ever changes, you'll be notified."

Bob held out his hand, and Simpkins accepted it reluctantly.

"In these parts we don't get many strangers that I take a shine to. I'm sorry to see you go, Mr. Hanson."

"Thank you, sir. I appreciate that. And best of luck to you both."

**PINEVILLE HAD BEEN** transformed in only twenty-four hours. Bob had to park over a block from the hotel and walk on foot. Cars with license plates from a half-dozen states were lined along the street, and the lobby was packed with men laughing, smoking and talking.

The recently evolved science of forensic entomology has established that after the death of a mammal, within an astonishingly short period of time there begins the ordered and sequential process of the laying of eggs thereon by flies of different species, allowing the time of death to be determined with amazing accuracy from a study of the status of the eggs and resultant larvae. The exact basis of the transmission of information in the process—olfactory and chemical—has yet to be established but operates with impressive efficiency, sometimes in the face of daunting environmental obstacles. An interesting comparative study could be made for reactions to an oil strike. The information transmittal would appear to be almost instantaneous, and timing and distances could easily be inferred by the sequence of hotel and motel registrations in the immediate area by "fly equivalents" from other areas and states, some from as far away as Louisiana, Texas and California.

Bob had seen a similar "swarming" once over in Webster County and remembered a few of the faces but passed unrecognized himself. Elbowing his way to the registration desk, he inquired as to the availability of a room for the night.

"I'm sorry, mister," said the clerk, who was looking down while leafing through a stack of reservation slips, "I can't help you. We're jammed to the rafters. I've been trying to place people in surrounding towns."

"Well, what about a rooming or boarding house? I'll be here only one night."

"All I can do, mister, is put your name on the list."

"The name is Hanson, Robert Hanson. I stayed here last night."

The clerk looked up immediately.

"Hanson? Why, of course, Mr. Hanson. Don't worry, sir. I have a room here for you, the best in the house—on the top floor."

"I thought you were 'jammed to the rafters,'" Bob said, beginning to fill out the reservation form the clerk had slid toward him.

"I just misplaced a reservation notice," the clerk said, grinning. "I'll put him in with someone else when he gets here. Maybe they'll like each other."

Bob closed and bolted his room door, placed his bag and briefcase on the dresser and, feeling emotionally drained and physically weary, lay down on the bed. His head had no sooner touched the pillow than the telephone calls began.

"Mr. Hanson, this is Sid . . ."

"Hi, Bob, you might not remember me, but . . ."

"Boy! Are you in luck, Mr. Hanson! I've got a friend of mine, Jack Ritchie, coming in from L.A. tonight, and we . . ."

At the first chance he had, Bob requested the hotel operator to hold all calls and then tried again to unwind, but rest would not come in spite of his fatigue. On the drive over from Lexington he had managed to benumb his feelings by channeling all of his mental energy into making the seemingly myriad decisions and plans necessary to resolve the concrete problems he faced.

But once he was insulated from external distractions and the need to make immediate responses, his defenses broke down and he was left to face alone the full realization of his loss and the implications of the events of the last twenty-four hours. The pain he now felt was of a force and nature with which his entire previous life had left him unequipped to deal. Out of stubbornness he refused to break down and weep, but as he paced the room the constriction in his throat almost choked off his ability to breathe. After two hours he felt he had to escape this chamber of self-torture, so he slowly walked down the four flights of stairs and made his way through the throng toward the coffee shop to order an early supper, since in the last thirty-six hours he had eaten only a package of crackers and a hurried plate of food at Windemere. He took a counter stool just vacated by another guest and ordered the day's special of fried catfish, hush puppies and cole slaw. While waiting for the filling of his order, he turned one hundred eighty degrees on his stool and with folded arms welcomed the distraction of observing the scene in front of him.

Every table was fully occupied. Not a vacant chair was in evidence. The crowd of men represented a motley assemblage of types and characters. Perhaps a minority were legitimate oil men. The balance was composed of every type of opportunist, charlatan, snake-oil salesman and naive neophyte. Bob knew that in the back of more than one of the cars or pick-up trucks ranged around the town square, there could undoubtedly be found a version of the ingenious "doodlebug machine" with its blinking lights, dials, horns and whistles that could be instrumental in duping some impressionable farmer into believing that the huckster-owner could actually ascertain on a scientific basis the existence of oil under his acreage.

Suddenly there was a commotion at the door, conversations were hushed and space was made available at the large, round, central "common table" in the coffee shop as J.P. "Big Daddy" Crawford from Bogalusa, Louisiana, made his typical entrance, as ostentatious and ceremonial as that of any potentate. At six feet and over three hundred pounds, Big Daddy was a legendary and imposing figure in the independent oil business. Supposedly he had been an active wildcatter in his youth, but no one could honestly state that he had ever seen him on his own acquire a lease or even look at an oil well, much less actually drill one. He was unquestionably the most successful "wheeler-dealer" in the game, however.

Bob knew that Crawford would take up his station at the center table and not budge for days except to go to the latrine or grab a few hours of sleep per night up in his room. The rest of the time he would sit and eat, drink coffee, eat, smoke cigars, eat, and talk frequently on a personal telephone strung to his table by his right-hand man, who served also as a chauffeur for the long light-blue Cadillac with the wide, custom-made rear door to accommodate the corpulent figure of the owner.

Ostentation was a principle by which the big man lived. When smoking, he would alternate his right and left hands in either putting the cigar in his mouth or taking it out, purely for the sake of the conspicuousness of the four gaudy diamond rings on each hand.

Whatever faults could be ascribed to him, however, he was the shrewdest trader in the marketplace. Never once having visited the sites or the acreages involved, he made his living and sometimes fortunes by buying and selling leases and production, at times even selling and buying the same property more than once in a given day. If he consulted geological maps, it must have been in the privacy of his room, for none were ever in evidence. But he had either phenomenal luck or uncanny instinct as to the probable location of additional deposits in the area of a strike, and only a bold or desperate man bet consistently against his judgment.

"Your dinner's ready, sir," the waitress said, touching Bob on the shoulder. He swung around on the stool and tried to focus all of his attention on the food in front of him. Twenty minutes later he tossed some bills on the counter to cover the check and the tip and walked over to the big round table.

"Mr. Crawford," he said.

The big man was saying something behind the back of his ringed hand to the man on his right and didn't even glance at Bob.

"Mr. Crawford," Bob repeated.

Again Crawford ignored him and began laughing softly at a private joke he was having with his neighbor.

"My name is Robert Hanson," Bob continued in an even tone. "I shall be available for three hours. If you ever have anything to discuss with me, send someone to my room to get me." With that he started for the door.

"Mr. Hanson!" Big Daddy almost shouted, getting to his feet and knocking over his chair in the process. "Forgive me, sir. I don't believe we've ever met. Please have a seat and join us here."

There was another flurry of activity as an additional chair was brought up and room was made at the table for Bob. When all had been seated, there was a ritualistic twenty-minute period wherein only trivia were discussed: Had there been enough rain for the spring planting? Did the late frost kill the fruit crop? Had Louisiana State University or the University of Kentucky had the best recruiting season for its football team? Then abruptly Big Daddy turned to Bob.

"What have you got, Mr. Hanson?"

"One well and sixteen adjacent leases," Bob answered in a matter-of-fact tone.

"Tell me about your well. All I've heard is rumors. Any idea of the reserves?"

"It's too early to tell. We just got it capped last night. The crew was to run a pressure test this afternoon, but I haven't got the figures yet. As close as we can estimate, before we got it closed down it had a flow of about twenty-five hundred barrels a day."

"I'd say that's a guess way on the high side, and it won't hold up."

"I didn't say it would."

Crawford lit a new cigar, the process allowing him to expose the rings on both hands at the same time.

"What do you want for the whole ball of wax?"

"As you know," Bob responded, "there's no accurate way to assess the values involved. Right now for a clean sale I'm looking for five hundred and a quarter."

"You're out of your mind. I'll give you three hundred thousand."

There thus began two and a half hours of talking, bluffing, bickering and hard trading, the scene at times taking on the aura of a high-stakes poker game in Nevada. Bob's cause was aided by the presence of several bidders in the crowd, including a man representing a big independent in Beaumont, Texas, and he was able to some extent to play them off one against the other. At ten o'clock, however, Bob felt utterly drained and exhausted. Getting to his feet and stretching, he announced, "Gentlemen, my final price is four hundred and sixteen thousand dollars with a retained interest of one and a half percent. Now if you all will excuse me, I'm going to bed."

"We can start again in the morning," Crawford said, motioning for the weary waitress to bring his check. "Shall we say ten o'clock?"

"You'll have to carry on without me," Bob said as he walked away. "I'm leaving first thing in the morning."

He took the jerky little elevator up to the fourth floor and after a quick shower fell into bed and mercifully into a deep sleep.

When he awoke in the morning, the sun was already up. For a brief moment he forgot where he was and simply enjoyed the feeling of being rested. Then reality surged back into his consciousness, bringing with it a return of his pain and anguish. Hurriedly he shaved, dressed and packed and took the stairs down to the desk. As he was checking out, the clerk handed him a stack of telephone messages. He shoved them into his pocket and walked into the coffee shop. Big Daddy was already at his station, talking on the telephone while efficiently washing down fried eggs, ham, grits and biscuits with an over-sized mug of black coffee. Bob sat at the counter and ordered his breakfast. While he was eating he idly flipped through the stack of messages, many of them repeat calls from persons he didn't know. At the bottom of the stack was a message to call Miss Nancy Garner in Lexington.

A constriction in his throat precluded his finishing his food. Consigning this last message to the pile of other rejects, he pushed his plate away and signalled for his check. He had picked up his briefcase and was heading for the door when Crawford's voice boomed out.

"Mr. Hanson, may I see you a moment, sir?"

As Bob walked up to the table, Big Daddy slid some stapled papers toward him. A glance through them confirmed that it was a contract meeting Bob's price.

"You know damn well that there might not be another drop of oil within forty miles of your strike," Crawford said, pulling a pen out of his pocket for the signing, "and that little hole you drilled could suck dry in a week. If my little grand-babies go hungry because of this mistake of mine, it's going to be on your conscience."

"I'll tell you what, Mr. Crawford," Bob responded as he signed on the appropriate lines, "if you still own these rights when you drive out of town in a few days, I'll quit-claim back to you my one and a half percent."

The big man was lighting a cigar and exploded with laughter, blowing a cloud of smoke toward the ceiling.

"Son, how did you get to know me so well in just one evening?"

"Sir," Bob answered as he picked up his copy of the contract and his check, "you know damn well everybody knows you. It would break your tender heart if they didn't."

As Bob walked out the door and down the street toward his car, he was neither elated nor disappointed. He was aware that he could have done better if he had persisted and planned to stay over another day or two, but he was no longer interested and felt a need to move on. He was willing to cede to Big Daddy the chance to turn a tidy profit for himself.

**ON THE DRIVE** up from Lexington the preceding day he had had the benefit of clear-cut goals to be attained and concrete problems that had to be dealt with, all of which had provided him with a cushion, a shield behind which he could emotionally retreat. Such was not the case as he drove westward toward Louisville. It's true that he had a plan of action that he was going to follow, but its details were not specific and the outcome was uncertain. In any case he approached it with a sense of dread. With no peripheral demands to distract him and no hope of joy or even relief in the near future, he was left with no escape from facing full-on the agony of the immediate past.

Bob had always enjoyed periods of being alone, but during his entire life, even in the jungles of Leyte, he had been a stranger to loneliness. Now for the first time he came to know this aching affliction, not just temporally but in a sense existentially. Severed—at least for a time—were the staunch, life-sustaining roots in family and homestead. He now felt adrift, floating in a hostile vacuum. To his eyes the lovely springtime landscape of Kentucky through which he was passing could just have well been a moonscape.

After he had shut off his engine in front of the Lorna Grey Home, he sat for a few minutes staring straight ahead down the tree-lined street, trying to prepare himself to deal effectively and humanely with awkward circumstances in a grim future. He took a deep sigh, got out of the car and walked up the concrete pathway, which was once again bordered with flowers. Stepping through the unlocked door into the hallway, he rang the bell on the table and a few minutes later saw Mrs. Waldron approaching from a back hall.

"Yes?" she said.

"I am Robert Hanson, Mrs. Waldron. We met when I was here last summer."

"Oh . . . yes, Mr. Hanson. Would you like to come into the office?"

After having taken a seat, Bob observed the woman closely as she rearranged papers and books on her desk and poured a little water from a glass onto a potted plant on the window sill, apparently purposely taking her time before seating herself behind the desk. From her manner and expression it was clear that the distaste he felt for her was mutual.

"Well, I see you came alone this time," she said in an obviously snide tone of voice and with her half-smile restricted to the lower half of her face. "How may I help you?"

Bob took a deep breath and repressed an urge to make a rude response.

"I have come here for Maria and the baby. I'm going to take them with me."

"I see," the woman responded, tapping a pencil lightly on the desk top, "but I'm afraid you're a little late. Maria left last week."

"She left? Where did she go?"

"I don't know. She did not say. I suppose she saw no need in leaving a forwarding address since she received no mail in the almost ten months she was here."

Bob felt distinctly uncomfortable under the pointed, harsh gaze of the woman.

"This may be of no interest to you, Mr. Hanson," Mrs. Waldron continued, "but we were all very sad to lose her. She is a warm, intelligent, giving person and was very helpful to many of the girls here during their periods of despondency. And it took us days to comfort the distraught children at the Center when they heard she was leaving. You did know, of course, that she worked full time with handicapped and disadvantaged children, did you not? I'm sure she described her activities in her letters to you."

Bob got to his feet, clenching his teeth.

"Well, I'm glad she felt productive while she was here," he said, moving toward the door. Then he stopped.

"Did she have any money with her when she left?"

"There was a balance of a little over a hundred and thirty-eight dollars in the account. She didn't want to take it, but we insisted."

Bob returned the steely gaze of the woman for a moment and then without another word walked out of the building and to his car.

## CHAPTER TWENTY-FIVE

**BOB HAD DIFFICULTY** finding the orphanage. He had spent over an hour in Kansas City, Missouri, before a police officer informed him that the institution was located in the sister city of Kansas City, Kansas. Finally he pulled up in front of an austere red-brick building in a grimy neighborhood of an industrial section of town. As he walked up the three steps of the front stoop, he saw above the door a wooden plaque with the inscription: *Suffer the little children to come unto me.*

At his second ringing of the bell the door was opened by a Catholic nun, who stared at him inquisitively.

"May I help you?"

"Sister Denise?"

"Yes. What can I do for you?"

"Please, is Maria Rodriguez here?"

The nun's expression did not change, but there was a slight pause.

"May I ask who you are and what your business is here?"

"My name is Robert Hanson. I'm from Lexington, Kentucky. I have heard Maria speak of you and thought she might have come here with the baby."

Sister Denise continued to stare at him for a moment and then stepped back, opening the door wider.

"Please come in. I will see."

She led him into a spacious, almost-barren room with a wooden table on one side and two ladder-back chairs on the other. There were no draperies at the lone window that looked out onto an alley and no carpet on the wooden floor, so the sound of their footsteps reverberated hollowly.

"Have a seat, Mr. Hanson. May I offer you a glass of water?"

"No, thank you.

The sister disappeared behind a door and left him alone. He sat on one of the chairs and listened to the slow ticking of a clock on the table and the muted sounds of children probably in a courtyard somewhere. Although the nun had not confirmed the fact, he was now certain that Maria was there and that the sister was determining whether the girl would consent to see him. When the door opened again, Maria walked into the room. She was dressed in the same white cotton dress she'd had on when Bob first saw her at Falcrest Acres. She was unchanged except that her hair, drawn back and secured behind her head, had grown longer and cascaded now almost to her waist. As he rose, she stopped and looked at him for a moment and then turned and nodded to Sister Denise, who had followed her into the room. When the woman had withdrawn and closed the door behind her, Maria turned to face him.

"How did you find me, Mr. Hanson?" she asked in a very quiet voice.

"You mentioned the sister and this place the first time we talked in Lexington. So when you were not in Louisville, I gambled that I might be able to find you here."

There was a long pause. Maria was obviously uncomfortable and searching for words.

"Sir, why have you come? I had so wanted to protect you and not cause you any more distress. Is it wise or kind to put me—to put us—through this? Is not your wedding to Miss Garner this Saturday?"

Bob had not gone over or rehearsed in his mind how he was going to explain things to Maria and found communicating with her difficult.

"The wedding has been called off. I am not going to marry Miss Garner."

She looked at him but made no response, as though allowing him to elaborate if he so chose.

"So I have decided that I want to give my child my own name. I want him to be my son in the eyes of the law in order to ensure his rights of inheritance."

There was another awkward pause. Maria folded her hands in front of her and looked down at them.

"Do you mean you want to adopt him?"

"No. I have come here so that you and I can be legally married. That will be quicker and accomplish my purpose more simply and directly."

This remark left the girl obviously agitated, although she didn't look up. "And you want my consent?"

"Why, yes. Of course."

Maria's hands were clenching and unclenching as she struggled with her emotions. "Mr. Hanson, what happened to your engagement? Why was it broken off?"

Bob looked at her in surprise. Being questioned by her was not something he had expected, and he was reluctant at first to be explicit. "She betrayed me," he answered curtly.

"*She* betrayed *you*?" Maria asked, raising her head and meeting his gaze. "Yes. With my best friend . . . I chanced upon them by accident. I left Lexington and have not talked to her since."

Maria was silent for a long time. She walked over and sat down on one of the chairs. When she spoke again, Bob could barely hear her. "Do you still love her?"

"Of course not."

"Of course not?"

"Of course—of course not!" Bob almost shouted. "Don't you understand what I'm telling you?"

Maria lowered her head and answered with a sadness to her voice. "Well, I know what you're telling me, but I admit I don't understand. I don't understand how love can be extinguished so quickly, Mr. Hanson. I don't understand how her yielding to temptation in a moment of weakness can be so totally destructive of your relationship, whereas yours was not. But I guess there are a lot of things in this world that I don't understand," she added, almost as an afterthought.

There was another long period of strained silence. Bob walked to the window and stood with his back to her. Her next remark caught him even more by surprise.

"You know, sir? I seriously wonder if you ever really loved her. Did you, Mr. Hanson?"

The question cut through Bob's chagrin and forced him to face squarely a question that perhaps had subconsciously haunted him for a long time. But he was in no mood for self-examination. He turned abruptly and looked at her. "Maria, I did not come all this distance to have my motives or attitudes analyzed. I came here to marry you and legitimize my son. Let's confine our discussion to that, if you don't mind. After an appropriate period we can quietly file for divorce and go on with our lives."

"Is legitimacy so easy to come by?" she responded, almost as though to herself. "Maybe so legally, but would that legitimacy be truly valid when we would knowingly be lying and falsifying when we took the marriage vows even in a civil ceremony?"

The vexation Bob had been feeling welled up more strongly. "Damn it, Maria! Stop all that moral pontificating! Let's leave off the mutual self-pity for a little while and think about our child. For the sake of his status and future, this is something we must do."

Maria looked out the window at the gray wall across the alley and said with a sad resignation, "If my son grows up to be the man I hope he will be, in twenty years I'm not certain he wouldn't feel that the price for his 'status' was too high . . . All right, Mr. Hanson, what do we do?"

The tension somewhat relieved, Bob took a seat in the other chair and pulled out a pen and small note pad.

"This is Tuesday. When I leave here, I will go to the courthouse and apply for the license. We can take our blood tests tomorrow. I believe the required three-day period starts from the application, so I'll make arrangements for a justice of the peace for Friday. Otherwise, we could wait until Monday."

Maria looked down at her hands.

"I think that Friday would be better, if it's possible. In that way you could be back with your family by Sunday."

Bob glanced at her.

"You don't understand. I'm not returning to Lexington. I'm going to take you and the baby west with me. I want to get the two of you settled comfortably and spend some time with him."

Maria looked up quickly, her face mirroring concern.

"Mr. Hanson, the Church will not recognize our marriage. I cannot live with you as your conjugal wife."

"I'm aware of that," he said brusquely, getting to his feet while sensing a return of a mild irritation. "Never fear, young lady, you won't have to worry about that. I promise. Now I had best get to the courthouse and then find a hotel room. I'll pick you up at nine o'clock in the morning for the blood tests."

As he headed for the door, Maria stood up.

"Mr. Hanson."

"Yes?" he responded, stopping and looking back.

"Wouldn't you like to see your child?"

Even with his agitation and preoccupation Bob was himself surprised at his oversight.

"Oh . . . yes. Of course."

Maria went to fetch their son and returned in a few minutes with him in her arms. The first sight of his own child made a profound impression on him, but he was also aware of a sudden transformation in his perception of Maria. The stereotypical image he had successfully maintained in his mind for almost a year was suddenly shattered. No longer was this a simple Mexican girl who had disrupted his life, but the mother of his child—a very pretty young woman radiating an inner beauty and serenity. Almost reluctantly he shifted his attention to the baby.

"Here, wouldn't you like to hold him?" she asked, showing Bob how to support him with his left arm. "Look, I think he recognizes you."

Bob had to smile. The little face was so serious as those eyes that had reached out to him from the photograph now stared intently into his. Bob took his index finger and touched the point of the baby's chin, and the tiny left fist closed firmly on the finger. At that moment the bond was permanently forged. Always his son actually, not yet his son legally, but now instantly his son emotionally.


**THEY DEPARTED KANSAS CITY** early on Sunday morning. Bob had spent Saturday afternoon checking over the station wagon and doing some shopping. He had asked for a list of things to get for the baby for the trip and in addition had bought some cheese and bread and fruit for them to eat for lunch on the way. It was a clear, sunny day, and the gently undulating countryside of eastern Kansas was resplendent on both sides of U.S. 40 with the brilliant green of new wheat and corn. With Bob driving, Maria sat in the front seat holding the baby. Within an hour the initial tension in the car had eased and almost-normal conversation became possible. Bob inquired concerning her experiences with handicapped children in Louisville, and Maria asked about news of the farm and of the number of friends she had made there in spite of her short stay.

"You haven't asked," Bob said, "where I'm taking us. Aren't you curious?"

"Well, I assumed that that decision has already been made and that I have no say-so in the matter," she answered with a half-smile.

"We may end up in Texas or California," Bob volunteered, "but I think we'll give Denver a try first. I liked the town when I was there. After you left Lexington, I dabbled a bit in the oil business in Kentucky, Illinois and Ohio. I realize that it's a different ball game out west—big league stuff—but drilling is drilling and, who knows? Maybe I can make a go of it. I've looked at some geological studies and projections for the area and think there are some good prospects. I'd like to take a crack at Colorado, Oklahoma and even Wyoming."

At midday, on the advice of a truck driver at a fuel stop, Bob left the main highway at Junction City and took State Road 18 due west. Several miles past Luray he pulled off the road and onto the side of a long driveway that led to a clump of cottonwoods and a farm house situated on a slight rise in the distance. There was an inviting patch of lush green grass on which they could have a picnic, so Bob began unloading what they would need—a portable cooler with apple juice, milk and soft drinks, the food basket and a large brightly colored cotton bedspread for them to sit on. Maria had laid the baby on the spread in the shade of an opened umbrella and was extracting paper plates and cups from the basket when a pick-up truck turned off the highway and stopped in front of the station wagon. A man and a woman stared at them through the open left window, and Bob assumed that they were the land-owners.

"Uh-oh," Bob said, getting to his feet. "We may have to move on. I think this is the farmer and his wife."

He stepped over to the truck and began explaining that they were stopping for just a few minutes and would leave the area immaculate but would be glad to move off the property if they were intruding. Dressed in their Sunday church-going clothes, the couple could have been a *Saturday Evening Post* cover. The middle-aged driver had a deeply tanned, rough-hewn face, and his wife, although small, gave the impression of being strong and wiry.

"Son," the man said, almost interrupting Bob, "you're welcome to use that spot, but it's gonna be pretty hot out there."

"Why don't you children come on up to the house?" the wife suggested. "We have a table under a tree out back, and it would be a lot more comfortable, especially for the baby."

"That's mighty kind of you," Bob said, "but we don't want to be any trouble. We appreciate your letting us use this spot, and . . ."

"Nonsense," the farmer said emphatically. "Now you all come on. Thelma here will get it set up for you." And without waiting for a reply, he put the truck in gear and drove off.

"Well, what do you think?" Bob asked, turning to Maria.

"They seemed sincere," she answered. "Maybe it would be rude if we didn't accept."

**THEY HAD STUMBLED** onto a gold mine. Typical of the rural people of the Midwest, the farmer and his wife could not have been kinder, friendlier or more hospitable. To enhance the communal picnic they provided copious additions from their kitchen, including ham, rice, chicken and freshly baked bread.

"I'm Calvin Anderson," the farmer said, as he placed his load on the outdoor table, "but all my friends call me 'Shoe.' And this is my wife, Thelma."

"I'm Bob Hanson," Bob said, smiling and shaking hands with each of them, "and this is Maria . . . my . . . wife."

There had been a hesitation in the introduction, because this was the first time he had had to think of her in terms of "wife." He did not feel married, and this identification of her did not come naturally.

"Where are you children from?"

"We've just come from Kentucky and are on our way to Denver," Bob answered, not totally accurately.

"Are you on vacation?" Thelma asked, arranging plates and knives and forks on the table.

"No, ma'am. We're going to be living in Denver—at least for a while. Here, let me help move the benches up to the table."

The lunch under the old cottonwood was extremely pleasant. From out of the west there was blowing a warm breeze, surprisingly gentle for Kansas. Thelma had had her husband go into the attic and bring down an oak crib on rockers, and its motion was soothing and apparently fascinating to the baby. During their conversation it was revealed that they had only one child, a son now in his third year up at Lawrence studying agronomy. After lunch when the women began gathering up the food and plates, Calvin stood up and stretched.

"Well, if you kids will excuse me, I've got to go change clothes and do a bit of work."

"Calvin," his wife scolded, looking up with a frown. "You know I don't like you working on the Lord's day. Besides, why don't you stop struggling with that old tractor and borrow Sam Whittaker's mules tomorrow?"

"Can't do that, woman. I'm already a week behind in my plowing and couldn't get it done quick enough with mules. I've got to finish that north section in the next day or so or I'll lose it this season. I apologize for leaving you kids," he added, turning to Bob, "but I can't put it off until tomorrow."

"What kind of trouble are you having with the tractor?" Bob asked.

"Aw, I dunno. The durn thing is just ornery. It started giving me trouble about a month ago, just when I needed it. Sometimes it won't run at all, and when it does, it runs rough. My boy always took care of the machinery and knew what he was doing, but he's so busy getting ready for exams I can't get him down here on a weekend to fix it."

"Mind if I go down to the barn with you?" Bob asked. "I probably can't help, but maybe we can figure out something."

"Why, that's mighty nice of you, son, but I hate to hold you kids up."

"You two go on down there," Thelma interjected. "Maria and I are going to straighten everything up and bathe the baby anyway."


**"YOU KNOW," CALVIN** said as the two men were walking toward the barn a little later, "farming's getting so complicated nowadays that you've got to be more of an engineer than a farmer just to keep things running. I had mules up 'til two years ago, and they were a lot more dependable. I never had any trouble getting old Seth and Sal started."

"I know what you mean," Bob laughed. "When I was a boy, we had mules too. They were beauties my dad bought down in Pulaski, Tennessee. I could drive the hay wagon with them by the time I was nine years old."

"You grew up on a farm?" Calvin asked, looking at Bob with enhanced appreciation.

"Well, it's a horse farm, but still a farm," Bob answered. "In the old days we also kept a henhouse for fresh eggs, a couple of Guernseys for milk and raised a lot of our own fruits and vegetables. We had ten acres in corn and rotated our pastures for hay."

Calvin raised the two-by-four latch on the barn doors and swung them open. When he engaged the starter on the old tractor, it coughed and sputtered and ran rough for a minute until it died completely.

"Mr. Anderson, would you have any tools in the barn here?"

"What do you need?" the farmer asked. "My son used to keep a tool box in that stall behind the plows."

"Not much, just general stuff—screwdrivers, socket wrenches, feeler gauges. Let me take a look."

He hauled out the well-stocked tool chest and found everything he needed. He removed and cleaned the spark plugs, adjusted the points and cleaned and replaced the fuel filter, which had been partially blocked by a gooey deposit. He drained the fuel tank and put in fresh gasoline from a ten-gallon tank.

"That's a pretty skimpy overhaul," Bob said apologetically, "but let's see if we did any good. Why don't you get up there and start it up again, and I'll check the timing."

When the engine was running smoothly, Bob helped hook on the brace of plows, and with a grin and wave of his hand Calvin drove off northward down a long fence row. Bob climbed up on a gate next to the barn and sat on the top, watching as the rig moved off into the distance. The beauty of the fields, stretching to the horizon, and the warmth of the afternoon sunshine on his back drained from him some of the tension that had been his constant companion for almost a week. For a brief period he was able to purge from his mind the pattern of concerns and troubled thoughts for the present, the immediate past and the uncertain future and indulge in disjointed memories of his childhood. His reverie was cut short by Maria's voice.

"What incredibly fertile land," she said almost dreamily.

She had approached so quietly that Bob had been unaware of her presence. She was standing on his right with her chin resting on her hands on the top rail of the fence and was gazing out at the greening fields.

"What did your family grow on your farm in Sonora?" Bob asked.

"You remembered!" she said, looking up at him and smiling. "We grew corn, of course, and we had pigs. But it wasn't our farm. We were just tenants. How beautiful and lucky America is!" she added, turning to gaze at the fields again. "I remember thinking the same thing almost a year ago when I came through here on the way from Texas to Kentucky."

Then she became pensive and rested her chin on her hands again.

"It is hard to believe how much one's life can change in just eleven months."

Bob's relaxed interlude was interrupted, and he felt uncomfortable again.

"Well, you are now legally an American yourself, so not all of your luck has been bad," he said, his voice taking on an edge of hardness that had not been intentional.

His regret at having made this rather callous remark coupled with her subsequent silence resulted in a brief period of unspoken tension, broken a moment later by a cacophony of squeals coming from the other side of the barn. When they went around to investigate, they saw that a small piglet had become stuck while attempting to squeeze under the bottom plank of the pig pen and could move neither forward nor backward. The maternal sow in the enclosure had become violently agitated by the squeals and in her frantic dashing around was threatening to trample the seven other minute members of the litter. Maria immediately sank to her knees and grasped the tiny animal by the shoulders.

"Mr. Hanson, try to lift the plank a little," she pleaded.

Bob was able to twist the board to the side sufficiently for her to extract the piglet, which she held close to her chest and caressed, resulting in the substitution of tiny grunts of comfort for the previous shrieks of terror. The sow sensed that the emergency had passed and also calmed down.

"It's getting your dress all dirty," Bob observed.

"That doesn't matter. It can be washed," she responded simply

Bob watched as she moved around the pen, unlatched the gate and gently pushed inside her tiny charge, who immediately joined his nursing brothers and sisters at meal-time. When she had re-latched the gate and turned to face him, Bob glanced down at her with grudging admiration.

"*Reverence for Life?*" he asked with a smile.

Maria looked up at him instantly and penetratingly.

"Maybe. But don't make fun of it. There are worse principles to follow, you know. I'm surprised that you have taken the time to read Schweitzer, Mr. Hanson."

"I'm not making fun of it," Bob responded soberly, "although it seems to me mankind has more of a 'reverence for death.' But as for my having read Schweitzer, there are probably other things about me that will surprise you. Incidentally, now that we're legally married, it's a little awkward for you to continue to call me Mr. Hanson. My name is Bob, you know."

"I know," she answered, "but I don't think I could call you anything else. I would feel it quite inappropriate."

"All right, if you insist," Bob said, starting back toward the farm house, "but two can play at that game. Shouldn't we be getting back to the baby and on our way, Mrs. Hanson?"

"No, there's no reason to rush," Maria smiled. "The baby's sleeping now, and Mrs. Anderson is having a good time playing dolls with him. She insists we at least stay for dinner with them."

"I hate to lose the time," Bob said, "but I guess a few more hours won't make that much difference. Let's rest on the grass here. That sun feels marvelous."

For several minutes they sat silently on a grassy hillock northwest of the house affording a wide view of the surrounding countryside. In the distance could be seen a neighboring farm house with a barn and grain silo and to the north a tiny dot representing Calvin's tractor and plow. Small lavender wild flowers were weaving and bobbing with the tall grass, and meadowlarks could be seen and heard in the fields below. Bob lay back on the turf and looked up at the blue sky.

"Tell me," he said, breaking the silence, "since Fate disrupted your dreams of nursing school and Lambarene, what were you planning to do before I came to get you and the baby?"

Maria watched the ant-like progress of Cal's tractor in the distance.

"Africa could never have been," she answered, "but I had not given up hope of becoming a nurse as soon as Roberto—I mean Robert—was old enough to be in school. In fact I had, and still have, an added incentive to dedicate myself and my life to doing things for others less fortunate than I."

"What do you mean—an 'added incentive'?" Bob asked, pulling up a long blade of grass and putting it between his front teeth, as he used to do as a boy.

"To try to cleanse myself and my son of my sins."

With a snort of exasperation Bob turned and looked at her.

"What the hell do you mean—'cleanse yourself of your sins'? What sin, for God's sake? If anyone sinned, I was the one, not you."

"No," Maria said, almost sadly, "life is not that simple. I sinned also. The teaching of the Church is very explicit."

"You're wrong on that," Bob said emphatically. "In fact there was an edict handed down by some Pope in the Middle Ages absolving the Roman women raped by the pagans who over-ran the Empire."

"I know," Maria added softly. "I read that in a course on Church history. But there was a condition to the absolution."

"What do you mean? What kind of a condition could there be?"

"The woman had to have been totally passive and to have experienced no pleasure," she answered and sighed deeply.

"I still don't get it," Bob said.

"I am not free of sin," she repeated. "I am very ashamed, but I also wanted you that day, Mr. Hanson."

Bob was temporarily silenced by the shock of this revelation. In the long months of his contemplation of the dire, threatening consequences to his precipitous behavior, this was one possibility that had not occurred to him. An even partial sensual complicity on her part had never entered his mind, so overbearing had been his own sense of responsibility and guilt. He looked up at the outline of her head against the clear sky and sensed the displacement of the lingering vestiges of resentment toward her by tenderness and compassion. He would need time to sort out these new feelings and deal with a vague confusion they had engendered, so he redirected the conversation somewhat.

"But this talk about you son's sin is a lot of malarkey," he blurted out. "How in hell can a little child be held accountable for an occurrence over which he had no control and for which he had no responsibility?"

"The sins of the father . . ."

"I know. I know that quotation. But that has to mean the *consequences* of the sins of the father will be visited on subsequent generations—not the sin itself. The other interpretation would be irrational and unjust. I couldn't accept an irrational, unjust God, and I don't think you could either."

"If we ever perceive a law of God as irrational or unjust, the fault lies in our perception of it, not in the law," Maria said assertively. "The important thing is that He has given us a way to work out our sins and still be accepted into His kingdom."

"Well, you can work off your imagined sins through dedicating your life to service to others if that's what you insist on doing, but I'm damn well going to see that you'll do it comfortably. You won't be struggling in want and poverty. I want the boy to go to the best schools he can get into, and you will be amply provided for. When you remarry, it will be because you want to and not because you have to."

"Remarriage will be for you," Maria said reflectively, "but not for me."

The conflict of emotions Bob had been feeling was in no way relieved by this trend in the conversation—in fact made worse—so he determined to break the pattern.

"Come on," he said, getting to his feet and reaching down for her hand to help her up, "let's go back to the house and see how the Crown Prince is doing."

"My hand is dirty from the little pig," she warned.

"Well, mine has grease all over it," he responded. "Maybe that's not such a bad combination after all."

## CHAPTER TWENTY-SIX

**BOTH THELMA AND** Calvin tried earnestly to talk them into staying overnight with them—Calvin out of gratitude from having been able to finish his plowing by late afternoon, and Thelma from a touching attachment to the baby. But Bob was insistent that they should push on, so after dinner there was a warm leave-taking accompanied by promises to keep in touch in the future.

"Stick to the state and county roads," Calvin had advised. "It'll be safer and quicker."

Bob had arranged all the bags and gear behind the front seat in order to make a wider bed out of the back seat for Maria and the baby, and after dark they settled down under the cotton bedspread while Bob guided the Pontiac westward across western Kansas and eastern Colorado as the hours slipped by. To him there was an aura of peace and tranquility encapsulated in the confines of the station wagon, an honesty and balance in harmony with the broad expanse of the western prairies. On those occasions when he stopped to refuel, after having paid the attendant for the gas and before getting behind the wheel again, he stood for a few minutes sipping coffee or a Coke and observing in the available light the sleeping mother and baby. He himself was at a loss to explain the feeling of warmth this gave him, a sense of purposefulness and inner wholeness he had not known for many months.

Dawn was breaking when he stopped the car on a rise west of Limon, got out and walked forward to stretch his legs and take in the panorama before him. In the distance the shoulders of the Rockies thrust abruptly up out of the plains, and their peaks, still glistening from the snows of winter, shone brilliantly against the darker western sky. Above the sage brush on both sides of the road there appeared the graceful flight of the first bullbats of the morning, and their plaintive cry could be heard on the freshening wind. Along the dark base of the mountain a diamond-like string of lights stretched for several miles to the north and south below the fading crescent of a waning moon.

"How beautiful that is!" came Maria's voice as she stopped by Bob's side. He had not heard her as she had gotten out of the car and approached. "Where are we, Mr. Hanson?"

"That's Denver, and I'm glad you like it, Mrs. Hanson, for that's where we'll be living for a while. What about the baby?"

"He's still asleep. I fed him not too long ago," she answered and shivered.

Bob took off his leather jacket and put it around her shoulders, and they stood for a long time, holding hands and watching as the first rays of the sun kissed the highest peaks and then gradually slid down the slopes toward the plain below.

After breakfast in Aurora Bob drove westward on Colfax, turned north on Twentieth and finally dog-legged over to Lawrence. The route taken by the taxicab eighteen months earlier had dimmed in his memory, but he still remembered the general location of the church and therefore of his destination. As he pulled up in front of the little house, he was pleased to see that his friend still lived there. In fact Vasquez was fastening paper lanterns to wires stretched across the narrow side yard and looked up as the car came to a stop at the curb. Probably because of the civilian clothes he did not recognize Bob until he had stopped at the front gate and given him an exaggerated salute.

"Captain Hanson!" he said with obvious pleasure and a wide smile while returning the salute and coming to shake his hand vigorously.

"Someone must have told you I was coming, but you shouldn't go to all that trouble," Bob joked, pointing to the colorful decorations festooning the yard.

"I must be honest: I never expected us to meet again," Vasquez said, "but since this is another important family day, I should have guessed that you would show up."

"Another important day? Are you getting married again or maybe divorced this time?" Bob rejoined and then immediately realized the poor taste of his attempted humor in this Catholic environment.

"Actually," his friend said, apparently ignoring his remark, "this is a double celebration for us. Today we have the Cinco de Mayo Festival and also our little daughter Conchita is to be baptized this afternoon. I hope that you will be able to be there."

Vasquez paused, looked over Bob's shoulder as Maria got out of the car with the baby, and then glanced back at Bob with a quizzical expression.

"These belong to you?"

"Well, to be more accurate, I belong to them. Sergeant Vasquez, this is my wife Maria and my number one son, Roberto the fourth. Maria, meet the man who saved my life one dreadful night many moons ago."

"What good luck!" Vasquez said, opening the gate for them. "We must have a real festival all our own today. Consuela!" he called, turning and going to the door to summon his wife.

The two wives hit it off immediately, and the rest of the morning was characterized by a warm and festive hubbub enveloping everyone but Bob. He had never previously heard Consuela utter a single word, but she and Maria now chattered away endlessly while they were tending to the babies or preparing the many food dishes for the evening party. Except for an infrequent remark to him by Vasquez or Maria, both of whom were very busy, Bob never heard a word of English spoken.

The christening was scheduled for four o'clock in the Sacred Heart Church, and since the fatigue of driving all night had begun to weigh heavily on him, after lunch Bob retired to the back seat of the station wagon and fell into a deep sleep. Maria wakened him in time to rouse himself thoroughly and wash up before the walk to the church. They entered by the main entrance and then walked down the left aisle toward the baptismal font. Bob held little Robert in his arms while Maria knelt and crossed herself before the icon of the Madonna in the nave and that of Mother Cabrini to the right. Father Versavel greeted all of the guests cordially but was especially warm to Bob and Maria. He had duties to attend to after the baptismal ceremony but promised to drop by the Vasquez domicile later in the evening.

It was fortunate that the weather was clear and warm, for otherwise the press of friends and guests could not possibly have been accommodated in the diminutive house. Even with the overflow into the yard there was such congestion that it was difficult to circulate enough to get near the tables loaded down with holiday delicacies. The mood of revelry was so deep and genuine that it probably would have prevailed even in the absence of the wine and tequila available, but nonetheless they did contribute to a none-too-restrained boisterousness.

Bob was able even to draw the taciturn Pedro Delgado and Juan Chavez into a conversation, and they actually became eloquent when he inquired concerning the origin of the Cinco de Mayo Festival.

"*Ah, sí, Capitan,*" Juan said excitedly, "we celebrate the Cinco de Mayo of 1864."

"*Stupido!*" said Pedro, hitting Juan on the shoulder. "It was in 1862. That was the day Benito Juarez defeated the French army at the city of Pueblo," he added proudly.

With the exception of this three-way conversation Bob felt out of place for most of the evening. Yet he was content to sit on a folding chair in a corner of the yard and watch the activity. The conviviality among the Mexican-American revelers seemed to him to be more genuinely open and spontaneous than that he had observed in the past among his own friends, and the legion of children mingling in the crowd were actively recruited to join in and participate in the singing and dancing.

But when Maria was in evidence, it was difficult for Bob to be aware of anyone or anything else. There was a radiance about her that made her conspicuous no matter where she was or what she was doing. The children especially tended to gravitate toward her, subconsciously sensing her patience and gentleness, and solace for a stubbed toe or spilled plate was immediately available and effective. Efficiently and unobtrusively she served as an alternate hostess, replenishing the supplies of food and drink as required, clearing away used utensils, periodically monitoring the babies in the back room and in countless other ways easing the burden of the grateful Consuela.

Pedro had taken up a guitar and begun singing a plaintive folk song when Vasquez came over to Bob's corner with a plate of food and sank lithely onto his haunches to eat. Peleliu flashed through Bob's mind, for this was precisely the motion and position the Marine had taken in the early morning hours underneath the F-4B so long ago.

"Sergeant," Bob began, "what kind of job do you have?"

"I work for the Highway Department, sir."

"Tell me something. Have you ever worked around oil rigs?"

Vasquez glanced up at him.

"Yes, sir. When I was in my teens, I was a sand-hog for several summers down in Oklahoma."

"Do you think you know enough to boss a drilling rig on your own?"

Vasquez put his fork down.

"I think I probably do, Captain, but it's not likely I'll ever have a chance to find out."

Bob was silent for a moment, then leaned forward and continued.

"Sergeant, I'm going to start up a little oil company here in Denver. I could farm out my drilling or lease a rig and crew, but I'd rather own my own. I've made enough recently to afford to buy a good rig and punch a few dry holes before I go broke. Would you consider coming on board to try out as my field boss?"

Vasquez put his plate on the ground, and his white teeth flashed.

"Captain, do I have to answer that?"

"Could you get together a good crew?"

"A good one. But their names won't be Hamilton or Stevens or Jones."

"I don't give a damn what their names are as long as they can get the goods out of the ground."

"You find it, sir, and if it's down there, we'll get it up."

Bob reached out and shook Vasquez's hand.

"Okay, we're on. I'm going to scout around for a bank and a good lawyer tomorrow and get started on incorporating. Hansoco. How does that sound? As soon as you feel you can quit your job, we'll start looking for a rig. I'll cover your present salary until we get a wet one. Then we'll renegotiate."

"Captain, Consuela suggested I ask you to put up here. We could move Conchita in with us, and you could have her little room in the back. I've tried to tell her it's too small—there's only a single bed and a little sofa—but she insists I ask anyway. I think she and Maria are already close friends."

"Thank you, Sergeant. That's a kind offer, and I will accept for Maria and the baby. That will be perfect for them, but as for myself, I'll go and find a room at a motel up on Colfax."

Vasquez rose to his feet and, leaving Bob alone again, went to the gate to welcome Father Versavel.

Bob sank back into his semi-reverie and again experienced a tinge of loneliness. Although he considered himself to be with friends, he felt himself to be a stranger, an alien here among these Spanish speakers, who sensed his differentness and of whose differentness he was aware. His sense of isolation was interrupted only at those times he was observing Maria. Then he would feel a unity, a bond, a sense of belonging. He realized her features were not classically beautiful, but there was an emanation of loveliness about her that shone forth from within. He himself was surprised at the extent and rapidity of the effect of her spell over him.

During the course of the evening Maria would occasionally glance in his direction and notice his solitary vigil. Finally she came over and knelt directly in front of his chair.

"Mr. Hanson seems quiet and pensive this evening—almost sad. Is there a problem?"

Bob smiled at her attempt to cheer him up.

"Yes. I think there is a problem," he answered.

Her smile was replaced by a look of concern.

"Do you think you could tell me about it?"

Bob looked at the slightly furrowed brow and the earnest eyes and leaned forward to whisper.

"Will you promise not to tell his wife?"

For a moment her face was frozen in incomprehension, and then the furrows vanished and the eyes smiled.

"I have never been known to violate a confidence."

"I can believe that," Bob said. "Well, I'm afraid there's a possibility—a small one, mind you, but nonetheless a possibility—that Mr. Hanson is falling in love."

Again her expression betrayed a momentary confusion, but then her eyes narrowed slightly.

"Oh? Again?"

"No. Not again. He thinks it might actually be for the first time."

There was a pause while she lowered her face for a moment and then looked up again.

"Why would that be a problem?"

"It could be a tremendous problem if the young woman in question would not agree to marry him. What do you think? In your honest opinion do you think this poor girl could be sufficiently insane or desperate enough to actually consider it?"

Maria jumped quickly to her feet, and it was obvious she was having difficulty trying to maintain a serious expression and not to laugh.

"Well, who knows? They say that all things are possible through love." With that, she turned quickly and melted back into the crowd.

When Bob noticed that Father Versavel was about to take his leave, he rose and walked over to him.

"Ah, good evening, Mr. Hanson. It was good to see you again. I know that Niwot appreciated very much your coming for the christening."

"I'm afraid that was purely coincidental," Bob responded. "Father, may I ask you a question?"

"Of course, my son. What is it?"

"Maria and I were married in a civil ceremony. If I, a non-Catholic, were to meet all the requirements, would you consider marrying us in the Church?"

"Why, of course, I would be glad to—once all the stipulations have been satisfied," the priest responded.

"As long as I am burdening you," Bob continued, "would you also consider instructing me?"

Father Versavel smiled and laid his hand on Bob's arm. "Certainly, Mr. Hanson. When would you like to begin?"

"Soon," Bob said. "Very soon."

**BOB'S EYELIDS HAD** grown oppressively heavy by the time the party had dwindled down to a few die-hard revelers. He stood up and stretched and made his way past Vasquez, Pedro and Juan, who were sitting on the front steps and talking quietly. He had wanted to inform Maria that he was leaving and tell her what time he would be back the next day, but when he opened the door to the back room, he saw her lying on her side on the small bed with her arm draped protectively across the baby, who was lying next to her. They were both sound asleep, and the baby's right thumb was only partially in his mouth, obviously having begun to slip out. Bob tiptoed over and pulled lightly on the little hand to complete the process. There followed a huge yawn with the face almost disappearing behind the open mouth, and then the slumber was resumed.

Bob stood and gazed down at them for a long time. He was aware that there had been many millions of renditions of the scene of madonna and child in the past but could not imagine that any could have appeared more hallowed than the one before him now. As he was softly closing the door behind him, one of the hold-out revelers was emerging from the tiny bathroom to the right of the bedroom and bumped into him. Swaying unsteadily on his feet, the man looked at him blearily and smiled.

"Ah, señor, I think I not know you. I am Cesar. *Como se llama?*"

"Paláran," Bob responded with a grin.

The man's drunken grin faded a little, and a somewhat puzzled expression passed over his face. "*Como?* Paláran?"

Bob laughed, put his hand on the man's shoulder and started guiding him toward the front door.

"*Sí, amigo,* Paláran. In fact, Paláran Na Paláran."


THE END

LaVergne, TN USA
25 March 2011
221732LV00002B/7/P